W9-BXY-845

704-814-0456

# Nothing to Fear

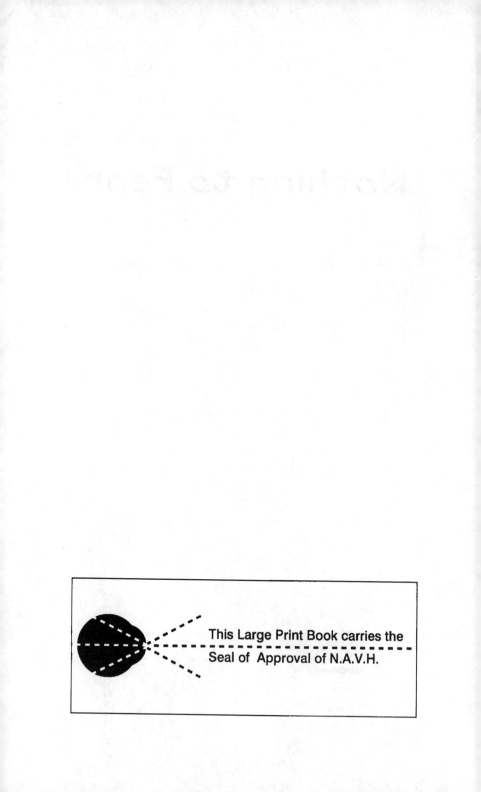

This Large Print Book carries the
Seal of Approval of N.A.V.H.

# Nothing to Fear

## Karen Rose

Published in 2006 by arrangement with Warner Books, Inc.

Wheeler Large Print Hardcover.

The text of this Large Print edition is unabridged.
Other aspects of the book may vary from the original edition.

Set in 16 pt. Plantin by Carleen Stearns.

Printed in the United States on permanent paper.

**Library of Congress Cataloging-in-Publication Data**

Rose, Karen, 1964–
  Nothing to fear / by Karen Rose.
    p. cm.
    ISBN 1-59722-178-3 (lg. print : hc : alk. paper)
    1. Women's shelters — Fiction.  2. Women social workers
  — Fiction.  I. Title.
  PS3618.O7844N68 2006
  813´.6—dc22                                    2005033295

For Martin. I love you.

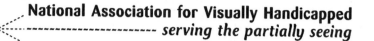

As the Founder/CEO of NAVH, the only national health agency solely devoted to those who, although not totally blind, have an eye disease which could lead to serious visual impairment, I am pleased to recognize Thorndike Press★ as one of the leading publishers in the large print field.

Founded in 1954 in San Francisco to prepare large print textbooks for partially seeing children, NAVH became the pioneer and standard setting agency in the preparation of large type.

Today, those publishers who meet our standards carry the prestigious "Seal of Approval" indicating high quality large print. We are delighted that Thorndike Press is one of the publishers whose titles meet these standards. We are also pleased to recognize the significant contribution Thorndike Press is making in this important and growing field.

Lorraine H. Marchi, L.H.D.
Founder/CEO
NAVH

★ Thorndike Press encompasses the following imprints: Thorndike, Wheeler, Walker and Large Print Press.

# Acknowledgments

Phyllis Towzey for the legal advice that kept my heroes on the right side of the law.

Staci Landers for the wonderful P.I. and police procedural information.

Marc and Kay Conterato for, as always, all things medical and for, as always, being my dear friends.

All the wonderful US military wives who told me about their men. Thank you for your sacrifices for our country.

My critique partner and best friend Terri Bolyard for helping me put the corkscrews in my plot twists and for everything else.

My fourth period Creative Writing class both for their patience as I finished this book and for their awesome creativity that continues to keep me inspired. You guys are destined for great things!

# Prologue

*Western Florida,*
*June 5, 2:30 p.m.*

It had been a traditional funeral. A few mourners wore green polyester golf pants, but most wore black despite the steamy humidity of the Florida afternoon.

From her vantage point five tombstones away Sue Conway could hear the minister intone the familiar, "Ashes to ashes and dust to dust." She dropped her eyes to the flowers she'd put on a stranger's grave, hiding her scowl. The damn funeral would be over soon and she still hadn't seen the one person she'd hoped to draw out.

The minister stepped back, letting the mourners say their final good-byes and wander away. The group was still in a state of stunned disbelief as evidenced by the murmurs Sue could easily hear through the surveillance device she wore in her ear.

"I used to feel so safe," said one.

"The community will never be the

same," said another.

"I never used to lock my doors before. I sure as hell will now."

No one in their cluster had been murdered before. And to be murdered so viciously . . . it was more than they could comprehend.

The murder hadn't been her first, but had given her more pleasure than any other. The moans, the sound of bones crunching in her hands. The blood spurting as she'd cut, just a little at a time. She'd dreamed of it for so long, fantasized each little cry, each slice into flesh and bone, each drop of blood. It had been pure, unadulterated pleasure. If nothing else, she had that to hold on to even as she continued her search.

Because even under extreme torture her victim had not given her what she'd demanded. She'd have to continue her search and when she found the real prize . . . this murder would seem like a walk in the park. She had years to make up for, a host of fantasies stored, an amazing amount of retribution to mete out. But nothing would begin until all the players were on the stage. Because once she started, she didn't want to stop.

She knelt, her pose prayerful as the service ended and the mourners dispersed. A few minutes passed, then she heard the rasping voice of the cemetery director.

"Lower it in, boys."

Sue pulled the earpiece from her ear before the amplified sound of the crane lowering the coffin shattered her eardrum. She sighed. This show was now over, and the guest of honor had never appeared. She stood up, brushed the dirt from her skirt, and set off for her car, only to slow her pace when a peripheral movement caught her eye.

She stepped behind a large monument and watched as a small car with an Avis sticker pulled into the access road servicing this part of the cemetery. The car stopped and the driver got out.

Sue's heart began to pound. A hundred different thoughts rushed in at once. *Finally,* was the thought that rose to the top of the pile. With difficulty she silenced what would have been a shout of triumph.

The guest of honor had come after all. Now, retribution could commence. But carefully, and according to the plan of her making. It would not be today. All the pieces needed to be in place, the destination carefully chosen.

But now she held all the cards. She was in control.

*Be afraid. I'm coming.*

# Chapter One

*Wight's Landing,*
*Isle of Wight Bay, Maryland*
*Wednesday, July 28, 2:00 a.m.*

*Ow.* That hurt. It was his first blurry thought as fingers gripped his shoulder and shook. Hard. That really hurt. *Stop it.*

The shaking continued, but he wouldn't open his eyes. It couldn't be morning yet. He drew in a breath, smelled her perfume. It wasn't fair. She'd promised him the whole week off. No lessons. No flash cards. No stupid word games or speech therapy. Just fun in the sun. Fishing, crabbing. Riding the waves. Video games all night. Sleeping in as long as he wanted. Yet here she was, shaking him awake.

He knew she'd break her promise. They all did, sooner or later. He'd just wait her out, just like he'd waited out all the other speech therapists. Sooner or later, they'd leave. Cheryl had stuck around longer than most. He had to give her credit for that.

He swatted her hand and tried to roll over, but she grabbed him and yanked him up by his T-shirt. Her hand clamped over his mouth just as his eyes flew open. Just as he took in her face, white as a ghost in the moonlight, and her dark eyes, wide and scared. Not just scared. Cheryl was terrified, and in that moment, so was he. He stopped struggling.

"Say nothing." She mouthed it. He nodded. She let go of his mouth and pulled him from the bed, shoving the processor in his hand. Normally he fought putting it on, put her off as long as he could. Now, he slipped it behind his ear without a word.

And flinched as the roaring began. As the processor "turned on his ears" as Cheryl would say, instantly changing the calm, quiet world of his deafness to a loud painful mess of sound. He concentrated to ignore it. To hear what he needed to hear in the ocean of noise. Now she didn't say anything, just pulled him across the room, into the closet.

She pushed him in the corner of the closet and to the floor. Crouched down to meet his eyes.

"Someone's downstairs." She whispered and signed it at the same time, her normally smooth hands shaking. Her whole body was shaking. "Paul went to check. Don't come out until I come get you." She gripped his chin. "Understand? Stay here. *Say nothing.*"

He nodded and she snapped upright, grabbing the stack of life jackets that his father had stored on the top shelf of the closet. Then they were covering him, smelly and musty. The door closed and he was left in the darkness.

He was hiding. Like a coward.

Temper began to simmer, mixing in with the fear. He wasn't a coward. He was going to be thirteen, for God's sake. She'd shoved him in the closet like a little kid. Buried him under a pile of smelly life jackets, while *Paul* went to check. Carefully he pushed one of the life jackets far enough away from his eye to stare at the door, trying to think of what to do. He wasn't going to just sit here while someone broke into his house. He certainly wasn't going to let *Paul* take all the credit for chasing them away.

Dim light appeared at the crack under the door and all his courage disappeared. Someone was in his room. He shrank back into the corner of the closet, his heart beating so loud he thought he could hear it. The hairs raised on the back of his neck. Painful shudders shook him. *No way. I have to do something.*

A scream cut through the ocean of sound. *Cheryl. I have to help her.*

But his body was frozen. Frozen into a useless lump in a closet under a pile of life jackets. He concentrated, listening. Pushed the roar aside like Cheryl had taught him to do. And listened.

There was nothing. They were gone. He should get up. He should.

Then there was a loud crack of sound, so loud it hurt. His head jerked back, struck the closet wall, that pain mixing in with the other.

A gun. They had a gun. Someone had shot a gun. Cheryl. They'd killed Cheryl.

And they'd kill him, too. Or worse. *Do something. Do something.*

What? He didn't know. Didn't know what to do. *Dad.* What would his father do?

He felt a sharp pain in his chest. He was too old to cry for his parents, but he wished they were here. Wished they hadn't picked tonight to go into Annapolis. It was their anniversary. They'd gone dancing. They'd come back and find him dead. Mom would cry.

He blinked, realized his own face was wet. He was hiding in a closet, crying like a baby, while they killed Cheryl. And he couldn't move.

He flinched at the second shot, quieter this time. Then more screaming.

She was screaming. Cheryl was still alive. Screaming. The sound stabbed his brain like a million knives. He could hear it. Feel it. A million knives slashing. Heart pounding, hands trembling, he yanked the processor from behind his ear.

And it was quiet. The minutes ticked by in his head. Then the closet door opened.

He shrank back into the corner, clenching his eyes shut, his teeth together. Trying not to make a sound. One life jacket was pulled away. Then another. And another. The musty smell no longer tickled his nose and he could feel the air on his face.

He made himself open his eyes, felt the whimper stick in his throat. Looked up.

She was tall, taller than Cheryl. Bigger. Her hair was wild.

Her eyes were crazy. White. *She has white eyes.*

Her mouth was smiling, an evil smile that made him want to scream.

But he didn't. Because her shirt was splattered with blood and in her hand she was holding a gun and it was pointed at him.

*Eastern West Virginia,*
*Thursday, July 29, 3:30 a.m.*

The shrill ringing of her cell phone woke her easily. She was a light sleeper. She hadn't always been, but prison had a way of changing little things like that. Even though she'd been out for six months now, it was one of the changes that stuck. Even though she'd been out for six months now, prison was still the first thing she thought of when she woke.

For that alone, there would be retribution.

Only her brother Bryce knew her cell number, still she cautiously answered, "Yeah?"

"It's me."

She sat up, cursing the stiffness in her back. Sleeping in the backseat of a small car was far from ideal, but she'd certainly slept in worse places. "They're home?" Her mouth curved and her heart began to beat a little faster. The Vaughns had come home. Found the wrecked house. The empty bed. The note pinned to the pillow.

The gift waiting for them in the shed. They'd be terrified. They'd cry. They'd be powerless.

*Powerless.* It wasn't nearly enough, but it was a damn good start.

"I'm n-not r-really sh-sure." Bryce stammered it out, fear lacing every stuttered syllable.

Visions of triumph abruptly fizzled. "What do you mean?" she asked, each word evenly spaced. If he'd fucked this up, he'd do a hell of a lot worse than shake. "Where are you?"

"In jail." She closed her eyes. Reminded herself that the throwaway cell she'd bought in Maryland was untraceable. Still, the thought of him calling her from a jail made her seethe. "They a-arrested me for r-robbing a store. I need you to b-bail me out."

Her laugh was cold and brief. They were on the verge of millions and he'd robbed a goddamn store. "You want *me* to bail you out. You've got to be kidding."

"Dammit," he hissed. "I called you because . . . *you know.* I c-could have called Earl."

He'd called because he was no longer at his post. No longer keeping watch over the beach house to report on the Vaughns' activities. No longer able to tell her when they came home and whether or not they'd called the fucking police.

"You're only seventeen. They'll slap you on the wrists and put you in juvie."

"No." Bryce's voice dropped to a terrified whisper. "They s-say they'll charge me as an adult. I'll go to p-p-prison. Please," he begged pitifully. "Get me out of here."

That she and Bryce shared DNA seemed an impossibility. And even the fact that they did wasn't enough to make her stick her neck out for him at this point. But she did need to get him out of jail before some slick DA got him to spill his damn guts. That Bryce would hold his stuttering tongue in the face of even the most civilized of interrogation techniques was too much to hope for. Growing up with Uncle Earl had mushed his brain. Growing up with Aunt Lucy had mushed his will. It was a pity she hadn't been around to see to his upbringing herself, but she'd been . . . indisposed. Incarcerated. And now Bryce was on his way there, too. Their father must be spinning in his grave like a rotisserie chicken.

"I'll call Earl," she snapped. "I'll tell him I'm a clerk at the jail." That her uncle would recognize her voice wasn't likely as they hadn't spoken in years. "Where are you?"

"O-Ocean City."

At least he'd had the brains not to do it in that little bumfuck town of Wight's Landing. Ocean City was an hour away. Nobody would think to tie the two together, even if the Vaughns did call the cops. "I'll call Earl. You keep your damn mouth shut and your eyes open." She smirked. "And if anybody drops any soap, don't bend over to pick it up."

"That's not f-f-funny, S-S-Sue."

Hearing him stammer her name wiped the smirk from her face. "No, it's not. Neither is you calling me from a damn jail." With that she disconnected and took a look out of the back window at the dark forest in which she'd parked to get some sleep. She was far off the beaten path and had been since leaving the Maryland Eastern Shore the morning before. She'd made terrible time on the single-lane roads, having to stop every few hours to give the kid water so that he didn't dehydrate in the trunk, but she was avoiding the interstates for now. She wasn't sure when the Vaughns would be home and even though she'd warned them not to call the cops, they just might. She wouldn't let herself be found.

She had too much at stake. The prize was just too sweet.

She climbed out of the car and popped the trunk. Eyed the two figures curled into fetal balls. They were still there, just where she'd left them. Still tied, just as she'd tied them.

Her prize. Her retribution.

Alexander Quentin Vaughn. A big name for such a scrawny kid. He was twelve, but he didn't look any older than ten. Bryce had summed it all up pretty well when they'd first laid eyes on the little brat cowering in that closet in the beach house. "Kid don't look like he's worth a million bucks," Bryce had said and in the strictest sense he'd been right. The kid was worth five times that.

But money wasn't everything.

Sometimes revenge meant a great deal more.

And when you could get them both at the same time . . . That was justice.

Alexander Quentin Vaughn. And his live-in speech therapist, who had put up one hell of a fight. The Vaughns owed Cheryl Rickman combat pay, assuming she lived to collect it, which she would not. Rickman knew it, too, from the look of dazed terror in her eyes. Sue had only kept

Rickman alive this long because she could communicate with the kid.

The boy blinked back tears now. Shrank back until his scrawny body bumped Rickman's. Tying him had probably been unnecessary. He couldn't weigh more than eighty pounds soaking wet and didn't fight worth diddlyshit. The gag was probably overkill as well, but Sue didn't know if he could scream. Just because he was deaf and mute didn't mean he couldn't scream.

That he was a deaf-mute had been a surprise. One of those glass-half-full things. He couldn't tell tales to people they'd meet on the way, but at the same time he couldn't make a terrified plea for his parents to pay his ransom. It was a damn shame. She'd been looking forward to hearing the kid making that terrified plea. But the plan moved on.

*Adopt, adapt, and improve.* It was a good motto. Her old man's favorite, ironically. She couldn't use the kid's voice, so she'd use his face. A picture was worth a thousand words.

She looked down at them, her prize, feeling control return. Bryce's arrest had changed very little, really. As long as she got him bailed out before he spilled his guts to some overzealous DA, the only thing that was impacted was her eye on the Vaughns. Hearing Bryce recount their pain and suffering firsthand would have been very nice, but ultimately unnecessary. Knowing if police cars lined the lonely road going up to the beach house would be valuable, but even if the Vaughns did go to the cops, they wouldn't find her. She'd be far, far away by then, tucked safely and secretly away in Earl's house. That didn't need to change either. Especially if Earl and Lucy were headed off to Maryland to bail Bryce's ass out of jail. Sue would have the run of the house to herself for a few days.

Then when they got back from Maryland, she and Earl and Lucy would have the reunion Sue had planned with such enthusiasm. She took out her phone and dialed Earl's number, noting the time. He'd be asleep, groggy. No way he'd know who he was really talking to.

The phone was answered on the first ring. "Yes?" a deep voice drawled.

Sue went still, every muscle tightening to its breaking point. He wasn't sleepy or groggy. He wasn't Earl. She said nothing, could say nothing. The voice just chuckled.

"Is this Bryce?" *James.* Sue's blood ran

cold. *Impossible*. James was dead. She'd slit his throat herself. Obviously, not well enough.

"Not Bryce?" he said genially. "Then this must be Sue. How the hell are you, Sue?" His voice hardened. "Free lesson. When you kill a man, you need to make damn sure he's really dead. Now, did you want to talk to your Uncle Earl?" A moan echoed in the background. "He can't come to the phone right now."

Sue gritted her teeth. "You sonofabitch. They were *mine*."

"I have to say I'm shocked, Sue. You, a dutiful niece." He sounded it. Shocked. "Protecting an aunt and uncle you hated?"

"Not mine to protect, you asshole," she hissed. *Mine to kill*. Mine to make moan and weep and wish they were dead. Mine to make *pay*. She'd had plans. *Damn him*.

James choked on a laugh. "You were going to kill your own aunt and uncle, just like you killed that woman in Florida. And I beat you to it. Sue, you're priceless."

He knew about the Florida murder. James Lorenzano knew too damn much. She should have stayed to make sure he was dead, but someone had been coming and she'd been forced to flee. Killing him a second time would be far more difficult.

She'd just need to stay out of his way. "Thank you."

"You're welcome. Don't forget I know far more about you than you know about me. I'll find you, Sue. You know I can. And when I do, you're dead."

A chill ran down her spine. He could. James knew how to find people. That's why she'd hired him in the first place. Then she stiffened her spine in resolve. She'd come too far to give up now. "No, you won't."

She hung up and seethed a moment. James was alive. That had been a bit of a shock. And he'd been to Earl and Lucy's. This was bigger than the lost pleasure of seeing Earl and Lucy writhe in pain. This meant she needed to find another place to hide with the kid.

*Adopt, adapt, and improve.* She would not change her destination. It had to be Chicago. No other city would suffice. No other place would be revenge.

She needed to find another place to hide in Chicago. Just long enough to get her money and her revenge. The money would be her ticket out of the country, away from James.

The revenge . . . Well, that was sustenance. Without it, there would be little reason to survive and little joy in doing so.

She needed to find a place to hide that James would never think to look. He was right about one thing. He did know more about her than she knew about him. He would visit all her old cohorts, most of whom would sell their own mother for a buck, so she couldn't call any of them. Not yet anyway. She had to hide the kid, because without him the whole plan fell flat. She stared down at the boy, her mind working. And as usual, the pieces fell neatly into place, a new plan forming.

Luckily James didn't know everything.

She glanced at her watch in the dim glow of the trunk light. She had things to do. With both hands she grabbed Rickman's shirt and hauled her out of the trunk with ease. Rock-hard biceps were about the only thing of value she'd gotten out of Hillsboro Women's Penitentiary. Well, that wasn't entirely true. Without Hillsboro, she never would have met Tammy, whom James did not know.

She dragged Rickman off the road and into the trees, thinking about her old cellmate. Twenty-five to life had been Tammy's sentence for killing her wife-beating husband, and hadn't Sue had to listen to her cry about it every damn night for the five fucking years they'd shared an eight by ten? But to be fair, without Tammy, Sue never would have heard of the place that would be sanctuary for the next few weeks. A secret place in Chicago that opened its doors to women in need. *I'm a woman,* Sue thought with a smile. And she sure as hell was in need.

*Adopt, adapt, and improve.* It was a good motto. A plan was only as strong as it was flexible. Sue pulled her gun from her back waistband and quickly pumped a bullet into the back of Rickman's head. Instantly the woman went limp. A few quick steps brought Sue back to the trunk where the kid stared up at her, terror in his eyes. She laid the barrel of the gun against his cheek for a split second, nodding when she heard his muffled scream. He *could* scream then. It was good to know. A red welt rose on his cheek, a burn from the hot steel. "C'mon, kid," she said, pulling him out of the trunk, dragging him over to where Rickman lay, her blood now soaking the ground. Tears rolled down the boy's face and she knew he understood the concept of death. At twelve, he'd better. She sure as hell had.

It was late. Or early, Dana Dupinsky thought as she slipped into Hanover House's kitchen through the back door. In any case, there didn't seem to be much point to going back to bed. Residents would be waking in two hours and the sounds of their morning routines combined with the aroma of brewing coffee would make it impossible to sleep.

She fastened the three deadbolts that provided some measure of safety — partially from the neighborhood but mostly from those who might be seeking the residents of Hanover House, the women whose lives she'd dedicated her own life to protecting. Dana winced as the third bolt screeched. It needed to be oiled. She'd get to it when she could.

"So where are they?"

Stifling a screech of her own, Dana spun, her hand over her heart. Her shock quickly became a glare at the young woman who sat at the kitchen table, her face bathed in the eerie blue light of a laptop computer screen. "Don't do that," Dana hissed.

Evie Wilson looked only mildly repentant. "I'm sorry. I thought you saw me.

28

Sshh," she murmured, dropping her eyes to her lap. "He's asleep."

Dana walked around the table, not surprised to see Evie holding the infant, the son of Ruby, one of their younger residents. Barely eighteen years old and unwed, Ruby was terrified of both the baby's father and her own. The bruises Ruby had worn when she arrived had more than substantiated her claim. But after a few weeks in the safe haven of Hanover House, Ruby was determined to get a new start. That's what women did here. They got new starts. Some, Dana thought, got newer starts than others.

"He woke up and Ruby was so tired, I told her to get some sleep. It's all right," Evie added, gesturing to her computer screen. "I had some work to do for my online classes."

Dana bit back a frown. Evie's online college classes were a source of disagreement between them. "I thought you were going to register up at Carrington for summer term."

Evie glanced up, then back at her screen. "I was, but . . . I changed my mind."

Dana's shoulders sagged. "Evie."

Evie shook her head. "Don't, Dana. Just . . . don't. I went up there, I really did. I even got out of the car and walked up to the registrar's office, but . . ." She let the thought trail.

Dana's heart squeezed even as she forced herself to say what she knew needed to be said. What she'd said so many times before. "You can't hide here forever, honey."

Half of Evie's face grimaced while the other half remained still as stone, legacy of a madman's attack two years before. "I know." She looked up, her dark eyes flashing. "Are you going to throw me out?" she asked, challenge lacing her tone.

"You know I'm not." Dana sank into one of the kitchen chairs, so exhausted. "For God's sake, Evie." That she'd even ask. Hell.

There was silence between them for a long moment before Evie finally spoke again. "So back to my original question, where are they?"

"They didn't show up. I waited for three hours and nobody that matched their descriptions got off any of the buses." Dana massaged the back of her neck wearily. She never questioned how women came to hear of Hanover House. She knew there were pockets of information out there. Nurses, cops, other victims. Sometimes women from outside Chicago would call and Dana would meet them at the bus station, but more than half of the women didn't show up. Like tonight. "But it wasn't all a total loss," she added. "I did get propositioned." One corner of her mouth lifted. "Guy offered me fifty bucks."

"Would've paid the telephone bill this month," Evie said lightly and rose to her feet. "Hold Dylan and I'll make you some coffee. You look like you could use it."

"Thanks." Settling the baby comfortably against her shoulder, Dana watched Evie fumble with the coffee filters with one hand. The nerves in Evie's right hand were damaged, legacy of the same vicious attack that left her face scarred and her mouth unable to smile. Three surgeries later, the scars were less noticeable, but her hand would never be the same. Yet Evie never asked for help. Wouldn't accept it were it offered.

Evie scooped coffee from the can. "I thought Caroline had bus duty tonight."

Caroline was Dana's very best friend. Her very pregnant best friend. A Hanover House success story, Caroline had made a wonderful life for herself and her son, Tom. Married for two years now, she was just six weeks away from having the baby

31

she and her husband Max had conceived in love. There were few things more successful than that.

"Nope, not anymore. She is officially off duty for the duration."

"And what did she say about that?" Evie asked wryly.

"The usual. That pregnancy was a natural state and how she was healthy as a horse. I told her to give it up. Max just threatened to tie her to the bed."

"Which is how she got that way," Evie quipped and Dana grinned.

"True. So, like it or not, I have bus duty for the next six months or so." Evie doing bus station pickup duty was not a possibility. She'd tried once, but the experience hadn't been a pleasant one for anyone involved, least of all for Evie. The client's child, terrified and exhausted, had taken one look at Evie's scarred face and burst into tears. The client refused to go with Evie and Dana ended up going to the station herself. After that, Evie never left the house without a protective layer of thick makeup that Dana thought looked worse than the scars. But it made Evie secure, so Dana never said a word about it. Dana could tell by the way Evie stared at the dripping coffee that she was remembering, too.

Changing the subject, Dana looked at Evie's laptop screen. "What are you taking?"

"Child psychology and statistics. The statistics course is required for a psych degree."

Dana's eyes widened. "You're majoring in psychology?" The thought of Evie following in her footsteps left her with a disturbing mix of pride and apprehension.

"I'd considered it. I was thinking of working with kids. And yes," she added crossly, "I know I can't hide here forever. I know the kids won't come to me." Evie jerked the partially dripped carafe from the machine, poured Dana the first cup. "I'm working on it."

Dana traded the baby for the full coffee cup with a sigh. "I know, honey." She could tell Evie that her scars were not that bad and even believe it herself, but Evie didn't and that was the issue. It was normal, but so very wrong. So wrong for a woman to be twenty years old and hiding in a women's shelter because she was afraid to face the world.

Evie didn't sit down, just stood rocking the sleeping baby. It was no secret that the babies were Evie's favorite, nor was it any great mystery. Babies didn't stare, didn't judge. Didn't cringe. They just cuddled and gave you unconditional love. What a deal.

It really was. Evie kissed the baby's forehead. "You'll leave soon," she murmured.

Dana regarded Evie over the rim of her cup. "You've become attached to him."

Evie looked up, her expression suddenly unreadable. "If you're thinking I want to keep him here, you're wrong. This is no place for a child to grow up."

Her voice was so adamant, Dana wondered if she was talking about the baby or herself. Evie had been brought to the shelter by one of Dana's policewoman friends when she was only fifteen, a terrified runaway with a quick mind and a sassy mouth who'd quickly wormed her way into Dana's heart. Dana had become Evie's legal guardian although Evie had always been more like a younger sister. "No, honey, it's not."

Evie rocked another moment or two. "He'll leave and we'll never know if he's safe. If Ruby stayed away from the baby's father or if she goes back to him." A pause. "It keeps me up at night, Dana. Does it keep you up at night, too?"

"Only all the time," Dana answered dryly and watched one side of Evie's mouth quirk up. "I wish I could take them all in, but I can't. So I do my best and pray it's enough."

"If Ruby left Chicago she'd be safer."

Dana nodded. "That's likely true. But Ruby rejected the idea. You know that."

"She might have said yes if she'd known she could have new papers."

New papers. Indeed, some of their residents left Hanover House with newer starts than others. A precious few left with a new identity. New birth certificate, social security card, and driver's license. Courtesy of Dana Dupinsky, full-time therapist and part-time forger. And she was damn good at both. Her documents had been withstanding scrutiny for more than ten years.

Dana knew exactly where this conversation was going. Still she kept her voice mild. "You know the policy, Evie. A client has to request help in leaving their old home city before we even bring up the possibility of papers."

Evie's jaw tightened. On one side. "*Your* policy."

Dana sipped more coffee, annoyed and determined not to show it. "My risk. My policy." What she did was illegal. She provided forged documents. Forged *federal* documents. Her reasons were pure, but she doubted any judge would take her side. It was critically important that the women she chose to help in this way were discreet, because once they started down the path of a new identity, the secret was out. If any one woman talked . . . *It would be my ass in jail. Not Evie's. Mine.*

Evie bristled. "*Your* policy could be putting *our* clients in danger," she said angrily. The baby whimpered and Evie went back to rocking him where she stood. "What about all the women right here in Chicago who have no idea that we could change their lives?" she whispered harshly. "How could you live with yourself if something happened to them?"

Dana drew in a breath. It wasn't a thought she didn't have herself. Every damn day. "Evie, I'll say this only once. You will not breach policy. You will not provide any resident of Hanover House with the possibility of papers. Are we clear?"

Evie's glare could cut through stone. "Yes, ma'am. We're very clear." Evie abruptly turned on her heel, waking Dylan who began to wail loudly. Dana glanced at the clock on the wall as shouts began to flow from the upstairs bedrooms. No, there was absolutely no sense in going back to bed. The day had officially begun.

# Chapter Two

*Wight's Landing, Maryland,*
*Friday, July 30, 7:00 p.m.*

Ethan Buchanan sat down at the table in the Vaughns' beach house kitchen and pulled his palms down his face in helpless frustration. He fought back the panic clawing at his gut. Little Alec was gone, as was his live-in interpreter and speech therapist, Cheryl Rickman. *Gone.* Little Alec who wasn't so little anymore. He was twelve. Old enough to know what was happening to him, to be terrified. Still too young to fight back.

And physically unable to call for help.

Ethan searched the stunned faces of his oldest friends, wishing he knew what to do next. He'd known Stan Vaughn for twenty-five years, Stan's wife Randi for ten. Yet the two of them seemed like strangers. Their son was gone, yet Stan and Randi had not called the police or the FBI. Randi sat clutching the phone to her chest and Stan looked as if he'd tackle Ethan when he'd reached for his cell phone.

Only after he'd promised not to call the police did Randi restore the phone to its place on the counter. Stan had taken up residence at the window, looking out at the bay. Ethan looked from Randi's pale face to Stan's rigid back. And sighed. "Let's take this from the beginning. When exactly did you realize Alec was gone?"

Silence. Ethan began to lose his patience. Time was ticking. "Stan?"

Stan leaned his forehead against the windowpane wearily. "Three-thirty this afternoon."

"Three thirty-five," Randi whispered.

Stan shot an angry glare over his shoulder and Randi returned it defiantly.

Ethan drew an uneasy breath. So this was how it would be. "Where had you been?"

"Annapolis," Randi murmured. "Wednesday was our tenth wedding anniversary."

A picture flashed in Ethan's mind, happier days. Stan in his tux; Stan's brother Richard in his dress blues as the best man; Randi, so beautiful in white lace. He himself had been holding wriggling toddler Alec, just hoping to keep his own dress blues free of slobbery Cheerio crumbs until they'd said their "I do's." Ten years. Gone by so fast.

Alec was now twelve. And gone, maybe for hours, maybe days. Hours Randi and Stan had done nothing. *Nothing except call me.*

"We should have come back yesterday," Randi bit out, angrily. "You *said* you'd called Cheryl. You *said* you talked to her." Randi took a step forward, her body quivering with rage. "You *lied* to me so you could keep me in —" She broke it off, spun, turning her face away.

Stan's lips thinned. "I left a message on the answering machine," he said harshly. "How was I to know? Dammit, Randi, you're acting like this is my fault."

"Go to hell, Stan," was her response. Quietly said, but very sincere.

Ethan cautiously interceded, putting his arm around Randi's shoulders, guiding her to one of the kitchen chairs where she sat, her hands locked between her knees. Trembling. He gave her shoulder a squeeze. "What happened when you got back here today?"

Stan waved his hand toward the window. "We smelled it as soon as we got out of the car. The first thing we did was check Alec's room. A note was pinned to his pillow."

*It.* The putrid odor of rotting flesh that had nearly bowled him over as soon as he'd stepped out of his car. Stan wouldn't say what *it* was. "What did the note say?"

Stan hesitated. Then he turned abruptly, waving Ethan to follow. "Come."

Together he and Stan walked through the back door that led to the beach. The stench grew stronger with every step as they crossed the sand to the little shed near the dock where they'd kept their summer toys. Stan opened the door. "See for yourself."

Ethan came up short in the doorway, his empty stomach heaving at the sight before his eyes. It had been a man. Who'd once had a head. A whole head. Buzzing flies now covered what was left. The body was bloated from the heat, nearly unrecognizable.

Shocked, he forced his eyes lower to where a shotgun lay sideways across the man's naked torso. Lower still to where a length of string ran from the shotgun's trigger across the man's boxers to the big toe of his right foot. The man had presumably put the end of the shotgun in his mouth and pulled the trigger with a wiggle of his toe.

Ethan turned to where Stan stood resolutely looking out at the bay, its serene beauty at diametric odds to the grisly sight in the shed. "Who —" Ethan's voice caught and he cleared his throat. "Who was he?"

Stan kept his eyes glued to the horizon. "Paul McMillan. Cheryl's fiancé." He swallowed, his throat working viciously. "It wasn't suicide."

No, Ethan hadn't thought so. But all he could think now was that whoever had done this had Alec. "What did the note say?"

Stan dug a crumpled piece of paper from his pocket and handed it to Ethan. Wincing at the evidence Stan had likely destroyed, Ethan took the note by the upper corner. The note had been made on a printer. Hard, perhaps impossible to trace.

" 'We have your son,' " he read. " 'Do not call the police or we will kill him. If you doubt our word, look in your shed. We made this look like suicide in case the body is discovered and the police ask questions. Make certain they get no answers. We will contact you with our demands. Do not call the police or any other authority. We'll know if you do.' "

Stan still stared at the bay. "Now you see

why we didn't call the police." His whisper was nearly lost on the wind that rippled the water. "We didn't know what else to do."

"So you called me."

Stan turned at that, and in his eyes Ethan saw fear and desperation and hopeless fury. And hate. After two years, Stan Vaughn still despised him. "We called *you*," he said deliberately as if spitting each word out of his mouth. "*You* have to help us find Alec."

"Stan . . ." Ethan lifted his hands, panic mixing with the shock at what Stan was asking him to do. "I run a security consulting business. I keep hackers out of computer systems. I set up surveillance. I'm not a cop." The only uniform he'd ever worn had been that of the United States Marines. God only knew how much he wished he were wearing it now.

Stan shook his head. "You have a P.I.'s license."

"Yeah, because I run background checks on my customers' contractors. *I'm not a cop.*"

Stan met his eyes with an icy stare. "You know how to find people."

The people he'd found had been terrorists hiding in Afghani caves, not little boys kidnapped by monsters. "Stan, look. I don't have a lab. I can't do forensics. Anything I touch would be contamination of a crime scene. I'd be destroying evidence the FBI could use to find Alec. Call the FBI and let them do their job."

In a blinding instant, Stan stepped forward and grabbed Ethan's lapels in both hands. Shook him hard. Ethan fought the wave of nausea and let him do it.

"Dammit, you have to help us. Whoever did that has my son. They'll kill him." He dropped Ethan's lapels, dropped his chin to his chest, his fisted hands to his sides, and for a long moment neither of them spoke. When Stan did, his voice was hard. "You and Richard tracked Taliban in the desert. He told me so. You know how to find people." He looked up, his eyes so very angry. "I'd ask Richard, but he isn't here." Stan's eyes narrowed, his jaw clenched. "My brother didn't come home."

*Because of you.* The phrase echoed between them as if it had passed Stan's lips. It had, of course. The last time they'd seen each other.

"That's not fair, Stan," Ethan said quietly and Stan exploded.

"*I don't care if it's not.* Those animals

43

have my *son*. They did *that."* He leaned forward, jerked his finger toward the corpse. "They'll kill him, Ethan." Stan straightened slowly. "If you won't do it for me, then do it for Richard. You owe him that much."

Ethan drew in a breath. He remembered those last moments before he'd lost consciousness after their vehicle hit the mine on the road out of Kandahar. Richard should have left him there, saved himself. But he didn't. He'd stayed and fought, his body shielding Ethan's from the bullets of the enemy, lying in ambush. Richard stayed when he shouldn't have, and would have for anyone, not just his best friend. Because that's the kind of man Richard Vaughn had been. Richard would have already been searching for Alec.

Ethan turned only his head to stare at the obscenity that had been a healthy young man. The body left behind to scare them senseless. And though terrified for Alec, Ethan was not senseless. He let the breath out. "All right. But I'm not going to do this alone. You have to let me call my partner. Clay was a cop after the Corps. He'll know what to do."

Stan shook his head vehemently. *"No.* No cops. He'll report it. He'll tell."

"Stan, look. I'm an electronics specialist. I do computer security and surveillance. Coded transmissions, for God's sake. I don't do forensics, but Clay did. He was a cop, a damn good one. I won't live with the guilt if I miss something that could have saved Alec's life. Clay won't put Alec in more danger. I promise."

Stan closed his eyes. "How soon can you get him here?"

"It's a three-hour drive from D.C."

"Call him then. Tell him to hurry."


*Wight's Landing,*
*Friday, July 30, 10:30 p.m.*

Ethan stepped out onto the front porch when Clay Maynard's car pulled into the driveway. The wind had shifted and the intensity of the stench had lessened. Or maybe he'd just become accustomed to it.

Clay got out of the car and flinched and Ethan decided it was the second one.

"This isn't right, Ethan," Clay said, his voice hard.

"I know." He'd thought about it in the hours since he'd summoned his partner. They shared a business and a friendship, both of which Ethan was risking by asking

Clay to become involved. "Give me my laptop and go back to D.C. I'll take it from here."

"Shit." Wearily Clay ran his hand down his face, his tan washed pale in the bright light of the moon. "This isn't going to bring Richard back. You know it as well as I do."

Ethan tightened his jaw against the flash of anger that Clay could trivialize the situation to a case of common guilt. "This isn't about Richard. It's about Alec. Now if you're not going to help, give me my laptop and get the hell out of my way."

Clay approached, stopped a few feet from the porch and glared up. "Get a grip on yourself, Ethan. This is a job for the FBI, not us. Every minute we're silent, Alec is in more danger. If you really care about the kid, you'll stop this insanity and call the cops."

Ethan took a breath, smelled McMillan's rotting corpse. Felt the terror bubble up anew and with it a cold fury. Deliberately he descended the steps until he could see Clay's eyes. "The *kid* is my godson."

Clay's eyes flickered. "I thought he was Richard's."

"That's right." He forced the words between his teeth. "He was Richard's. But

Richard's *dead* and as you so noted, nothing I do can bring him back. When he died Randi asked me to take his place. And Stan said no, that I wasn't worthy of the responsibility. But Randi said yes, so I am." His breath hitched when he remembered the moment two years before, a moment that severed what little had been left of his friendship with Stan.

"My *godson* has been kidnapped by people who murdered an innocent man. If we go to the police, they will kill him." Doubt began to creep into Clay's eyes and Ethan swallowed, unable to keep from thinking about Alec in the hands of monsters. "He's just a boy, Clay," he whispered harshly. "He'll be terrified, confused." *Unable to call for help.*

Clay's eyes hardened again. "If he's still alive."

*Alec could be dead right now.* It was a picture Ethan had to force from his mind. "He is alive. He has to be. Look, if anybody is watching this place, we're giving them an eyeful. Either stay or go, but we can't stand out here talking."

Clay leveled a long stare, then pulled his gym bag and Ethan's laptop from his front seat with a sigh. "Hell. Please say they have air-conditioning."

"It's better inside," Ethan confirmed, his nerves settling. Clay was in. He led Clay directly to the kitchen where Randi sat with the phone on her lap and Stan paced the floor, a glass of whiskey in his hand.

Randi looked up at the sight of them, her face still so pale. "You're Ethan's partner. Thank you for coming."

"I served with Richard," Clay replied simply. And that was all he needed to say. Marines took care of one another. Even when they no longer wore the uniform.

"Richard and I served with Clay during our deployment to Somalia, right out of the Academy," Ethan explained. Stan's spine stiffened. Stan had never understood Richard's dedication to the Marines and it had become a source of division between the brothers. That it was a common bond Ethan and Richard had shared only served to widen the gap between Stan and Ethan. Richard's death turned that gap into a chasm.

"Good old *Semper Fi,*" Stan said bitterly, tossing back what was left of his whiskey. "Hell of a lot of good all that brotherhood and devotion does him now." He slapped the glass on the countertop and stalked from the room.

Randi closed her eyes. "I'm sorry."

Ethan squeezed her shoulder. "It's okay."

Clay crouched down in front of her chair. "Randi, who knew you'd be here on vacation?"

Randi's eyes flew open at the implication. "Oh, God. It could be somebody we know." She covered her mouth with her hand. "I don't know. I can't think."

Ethan rubbed a comforting hand over Randi's back. "You sit here and try to think of anybody that knew you'd be here, and more importantly, anybody that knew you'd be gone to Annapolis the last few days. I'm going to take Clay outside, then I'll trace that e-mail."

She flinched at the word *outside,* but nodded. "All right."

Clay waited until they were on the path to the shed. "They got an e-mail? When?"

"Came through Thursday morning at seven forty-five from Rickman's e-mail address. It said Alec was alive and reminded them not to call the cops. It came with an attachment."

"It came from Rickman's e-mail address?"

"Yeah. Her laptop was missing from her room. So was her digital camera."

Clay shot him a sideways look. "And the

attachment? Picture of Alec, bound, gagged?"

"Yeah. Taken at night against a background of trees that looked like northern pine."

"Ethan, I know this boy is important to you, but this is a job for the FBI. You know it."

Ethan knew. He also knew what was inside the shed. "Just wait another minute." In another minute they arrived at the little wooden shed. "There's no light inside." He bent down to retrieve the flashlight he'd left next to the shed. "Use this."

Clay opened the door and for a moment there was only the sound of the night wind and the waves gently lapping at the sides of Stan's boat, moored at the dock. His partner shone the light around, lingering on the body inside.

"His name is Paul McMillan," Ethan said quietly. "He was an architect in Baltimore. He and Cheryl Rickman planned to get married next Valentine's Day."

Clay switched off the light. "Any chance Rickman had anything to do with this?"

"We can't rule it out, but it seems unlikely. Randi swears Cheryl would protect Alec with her own life and there's been a hell of a struggle in one of the bedrooms.

Lamps smashed, pictures knocked off the wall. There's a slug in the bedroom wall. From the size of the hole it looks like it came from a nine mil."

"The shotgun they used on McMillan is old and rusted, but they didn't need too much accuracy for this," Clay said grimly. "They wouldn't have carried a weapon like that for themselves. It's useless except in the way they used it. They planned ahead to leave McMillan behind, which means they knew he'd be here."

"He was staying with Cheryl while Stan and Randi went away for their anniversary. If they were watching this place, they would have known McMillan was here. They took Alec sometime between Tuesday night at eight and Thursday morning at seven forty-five when that e-mail came through. Randi called Tuesday night and talked to Cheryl, told her to say good night to Alec. He doesn't use the phone."

Clay started walking and Ethan followed, stopping on the dock. "Alec's deaf, right?"

"Among other things, yes. Alec got meningitis when he was two, barely a month after Randi and Stan got married. He almost died. As it was, it left him deaf and epileptic. He takes medicine to control the epilepsy. Randi says the bottles are gone from the bathroom. Alec had surgery for the deafness three years ago, when he was nine. They gave him a cochlear implant."

"Explain," Clay bit out. "In laymen's terms, please."

"In layman's terms it's a device that's surgically implanted in the bone behind the ear. It gathers sound like a hearing aid, but instead of amplifying, it translates it into signals that the brain can interpret as speech and any other sound. Alec wears a piece behind his ear that does the gathering and translating. I found it in his bedroom closet. Without it, he's completely deaf." *And unable to find help.* Ethan grimaced. He had to stop thinking that.

Clay gestured at the air. "Where is this thing now, this . . . piece?"

"Still on the closet floor. I didn't disturb anything. I thought we'd want to take prints."

"Can Alec speak?"

"No. That was Rickman's job — teaching him to use the device to learn to listen and speak. Alec isn't very receptive to the device. He's used sign language for a long time." Ethan thought of the e-mails Alec had sent, complaining about the implant. "He said the implant was too loud, that the sound made his head hurt. The doctors told Randi that he'd get used to it. He hasn't yet. He ran off his last three therapists."

"He's a bad kid?"

Ethan shook his head. "Stubborn maybe, but not bad. He's thoughtful. E-mailed Richard every week when we were at the front. E-mailed me when I was in the hospital." His throat closed and he cleared it harshly. "He calls me Uncle Ethan."

"I'm sorry, Ethan. I didn't realize you two were close."

Looking out at the quiet water where he'd spent the best years of his childhood, regret surged, and Ethan sighed. "We should be closer, but when Richard died, everything just seemed to disintegrate, with Alec caught in the fray. We e-mail, but Stan never lets me visit him. I didn't want to drive a bigger wedge between Stan and Randi, so I didn't push it. I should have just visited Alec anyway."

"Ethan, why does Stan hate you so much?"

Ethan grunted. "Good question. He says Richard never would have requested Afghanistan if I hadn't asked him to, that he'd still be alive. But Richard wanted to go. He'd prepared his whole career for it.

53

He spoke Farsi, for God's sake. We needed him to decode communications. I think Stan hated me a long time before that, though. When we were kids they'd come down for the summers and we were the three musketeers. By the time we were teenagers, Stan's interests were different from ours. Richard and I were headed for the Academy. Stan bought a motorcycle right out of high school and went cruising. Got into some trouble. A misdemeanor, I think. Nothing too big, but his parents were so disappointed. Stan buckled down in his father's business and Richard and I went on to the Academy. Nothing was really the same after that. Stan saw me and Richard as his parents' favorite sons." Ethan shrugged. "And I wasn't even his parents' son."

"Alec isn't, is he?" Clay asked. "He's not Stan's biological son."

"Not biological," Ethan answered, again remember back ten years, to happier days. "When Stan met Randi, she was a single mom struggling to make it on a waitress's salary. She'd never married Alec's father. Stan married Randi and legally adopted Alec." He sighed. "They were a happy family once, Clay. Really happy."

Clay was quiet for a long moment. "Why

did Stan and Randi wait so long to get Alec the implant? If he had meningitis when he was two, why'd they wait until he was nine?"

This Ethan remembered clearly and he'd already started making conclusions. "The surgery's expensive, over fifty thousand dollars, and it wasn't covered by their insurance. Stan and Randi didn't have any money back then. Stan was working at his dad's electronics store, barely making ends meet. We all worked to add to the savings account for Alec's surgery, but Richard couldn't afford to add much. He had a family."

"Three girls, right?"

Ethan thought about them, the little girls that had been the foundation of Richard's life. The little girls that would grow up without a father. The grief welled up, but Ethan pushed it back. "Yeah. Then Stan started growing his dad's business, adding new stores. Made enough to get Alec the surgery."

"And in the process made an enemy that hated him enough to kidnap his kid?"

"The thought occurred to me. Stan promised a list of his customers and suppliers."

Clay nodded briefly. "Do you believe

they'll kill Alec if we call the cops right now?"

Ethan had expected the question, asked it of himself a hundred times since he'd agreed to help. "They've already killed one man. They don't have a lot to lose. I know Stan and Randi believe it and I *know* there's no way they're calling the cops. If the cops or the FBI get involved, it'll be because we called them. I couldn't live with myself if Alec got killed because we did."

"What about him?" Clay jerked his head toward the shed.

"McMillan? Stan needs to report finding him. He can say he found a suicide on his property. Maybe the locals will be able to find something on the body that will help."

"Will Stan do it?"

Ethan pursed his lips. Tried to reconcile his memories of Stan with the man who'd stood on this very dock planning to use his boat to drag the body of an innocent man out to sea. "If he wants our help he will."

Clay was silent another long moment. "Then let's go trace that e-mail."

Dana stood in the shadows at the east exit of the bus terminal. It was the most inconspicuous place to wait if one didn't want to be seen. She'd lost count of the number of times she'd waited here over the years, but never forgot the women she'd met here. The face of each one was indelibly stamped in her memory. They came from all walks of life, different backgrounds, places, ages. Their paths might never have crossed under normal circumstances, but these women didn't live under normal circumstances. Too many had never even known normal circumstances. All had been battered, some worse than others. Most wore the evidence where it could be easily seen by anyone who cared to look. Their cuts and bruises would be treated and in time would heal.

The scars to their souls were much harder to treat. Some would find the strength to pick up and go on and others would not. It was as simple and as complicated as that.

Tonight she was to meet a woman named Jane Smith. Not terribly original as an alias went, but it would do for the time being. Jane was coming from downstate and she had a ten-year-old son. Erik was his name.

The children were always the hardest for Dana to personally deal with. The fear she saw in their eyes, the utter desolation. The defeat and the shame. The knowledge that regardless of what she personally did, each child would grow into an adult who would always carry those internal scars. This she knew all too well.

She straightened, watching. The bus had just come in and passengers were starting to trickle through the terminal. Old women, old men. A mother with her child. Dana watched them from the shadows, quickly determined they were not the two she sought. The mother smiled too readily, the child's eyes were too bright.

Then she saw them. The woman was of medium height. It was hard to tell her build as she wore a pair of shapeless beige coveralls. Her head was down and she wore a baseball cap with a large bill. She held the hand of a thin little boy, tugged him forward. He stumbled a little and the woman all but lifted him to his feet.

Dana hoped the child's sluggishness was due to the late hour and a long journey and not illness. The woman was looking around, her tension almost palpable. Dana stepped from the shadows and watched the tension ease. "Jane? Erik?"

The woman looked up long enough for Dana to see a heavily battered face before dropping her eyes back down to the ground. This woman had been beaten, and recently. But the child was of an even greater concern at the moment. He refused to look up when she called his name, but that in and of itself wasn't unusual. What disturbed her was the intensity of his withdrawal, as if he concentrated on not making eye contact. She dropped to one knee, tried to hook a finger under his chin, but he jerked away, trembling, his thin shoulders hunched so hard. It was enough to break her heart. It always was.

"It's all right," Dana murmured. "No one will hurt you here. You don't have to be afraid anymore." She rose to her feet, lightly touched the woman's shoulder, felt her stiffen. Even more lightly touched the woman's chin, tilting her face up. Bruises and welts covered her face, both vicious and recent, but it was the woman's eyes that made Dana flinch. In the dim light they appeared almost white. Quickly Dana threw off the chill and made her mouth smile warmly. "I'm Dana. Welcome."

Ethan sat down at the little desk against the wall and prepared to trace the e-mail while Clay checked out the upstairs. Working quickly, he networked his computer to Randi's and opened the e-mail with its hideous attachment. On his computer, he ran software he needed to trace the e-mail.

"You do this a lot?" Randi murmured from the couch.

"Tracing e-mails? Enough."

She got up and stood behind him, crossing her arms over her chest, hunching her shoulders. "Ethan, what exactly do you do?"

His lips quirked up at her hesitant tone. "Clay and I work with companies to improve their security. I make sure that hackers can't get into their systems and steal information. And that they have surveillance on their employees to prevent theft as well."

"You mean you help bosses spy on their employees."

"Essentially, yes. A lot of our customers are defense contractors. Their secrets need to stay secret. Their government clearance and the country's security depends on it."

"What does Clay do?"

"He trains their security guards. Sometimes he trains police departments in small towns on use of assault weapons and personal defense."

"And you're successful at this?"

Ethan's smile was grim this time. "Yeah, Randi, we are." They were good at what they did, he and Clay. He could only pray they were good enough to find Alec.

He finished entering the information and let the software do what it had been designed to do — trace e-mails to the point of origination. Felt a surge of relief at the result. "Well, at least we're not dealing with anybody who knows anything about servers. This message came straight through." A more sophisticated person might have rerouted the message a few times before landing it on Randi's server.

"Then . . . then that's good?" Randi's voice was small, but Ethan heard a flicker of hope.

He looked over his shoulder, met her eyes. "Yeah, that's good." He did a reverse search. "This e-mail came from . . . Campus Joe's Copy Store, Morgantown, West Virginia." He swiveled the chair abruptly. "Do you know anybody there?"

Eyes wide and haunted, she shook her

head. "No. I've never been there."

Clay came down the stairs, a frown on his face. "You find anything?"

Randi wrung her hands. "It came from West Virginia. They have Alec up there."

Clay's frown deepened. "They're on the move."

Ethan shut down his laptop. "I need to get to Morgantown. Can you stay here in case they call with ransom demands? Did you bring that case from my office?"

"It's in my car."

"Good. I'll set up the tracing equipment on the phone line before I go."

He stood up and Clay grabbed his arm, his dark eyes worried. Clay darted a look at Randi, then looked back at Ethan. "You've been working eighteen-hour days. I'll go."

Ethan tried not to let annoyance flare. For all his tough-guy image, Clay Maynard worried about him like a mother. "Thanks, but I'm fine."

Clay let go of his arm. "Fine," he muttered. "Have an episode behind the wheel."

Ethan kept his tone mild. "I haven't had one in months, and you know it."

Randi was watching them warily. "What's wrong?"

Ethan patted her hand. "Nothing. Now I want you to listen to me. While I'm gone I want you to eat, even if you're not hungry. I want you to sleep, even if you have to take a pill to do it, because Alec needs you to be strong, not exhausted. Okay?"

She'd seemed to shrink as he talked. Solemnly, she nodded. "Ethan, will you find him?"

Statistics raced through his mind, none of them good. The first few days were critical in tracking prey and those days were already gone. But Randi was looking up at him with trust and tears in her eyes and he found himself nodding back. Saying words he hoped wouldn't be a lie. "I'll find him."

# Chapter Three

*Chicago,*
*Saturday, July 31, 5:45 p.m.*

"You're going to break your neck."

Startled out of her thoughts, Dana's grip tightened on the sides of the ladder and she glanced down from her perch even though she knew full well who was down there. David Hunter stared up, hands on his hips, a look of annoyance on a face that had most women instantly falling in love. Dana had often questioned her own sanity at not being one of those women. Instead, David was a treasured friend, one of a few who knew what she did here, lending his hands to the effort whenever he could. "I will if you keep scaring me like that," she responded, turning back to her inspection of the shingles. "We have a leak."

"Dammit, Dana, I told you I'd be by in a few days to check that for you."

"You've been busy working. I didn't know when you'd get a chance to come by."

But the truth was, she was on the roof because she couldn't sit still. She'd been fidgety since her argument with Evie, wondering if she could do more. If she should.

"Well, I'm here now," David countered. "Come down and let me fix it *right.*"

Dana pursed her lips. "I was fixing things *right* long before you came along, big boy."

"True," he acknowledged. There was a short pause, then slyly, "I can see up your skirt." Dana snorted a laugh and pulled at the loose shingle. "Not that I'm complaining," David continued helpfully. "Just thought you'd want to know."

"Go away or I'll tell your mother you go around looking up girls' skirts."

"Go ahead. Ma's just going to lecture you not to climb a ladder in a skirt."

He was right there. But Phoebe Hunter wouldn't stop there, going on to cluck her tongue at the fact that Dana was too independent. If she had a man in her life she wouldn't have to do her own repairs. Which would be followed by a meaningful glance at David, her only unmarried son. Which both Dana and David would just ignore with a smile.

They were friends. David had his own life, his own girlfriends. And she had her life and Hanover House was the core of it. She climbed down, frowning at him when she reached the ground, even though David always made her want to grin. It was part of his charm. "You didn't have to look up my skirt."

David beamed a beatific smile. "We'll just have to disagree. Now let me have a look."

She watched him start up the ladder, grateful he'd come by even as insufferable as he was. She could fix all manner of small things, but a roof was a bit more of a challenge than she was willing to tackle at the moment. "Well?"

"You've got some slippage. I'll get some roofing tar and shingles and put it back to rights." He started back down. "I'll come back tomorrow afternoon." He gave her a hard stare when his feet hit the ground. "You've got circles under your eyes. What's wrong?"

Dana grimaced. "If you notice, you're not supposed to mention it. It's not polite."

His sideways grin nearly disarmed her. "Since when have I ever been polite? I'm the one who looks up girls' skirts." He sobered, dropping his gaze to the toe of his work boot before glancing up from the corner of his eye. "You and Evie have a fight?"

Dana blew out a sigh. "You talked to her?"

"Didn't have to. I asked where you were and she just pointed without saying a word, like the Grim Reaper. What happened?"

Dana made herself smile. "Evie thinks I'm not doing enough to ensure client success."

David's face darkened. "In whose universe? If anything you do too much." He considered her for a long minute, his jaw tightening. "You're wondering if she's right, so you fussed and obsessed until climbing a ladder in a skirt and open-toed sandals sounded like a good idea."

He knew her well. "Maybe just a little."

"Well, she's wrong. You do more than enough. You do too much."

The forced smile eased into a natural one at the vehemence of his defense. "Thank you. I needed to hear that. Let's go inside, get some iced tea. It's too damn hot out here."

David didn't move, just stood blocking her path. "I'm serious, Dana. I think you do too much and it worries me." He glanced from side to side and lowered his voice. "I know what you do is necessary, vital. But that won't help you if you get caught."

She stepped around him, not willing to have this conversation today. Again. "I don't plan to get caught." He caught her upper arm and gently squeezed until she looked up at him over her shoulder. His gray eyes were serious, bordering on grim.

"Nobody plans to get caught. Promise me you'll stop going to the bus station in the middle of the night."

"I can't promise that, David. You know that."

"You mean you won't."

She quirked her mouth in a half smile. "A little of column A, a little of column B?"

He didn't smile back. "It's not funny, Dana. It's dangerous there at night. If you won't promise me, at least call me so that I can go with you."

"No. You're a hell of a guy, David, but these women are running from men. They wouldn't trust me if I brought a man with me. Even you. Now how about that tea?"

With a frustrated shake of his head, he gave it up, following her into the kitchen. He closed the door behind them, wincing when the deadbolt screeched. "I'll fix that for you when I come to do the roof."

"Thanks. It made an awful racket when I came in last night."

David narrowed his eyes as she poured their tea. "When you were coming back from the bus station in the middle of the night?"

"I was home before midnight." With Jane Smith with the odd-colored eyes and facial bruises and her son Erik with the nasty burn on his cheek and refusal to meet anyone's eyes. When Dana had applied ointment to the burn, the boy had kept his eyes clenched shut, not responding to a single question or offer of food. He'd been terrified, even though his mother had kept her hand on his back the entire time. She'd seen Jane only once today. She'd taken a plate back up to the boy, saying he was too tired to come down on his own. It wasn't exactly normal, but by no means unusual. Jane would come around. Dana worried about Erik.

"Well, all right," David grumbled. "Before midnight's not so bad."

"I'm so glad you approve," Dana said dryly. *Tonight* she would go to the bus station in the middle of the night, but thought that best left unsaid. The woman who hadn't shown on Thursday had called to say she was unable to escape, but that she was coming tonight. Dana didn't believe she would, but would of course be there in the event that she did.

David lifted his tea to his lips, then stopped, his gaze fixed over her shoulder. "Dana."

Evie stood in the kitchen doorway, her face carefully blank. The petite blonde standing beside her looked way too sober and Dana felt her knees wobble and her heart race.

"Mia." Dana's voice was unsteady. It was never a good thing when old friends looked too sober, especially when those friends were homicide detectives. "What's happened?"

Dana and Mia had met years before, when Mia was a beat cop and Dana the new manager of Hanover House, and had quickly become friends. A good number of her clients had been referred by Mia over the years. Dana often wondered if Mia knew about the papers Dana provided, but if she did, Mia never said a word.

Mia Mitchell hadn't come on a social call. One look at Dana's pale face told her that her friend knew it. Mia hated these calls. They normally started with *I'm Detective Mia Mitchell* and ended with *I'm sorry for your loss*. It was a hard enough conversation to have with a stranger. When it was a close friend . . .

"Dana, I need to talk with you." Mia glanced over meaningfully at the tall dark man wearing a tool belt. It was unusual to see a man at Hanover House. She didn't think she ever had before. "Privately."

"It's okay, Mia. He knows. David, this is Detective Mia Mitchell."

He reached around Dana to stick out his hand. "I'm David Hunter."

"Caroline's brother-in-law," Dana clarified.

Mia's brows lifted as she shook his hand. Max Hunter's brother. She should have seen it immediately, but she was . . . distracted. She was about to deliver news that would tear Dana into pieces. "Dots connected. Good to meet you, Mr. Hunter. How is Caroline?"

"It's David and she's as big as a house," David answered quietly. "But healthy."

"I'm glad to hear it." She straightened her spine. "I need to give you some news, Dana, and it's not good. You might want to sit down."

Dana crossed her arms over her chest, resolute, but trembling. "I'll stand. Who, Mia?"

Mia sighed. "Lillian Goodman."

Over by the door, Evie gasped. "No."

Dana closed her eyes, the remaining color draining from her face. "When?"

"Thursday. A squad car got a call to her mother's apartment and found both Lillian and her mother dead." Mia grasped Dana's shoulders, squeezing hard. "I am so sorry, Dana. I wish I didn't have to tell you this."

"How?" she asked, her voice harsh.

"Her husband beat them to death. Both Lillian and her mother."

Dana's throat worked viciously. "The kids?"

"Both of them alive."

"They left here last Friday," Dana murmured, looking away. "Lillian found a job. She was going to make it on her own. She lasted less than a week."

This next part, Mia knew, would be the hardest for Dana personally to bear. "One of the units responded to the kids' 911. The oldest, Naomi, told the uniforms that she and her brother came home from playing at a friend's house and . . . found her."

Dana slowly lowered herself into a chair. David Hunter's hands covered her shoulders protectively. Evie, Mia noticed, hadn't moved a step. She stood alone, apart, tears rolling down her face. Something was very wrong here.

"Where are they now?" David asked, his voice rough. "Naomi and Ben?"

He'd known them, too, Mia thought. And had cared. "In a safe house." Mia crouched down, caught Dana's chin. "If you want to see them, I'll arrange it. But wait a day or two."

Dana nodded, dully, Mia's words sinking in. Those babies were hiding yet again, with strangers this time. When they'd hidden at Hanover House it had been with her and Evie and, and their mother. Who was now dead. She could only imagine how scared they must be right now. But that day, Thursday . . . Finding her broken body . . . Dana didn't have to imagine that. "When can I see them?"

"I'd like you to wait until we have Mr. Goodman in custody."

David's hands clenched on her shoulders. "You mean you don't have him yet?" he hissed. "Dammit. Does he know about Dana? About this place?"

Mia straightened. "I don't know. I don't think so, because I think if he had, he'd have been here already. Just be careful and keep your doors locked. I'll call you when I have more information. If you hear something, I need to know about it." Mia handed David one of her cards. "I know the way out."

"Mia." Evie held up a hand to stop her. "When is the funeral?"

Mia frowned. "Tomorrow. But I don't want you there. If Goodman shows up he could follow you back here. Understood? I'll let myself out. Dana, call me if you need me."

Evie waited until the front door closed behind Mia before turning to Dana with glittering eyes. "He wouldn't have found her if she'd had papers."

Dana's eyes widened, the words like a physical blow to her gut. "Evie, that's not true."

Evie's eyes hardened. "What's true is that Lillian's husband killed her like she was nothing." Her hands clenched at her sides. "*Nothing.* If you hadn't been so damned high and mighty and stubborn with all your damn *policies,* she might be alive today."

"Evie, that's enough," David bit out.

"She wouldn't leave Chicago, Evie. I begged her to leave, but she wouldn't."

"She might have if she'd known she could really, truly disappear." Evie turned on her heel, paused at the kitchen doorway to lob the final verbal grenade, tears coursing down her cheeks. "But now we'll never know, will we?"

There was silence in the kitchen, then David pulled up a chair next to her and sank into it heavily. "Dana —"

"Don't say it," she interrupted him. "Don't tell me this wasn't my fault, David. Don't tell me there wasn't anything I could have done."

"Okay, I won't. Seems to me you said it just fine yourself."

He put his arm around her and for just a moment she rested her head on his strong shoulder. For just a moment she allowed herself to wish she had someone of her own to hold her in the middle of the night when she was sure to wake with nightmares. Then shoved the self-pity aside to focus on the real issue. "Those poor children," Dana murmured. "They'll never be the same."

"I know." He gave her a squeeze. "You want me to stay with you?"

She shook her head. "No, you go on. I'll be fine."

"I don't want to leave you alone."

"David, Mia's right. If Goodman knew about us, he'd have been here already. He's probably hiding out with some of his friends, drunk. He'll stagger out sooner or later and CPD will pick him up. I'm more worried about the kids. I don't know who'll take care of them now. Lillian didn't have any family other than her mom. She stayed in Chicago to take care of her mother." Dana swallowed hard. "That's why she wouldn't leave town."

"But you'll wait until Goodman's caught before you go see them, right?"

Dana heard the warning in his voice and forced her lips to curve. "Of course. I'm not stupid, David." *Just high and mighty and stubborn.* The words had hurt. A lot. As Evie had meant them to. Knowing that perhaps hurt more.

David stood up, slid Mia's card in his wallet. "I'll be back tomorrow to fix the roof." He hesitated, then blurted, "Do you still have your gun?"

Dana shivered. "Yeah. At my apartment."

"Bring it here. Call me if you need me. I mean it. I don't care what time it is."

"I will."

"I'll see you tomorrow. Lock the door behind me."

Dana followed him to the door, flipped the three deadbolts. Then jumped when she heard her name called, so softly.

Turned to find a woman standing in the kitchen doorway. "Jane." The client she'd picked up last night. Quickly she searched Jane's face, wondered how much, if any, she'd heard. But Jane just blinked out of those pale, pale eyes that sent new shivers down Dana's back.

"I just wanted to get some Benadryl for Erik," Jane half whispered. "He's having trouble breathing. Allergies, I think. But if this is a bad time . . ."

Dana made her feet move. Lillian was gone and that she could not change. Jane was here now and needed her help. "It's not a bad time." She unlocked the cabinet where they kept the over-the-counter medicines and took out a bottle of Benadryl and a plastic cup. "Erik weighs, what, about eighty or ninety?"

Jane's eyes had narrowed at the plastic cup. "About. What if that's not enough?"

Dana managed a smile. "Then we'll get him some more. Hanover House policy is to dispense medicine by the dose. I'd hate to have a kid get sick because we left a bottle out where they could get hold of it."

Jane's eyes dropped to the floor. "I understand. Thank you."

Dana watched her take the little plastic cup. Heard Jane's footsteps as she went up the stairs. And rested her forehead against the cabinet as she locked it back up. Policies. Without them they'd have chaos.

Thoughts of Lillian and Ben and Naomi flooded her mind and grief stabbed sharp into her heart. Lillian had been so brave, the children so hopeful. Now those beautiful children would grow up with no one. It seemed that they had chaos anyway.

*I'm so tired.* She'd sleep, she thought, but just for a few hours. She needed to be back at the bus station by four a.m. Life would go on. *And so will I.*

# Chapter Four

*Chicago,*
*Sunday, August 1, 5:30 a.m.*

"Excuse me." Ethan flagged the security guard. "I need to speak with the manager."

The young man lifted his sandy brows. "About?"

Ethan reached for his wallet and held up a calming hand. "My credentials." He'd applied for the P.I. license to do background checks for his customers. He never dreamed he'd ever be flipping it out in true Magnum, P.I. style, but that's exactly what he'd done. Six times in the past thirty-six hours. If the situation wasn't so grave, he'd feel ridiculous.

"I'm looking for a woman and a little boy." He gave a careless shrug. "Custodial thing. The mother picked the kid up from school and disappeared." He uttered the lie smoothly, understandable as it was the sixth time in thirty-six hours that he'd done so. "She might have come through here and I'm hoping to check your surveillance tapes."

He then held his breath. Technically nobody had to let him view the tapes without a subpoena. So far though, he'd been lucky five times. He silently prayed for a sixth.

The guard narrowed his eyes. "I'll need to talk to the manager on duty."

Ethan leaned against the counter, his elbow taking the weight of his whole body. Before Kandahar, four hours' sleep would have lasted him forty-eight. Not anymore. He didn't need to glance at his watch to know he hadn't slept since Friday. The brass band marching through his head was clue enough. His cell phone buzzed in his pocket, prodding him to alertness. The incoming number revealed it to be Clay. "What's up?"

"Where are you, Ethan?" Clay asked.

"In Chicago. Finally."

"And?"

From his position against the bus station counter, Ethan watched the security guard lean in to murmur to the man who sat in the manager's office. The man lifted his head and Ethan could feel the pinch of his scrutiny from twenty feet away. "I don't think they're going to allow me access to the security tapes until I get a shower and shave."

"So go get a hotel and catch a few hours' sleep," Clay said sharply. "You're going to get so tired that you'd miss Alec if he is on the tape."

"Maybe." Probably. "Did we get another e-mail?"

Clay's sharpness quickly faded to concern. "No."

Which wasn't good. Neither of them had to say it aloud. It had been four days since Alec's kidnapper had taken him and in that time sent only one e-mail. Not one iota of communication since. No ransom demands. No phone calls, no e-mails, nothing.

"We have to get something soon." Ethan rubbed his sore forehead. "I just need to pinpoint what city she's actually in. I know she's not in St. Louis," he added bitterly.

"You have to stop blaming yourself for that, Ethan. You made a logical choice."

Ethan gritted his teeth. "I hope my *logical choice* doesn't get Alec killed."

"Stop it." Clay's voice was back to sharp. "You've done everything anyone could have done at this point. In the last thirty-six hours you've tracked her from that copy store in Morgantown all the way to Chicago. That's something, so stop beating yourself up."

Ethan drew a breath. "I know, Clay." He

let the breath out, made himself calm. "I'm just frustrated. I've been chasing this woman for a day and a half and I still haven't seen her face." Every shot of her face on every surveillance video was blocked by a large-billed cap. Nothing to set the cap apart other than it covered ninety percent of her face.

"Because she hasn't wanted you to," Clay said reasonably. "How many times have you told me that you can't see what the camera doesn't catch?"

"You're right. I know you're right." But in his past life Ethan had been professional, even dispassionate, as he traced terrorist e-mails, searched aerial surveillance photos of what had seemed an endless maze of tunnels and caves. This was so different. This time it was Alec. "But now she's got an even bigger lead. Dammit, what was I thinking?"

"Don't make me come and kick your ass, Ethan," Clay warned. "She bought two tickets to St. Louis via Columbus, Ohio. It made sense for you to drive straight to St. Louis to try to make up some of her lead."

"Which was just what she wanted us to do. I lost at least fifteen hours on that detour." He'd had to call Randi and tell her he'd lost her son, then drive to Columbus, Ohio, Randi's terrified whispered pleas still ringing in his ears. In Columbus the video-tapes showed the kidnapper had disembarked with Alec, the child still looking to be in shock and numb. This time the woman bought two tickets from Columbus to Indianapolis. Both times she'd paid for the tickets with cash. Neither time had she shown ID.

"She planned this, Ethan. She faked us out. At least you found her in Indianapolis. And at least now we know she's definitely not Cheryl Rickman."

The woman had worn shapeless cover-alls all the way from Morgantown to Columbus, finally shedding them somewhere before reaching Indianapolis. Her build was not Rickman's. Rickman was slender and fine-boned. This woman had well-developed arm muscles and was at least a C cup. The Indy ticket-counter attendant confirmed she'd bought tickets for Chicago. The next bus should have arrived late Thursday night.

"Which means Cheryl is still missing and not with Alec. How did Randi take the news?"

"Not well. I think she hoped it was Cheryl even while claiming it couldn't have been."

"Because if it was Cheryl, Randi would

have a harder time visualizing her hurting Alec." So had he, Ethan thought grimly. "Now, all bets are off."

"True. But now we have to look for a female connection other than Rickman. After you called to say that it definitely wasn't Cheryl, I got Stan and Randi together to brainstorm other women who could have had a reason to plan a kidnapping. Randi took one look at Stan's guilty face and went ballistic. Leaped at Stan, pounding him, scratching his face."

Ethan blinked in surprise. "She accused him of having an affair?"

Clay's sigh was pained. "Does 'You fucking sonofabitch, why couldn't you keep your dick in your pants' count?"

Ethan coughed. "Yeah, I guess it does. What did you do?"

"I pulled Randi off Stan and made her take something for her nerves. She had quite a collection, by the way, Ethan. Tranquilizers, antidepressants, you name it."

"Wonderful."

"Then Stan and I had a little talk. He came clean with a list of names."

"Names?" Ethan winced. "As in more than one affair?"

"As in more than ten," Clay said flatly, his tone clearly communicating his disgust.

"And those were the ones whose names Stan knew. Seems like our boy Stan has a bit of an addiction. He'd promised Randi he'd stopped some time ago, but he lied."

"Imagine that," Ethan muttered, glad he wasn't there with Stan. He might let Randi finish what she'd started. Hell, he'd do it himself.

"I'll start checking financials on the women and do the background checks for priors."

"What about Stan's business associates?" They were interested in anyone who had been disgruntled. Anyone who could have benefited financially from a ransom.

"Nothing so far. I'm still working through his list of suppliers and customers. There are a lot of them. I'll let you know when I have something."

Ethan hesitated over the next question. "What about Alicia Samson?" It was the name on the credit card the woman had shown in the Morgantown copy store when she'd sent her e-mail, the only time she'd shown an ID.

"Samson's a student at the university in Morgantown. I called her place a few times yesterday, but didn't get any answer. I'll keep trying today, but it doesn't look good."

"No, it doesn't. Damn." Another missing person on his conscience. He could only hope her wallet had been stolen and she'd spent the week on vacation. It was summer after all. "See if you can find out where she works and if she's been there since Thursday morning. If not, report her missing to the local authorities. Anonymously, of course."

"That was my plan," Clay said. "I called in a marker and got an old pal to run the ballistics on that slug from the bedroom wall."

"Timing for the analysis?"

"Two, three days. Maybe four."

"This marker you called in, can he be trusted to be discreet?"

"She always has been before."

*She.* Well, that made sense. "Old flame?"

"More like a little spark. But no hard feelings so she's willing to do this for me."

"And the shotgun in the shed had nothing?"

"Nothing that I can see without disturbing the scene. Vaughn's got to call the authorities, Ethan. *Today.* That body out there is putrefying. Nobody will believe he just discovered it."

Stan was supposed to have done it yesterday. Ethan felt a surge of anger that he hadn't. "Tell him that. And if he doesn't comply, report it yourself, anonymously." It was part of their deal. Stan had to report McMillan's body to the authorities. That young man had been murdered. He deserved more than having his body dragged out to sea.

"Maybe the local coroner will find something," Clay muttered. "We could use a lead."

"As I recall the local coroner is a retired ME out of Baltimore. Smart old guy. He should be able to help." Ethan straightened with considerable difficulty. The security guard was headed back his way. "I have to go. I'll call you all again later."

"Ethan, go get some sleep." Clay hesitated. "Are you all right?"

Ethan hissed out an impatient breath. "No episodes, Clay. Nothing. Nada. Goodbye." Smoothing the frown from his face, he turned to the baby-faced guard.

"I'm sorry, Mr. Buchanan," the guard said. "The night manager and I are both new. He says you'll need to come back when the head security manager comes in."

Ethan massaged the corded muscle in his neck, both frustrated and grateful for the forced break. The woman who had Alec would have an even bigger head start. Alec could truly be anywhere. But he was so tired. He'd use the time to get something to eat and check into a hotel for some sleep. "What time does the head manager come in?"

"Usually after nine, but his kid's got a baseball game this morning so it'll be at least noon. You might want —" The guard spun around when a scream echoed through the terminal. The guard started toward the sound, pulling his weapon from its holster.

Leaving his own weapon securely tucked against his kidney, Ethan followed, a sudden surge of adrenaline fueling his legs to run. A young woman in her early thirties lay on the floor next to one of the metal benches. A thin stream of blood trickled from her temple down her cheek, clashing with the rich copper of her short hair.

An old woman wailed while a handful of shocked travelers pointed mutely at the nearest exit. The guard took off in that direction, calling the incident into the police.

"She's dead, she's dead," the old woman sobbed. "He's killed her and it's all my fault."

Ethan dropped to his knees beside the woman, took her wrist, and exhaled in relief when he felt the slow steady throb of her pulse. He'd just pulled his cell phone out to call for help when her eyes flew open. Wide and brown, they flickered with alarmed confusion when she saw him, then the confusion gave way to wary assessment as she searched his eyes, his face. Then, as if she accepted what she saw there, she seemed to simply . . . settle.

And incredibly . . . so did he. Everything inside him, all the turmoil and confusion and the fear . . . it all stilled, focused. It was as if she soothed it all away with a palpable touch, although through the entire exchange she'd never moved a muscle.

Neither had he. Nor had he breathed. He did now as she slowly straightened, one hand coming down to tug at her skirt, drawing his eyes down long, statuesque legs.

"Tell her I'm not dead." Her voice was soft and husky, like she'd just woken from a deep sleep and the sound dragged his eyes back up her body, up those long dancer's legs, past curvy hips, generous breasts, back to warm brown eyes that held him. It wasn't until she started struggling to sit up that awareness of the situation returned like a hammer to his head. She was hurt and he was gaping like an idiot while the old woman continued to wail. "Tell her I'm not dead," she said again, more insistently. "Please."

Ethan looked up sharply, found the old woman had come closer and now stood a few feet away, wringing her hands. "She's not dead. Calm down, ma'am, please." He looked back down to where she'd struggled up on her elbows and placed one hand on her shoulder. "You need to keep still," Ethan said quietly. "Where do you hurt?"

She blinked. "Just my head." Gingerly she touched her temple, grimacing when she saw her fingertips covered in blood. "Damn."

"I'd say that about sums it up." Ethan held up two fingers. "How many?"

She blinked again. Her eyes were a little dilated, but not alarmingly so. Once again she met his gaze and steadily held it. And his heart skipped a thump.

"Two," she said. "Who are you?"

He studied her for a moment. Her color was coming back, her eyes becoming brighter, sharper, more intelligent by the moment. She was attractive, but by no means classically beautiful. She was something . . . *more,* and he couldn't seem to make himself look away. The air around her practically vibrated. He could actually feel the blood coursing through his veins. "I'm Ethan. I was a bystander. The guard chased whoever did this out of the building. He's called the police."

Something moved in her brown eyes, rapidly elusive. "Wrong place, wrong time," she murmured, gently pushing his hand from her shoulder and herself to a sitting position. She then gingerly turned her head to where the old woman still stood wringing her hands. "Did he hurt you, ma'am?"

The old woman shook her head. "No. Did he hurt you?"

Unbelievably the woman sitting in front of him smiled. "Not too bad. Just knocked the wind out of me. Did he get your purse?"

"Yes." The old woman's lips quivered and Ethan felt a spurt of outrage on her behalf as he realized what had happened. The outrage was followed by disbelief that the redhead had stood in the way of a mugger.

With a frown he looked down at her. "You tried to stop a purse snatcher?"

Mildly she looked up at him. "He had his hands around her throat. I wasn't terribly worried about her purse until he grabbed it. Do you have a last name, Ethan?"

Ethan sat back on his heels. "Buchanan. And you are?"

"Dana Dupinsky. Do you think you could help me stand up, Mr. Buchanan?"

He opened his mouth to suggest she stay put, then closed it. Already he could tell she was a woman who would do only what she wanted to do. "Give me your hand."

For just a moment she faltered, her brown eyes flickering uncertainly. But then she squared her shoulders and extended her hand. Before he touched her he knew. Knew it would be more than he expected. Knew that she knew it, too. Then knew he'd been right when he took her hand and felt a jolt that skittered straight down to his toes. His heart skipped another thump.

*Wrong place, wrong time,* she'd said. Perhaps, perhaps not. But he sure as hell wanted to find out. Placing a steadying hand on her back, he pulled her to her feet, feeling her muscles tense under his hand as she found her balance, watching as her eyes changed yet again. Heated. Narrowed. She felt it, too, the electricity between them, and he could see she was not at all happy about it. And that intrigued him more than anything else.

Was she attached? Deliberately he lifted her left hand, dropped his eyes to her bare fingers. She was unmarried, at least. And if she did have a boyfriend, he had to be a real louse to let her come to the bus station alone. *If she were mine, I wouldn't.* He looked up with arched brows and her brown eyes flashed, as if she'd read his mind.

Politely but firmly she disengaged her hand. "Thank you, Mr. Buchanan. I appreciate your help, but as you can see, I'm fine. I won't take up any more of your time." She turned to the old woman and put an arm around her thin shoulders. "You need to sit down," she said and led her to an unoccupied row of seats. "How's your heart? Are you on any medication? Are you waiting for someone?"

Ethan followed, concerned, but even more curious. He heard the old woman say her heart was as strong as Dana's and that she was waiting for her grandson to come.

"Did you have anything valuable in your purse?" Dana asked her.

"I don't carry anything valuable anymore. The world's filled with too many crazies." She patted Dana's hand, so much calmer now. "I just hate that awful man knocked you down."

"Well, I'm fine, so don't you worry." She stood up and Ethan watched her close her eyes for a few seconds. When she opened them he could see the pain brewing. "The security guard will be back soon, ma'am. I hope he gets your purse back."

"Thank you." The old woman caught Ethan's eye. "Your Good Samaritan is waiting."

Dana's eyes glanced his way, then back down to the old woman. "I really have to go." She took one of the woman's gnarled old hands in hers. "Take care." Then she made a beeline for the exit and Ethan had to quicken his pace to keep up with her.

With a hand on her arm, he stopped her at the door. "Maybe you should stay put for just a few more minutes, Miss Dupinsky."

Again her brown eyes flashed. "Are you a doctor, Mr. Buchanan?"

"No."

"A lawyer?"

"God, no."

She smiled again, but it didn't reach her eyes. "Good. We've established that you have no medical or legal basis for your opinion. What I am is tired and now I have a headache. What I could use is a place to clean up and some coffee to wash down an aspirin or two."

"I passed a coffeehouse on my way in here." He glanced at his watch. "It's after six now, they should be open."

"I know the place. They're open twenty-four/seven, so I'll be on my way and you can go back to doing whatever it was you were doing before you became a by-stander."

She was dismissing him, politely but firmly. Trouble was, he wasn't in the mood to be dismissed. Somehow he'd pushed his fatigue back and his headache had ebbed enough for him to want to see where this chance encounter led if only for the next hour. Then he'd have to get some sleep so he could be back here looking at videos by noon. He was here to find Alec. But prag-matically speaking, he had to eat. And while he ate, he could decide what he wanted to do next about this woman who set his skin on fire with a simple touch. "I'd finished my business here for now. I was just leaving when I heard you scream."

"That wasn't me." It seemed a point of pride. "It was her." Then her eyes softened and his heart took a slow roll in his chest. "Thank you for helping me, Mr. Bu-chanan. Not many strangers would take the time to be a Good Samaritan these days."

"You did. So did I." He paused, let the simple statement sink in before adding, "My next stop was going to be to get breakfast at that very coffee shop."

She sighed and her shoulders slumped. "I don't mean to be rude, but while I really do appreciate your help, I'm not interested in any relationships. I don't want to lead you on."

Ethan felt some sympathy for the women who'd approached him over recent months. If he was a fraction as dismissive as Dana was, he'd probably hurt quite a few female egos. His might have been bruised as well if he hadn't seen that she'd been as affected by that brief physical contact as he. "I didn't ask you to marry me, Miss Dupinsky." Her eyes widened at his bluntness and he shrugged. "At this moment all I want to do is to eat breakfast and make sure you don't have a concussion. If I can do both at the same time, that's a good use of my time."

She closed her eyes. "I don't have a concussion," she said tightly.

"Are *you* a doctor?" he asked, injecting mild humor into his voice.

She opened her eyes and regarded him

levelly. "No. I'm not."

"Then how do you know you don't? Are you hungry?" he added before she could come back with another put-off.

She huffed a very tired, almost mirthless chuckle. "I could eat."

"Then when the security guard gets back, we'll go have some breakfast."


*Chicago,*
*Sunday, August 1, 6:15 a.m.*

Dana closed the coffee shop's bathroom door and leaned back against the painted plywood. Her head hurt, a dull throbbing pain, but she was lucky.

She'd been standing in the shadows waiting for the woman who was supposed to have come Thursday night, about ready to go home. It had been risky to venture out alone when Mia had told her to be careful, but she wouldn't have told the woman not to come even if she had known how to contact her, which she did not. She'd considered calling David, but in the end decided against it. The women she met distrusted men. Even a gentle man like David Hunter would send them running away.

So she'd gone herself and stood there, nervous at every noise, carefully watching every face, waiting. She'd turned to leave when she saw the young man approach the old woman, a crazed light in his eyes with which she was unfortunately too familiar. Her own ex had come home that way all too often, a junkie, desperate for his next fix. He'd put his hands on the old woman's throat, and Dana had simply reacted. It hadn't been intelligent or particularly well planned and the next thing she knew she was sailing through the air, crashing her head into the bench. Dammit, it hurt like a bitch, too.

She'd lain there, trying to get her bearings, listening to the old woman's wails, when she felt the warmth of a big body kneeling beside her. And then she'd found herself looking up into a pair of steady green eyes. Not the brilliant green of jade or emerald, but the soft green of new leaves after a long winter. And everything inside her, all the turmoil of Evie and Lillian and even the old woman . . . all of it calmed. It didn't disappear, but it was suddenly manageable. In that one moment, she wasn't alone.

And then he'd held her hand and suddenly, unexpectedly, everything inside her turned upside down. Even now, it still was. Even now, her heart still thundered in her chest, her skin still almost painfully sensitized. She could try to tell herself it was the shock of being knocked down, but Dana Dupinsky didn't lie. At least not to herself.

She made her way to the sink and stared at her reflection in the mirror. Blood was crusted in her hair, on her face, smeared on her plain polo shirt. A bruise had formed on her cheek where she'd taken the brunt of the fall. The bruise would fade in a day or two. *I've had worse,* she thought. And she had. Still, she'd been lucky.

Hands shaking, she turned on the water, splashed her face. Grabbed a paper towel and dabbed at the blood on her face until she'd uncovered the cut. It was worse than she'd thought. She probably needed stitches. Buchanan had been right.

Buchanan. He was out there, with his steady green eyes and gentle hands. Waiting for her at one of the tables. She didn't believe for a moment that he'd given up and left. And to her own consternation, she wasn't certain she wanted him to. No, she couldn't lie and pretend nothing happened when he'd taken her hand. She'd felt it. Hell, she would have had to have been dead not to. It was as if a current had passed through her body, strong and very real. It certainly wasn't something that happened to her every day.

It certainly wasn't something that had happened to her, ever.

So she'd agreed to breakfast. Then she'd walk away and he could return to whatever business had put him in the Chicago bus station before dawn. She couldn't lie and pretend she wasn't the smallest bit curious about that as well. Why had he been in the bus station at five-thirty in the morning? Why did his suit look like it had been slept in while his eyes looked like he hadn't slept in days? And why had he taken the time to be a Good Samaritan? There was only one way to find out.

The coffee shop was starting to fill up when she slipped back into the dining room, but it took only a second to locate him. He would be the golden giant of a man politely rising to his feet by the table against the wall. Watching patiently as she came to him.

She couldn't shake the feeling that she'd done so before. It was the same feeling she'd had looking up at him from the bus terminal floor. Like she'd known him forever.

He didn't sit when she reached him, but instead gently grasped her chin and pulled her closer, tilting her head toward the light. Giving her a close-up view of the strong, tanned column of his throat. The loosened knot of his tie. The hint of golden hair at his open collar. She couldn't control the shiver that raced down her back. His chest expanded suddenly as he drew a deep breath. "You need stitches," he pronounced. Huskily.

"Butterfly bandage," Dana responded. Unsteadily. She gulped at the air. "It stopped bleeding a long time ago." Although the way her heart was pumping, it was small wonder it didn't start spouting like a geyser. He didn't let go. If anything, he pulled her closer.

"It'll get infected." It was the barest of murmurs. Another shiver arced across her skin.

"I'm . . . I hate needles," she confessed.

His chest moved again, this time in silent laughter. "Well, I guess I can't argue with that." He let her go and she wished he hadn't. "Sit and eat," he said quietly and slid onto the vinyl bench on his side of the table. "It appears you've been here at least once or twice before," he added wryly, pointing to her place where a plate of steaming French fries sat waiting, and Dana instantly regretted having chosen this shop. It was so close to the bus station, she came here whenever a bus was arriving later than scheduled. She never had enough cash for more than a plate of fries and a Coke, so that's all she ever ordered.

Dana glanced over at the counter where the coffee shop owner stood grinning. Fifty-plus and man-hungry, Betty's eyes moved lasciviously over Buchanan before turning to give her the thumbs-up sign. Buchanan just smiled politely at the busybody and gave her a crisp military salute.

Dana rolled her eyes and sat down. "Pay no attention to the woman behind the counter, Mr. Buchanan. She's been committed three times just this year."

His brows lifted as he liberally salted his eggs. He shot a curious glance to where Betty sat openly staring, agog. Not that Dana could blame her, really. "Oh, yeah?"

Scowling, she squirted ketchup on her plate. "No. She's just nosy."

Buchanan smiled and Dana drew another gulping breath at the sight. The man was going to give her heart failure. Even with a rumpled suit and unshaven cheeks the man was gorgeous enough to take the breath of any woman with a pulse. And

Dana found she definitely had a pulse, which at the moment was scrambling to beat all hell.

"Well, I figured you must come here fairly often even before she brought the fries," he said, spearing his fork into his steak. "When we came in and you went straight to the rest room, she marched over here and gave me grief about the blood on your face. I had to tell her what happened before she would let me sit down. But I think she likes me now."

Dana glared at Betty who just beamed. "Please, let's just change the subject." She dunked her fries and watched him consume huge quantities of food, like he hadn't eaten in days. "So why were you in the bus station at five-thirty in the morning?"

"Um . . ." He swallowed and patted his lips with the napkin, which of course drew her eyes to his mouth. It was a very, very nice mouth. Very nice lips. "Business."

"What kind of business?"

"I have a security consulting business."

Dana frowned. "Securities — like stocks and bonds?" If he was an investment banker, she was the Queen of England. No investment banker had shoulders like his.

He shook his head. "No, like secure networks. I help companies make their computer systems as hack-proof as possible. I also set up video surveillance and along with my partner, Clay, assist in training their security guards."

She regarded him thoughtfully. Well, that made more sense, now that her mind was working a little more clearly. "So do you normally call on potential clients in the middle of the night wearing a rumpled suit and two days' beard?"

He coughed. "Observant, aren't you?"

"Normally, yes."

He narrowed his eyes. "So why couldn't you describe the guy that knocked you down in there when the security guard returned empty-handed?"

Dana met his gaze head-on. "I did."

"Um-hmm. Tall, twenties, no eye color, brown hair. The old lady who screamed gave a better description and she wore glasses as thick as my thumb."

The truth was, Dana didn't really want the guy caught, because then she'd have to go to court and admit why she was in the bus station to start with. She would have if the lady had been hurt or if anything of value had been stolen, but she wasn't and it hadn't and Dana was keeping her mouth closed. "It happened too fast."

Buchanan wasn't buying it. "Uh-huh. And why were you in the bus station so late?"

This one at least she was ready for. "I was waiting for a bus."

"To?"

"From. I was meeting a friend."

"Who is where?"

"She didn't get off the bus, so I guess she's not coming after all." She'd waited for tonight's client for two hours, but the woman had never gotten off the bus. Again.

He raised a blond brow. "Impolite friend."

Dana shrugged, laying it on a little thicker. "More like flaky. She says she's going to come and gets the dates mixed up. Tomorrow she'll call, crying her eyes out in apology."

"Which you'll accept."

"Naturally. She's my friend."

He tilted his head. "So what do you do when you're not meeting flaky friends at the bus terminal, Dana?"

"I'm a photographer. You know, mothers and babies, that sort of thing." This was actually true. Sort of. She'd been worried that the constant flow of women and children in and out of Hanover House would attract unwanted attention from her neighbors. It had been Evie's idea to put out a small, discreet sign advertising family photography. Dana already had the camera equipment she used to produce new driver's licenses and it did explain all the women and children, but to Dana's annoyance and Evie's amusement, sometimes they drew real business. Normally enough to pay the monthly phone bill, but not enough to threaten the true mission of Hanover House, so everybody was happy.

She leaned back, studied him. "So why *were* you calling on customers with a rumpled suit and two days' beard at five-thirty in the morning?"

He lifted one corner of his very nice mouth and every square inch of her skin sizzled, some square inches a lot more than others. "Nice. I was just about to cut you a handicap."

She bit back a smile of her own. "Keep your handicap. Just answer the question."

"I just got into town and wanted to check out their night talent before calling on the boss during the day. It's the best strategy for winning new business. Evaluate their vulnerabilities" — he leaned forward conspiratorially — "and offer something better."

His voice had softened to something

close to a purr and all Dana could think of was a big golden cat, stalking his prey. But she didn't feel threatened. Not in the conventional sense anyway. She felt . . . powerful, like he'd given her a secret key.

"Are you . . . evaluating my vulnerabilities, Mr. Buchanan?"

Those steady green eyes gleamed. "Ethan."

She acknowledged his point with a small nod. "Ethan. Well, are you?"

He said nothing for a moment, just held her gaze. Finally he leaned back, and when he spoke all smooth texture and pretense were gone from his voice. "Do you want me to?"

It was not the answer she expected and she blinked. "Me?"

"Yes, you. I get the impression that you don't say or do anything you don't want to do. And if someone tries to make you, you duck the issue like a pro."

She blinked again. "What a strange thing to say." *And reasonably true.*

"Astute, I'd think. Well?"

She drew a breath and gave him the most honest answer she knew. "I don't know."

He nodded. "That's fair, I suppose. One more question and I'll let you go."

Disappointment speared her heart at the very thought of his leaving. "Okay. Ask."

"Do you have a boyfriend, husband, or significant other . . . of any kind?"

It was her turn to cough at his implication. "No current husbands or boyfriends and I'm heterosexual, thank you very much."

He smiled at that. "Good to know. Can I then assume you have an ex-husband?"

She thought about her ex-husband, the years she'd suffered under his abuse. The relief at breaking free. She'd never looked back. "Very ex. So ex he's way past Z. You?"

"Ex. Not as ex as yours. She's probably only halfway to Y." When she smiled back he leaned forward, his nice mouth gone totally serious. "You felt it back there, didn't you?"

Instantly she sobered. Opened her mouth to deny it, but couldn't. "Yes."

It wasn't until he exhaled that she realized he'd been holding his breath for her answer. Realized that he'd just exposed one of his vulnerabilities. He slid his hand across the table until it covered hers. "I have to go now. Meet me here. Tomorrow. Same time."

It wasn't a question. It was a demand,

insistently offered. Dana sat staring at him, feeling it all over again, that surge of current at just the touch of his hand. And suddenly she stood at the edge of a precipice, somehow knowing that her answer was very important. The wariness with which she lived every day of her life inserted itself. "I don't —"

He shook his head, interrupting her. "You're cautious, I understand that. I won't ask for your number, or your sign, or even your favorite color. I promise." He clenched his jaw for a moment, then visibly relaxed it. "Life is too short, Dana. Too damn short not to seize opportunities when they present themselves."

Something had changed. Gone was the stalking cat, in its place a man as honest as she thought she'd ever met. *It's just fries and a Coke. How much safer could it be?*

Her eyes dropped to his hand, still covering hers. Still hot. Electric. She raised her gaze to find his intently focused on her face. "Green." The word was out of her mouth before she realized it.

His eyes narrowed. "What?"

"My favorite color is green."

He leaned back, relief in his green eyes. "Tomorrow then? Same time?"

His hand no longer covered hers and she

wanted it back. And because she wanted it back, she wanted to run. "I'll think about it."

His blond brows furrowed ever so slightly. "Think hard. I'll be here."

# Chapter Five

*Wight's Landing, Maryland,*
*Sunday, August 1, 8:30 a.m. Eastern*
*(7:30 a.m. Central)*

Sheriff Louisa Moore shook her head in disbelief, her eyes watering from the stench of decaying flesh. Mr. Stan Vaughn had placed a call to her office this morning, clearly in a panic. He'd found a body, he'd said. Well, he'd certainly been right on that score.

Lou covered her mouth and stuck her head in the little shed. "Find anything, Doc?"

County Coroner John Kehoe looked up, the top half of his face covered with goggles, the bottom half with a surgical mask. "Not yet."

Her first partner back in Boston told her she'd get used to the bloaters, but ten years and a major career change later, she still had not. "Then at least a time of death?"

John sat back on his haunches. "Three days, maybe four. Sometime between Wednesday and Thursday, I'd guess. The bugs will tell the true tale."

Lou fought back the urge to gag. "Bugs?"

"Sure. I'll send samples of the bugs and their larvae to the lab." He rocked forward to his knees. "Give me another half hour, then we'll be ready for tag 'n' bag. I don't need you here if you want to run on up to the house."

"Thanks."

She made her way up to the house, scanning the beach as she went. Her deputies had combed every inch of sand for several hundred yards on each side of the body. They'd had a bad storm Thursday night. Any evidence outside the shed would most likely have been washed away.

But it looked like a suicide, so that would probably not be a major concern. But the boxers bothered her. Why would a man come to a stranger's shed wearing only his boxers to commit suicide? And where was the note? And could the Vaughns really have ignored *that* smell for almost two days? She let herself in the kitchen. "Mr. Vaughn?"

"We're in the living room."

They were, sitting side by side on an old sofa. Lou studied the Vaughns for a moment. Both looked pale. It was understandable, of course. It wasn't every day vacationers found a dead body in their shed. Still, there was something about these two that bothered her. "Dr. Kehoe is examining the body right now," she said and the two nodded. "Can you tell me how long you've been staying here?"

"For about a week," Mrs. Vaughn said, her voice quavery. "We got here Sunday, but we left again on Tuesday."

Lou slipped her notepad from her breast pocket, not breaking eye contact. "Why?"

Mr. Vaughn covered Mrs. Vaughn's hand with his. "We went to Annapolis for our tenth wedding anniversary."

If she hadn't been watching she would have missed it, missed the way Mrs. Vaughn flinched when her husband touched her. Still, the woman had discovered a suicide in her backyard, a grisly one at that. "When did you come back?"

"Friday afternoon," Mr. Vaughn answered.

*Just the facts, ma'am,* Lou thought. She smiled pleasantly. "What time?"

Mrs. Vaughn moved her shoulders back and forth. "Three-thirty. Or so."

"And where did you stay in Annapolis?"

Mr. Vaughn frowned. "Statehouse Hotel,

but why are you asking?"

Lou shrugged. "Just gathering all the information. Did you see anyone lurking around?"

Mr. Vaughn was still frowning. "No."

"Mr. Vaughn, Mrs. Vaughn." Lou shook her head, giving a friendly grimace. "I'm curious as to how you could have ignored that smell for a day and a half."

"We did," Mr. Vaughn replied smoothly. "Sometimes after a storm we find dead fish littering the shore. Once, a small shark washed up. The tide always comes in and takes it away. There was a storm Thursday night. We just assumed . . ." He let the thought trail with a grimace of his own. "I have to say my brother had the iron stomach of the family. I get queasy thinking about dead things. I just prefer to let the bay do the work for me. But it didn't and we couldn't stand it anymore, so I went down to investigate. And found that poor man."

Lou glanced down at her notepad, irritated by the polish of his reply. "Well, I won't take any more of your time. But, please let me know when you plan to go home." Outside again, she covered her mouth with her handkerchief as she made her way back to the shed. Dr. Kehoe was directing her deputies as they rolled the gurney bearing the body bag.

He pulled his mask off. "I'll call you when I know something."

"And I'll check the missing persons reports," she said. "That's all we can do for now."

*Chicago,*
*Sunday, August 1, 8:00 a.m.*

Dana smelled the beef stew before she slipped into Hanover House's kitchen. Caroline was here, doing her normal Sunday cooking that would last them well into the week.

"I was wondering when you'd get back," Caroline said. She looked over her shoulder and her eyes widened. "What happened?"

"I had a little accident in the bus station."

Caroline found the first-aid kit and pushed Dana into a chair. "You need stitches."

"A butterfly bandage will do."

"That's what you always say." She started cleaning the cut with peroxide. "David came by last night after he left

115

here. He told me about Lillian. I'm so sorry."

Dana drew a deep shuddering breath. "Me, too."

"David also said you and Evie had words."

"You could call it that, I guess."

"Dana, you know Evie is wrong. I worked with Lillian, too. She wasn't going to leave Chicago. New names would not have helped her."

"I know."

"Then you also know you've stalled long enough. What happened, honey?"

From the corner of her eye, Dana watched Caroline exchange the brown bottle of peroxide for the disinfectant. "Just a little accident. *Ow.* That stings."

Caroline tilted Dana's face up to the light, her blue eyes troubled. "You have a bruise, too. Did somebody's husband do this to you? Lillian's husband?"

"No. It really was an accident. Some junkie tried to rob an old lady."

Peeling a length of adhesive tape, Caroline sighed. "And you just stepped right in?"

"It was reflex. He gave me a shove and my head hit a bench." Her eyes teared as her hair was pulled back from the cut.

"*Ow.* Dammit, Caro, that really hurts."

"Sorry. When was this?"

Dana glanced at the kitchen clock. "About two and a half hours ago."

Caroline drew back, surprised. "What took you so long to get here?"

Dana hesitated, then shrugged. "There was . . . this guy."

Caroline's hands stilled. "Did this . . . *guy* have a name?"

"Ethan Buchanan."

"Hmm. Nice name." She gently pressed the bandage into place.

"His name wasn't the only thing that was nice," Dana responded dryly and Caroline huffed a chuckle before carefully lowering her pregnant body into a chair.

She sat back, arms propped on her rounded stomach, her eyes sober. "Tell me."

"Well, it was right after the junkie hit me. When I opened my eyes . . . he was there."

Caroline held up her hand. "Wait just a minute. You mean you were unconscious after you hit your head? And you didn't go to the hospital? Are you *insane?*"

"If I was out, it was only for a few seconds. And I didn't go to the hospital because I don't have insurance. Not everybody has a rich husband, you know."

Caroline looked pained. "You know we'd pay for your insurance, Max and I."

"And you know I don't take what I don't earn. You want to hear this or not?"

"You know I do. So *he* was there, this Ethan Buchanan. Then what?"

Dana moved her shoulders uncomfortably. Now that she had to say it, it sounded pretty stupid. *Then he looked at me.* It sounded so childish. But he had done no more than that, not at first. "I don't know. It's hard to explain."

"Try," Caroline drawled.

"Dammit, I don't know. I was all mad and upset and my head hurt and then, there he was, all of a sudden. He . . . he looked at me. And then . . ."

Blonde brows lifted. "And then?"

"I felt like everything would be all right. Like I'd always known him. Dumb, huh?"

"No." Caroline's voice was gentle. "Don't even think it. So what happened then?"

Dana drew a very deep breath. "He touched my hand to help me up and it was like . . . electricity. Like when they use the paddles to start your heart."

Caroline's eyes had grown wide. "Mercy."

Dana had to chuckle at the subdued exclamation. "Yeah. I tried to leave before the security guard came back from trying to catch the junkie, but Ethan wouldn't let me go. Said he was afraid I had a concussion. Then he made me go get breakfast with him."

"*Made* you, huh?"

Dana shot her a foul look. "You're enjoying this, aren't you?"

"Immensely. So what will you do next?"

"He asked me to meet him there tomorrow. I said I'd think about it."

Blond brows arched. "Which means yes or no?"

"I'm not sure."

Caroline touched her hand. "What's really bothering you, honey?"

Dana blew out a breath. "I don't know. I've just got . . ." She rubbed her hand over her chest to relieve the pressure building there. "Do you believe in fate?"

Caroline didn't blink. "Yes. And no."

"Well, that's definitive."

Caroline smiled. "I know. I learned it in law school last semester. How to Dodge Secret of Life Questions 101. I got an A."

Dana's lips curved in spite of herself. "I'm serious."

"So am I." Caroline sobered slightly, flinching. "That was a swift one." She shifted in her chair, rubbing the side of her stomach with the heel of her hand. "He/she's active this morning." She leaned back, her gaze sharp, her palm resting atop her unborn child. "How can I sit here today and tell you I don't believe in fate? I met Max at just the right time . . . for both of us. I think the fate part is where we met. But I distinctly remember the moment when I decided not to walk away." Her eyes sharpened. "Fate is the opportunity. Choice is what you do with it."

"That's what I thought," Dana said quietly.

Caroline tilted her head. "Ethan Buchanan made a pretty big impression on you."

Dana's chuckle was mirthless. He had. She just had no idea what to do about it. "I was thinking about you and Max and then I wondered — what if I never meet anyone of my own?"

"Dana —"

Dana shook her head. "No, really. And then I thought, so what if I do? Would it really matter? Would I walk away from what I do? Could I? It's what I am."

"You are a great deal more than the director of Hanover House, Dana. But that aside, why should you have to give up what you do?"

"Please, Caroline. I practically live at the House. I sleep in my own apartment maybe once a week. I could never give someone the time a relationship deserves."

"Well, then, I suppose that's the choice." Caroline drew a breath, let it out. "Did it ever occur to you that you don't have to work at Hanover House forever?"

Dana's mind was flooded with the picture of Lillian's children discovering their mother's body. Even as she desperately tried to push the picture away, it morphed into the image that still managed to rip her insides to shreds. She stared down at the backs of her hands, then her palms. "No, this is something I have to do. It's . . . it's my life. That's all."

Caroline grasped Dana's hands, kneaded her palms with her thumbs. "Look at me, Dana. Look at me." Dana raised her eyes slowly, saw Caroline's face focused with singular intent. "Your hands are clean, Dana. Don't you think you deserve a life of your own? Don't you think you deserve to be happy, too?"

The question hit harder than the bench. Dana opened her mouth, but not a sound came out and Caroline's blue eyes went sad. "Go get some sleep, Dana. Maybe things will be clearer when you're not exhausted."

Evie stopped in front of the mirror in the front hall. Examined her reflection. Her makeup was good. No sign of the damn scar. She wouldn't be expected to smile. Funerals were good in that regard. Her lips thinned as she stared at her reflection.

She'd be damned if she didn't go to Lillian's funeral. If they'd done their jobs, Lillian would be alive today. She'd sit in the back. Slip in after the funeral started and slip out before it was over. No one would see her and Dana's paranoia would be upheld.

She turned for the door when she heard a quiet "Ahem" behind her and she jumped.

"Jane." Her pulse settling, Evie regarded the woman who'd been standing behind her. She'd been here since Friday, the tenth Jane Smith to arrive in the last year. Evie wished their clients would show more creativity when choosing an alias. "What can I do for you?"

122

Jane wrung her hands nervously. "It's nothing. I'll just wait until you get back."

Evie lifted one corner of her mouth in the three-cornered smile she'd practiced in the mirror. "I'm going to be gone for a while. I have a funeral to go to. What do you need?"

"I just was wondering if I could get some Benadryl for Erik. He gets hives."

Poor kid. Curled into a ball like that. Evie's lips thinned. Somebody should pay for whatever had happened to that little boy. "You go to him. I'll bring it to you."


*Chicago,*
*Sunday, August 1, 11:15 a.m.*


As setups went, this one was perfect. Sue was here, in a place James would never even think to look. She crept up to the little room she'd been given on her arrival Friday night, found the kid on the twin bed where she'd left him. He was waking up.

"Can't have that," she murmured. She retrieved one of the kid's pills from her backpack and made him swallow it. There had been two bottles in the Vaughns' bathroom. She'd tried to pry details from

Rickman regarding the kid's meds, but having never fully recovered from seeing her fiancé lose the top of his head, she'd been very little help.

A quick Internet search while she'd been connected at Morgantown had yielded better results. Keppra was the more powerful drug, but Phenobarbital could dope a kid up if given in too large a dose. She did want the kid to sleep. She did not want him going into seizures that would make them noticeable in a crowd. Or perhaps make him dead.

Sue needed the kid to keep breathing. At least for another week or so. So she gave him just enough of the Keppra and doubled up the Pheno. And he'd slept like a baby all the way to Chicago. But she was running low on both drugs.

*Adopt, adapt and improve.* Her mother had used garden variety over-the-counter Benadryl mixed with wine to shut Bryce up when they were kids, and if it was good enough for Mom, it would be good enough for her. She'd stretch the Pheno with Benadryl until she could get a refill. A refill was something the other mothers in the shelter had assured her would be easy to do. "Just ask Dana," the mother in the room next door had said.

Dupinsky had been stingy with the Benadryl last night. Only gave her a single damn dose. But Scarface had given her the whole damn bottle.

So now Sue chased the pill with a big spoonful of the Benadryl. The kid struggled at first, weakly, but a single hard look had him complying. She watched his throat work as he swallowed, but something in his eyes, just the tiniest flicker of defiance, made her check to be sure. He fought, pulling his face away from her hands when she grabbed him, nearly choking when she forced his mouth open to find the red liquid still pooled in his cheek.

"Swallow it," she muttered, before realizing it would do no good to threaten the child with words. With one hand clenching his scrawny jaw, she wrote him a note on the pad of paper someone had so thoughtfully left next to the bed. Showed it to him.

Watched his face blanch. Without another flicker of his eyes, he swallowed.

She tipped him a nod, shoved the note in her pocket, and shoved his head forcefully to the pillow. Dumb kid. Thinking he could get the better of her. He was twelve, for God's sake. And how smart could he be? Considering his father, after all.

For a moment she stood looking down at the boy, contemplating. By the time the final curtain fell, he'd be dead. On some level, the notion should bother her. It did not.

She clenched her hand slowly. It was sticky from the Benadryl. She needed to wash her hands. And she desperately needed a smoke. With a final warning glare at the kid, she grabbed her cigarettes and lighter and headed for the bathroom.

Alec watched her go, then closed his eyes, pulling himself into a miserable little ball. He remembered the man who'd been with her at the beach house. The one who'd held a gun to Cheryl's head while the white-eyed woman tied him up. Bryce was his name. Alec knew that now. Alec knew that Bryce had stayed behind, waiting for his parents. And Alec knew that Bryce now held that gun to his mother's head. The note had said so.

Alec couldn't take a chance that the white-eyed woman was lying.

His mother would die. Just like Cheryl died. And Paul. Unless he cooperated.

Alec swallowed again, this time feeling the burning of tears in the back of his eyes. He was crying like a stupid little baby when his mother needed his help. He'd let that bitch drug him, while his mother needed his help.

He had no idea of where he was, or who all the people were around him. The red-haired lady treated the white-eyed lady nice. So she must be bad, too. For the first time he desperately wished for his processor. He could slip it behind his ear and listen, like Cheryl had taught him. He would know if the red-haired lady was good or bad. But he didn't have his processor. Cheryl was dead. And his mom needed his help.

But the meds made his arms feel like lead and the inside of his head like molasses. He struggled hard, but in the end he drifted.

Satisfied, Sue sat down on the edge of an ancient tub in the equally ancient bathroom. She fished a cigarette from her pocket, flicked her Bic to its tip, and took a nice long drag. With a flourish, she pulled the note from her pocket and touched the burning end of the cigarette to the paper, watching fascinated as it smoldered, then burned, the red edge of the flame racing to the paper's edge. Just before the flame reached her fingers, she dropped it in the toilet and flushed the ashes. The note had done the trick, threatening to have Bryce kill his mother. That Bryce was rotting in some Maryland jail was something the kid didn't know, and what the kid didn't know wouldn't hurt either of them.

Another drag filled her lungs, and she relaxed for the first time in days. Then her cell phone rang, nearly sending her off the edge of the tub. She dug the phone from her pocket, her pulse quickening. *Bryce. Or worse, James.* "Yeah."

"Baby, it's Fred."

She blew out a lungful of smoke, now annoyed. "What do you want?" she hissed.

"Now is that any way to talk to your personal delivery service?" he mocked.

She'd been afraid of this. One damn favor, that's all she'd asked. A favor she'd paid for in more ways than one just two days before. "What do you want?"

He chuckled. "Just checking in on you, baby. You find the place all right?"

"Yes."

"And? Did they believe you? Was my work acceptable?"

Sue eyed her reflection in the mirror over the sink. The bruises he'd applied to her face with such relish were just now beginning to fade. But they'd been necessary, both to convince Dupinsky and Tammy.

She'd needed to know how to contact the shelter Tammy had told her about so many times during their five-year Hillsboro cohabitation, the shelter where Tammy herself had hidden for weeks before returning home to kill her husband. Tammy would never have believed her story without the bruises, never would have given her the phone number for Hanover House had she not been certain Sue was really in danger. That was the thing about people who murdered in the heat of passion, like Tammy. When they were in their right minds, they tended to have . . . scruples. Sue grimaced, finding even the word distasteful. "Yeah, they believed me. I have to go."

"Not so fast, baby. I was walkin' my rounds today and Tammy asked about you. She wanted to be sure you were all right." Laughter filled his voice and she knew what came next would not be good. "I told her I'd check on you myself."

Fred had been the best way to get a message to Tammy. Sue hadn't been about to return to Hillsboro during visiting hours, even if she'd been allowed through the front gates, which as a paroled felon, she was not. That's where Fred had come in. He'd been a guard in her cell block, a dependable supplier of anything they'd wanted from the outside — for a price, of course. Fred wasn't Hollywood material, but no troll like some of the other guards, so most of the girls hadn't minded paying his price. Sue had. Every damn time.

The morning of Sue's release, he'd taken her into the supply closet for one more little "heart-to-heart" as he liked to call them — just for old times' sake. When he was done, he'd told her if she ever needed anything to just give him a call.

So she did. She'd called him from Columbus, asked him to meet her at the station in Indy, but he hadn't shown, the bastard, and she'd missed the next bus to Chicago, waiting for him. She'd ended up taking the Friday morning bus to Chicago, where she and the kid transferred to the bus the regular visitors called the "Prison Express." A cab ride later she was on Fred's doorstep. She told Fred she needed some convincing bruises on her face, a Polaroid to show them off, and a letter containing the photo delivered personally to Tammy. After locking the kid in the bathroom, she paid Fred's price, gritted her teeth as he obliged her need for bruises, and waited until he made a trip up to the pen.

A few hours later he was back. Tammy had bought the story and Sue had the telephone number she needed. She and the kid had gotten back on the bus to Chicago and a few hours later met Dana Dupinsky at the bus station. All in all, a smooth operation. Except for Fred. He was a loose end. Loose ends were normally a bad thing. She should have dropped him in his apartment Friday afternoon, except he'd been armed, too.

"Tell Tammy I'm fine. I have to go."

"Not so fast." His voice hardened. "Now that you're there, you'll do a favor for me."

"Evie!"

Sue started at the yell, which had come from right outside the door. "Somebody's coming," she whispered. "I have to go."

"Just remember, I have the phone number, too, sugar. One phone call from me will expose you and the kid, whoever he is. Call me later." *Damn.* She'd have to take care of him and soon. She dropped the butt in the toilet and flushed it.

"Evie! Where are you?" There was a light knock. "Evie?"

Shrugging back into character, Sue opened the bathroom door and came face-to-face with a very pregnant woman she hadn't met yet. Her blond hair was too

131

shiny, her eyes too calm, her face too serenely content to be a "client," which was what Dupinsky called the women she took in. Blondie must be one of the wardens. The woman's brows went up in surprise. "I guess Evie's someplace else," the woman said with a soft drawl and a kind smile. "You must be Jane. Dana said you arrived just yesterday. I'm Caroline."

Sue dropped her eyes, glanced up through her lashes. Managed a trembling nod. "I did," she murmured. "Me and my son."

"Erik, right?" Caroline, still with the soft smile. "Dana says he's ten."

"That's right." That's what she'd told Dupinsky. The kid was so scrawny that Sue was afraid they'd insist on a doctor if she said he was twelve. "You work here?"

Caroline smiled. "Sometimes. I'm looking for Evie. Have you met her yet?"

Evie was Scarface, the one who'd run from the kitchen the night before. Sue had been eavesdropping outside the door, heard the little blond cop break the news of the woman's murder. If the argument between Dupinsky and Evie had provided an earful, the brief peek into the kitchen after Evie's stormy departure was an eyeful — Dupinsky in the arms of a delicious

132

specimen of man. Even now the thought of him made Sue want to drool.

"She . . . um . . . she left an hour or so ago." To go to the funeral Sue had heard Dupinsky and the lady cop expressly forbid. "She said she was going to a funeral." And from the corner of her eye she watched Caroline's face go dark for just a moment, then the wrath was smoothed away, serenity restored.

"Thank you, Jane. Is there anything else you or Erik need?"

A computer connection for my laptop, Sue thought. It was past time to send another communication to the Vaughns. Two uninterrupted hours with the Adonis that had been in the kitchen with Dupinsky last night . . . She ducked her head. "No. We're fine."

Caroline lightly touched her shoulder and Sue had to fight the urge to knock her hand away. She really hated social workers. Always trying to get into your head.

"Everything's going to be okay now, Jane," Caroline said. "You're safe here."

Sue made her eyes tear, her lips quiver. "Thank you," she whispered.

"We're doing some work on the roof later today. Will the banging bother Erik?"

An atomic bomb wouldn't bother Erik.

Even if he weren't drugged, the kid was deafer than a rock. Sue had tried many times to catch him faking his deafness, but he wasn't. "No, Erik will be fine." Her brows furrowed. "Who will be working on the roof?"

Caroline's smile was a tad too bright and Sue could see anger simmering beneath her calm exterior. She was still pissed at Evie. Most excellent. Diversions among the wardens would keep the spotlight off Sue.

"My brother-in-law David. He's the most trustworthy man I know. Well, after my husband, of course. He'll be done quickly, so you'll get a good night's sleep tonight."

The Adonis was her brother-in-law? If her husband was half as good-looking as his brother, it was just one more reason to hate Caroline. Sue lowered her eyes to the worn carpet that covered the floor. "Thanks. I need to get back to Erik now."

"Of course. Oh, Jane?"

Sue turned to find Caroline's smile still firmly in place. "Yes?"

"I couldn't help but notice the smell of smoke in the bathroom. We don't allow smoking here at Hanover House. It bothers the children and it's a fire hazard.

It's an old house. One spark . . ." She let the thought trail with a friendly grimace. "Okay?"

Sue drew a breath. Shoved the anger back down from where it boiled up. *Little bitch, trying to tell me what to do.* Sue nodded at the carpet. "I'm sorry." She gritted the apology through her teeth, trying like hell to re-affect the put-upon Jane.

"It's not a problem. I just needed you to know. I'll see you later."

Sue jerked a nod. "Later." Quickly she escaped back into her room, glancing in the mirror on the wall. Caroline was still standing in the hall, staring after her with a troubled frown on her face. Sue shut the door. Carefully.

She would regain control of herself. *You will calm down.* She came to an abrupt halt, realizing she'd been pacing the floor with quick, savage steps. She drew a deep breath.

*I only need a week,* she thought, looking at the kid peacefully sleeping. But first, there were still things to do. She dug the digital camera she'd stolen from Rickman from her backpack and snapped a picture of the sleeping kid. Nothing dramatic, just a little reminder to the Vaughns that she still held all the cards. She pulled the laptop from her backpack, flipped its power button. She'd give them her terms now. Five million wired to an offshore account. She'd learned all about offshore accounts in the prison library.

She frowned. The laptop screen was still blank. Shit. The battery was dead.

The computer had plenty of juice when she'd sent the first e-mail from Morgantown. *I must not have turned it off when I was finished,* she thought crossly and pawed through her backpack, but found no electrical adapter. Fuck. That idiot Bryce had put it in his backpack, which now resided somewhere with the Maryland police. Her heart went still. Had she touched it? No, she was certain she had not, so her person was still in the clear. She just had to find another way to reach out and touch the Vaughns.


*Chicago,*
*Sunday, August 1, 2:00 p.m.*

Dana closed her office door, wincing when Evie's bedroom door slammed upstairs, hard enough to shake the whole house. Caroline had shaken her awake,

136

told her that Evie had gone to Lillian's funeral. Dana tried to intercept her, but had been too late. Instead, she'd waited until Evie came out of the church, her heavy pancake makeup streaked with tears. The ride back had not been pleasant. They'd argued bitterly and Evie's tears flowed again — until a glance in the visor mirror had Evie's accusations shuddering to an abrupt halt.

Without the makeup, Evie was scarred. With it, Dana thought she looked fake. But when it was melting off her face . . . Dana had to admit Evie looked scary. Like the Phantom of the Opera. Understanding her dismay, Dana had stopped at her apartment to allow Evie to fix her makeup so that no one else could see her that way. And after that, Evie hadn't said a word.

Dana sat down at her desk and closed her eyes. Her head still hurt from this morning. And she was hungry. French fries at Betty's with Ethan Buchanan had been a long time ago. Ethan Buchanan. He wanted her to meet him tomorrow. She'd thought about it, sitting out in front of Lillian's funeral, waiting for Evie. She knew nothing about the man except his name and that he could make her heart calm with a look and her nerves zing with a touch. But she could learn more. The resources of the Internet were a click away.

She eyed her dormant computer screen. She could do a search on him, but that seemed rude. An invasion of privacy. She nudged her mouse with one finger.

And sighed when her screen woke up to the Google search result screen. One of their residents, Beverly, would be going west this week and Dana had been searching low-cost housing in California the night before. It seemed to be a sign. If her screen had woken up to solitaire, she could have laughed it off and gone on with her business. But the Google screen beckoned. Tentatively she typed in his name. And hit SEARCH.

Dana stared at the screen as the results came up. Nothing caught her eye. She was being silly. But the arrows at the bottom of the page beckoned and she clicked to the next page, and the next. She was about to give up when a few bolded words caught her eye. And caught her breath. The words *Kandahar* and *casualty* jumped off the screen. She remembered the crisp little salute he'd given Betty that morning. He was military. Or had been. Her palm sweaty on the mouse, she clicked. And watched as her dial-up connection slowly loaded a page from what appeared to be a newsletter. Very slowly.

There was a light knock at her office door and Caroline poked her head in. "Did you eat while you were out?" Not waiting for an answer, she set a bowl of stew on the desk. "What are you looking for?"

Dana shot her a veiled look. "One laugh, one little chuckle, and you're toast, Caro."

Eyes wide, Caroline pulled up a chair. "I wouldn't. It's too important."

"It's from a Marine Corps base in California," Dana murmured. Another minute that seemed like an hour passed while a photo loaded, and Dana found herself staring into those steady green eyes again, this time serious under the brim of a Marine cap. Her pulse once again scrambled. Her heart lodged somewhere in her throat. He was every bit as beautiful as she'd remembered. He'd been a Marine. He'd been wounded. But he was fine now. Very fine. Very much alive. Which is just the way she felt at the moment. *Alive.*

"That's him?" Caroline asked.

Was it ever. "Yeah, that's him."

Caroline squeezed her shoulder. "Looks like your Ethan Buchanan is a war he-ro."

Dana's lips curved at Caroline's twang as her eyes scanned the article. "He was part of a Marine Expeditionary Unit sent into Afghanistan after 9/11."

"He was wounded. He's okay now?"

"Oh, yeah."

"So find out what he's doing now."

Dana refined her search, looking for security consultants, and blinked when her search yielded his Website. "Maynard and Buchanan. He does have a security business."

"So he is who he says he is. You didn't think he would be, did you?"

"Sitting there talking to him, I did. Later, I had my doubts."

Caroline reached over and grabbed the mouse. "Let's look at the staff." She clicked and hummed in approval when a more recent picture of Ethan loaded, minus the Marine cap. "He's a blond. You didn't tell me that."

Dana crossed her arms over her chest to keep her thudding heart contained. She remembered that golden hair at his open collar. "He's a blond, okay?" *He's blond all over.*

"And built. You didn't tell me that, either."

Dana fought the urge to fan herself. The

picture didn't do him justice. "Yes, he's built."

Caroline's eyes twinkled. "And there's a phone number for his office."

"It's Sunday. No one will be there. Besides what would I say to anybody who answered? Hi, my name is Dana and I want to know if your boss is a homicidal lunatic?"

"It does have a certain ring to it." She turned back to the screen with a slight frown. "But you're right. If you're going to be careful, he's the kind you'd need to be careful about."

"What are you talking about? He's a damn war he-ro. You said it yourself."

Caroline tapped the screen next to his picture. "Look past the pretty face and the chest full of medals, Dana."

With difficulty Dana did so, and saw what she meant. "Damn. He's got a brain, too."

"Electrical engineer, electronics specialist, communications expert . . ."

Dana scowled, torn between admiration and annoyance. "He could find out anything about me he wanted to."

"Not like you just did," Caroline said, her tongue tucked in her cheek.

Dana chewed on her lip. "Yeah, but he

can't get thrown in jail for what he does."

Caroline sighed. "We getting too old for all this cloak and dagger stuff, Dupinsky."

"I know."

# Chapter Six

*Chicago,*
*Sunday, August 1, 5:15 p.m.*

Ethan glanced up when a cup of coffee appeared on the table in front of him. "Thanks."

Security Manager Bill Bush grunted. "I can't believe you're still staring at that monitor."

"Me either," Ethan said dryly. His eyes burned, his head ached, and his stomach growled. The sandwich he'd fished out of a vending machine three hours ago was history.

"Anything?" Bush asked, not unkindly.

"Nothing." Ethan took a sip of coffee and winced. It was hot and strong but not enough to combat his fatigue. The few hours' sleep he'd gotten after leaving Dana this morning hadn't been nearly enough. Especially since he'd tossed and turned for most of it. Every time he closed his eyes he'd see that body in the shed. Or Alec, cowering. Or Dana. She was at the edges of his mind as he searched for Alec, an inch of tape at a time. "I wish I could be sure the kid's mom even took this bus. She gave me the slip once before."

Bush sat down behind a desk that held only his Chicago PD retirement plaque. "The driver isn't back on duty until to-morrow. I'll let you know when he calls in."

"I appreciate you checking it out for me," Ethan said.

Bush nodded grimly. "I've got grandkids that age. We were worried my daughter's ex would take the kids. Not because he wanted them, but to make her suffer."

Ethan's custody story had been once again accepted without question. Appar-ently, he was just one of a string of P.I.s to request access to the surveillance tapes for the same purpose. He wished he could come clean with Bush, who seemed like a really decent guy. But he'd promised Stan. No cops, and even though he was retired, Bill Bush was still a cop. Trouble was, searching the tapes would go a lot faster with more eyes than just his. His eyes were becoming too tired to focus. "I think I need to take a break and get some air before I look at any more. I'll be back in a few."

Ethan took his leave, blinking when he stepped into the sunlight. He glanced across the street to the coffee shop. Thought of Dana again, of the way she'd fit just beneath his chin. Of the way she'd let him draw her close, just like she'd known him her whole life. Of the way she'd shivered, the way her voice got all husky and breathless from a simple touch to her hair. She'd been as affected as he was, physically. But there had been so much more. The humor and intelligence in her eyes. The warmth.

Dana Dupinsky had, simply put, intrigued him.

He blinked hard when sweat dripped into his eye. He'd been standing in the August sun, staring in the windows of an all-night coffee shop. He pulled out his cell phone and dialed Clay as he started walking.

"If you hadn't called in another half hour, I was going to call you," Clay said sternly.

"Sorry. I've been checking surveillance tape at the bus station for the last five hours."

"Nothing?"

"Not yet. My eyes were getting blurry so I took a break. Anything on your end?"

"Well, Stan finally called the local police and they came and took McMillan's body."

"When?"

"This morning, after you and I hung up."

"Were you there at the time?"

"No, I didn't want the police to start asking why I was there, so I took a drive . . . well, right after I convinced Stan to make the call. I waited until the coast was clear before I came back to the beach house."

Clay had left a great deal unsaid. "What happened?"

"I heard Stan revving up his boat this morning while you and I were on the phone. Accused him of getting ready to drag McMillan's body out to the middle of the bay where he could dump him. Stan denied it."

Ethan's shoulders sagged. "But he was going to, wasn't he?"

"Of course he was. Stan did *not* want to call the cops. Accused us of not caring what happened to Alec. Then Randi threw his affairs in his face again. It was . . . unpleasant."

"I'm sorry you got pulled into the middle of this, Clay. Stan's not the man he used to be."

"For whatever it's worth, I'm not sure he ever was the man you thought he was. People don't change, Ethan, not like that. He's under strain now, and that might explain his not wanting to report McMillan's murder. It might even explain his trying to dump that poor man's body in the bay, but not the women. Dammit, if you could have seen Randi's face when she saw the list I was working through."

Ethan's anger boiled. "Sonofabitch. She needs to get tested, right away."

"Somehow I don't think that's uppermost on her mind right now," Clay said mildly.

*Alec.* "I guess not." Ethan came to an intersection where sunlight cut through the tall buildings and he winced at the light. He stood staring up at the traffic signal broodingly as the reality of the situation seeped into his mind. "This is impossible. We're looking for a damn needle in a haystack. I should never have let Stan talk me into this. What was I thinking?"

"That you didn't want Alec to end up like Paul McMillan," Clay said flatly. "Look, if it's any consolation, we're doing everything the police would be doing."

"With the exception of posting Alec's picture across the country as a missing person."

"They may not have done that either, E. Not if they were afraid of retaliation. Whoever took Alec didn't leave any major clues behind except McMillan's body and the police do have that. We just need to wait. Go get something to eat and a few hours' rest."

"Do me a favor. Run a check on a William Bush. Retired sergeant, CPD, now working security at the bus terminal. I want to know what kind of cop he was. My gut says he'd make a good right hand, but my gut's really tired right now."

"Will do. Any other names you want me to run while I'm at it?"

"Yeah." *Dana Dupinsky.* Ethan opened his mouth to say her name, then closed it on a snap. Somehow the thought of Clay checking into her background seemed too . . . personal, too intimate. No, if he decided to have Dana checked out, he'd do the checking himself. "Never mind. Call me when you have something on Bush."


*Chicago,*
*Sunday, August 1, 8:15 p.m.*

Dana stood at the open doorway to their newest client's room. Evie sat on Erik's

148

twin bed, stroking his hair. Jane was nowhere to be seen.

"How is he?" Dana murmured and Evie's back stiffened. They hadn't spoken since returning from Lillian's funeral hours before.

"Still asleep. Jane said he'd been awake most of their trip, so he's just catching up."

"No healthy child needs that much sleep," Dana said with a troubled frown. Something was very wrong with this little boy. "And all that banging David did on the roof should have been enough to wake the dead. I'll call Dr. Lee tomorrow, have him come check on Erik."

Evie's hand continued its gentle stroking. "Thanks."

"Where is Jane?"

"Out back smoking."

Dana sighed. "Were Naomi and Ben at Lillian's funeral today?"

Evie's dark head wagged side to side. "I didn't see them, but I stayed in the back. Mia was there. If it's any consolation, she looked right at me and didn't recognize me."

"Yes, she did. She called me this afternoon. She acted like she didn't recognize you because if Goodman was watching, she didn't want to tip him off. Evie, you're old enough to think before you act. You endangered the lives of every woman and child in this shelter by directly disobeying me and Mia today."

There was nothing but thick, thick silence.

"I did ask Mia about visiting Naomi and Ben," Dana finally said and Evie's head half turned, just a minor indication she was still engaged in the conversation. "She said she'd do her best to get us in to see them in a day or two, even if they haven't caught Goodman."

More silence

"Tomorrow I'll call Dr. Lee about Erik. I need you to stick around here tonight. I got a call from the woman I was meeting this morning. She'll be on the eleven-thirty bus tonight."

Again Evie's back snapped straighter. "So you'll go where you want even though Goodman is still out there, but I have to stay here, locked up in this . . . *house,*" she whispered harshly. "Is that the way we're playing this game, Dana?"

Dana gritted her teeth. "You're free to go at any time, Evie. You always have been."

"Maybe I will. God knows I could be

working a real job with real pay anywhere else."

Knowing Evie was striking out in her own pain didn't make the jab sting any less. Struggling to keep her voice even Dana murmured, "You're free to find another job any time you choose. Just let me know in advance so I can hire another assistant."

Evie's quiet laugh was rife with discontent. "So I'm just an assistant? Do you have a *policy* that pertains to me, too?"

Dana sighed. "You know I don't mean that. And you know you're more than an assistant. You're . . ." *My friend. My sister.* But staring at the rigid set of Evie's back, Dana couldn't force the words from her throat. "You're important to me. I worry about you."

"Well, don't," Evie said bitterly. "I've been through hell and lived to tell the tale. Anything else is just a walk in the park. Even Goodman. I say let him come. I'm not afraid of him."

Dana flinched at the venom in Evie's voice. Had no idea how to diffuse it. "Evie . . ."

"What?" Evie stood up and turned, one side of her mouth set in a firm line while the other side drooped. "Don't be bitter?

Sorry, I can't help that. Don't do anything else stupid? That I think I can manage. I'll let you know if I choose to leave. For now . . ." She let the thought trail off as her eyes focused over Dana's shoulder, her expression suddenly uncomfortable. "Hi, Jane."

Dana turned to find Jane standing in the open doorway, her pale eyes narrowed, twin flags of color staining her cheeks as she flicked her gaze from Dana to Evie to her son sleeping on the bed. "Jane, Evie and I were just checking on Erik."

Letting out a breath, Jane's shoulders sagged and her eyes dropped to the floor. "I just got scared when I saw you here," she mumbled. "I was only gone a minute."

Dana risked squeezing Jane's hand, then abruptly released it when the woman's shoulders went stiff. "Erik's safe here," she said softly. "I was just worried when he didn't wake up. He's been sleeping a long time. Should we call a doctor?"

Jane shook her head, her eyes still focused on the carpet. "He was up most of the night. His schedule's off, what with the trip. He . . . he's not like other boys."

Dana glanced back at the sleeping boy. "How so, Jane?"

"He sits and stares for hours. He did that last night."

"Have you ever had him tested?" Evie asked, lightly stroking his hair.

"A few times. They always said the same thing. They didn't know what was wrong with him. They always wanted to run more tests we couldn't afford. So, I'd always just bring him home." She looked up, her odd eyes filled with tears, and Dana bit back the flinch that seemed to be reflexive now. She'd have to work on that. She couldn't be flinching every time she looked into this woman's milky eyes.

"I can make some calls if you want."

Jane shook her head. "Maybe in a little while. I just want to get us settled first."

Evie attempted her three-cornered smile. "We're just trying to help."

Jane hesitated. "Thank you," she finally murmured and dropped her gaze to the worn carpet as she pushed by Dana and into her room. "I'm tired. I think I'll sleep now, too."

Evie backed out just as Jane pushed her door closed in their faces. Dana gestured Evie to move to the other end of the hall. "Whatever you decide to do is fine with me, Evie. You know that. But while you're here, help me keep an eye on Erik. I was up most of the night, too, and I didn't hear them. Despite what Jane says, I still don't like that he hasn't woken and that burn on his face is fairly new. She never even asked for medicine for it."

"I put some antibiotic cream on it this afternoon," Evie said quietly. "I'll see if she'll let me put on some more tomorrow. I'm tired, too. I think I'll turn in for the night."

With the quiet closing of Evie's door, Dana found herself alone in a filled house. With a sigh she started down the stairs. There weren't enough hours between now and the time she had to be at the bus station to bother trying to sleep, but she had work to keep her busy. Beverly would be leaving Wednesday and she still had to finish Beverly's papers.

Locking herself in her office, she pulled on a pair of white gloves and removed the tools of her trade from her desk drawer. Pens, razor, laminating film. And frowned. Caroline's words had been nagging at her all day. *Have I ever considered that I don't need to work at Hanover House forever?* Dana knew it didn't matter what she did or did not consider. This was her life. She had forfeited the right to any other. In the end there would be the work and that would have to be enough.

Resolutely she shrugged off the intangible dissatisfaction and began assembling the pieces of Beverly's driver's license. And had to blink when the face staring up at her from the photo was not Beverly's, but Ethan Buchanan's unsmiling face under his Marine cap. She wondered if he missed it. Missed being a Marine.

He was a very attractive man. She hadn't needed Caroline to tell her that. Just remembering how attractive was making her palms sweat inside her white gloves. And it had been a very long time. She might not have a life of her own, but she did have needs. Highly unmet needs. He seemed interested. And he didn't live here. When his business was finished he'd go home. Back to Washington. Never to be seen again. Never to need anything more from her again. It could work.

She closed her eyes and splayed her gloved palms on her desk. A fling. She was actually considering a fling. She swallowed as the reality of the situation struck her hard. She was contemplating an affair with a man she barely knew. A man who made her heart race and her skin tingle and her mind conjure all kinds of mental images of rolling around on tangled sheets. Long bouts of hot, sweaty sex. She squeezed her thighs together and took a deep, deep breath. It had been a long time since she'd engaged in any sex at all, sweaty or otherwise. And she missed it. A whole hell of a lot.

She was certain he'd be extremely good at it. Good enough to top her off for a good long while. Because who knew how long it would be before another man like Ethan Buchanan came along? Whatever kind of man he was.

She was contemplating an affair with a man she barely knew. *Well, get to know him better,* urged the voice in her head. She pushed aside the hem of the glove to glance at her watch. Less than ten hours until breakfast. When the getting to know him would commence. Then she'd decide. For now, she had a driver's license to forge.

Sue's palms stung as the nails of her clenched hands dug deep, the pain a welcome distraction. It would have been such a pleasure to tell those two interfering bitches what to do with their help. It would have been a greater pleasure to see their smiles wiped away. Permanently. But that wouldn't do. Not today. Today she needed them, no matter how much she hated to admit it. No matter how much she hated them.

Sue hated social workers. She'd forgotten just how much until today. They were nosy and poked their fingers into everyone else's business. Telling you to stop smoking and checking on your kid like you weren't smart enough or good enough to take care of him yourself. They were high and mighty and interfered where they were not wanted. She narrowed her eyes at the door she'd closed in Dupinsky's face.

Sanctimonious bitches, all of them. Her mother had managed to keep them at bay for years. Moving from one ratty apartment to the next when she could no longer lie her way out of a referral from a "well-meaning" neighbor or teacher or some other busybody with too much time on their hands. They'd gotten along just fine. Until the day a social worker invaded their apartment with the cops and took them away. Her mother had been too stoned to protest. Bryce had been just a baby, screaming as they took him away.

She'd been twelve. The same age as Alexander Quentin Vaughn. Sue turned from the door to sneer at the sleeping boy. A few lousy threats and he folded like a kicked puppy. At twelve, she was already hard.

She'd escaped the foster home with its rules, found her father who hated social workers as much as she did.

Together, they'd gotten Bryce back and gone on the road. Until her father had the bright idea of knocking off a convenience store one night with his kids in the car. Like father like son, she supposed, wondering how much of his guts Bryce had already spilled to the cops. Remembering how her father had spilled his guts, quite literally, on the store's floor when the owner blew him open with the rifle he kept behind the counter.

And she and Bryce had gone to live with Lucy and Earl. They'd been better off with their mother. She looked at the kid dispassionately. So had he.

Calmer now, she considered her next steps. She was here in a place Dupinsky assured her was "safe." There was a sweetness to the irony, even if she did have to put up with Dupinsky for a few days. Social workers defending her, keeping her safe. It was justice.

Now for a little more justice. From her backpack she pulled a sheet of paper, each name on the list bringing back memories. Bad ones. Vaughn's name was there of course, or the name as she'd known it back then. Next was Vickers, the slimy sonafabitch who'd testified against her at her trial. She'd faced ten years for drug trafficking, same as all the boys — except Vickers, who'd copped a damn plea. He'd testified against Sue in exchange for a reduced sentence. That she'd be convicted for drug trafficking had been a done deal. She'd done it. The cops found the proof. That she'd been arrested to begin with wasn't Vickers's doing. But his story wasn't about simple drug trafficking. Oh, no.

She'd used mules, Vickers said on the stand. Drug couriers. But not only had she used them, she'd *killed* one of them. They couldn't prove it. They found no body, because there'd been *no damn murder.* Still, the prosecutor was determined to get a conviction and managed to tack another five years onto her sentence for "reckless endangerment." Fifteen years was her sentence, longer than everyone else's thanks to that little fucker Vickers. She'd *recklessly endanger* him, she thought savagely. He'd pay, and soon.

There were a few others who'd played significant roles. An old neighbor. The arresting cop. The damn prosecuting attorney. They'd all conspired to steal those years of her life. And they'd pay before the week was over.

Then there were other names that brought back better memories. Her partners in moving the stash. Their product had been so fine. They'd done the importing themselves. Walking right by the airport dogs, knowing the cops would never find their hiding place, knowing they'd won . . . What a rush it had been. But then they'd been betrayed. Caught.

As far as Sue was concerned, Vickers and the others were merely side items. The main course, the focus of the revenge was their betrayer, the one who'd set it all in motion. The one who'd destroyed their business. Their lives. *Let's see if they still feel as strongly about our common tie as I do.* Donnie Marsden had been their leader and a long time ago, her lover. Donnie had served seven of his ten-year sentence. He was a bookie now, but rumor had it he still kept his hand in the old candy jar. She dialed his number, hearing a flurry of activity in the background. "Donnie. It's Sue."

There was a beat of stunned silence that stretched on just a little too long and then Donnie sighed. "Hell, Suze, what'd you do?"

Her teeth clenched. *James.* "You got a visit from my pal. How much did he offer you?"

"Fifteen."

Sue wasn't sure whether to be annoyed or insulted. "Shit."

Donnie chuckled. "Don't pout, Suze. And don't worry, I'm doing well enough that I don't have to sell out for fifteen. Sixteen maybe. But your friend wouldn't budge."

"Good of you, Donnie," Sue said dryly. "Can't tell you how much I appreciate it."

"Why are you callin' now, Suze? I heard you got out months ago."

"How would you like to get your hands on the little bird that put you in a cage?"

Donnie's voice was perfectly sober, perfectly cold. "You know who set us up?"

She'd always known. But she'd hoarded the secret, just waiting until she could exact revenge her way. *I'm pulling the strings now.* "I do. You interested?"

"In dealin' the bastard that stole seven years of my life? Hell, yeah. What's the plan?"

"I'll tell you in time. Just clear your calendar for the weekend."

"True. Okay, I'll wait. But, Suze, you need to watch your back. That friend of yours seriously wants a piece of you. What does he have to do with all this?"

"Nothing. I just have to steer clear of him until the deed's done." Until the game was completed. *Until I win.*


*Chicago,*
*Sunday, August 1, 10:45 p.m.*

Dana eased back into the shadows, wearily leaning against the wall of the bus station. The bus was an hour late, all she needed tonight. Her shoulders were stiff from hunching over Beverly's license, but worse was the chill from Evie's cold shoulder.

"What took you so long, honey?"

Dana jumped at the amused drawl, nearly cracking her head against the wall. Caroline stood a few feet away. "What are you doing here?"

"Ruby heard you tell Evie you were coming and Ruby told Beverly who called me. Under the circumstances, we didn't think you should be venturing out alone anymore."

Dana eyed Caroline's bulky middle balefully. "So you're going to protect me from Goodman? With what, a belly-buck? Or maybe you'll grab him and let the baby kick him?"

Caroline merely raised a brow. "*I* didn't come alone." She looked into the waiting room where Dana saw a familiar cane and a tall man reading a newspaper.

"You brought Max," Dana muttered. "You're insane, you know that?"

"And you're not? Coming out into the night alone? Do you think you're bullet-proof?"

With a sigh Dana let her head fall back against the wall. "No, I'm not bulletproof."

"You can't lecture Evie about going to Lillian's funeral and then run around at night by yourself. If you don't want to think about your own safety, think of mine." She crossed her arms over her belly. "All this stress is bad for me. I'm delicate."

Dana snorted. "Hell." She rolled her head sideways to look at Caroline in the shadows. "Evie's pissed at me again."

"I'd say she has a right this time. Why didn't you call me?"

"Because you're delicate," Dana retorted and Caroline's dimple flashed.

"Touché." She sobered. "You go home. I'll get this one and deliver her safely."

"She'll be afraid of Max."

Caroline shook her head stubbornly.

"You always say that. I think we can manage."

"No." Fatigued, Dana let her eyes slide closed. "End of discussion."

"But —" Caroline didn't finish, instead widening her eyes and staring. "Mercy. It's him."

Dana's eyes opened and grew wider than Caroline's. "Holy hell." It was. Ethan Buchanan in the flesh, walking out of the security office with the man she knew to be the head of security at the bus station. Ethan shook hands with Bush and started their way, headed for the exit they were hiding next to.

Dana pulled her from the shadows. "Come on. I don't want him to think I'm always hiding in dark corners. You and I are here to meet a friend who's so flaky she gave the wrong bus this morning. That's why I was here this morning and again tonight. Got it?"

"Got it. Ouch. Stop pulling so hard." Caroline was grinning. "I'm delicate."

"Hell." Dana stopped them next to a bank of chairs. "Sit, then." She looked up to find Ethan had already seen her. He stood staring and once again she felt his gaze as palpable as a touch. It raked across her skin, leaving her tingling head to toe.

He started walking again, this time closing the distance between them in purposeful ground eating strides. And her heart fluttered. She wondered what to say, then felt her cheeks heat as her mind flooded with all of her earlier daydreams of a fling with him.

And then he was there, standing inches away. Looking down at her with those steady green eyes. And damn if she didn't want to swoon. "Hi."

He smiled. "Hi, yourself. Are you stalking me, Dana?"

Dana smiled back even as every nerve in her body zinged. "No, nothing so deliberate, I'm afraid. My friend called back, just like always."

He looked over her shoulder down at Caroline. "She doesn't look too flaky to me."

Caroline chuckled. "Haul me up, Dana, so I can meet your war he-ro with dignity."

Dana didn't miss the way his eyes widened as he held out his hand to pull Caroline from the chair. "Easy there, ma'am. I've done many things in my life, but labor and delivery are not among them."

Caroline smoothed her maternity top in place, then shook the hand he offered. "I'm not the flaky friend. Her bus is an hour late. Nor am I about to go into labor. I'm Caroline Hunter, Dana's not-flaky friend."

"Maybe," Dana grunted. "Jury's still out on that one. Caroline, this is Ethan Buchanan."

"Nice to meet you, Mr. Buchanan."

"Please call me Ethan." He met Dana's eyes and she could now see the shadows of fatigue on his face. But it was more than simple fatigue. There was worry and something akin to despair. The smile that still curved his lips didn't come close to reaching his eyes. "So there really is a flaky friend. I admit I had my doubts."

She so wanted to lift a hand to his face, to smooth away the worry. But she didn't, keeping her hands fisted at her sides, keeping her voice light. "So you really are a security consultant. I admit I had my doubts."

"You were busy today," Ethan remarked. "Checking up on me."

"It's only prudent. I'm a single woman. I can't be too careful."

He looked surprised at the notion. "I guess you're right. Did I pass muster?"

"For now. You look tired, Ethan. Have you been working all day?"

"Not all day. After I left you this

morning I caught some sleep, then made some more calls." He gestured to the security office with a jerk of his head. "I got an appointment with the head of security here."

"At ten-thirty at night?" Caroline asked. Dana had almost forgotten she was there.

Ethan shrugged. "You take a sales appointment when you can get it, ma'am."

Caroline was boldly assessing him. "So you got injured in Kandahar."

Ethan's brows lifted. "Thereabouts."

Caroline's eyes took him in head to toe and back again. "What did you injure?"

He grinned now, a slow sure grin that made every ounce of sensation pool between Dana's legs. "Nothing I can't live without, ma'am."

Caroline laughed, then pursed her mouth. "What are your intentions, Ethan?"

Dana blew out a breath, mortified. "Caroline," she gritted. "Don't."

Caroline just shot her a look. "Hush." She turned back to Ethan who stood looking mildly perplexed. "Well?"

"I'll be a gentleman, if that's what you mean. Is that what you mean?"

Caroline looked satisfied. "Close enough. Do you see that man over there? The one behind the newspaper?"

Ethan looked over his shoulder, then back. "The big one?"

"Yes. He has two brothers almost as big as he is. Dana's our family."

His very nice lips curved and this time the smile crept up into his eyes. Dana's knees went weak at the sight. "I'm glad Dana has family that cares about her. You won't have to sic them on me. That I can guarantee."

Caroline smiled back. "Good. Dana, have you eaten dinner?"

Dana coughed. "No. Caroline, I —"

"Hush. Ethan, have you eaten dinner?"

Ethan shot Dana a slow smile. "No, I haven't. I was just going to grab a burger."

"Well, Dana loves burgers. Make her eat a salad, too. I swear if I didn't make her eat vegetables she'd have scurvy in a week. Woman lives on French fries."

Ethan's lips twitched. "Scurvy comes from lack of vitamin C, ma'am."

Undeterred, Caroline nodded briskly. "Make her eat that, too. Dana, give me the keys to your car. I'll take our friend home." She held her hand out, snapping her fingers. "Well, I haven't got all night and Ethan hasn't had supper. Give me your keys."

Dana frowned. "Ethan, would you please

excuse us?" She dragged Caroline over to where Max still read his newspaper. "What are you doing?"

"Helping you. You said you didn't want tonight's client frightened by Max, so that's fine. I'll drive her to Hanover House in your car and Max can follow in ours. I'll get her settled in and Evie can take over."

"How will I get home?"

"Take the El. Or take a cab." She dug into her purse and pulled out two twenties. "Cab fare. Dana, don't argue with me. Go eat dinner with that man."

Dana pushed Caroline's hand away. "Keep your money. I have enough for a burger with enough left over for a token. Why are you doing this? He could be an ax murderer."

Caroline sniffed. "Man hasn't had so much as a parking ticket. He's squeaky clean."

Dana narrowed her eyes. "And you know this how?"

Caroline's eyes took a tour of the ceiling. "Mia ran a background check."

Dana pressed her fingers to her now-throbbing temple. "A background check."

Caroline grinned. "It was prudent. You're a single woman. You can't be too careful. Keys, please."

Max lowered his newspaper. "Dana, just do it. I don't want to have to listen to her gripe all the way home if you don't." Up went the newspaper before she could protest.

Dana slapped the keys into Caroline's palm. "Her name is Shauna Lincoln."

"I'll take care of it." Caroline gave Dana a hug. "Call me tomorrow."

Dana hugged her back, more grateful than angry. It was a step she might not have gotten around to herself for several more days. If ever. "Don't ever do this again." She rattled Max's newspaper. "Thanks, Max."

"Don't eat onions in case he wants to kiss you," he said evenly.

Dana rolled her eyes and walked away, hearing Caroline's chuckle behind her. Ethan stood watching as she approached, his eyes slowly lifting to hers and just that fast her body heated. He'd been staring at her breasts. The very notion sensitized them and Dana didn't have to look down to know her very modest polo shirt was now showcasing her very erect nipples. She nearly crossed her arms over her chest, then decided no. He was obviously interested and so was she. Flings didn't happen for shy women.

He swallowed hard when she stopped in front of him. Tried to smile. The fatigue and worry still shadowed his eyes, but now there was a sharpness that hadn't been there before. Perhaps they could make each other's worries go away for just a little while. And what harm could there be in that?

He glanced over to where Dana knew Caroline stood watching. "Was she trying to pay you to go to dinner with me?"

Dana shook her head. "Mad money," she said, her voice gone husky.

"You didn't take it."

"I never take her money. Besides, I have enough to get home on the El."

"I'll take you home."

His voice had dropped to a caress and she shivered. "We'll see. For now, how about a real taste of Chicago?"

His lips curved. "Can you eat vegetables there? Wouldn't want you getting scurvy."

"French fries are potatoes. Come on. Let's go to Wrigleyville. We'll take the El."

"I have my car."

She shook her head. "We take the El." And waited for his temper.

Instead he considered her with those steady green eyes, turning up the heat several notches. "Single woman. Prudent. Got it. The El it is."

# Chapter Seven

Sue quietly closed the office door behind her. Dupinsky was gone to pick up a new client and Scarface had shut herself in her room in a pout. Dupinsky had a good lock on this door. She could pick most locks in ten seconds. This one had taken eleven.

Sue could get a new identity if she asked. Dupinsky apparently thought it was a huge secret, but according to old cellmate Tammy, everybody knew. Nobody said a word out of loyalty to Dupinsky. Nobody knew where Dupinsky got the fake IDs, but based on the laminating film and the razor blades on the desk, Sue had a good idea.

She picked the lock on the desk drawer easily. Inside was a finished driver's license. Sue lifted her brows. Dupinsky could make some real money doing this full-time. The woman had a gift. Sue recognized the picture on the license. It was Beverly, two doors down the hall. There was also a passport with lots of stamps. Again, with Beverly's picture inserted. So, Dupinsky could make passports, too. Good to know. Sue would need one when all this was done, when the Vaughns' ransom money was safely tucked away in an off-shore account. She wouldn't want to stick around the good USofA, always looking over her shoulder. She'd go overseas. Paris sounded good. She'd planned to buy a passport, but if Dupinsky's passports were as good as her licenses, well . . .

She studied Beverly's license. Her facial structure was similar to Sue's. A little makeup, contacts, and a dye job . . . It could work. Beverly was leaving this week for California, according to Ruby. The timing was perfect, as were the circumstances. Once Beverly left Hanover House, no one would expect to hear anything from her for days, if at all. Nobody would file a missing person report or check the morgues.

It was a sports bar. TVs hung from every corner, each playing something different. It was a welcome distraction from the fuzzy video Ethan had been staring at for nine of the last ten hours. Desperately needing a break to rest his eyes and fill his stomach, he'd just gotten Bush's permission to come back later and was headed for the door when he'd seen her. For a split second he'd thought he was imagining her, he was that tired.

Then she met his eyes and it was the same as it had been this morning. Electricity in the air, raising every hair on his body on end, the sudden rush of adrenaline propelling him across the terminal. And just like this morning, she'd felt it, too. He'd left Bush's office looking for a diversion, a way to clear his mind so that when he came back to search for Alec he'd be fresh and sharp. He'd certainly found what he was looking for.

Possibly in more ways than one.

Cubs fans were everywhere, poor, deluded souls. Seemed like a couple hundred of them crowded the bar, but he couldn't complain. The cramped quarters put

174

Dana's back squarely against his chest, her curvy rear end right up against his groin. Yet even so close he still had to shout to be heard. "You're a Cubs fan, I take it?"

Dana turned, the grin she threw over her shoulder more warning than amusement. "I am and if you're not, I wouldn't advise saying it too loud in here. Crowd's pumped." She turned, pointing at the scoreboard mounted over the bar. "We won tonight."

Ethan dipped his head to her ear. "Enjoy it. It might be a while before it happens again."

Her head whipped around, her brown eyes narrowed. Her pursed lips mere millimeters from his. After a stunned split second, her eyes widened, filling with hot awareness. Her lips relaxed, falling apart just a hair, full and moist, making one of the most provocative, inviting pictures he'd ever seen. And his body, still half aroused from the sight of her walking toward him in that damn bus terminal with her nipples pressing against the soft material of her shirt, roared to full throttle. Just a tiny movement and he'd know what it was like to kiss her. And she wanted him to. Of that he was certain.

But her eyes narrowed again and her

kissable lips curved into a smirk, her words barely registering through the noise of the bar and his own thick fog of lust. "For your own safety, I think we'd better take this outside." She moved toward the bar, leaving him leaning forward, hard as a damn rock. With no small difficulty he straightened and followed her, wordlessly paying the bartender for the beers that came sliding across the bar. Dana took both mugs and gestured to a back door with her head. "Outside."

Again he followed, noting more than one man eyeing her, pushing back the unfamiliar urge to poke them all in the eye just for looking. But he couldn't blame them. Curves in all the right places, she was raw sensuality in a sleeveless polo shirt and plain cotton skirt.

He wanted her. It was as simple as that. And complicated as hell. He'd promised himself he'd take time for dinner. He had no time for anything else. No matter how much he wanted it or how long it had been. He'd eat, and then he'd take her home. Then back to the tapes. Until it was time to eat again.

There was symbolism there, on way too many levels.

She snagged a table on the edge of the

patio that would sit in the shadow of Wrigley Field on a hot summer afternoon. He took his beer from her hand and lifted it in a toast. "To what could become a winning streak," he said and her lips twitched.

"So you like baseball, Buchanan, or you just like to poke at the underdog?"

"You don't know? I thought you checked me out. Me and my . . . injured parts, that is."

Her cheeks flushed. "Your Website said nothing about your baseball preferences."

He sipped his beer thoughtfully, watching her. "Orioles fan."

She grimaced. "Ah, yes. You live in D.C. Baltimore would be the closest team."

"I live in D.C. now, but I've always been an Orioles fan. Have you always rooted for the underdog?"

Something changed in her eyes. "Yes," she murmured. "I guess so." Then her full mouth curved in a smile. "So if D.C.'s just where you live, where's home?"

"Maryland. Little town on the Eastern Shore called Wight's Landing." And his mind instantly flashed to the picture of the body in the shed. Followed by that picture of Alec, tied and gagged by the side of the road. Restlessly Ethan cast his eyes on the lights of the skyscrapers poking up in the distance, wondering if he was even in the right city. If Alec was here or a thousand miles away. If Alec was hurt . . . or killed . . . *I'll never forgive myself.*

He jumped as Dana's palm covered the hand he hadn't realized he'd clenched into a fist. Found himself staring into warm brown eyes that searched his face. Found the turbulence in his soul once again calming. "What's wrong, Ethan?" she murmured.

And he actually considered telling her. "Nothing either of us can fix right now."

She tilted her head, her eyes still on his. "I'm a good listener. If you want to talk."

There was something in the way she said it. It was practiced. Not false or phony, but like she'd had cause to say it many, many times before. And suddenly he wanted to talk. To have her listen. Maybe just to keep those warm eyes looking at him, to hear her smooth voice. Just to keep the feeling of calm in the storm. So he shrugged. And talked. "Whenever I think about home I think about two friends of mine. Brothers."

Her brows rose. "Your brothers?"

"No. They were brothers. I grew up in Wight's Landing with my grandmother and they'd come down from Baltimore every summer. Richard and Stan."

"Where are they now, Richard and Stan?"

Ethan gritted his teeth. "Richard is dead. Enemy fire outside of Kandahar."

"Where you were injured," she said softly. "The newsletter I found said your vehicle hit a land mine and you were caught in enemy crossfire. I take it Richard didn't make it."

"He died protecting me." Ethan looked away. "We were thrown from the vehicle and I was knocked out, but Richard wasn't. He could have crawled back and used the Humvee as a shield until the medics came through to pick us up."

"But he didn't. He stayed with you." She tapped his fist until he met her eyes. "Just like you would have done had the situation been reversed. But you know that, don't you?"

"Yeah," Ethan said bitterly. "I know it."

"But at three a.m. it still gets to you. It can be hard to be the one that lives. Guilt and all that added responsibility . . . You were spared. He wasn't. It makes a lot of people wonder why, makes them search for a purpose they weren't as sensitive to before."

Ethan blinked slowly. "You sound like the hospital shrink." Better actually. The shrink had stopped at guilt. The responsibility was something he'd grappled with on his own.

She lifted a shoulder. "Was Stan in the Marines with you and Richard?"

Ethan's smile was grim. "No. Stan was never very disciplined."

"Do you still see him?"

*Only when he needs something.* "We haven't been on great terms since Richard died."

"He blamed you." It was murmured softly.

"You could say that." Ethan took a healthy swallow of beer. "In fact, he did."

She rubbed his hand with her palm until his fist relaxed. "That was . . . unkind."

Ethan laughed harshly, thinking of Stan cheating on Randi, forbidding Alec's visits, trying to drag poor Paul McMillan's body out to sea. "Well, that's Stan for you. Unkind."

Her fingertips stroked the back of his hand. "So was Richard an Orioles fan, too?"

Ethan looked up, found her smile still in place. "Yes, he was. We never missed a game on TV. Bought tickets in the nosebleed section every chance we got." She said nothing and in the silence he stared at the outer walls of Wrigley, seeing himself and Richard as young boys, hiking up to the cheap seats in old Memorial Stadium in Baltimore, saving their money for hot dogs. Then he smiled as a nearly forgotten memory bubbled to the surface. "Back in '85, Richard caught a foul ball. I was so jealous, but I stood outside the team entrance with him anyway, waiting for Eddie Murray to come out to sign it."

Her lips curved. "Steady Eddie. 'Eighty-five was his best year. He hit what . . . 125 RBIs?"

He lifted his brows. "One-twenty-four. Most girls I knew didn't follow the teams."

"I knew my stats better than any boy in my class. So did he? Sign the ball, that is."

"Him and four other players."

She smiled again. "You guys must have been on a cloud."

"We were, but by the time we got back to Wight's Landing, Richard was feeling guilty. We'd switched seats midway through the game because there was a girl he'd wanted to talk to. If we hadn't, I might have caught the ball."

"And you weren't interested in the girl?" she asked.

"Nah. Not then. Cal Ripken was on the field."

"I understand completely," she said. "Girls paled in comparison."

"Well, then, maybe. Richard was always a little faster on those things than I was. First to get a girl, first to get —" He stopped short, but her low laugh told him she'd figured it out. "First to get *married* I was going to say." He shook his head with a smile. "Anyway, by the time we got home, we were fighting over who should keep the ball. We flipped a coin."

"And you won?"

Ethan's throat suddenly thickened and he had to clear it before answering. "Nah." He swallowed hard, appalled that the memory stirred him so deep. "He did. Apologized every damn day for the rest of the summer, until I wanted to deck him."

Her fingers squeezed his hand. "And the girl? What happened to her?"

"They started going steady that fall and got married eight years later, right after we graduated from the Academy." Again his throat closed. "I was his best man."

"And the ball? Whatever happened to the ball?"

"It's in a glass case on a bookshelf in my bedroom. He left it to me in his will."

"Did you begrudge him the ball, Ethan?"

There was something in her voice, an authority he couldn't deny. "No."

"But you switched places. He had your seat."

Something inside him stirred. "Richard was in the right place at the right time."

"So conversely, you were in the wrong place at the wrong time. Kind of like that day."

*That day.* It was how he thought of it in his own mind. "When I was in the wrong place at the wrong time." The words were out before he knew they were coming.

"Really?" Her brows went up. "You wanted to die?"

"No." Angry now, he pushed his beer to the middle of the table. "I did not want to die."

"Do you think Richard would begrudge you your life?"

"There's a hell of a lot of difference between a damn ball and a life."

"Yes, there is. But would he?"

"No." He let out a shuddering breath. "That's not the kind of man he was."

"Ethan . . . Some people never find a friend like that their whole life. You did."

His heart warmed, remembering Richard for the friend he'd been. "Is Caroline that friend for you?"

Her lips curved. "She is. But Caroline wouldn't have accepted a single coin toss. It would have been best two out three, then three out of five. She's the tiniest bit stubborn."

"I figured that out. I have to say I haven't been threatened by a date's family since my Academy days. I decided that girl wasn't worth the risk."

"And tonight?"

He turned his hand over and threaded his fingers through hers, realizing there wasn't an army of brothers big enough to keep him from her. "I'm here, aren't I?"

She dropped her eyes to their joined hands, staring as if the sight were a foreign one. Then looked back up and nodded. Slowly. "Yes. Yes, you are."

The brown eyes that had encouraged him were suddenly vulnerable, unsure. Sad. And he wasn't sure what to say to give to her some measure of the peace she'd given him.

But with a hard blink, she made the look disappear, smiling brightly over his shoulder at their waitress who deposited a huge plate of hot wings and two enormous burgers on their table. Dana lifted a limp celery stalk from the plate of wings.

"Vegetables," she said. "I can now honestly tell Caroline I had some." With zeal she dug into the hot wings, sighing at the first swallow. "I was hungrier than I thought."

As Ethan loaded his plate he considered the sad look he knew he had seen. Wondered what prompted it. And where she'd stowed it. She'd claimed to be a good listener and that she most certainly was. He wondered if she was nearly as good at talking.

*Chicago,*
*Monday, August 2, 1:00 a.m.*

Sue slipped into Scarface's bedroom and stood there a moment, contemplating the sleeping girl. It would be so easy to get rid of a parasitic social worker in training. But although satisfying, such an action would cause undue scrutiny she couldn't afford.

Sue slipped Scarface's pancake makeup into her pocket. She'd need it to cover certain identifying features before she went out to send the Vaughns' latest e-mail in the morning. She turned from the girl in the bed. Soon enough her day would come, along with Dupinsky and sweet

185

Caroline. First, she had to reach out and touch the Vaughns.

And then, she had an appointment to keep. Her blood was already rushing. It would be the first name on her list she'd cross off. Leroy Vickers.

*Chicago,*
*Monday, August 2, 1:45 a.m.*

It was one of those trite but true things, Dana decided glumly, watching Ethan Buchanan sleeping in the train seat beside her. She was not that kind of a girl. She'd gotten to know him better and now knew there could be no fling. No sweaty bouts of sex.

No relief from the little sizzles that had become major yearnings as the night wore on. Hell, who was she kidding? They'd never been little sizzles. They'd started out as lightning bolts in the bus station and had just increased in intensity from there. And for that moment she'd been pressed against him in the sports bar . . . *God.* Just the memory of his rigid arousal pulsing up against her rear end was enough to make her shudder now, hours later. She should have kissed him then, right after he'd made

186

that half-assed jab at the Cubs. They would have combusted, found a room, and fucked like weasels. She could have gotten him out of her system. Topped off her tank. But she hadn't.

Nope, she'd pulled away. Sat down and talked to the man. And found him to be good and kind and . . . honorable. Not the kind of man a woman used for her own sexual purposes and tossed aside. *Not this woman, anyway.* Shit. He'd put his gut right there on the table, telling her about his best friend. Trusted her. Her heart still squeezed at the misery she'd seen in his eyes. Two years and he still felt guilt over Richard's death. But there was no statute of limitations on that kind of guilt. Dana knew that all too well.

But talking about his friend had helped, as she'd known it would, and for the rest of the dinner he'd been downright chatty. He liked baseball and movies, just as she did. He liked *Die Hard* and *Terminator* and could give the stats on any player in the league. She searched his face, relaxed in slumber. Any player up until two years ago, that was. More recently, he knew nothing. At first she'd wondered about memory loss from his injury.

But the reason was far more basic than

that. Since his release from the hospital, he'd started his consulting business and Ethan had simply worked himself into the ground. Keeping busy kept the guilt at bay. Hell, she was seeing his obsession with his work right now as he sat in the ratty old train seat, snoring softly. He'd worked last night and most of Sunday before going to dinner with her. He'd insisted on seeing her back home, instead of going straight back to the bus station for his car. But he'd lasted less than five minutes on the El, his eyes sliding closed at the swinging rhythm of the train. He was exhausted.

He was also gorgeous. And although her fingers itched to touch, he was off-limits.

Thankfully, her station was approaching. "Ethan." She shook his shoulder. "Wake up."

Ethan jerked awake, bolting upright in his seat, his pulse shooting through the roof.

"You fell asleep," she said. "Five minutes out of Wrigleyville."

He'd been sleeping. Dreaming. Of Richard and McMillan and Alec, but through it all had been Dana, drawing her to him, letting him sink into her, letting him find peace in the softness of her body. He'd been rocking inside her, in and out, a

188

slow easy rhythm . . .

The rhythm he now recognized as the sway of the train. He was awake and she was staring at him with those warm brown eyes. He bit back a groan. He was stiff as a pike.

"This is where I get off," she said.

Ethan blinked, her words some surreal extension of his dream. "Excuse me?"

She gestured to the window as the train pulled into the station. "My stop. I get off here."

"Okay." He started to get up, but she gently pushed him back down.

"You don't have to get off here. It's a short walk to my place from this stop. I'll be fine."

He stood, nearly wincing at the sharp ache in his groin. "I will see you home, Dana," he said through his teeth and her eyes narrowed.

"Fine. No need to get testy." He followed her off the train, nearly hobbling in pain.

"I'm not testy." The train continued on, and he got his first look at Dana's neighborhood. "You've got to be kidding," he said harshly, because he still hurt.

She'd already started walking and he hurried to keep up with her, his sexual discomfort rapidly easing in the face of his growing alarm. Most of the windows were boarded up, and he didn't have to be a cop to recognize gang symbols in the graffiti covering the walls.

He gripped her arm, bringing her to a halt. "You really do live here, don't you?"

Her cheeks flushed and her eyes flashed. "Yes, I do."

"Why?"

She pulled away. "I'm sorry it's not a penthouse, but it's what I can afford."

He'd embarrassed her when that had been the last thing on his mind. "Dana, I'm sorry. I don't want to ruin a very nice evening. Look at me please." He squeezed her arms when she kept her eyes down-turned. "I'll take back every nasty thing I said about the Cubs."

One side of her mouth quirked up. "Every single one?"

He pretended to hesitate. "Oh, all right. Every one." He tipped her chin up and her lashes lowered, still hiding her eyes. "I'm sorry. I didn't mean to be a jerk."

"It's all right," she murmured. "I put most of my money back into the business. There isn't a whole lot left over for frills."

He wouldn't call basic safety a "frill." "Your photography business?"

"It's the only one I have," she said slowly. Almost cautiously, he thought.

"Your business is important to you."

She lifted a brow. "From the man who spent most of the last twenty-four hours working."

If she only knew. "Touché." He held out his hand. "Can I walk you home now?"

After a beat of hesitation, she put her hand in his and started down the street. Ethan was determined not to say another word, but felt his resolution slipping when she stopped in front of a seedy-looking building. Two drunks were sleeping it off just outside the door and a third scurried into the shadows. *Holy hell,* he thought. Every night she comes *here.*

"Thank you, Ethan," she said simply. "I had a wonderful time with you tonight."

He glanced up at the building and back down to her. "Let me walk you up."

"It's not necessary."

"It is to me." He tried for a smile. "My grandmother raised me right."

With a sigh she led him up the stairs. The number of winos and junkies loitering in the hallways climbed along with his temper. Having her own business was one thing. Putting herself in jeopardy every time she came home from work was something else entirely.

Mechanically she unlocked the dead-bolts on her front door, not even seeming to notice the stinking drunk curled up asleep not five feet away. "Thank you, Ethan." Her lips curved into an utterly false smile. "Your grandmother would be proud. Good night."

Completely gone was the warm, compassionate woman who'd pulled such emotion from him not two hours before. And he wanted to know why. "Invite me in. Please."

Dana's gaze flicked to the hall, the low-lifes registering along with his implacable tone that said he would not be dissuaded. The effort of keeping her sexual frustration hidden away combined with her dread of this very reaction made her grimace in weary surrender.

"Please come in." She watched him take in her living room. Knew what he was thinking. How could she live like this? Only a trusted few knew why. It was not something she intended to blurt to a man whom she'd likely never see again.

This was what she'd hoped to avoid. Ethan's reaction to this place. But she couldn't very well have taken him to Hanover House and he'd insisted on seeing her home. He now stood in front of her ancient television set. "I haven't seen rabbit ears since I was a kid," he said, running his fingers lightly over one of the antennae.

She wondered how it would feel to have his fingers run over her that way and her mouth went dry. "I don't watch enough television to make cable worthwhile."

He shot her a look from the corner of his eye. "You put all your money in the business."

She leaned her head back against the door. "That's right."

"That good night outside sounded more like good-bye. Are you telling me good-bye?"

"It certainly would be easier that way," she murmured.

His shoulders stiffened and he set the antenna down on the television. "When we left the restaurant, you were smiling. When I woke up on the El, you weren't." In two long strides he crossed the room to stand before her. "I know I snore, but it's never been enough to chase a woman away," he added in a teasing voice meant to make her smile.

She did, in spite of herself. Shook her head. "Ethan."

He lowered his brow to hers, so gently

she wanted to weep. "Dana." He cupped her cheek, caressing with a sweep of his thumb. "I'm a good listener, too. Just give me a try."

And therein lay the problem. She desperately wanted to give this man a try. She lifted her eyes to his in resignation. "I'm not looking for a relationship, Ethan. I told you that."

He straightened, his eyes flickering as he looked down at her. "Yes, you did. Why not?"

She swallowed hard. "You live somewhere else. And I have other priorities."

His lips thinned. "Your photography business."

"Among other things." She closed her eyes. "Although I did consider a fling with you."

She could feel him tense even though now he touched her nowhere. "You did."

"I did. It's been a while for me and . . ." She exhaled carefully. "You're very attractive."

He cleared his throat. "I am." It wasn't a question or an agreement. She wasn't sure what it was so she opened her eyes. And sucked in a sharp breath as his steady green eyes flashed and burned. Smoldered. Scorching her already sensitized skin.

"So you were going to have your way with me and dump me," he said thickly.

"No." The word emerged a harsh whisper. "I was going to have my way with you and then you were going to go home. No harm, no foul. No strings."

Color rose in his cheeks and his breathing quickened. "What changed your mind?"

Dana rolled her eyes heavenward. "It's dumb."

"Try me," he drawled, settling his fists on his hips. The pose revealed exactly how much her words had bothered him and she crossed her arms to keep her hands under control.

"You're a nice guy."

His brows shot to the top of his forehead. "That's it?"

She scowled. "You're a nice guy and a war he-ro."

His lips twitched now and she wished he'd be angry. "So you'd have a fling with a cowardly bastard over me?"

When he said it that way she wanted to sink into a hole. "I told you it was dumb."

He ran his tongue over his teeth. "No, I think it's pretty remarkable, actually. Dana, you said something tonight that really struck home. That the survivor feels a heightened sense of responsibility. Do you know what Richard and I were talking about right before we hit that mine? Marriage. Specifically his success and my failure."

"You said your ex-wife was only halfway to Y," Dana murmured.

"Jill's a wonderful woman. We just got married for the wrong reasons. Richard was married to Brenda and Stan had just married Randi. I felt . . . out of the loop. So I went out and found a wife. Trouble is, I didn't take the time to fall in love first and I guess she didn't either. I knew it was a big mistake from day one. Jill and I started to drift apart the day we got back from our honeymoon and being stationed on two different continents didn't help."

"She was a Marine then."

"She's a Navy pilot." Pride was in his voice and Dana felt a twinge of envy. His first wife had a valiant career and he thought she slaved herself into poverty over a damn photography business. "About a year into the marriage, she called and told me she'd met someone else. It was almost a relief. I wished her well and that was that."

"Is she happy?"

His face softened for a moment. "Yeah,

she is. And I'm happy for her. While we were married, I never strayed, but after the divorce . . ." He shrugged. "I guess I made up for some lost time. I was careful, but I was not Mr. Commitment. Richard had just arrived on base a few weeks before and was . . ." He frowned. "Disappointed in me. Gave me hell. Told me I'd been wandering long enough, that it was time to buckle down, start a family." He blinked hard. "Leave a legacy," he said unsteadily. "It was the last thing he said to me."

The sheen in his eyes made her falter all over again. "Final words like that are hard to live up to," she said softly.

"So I've found. I stopped wandering, Dana. I started waiting for someone special."

Panic began to well in her chest. "You can't think I'm special," she said. "I'm not."

He shrugged. "Maybe you aren't. But I'd sure as hell like to find out." He shot her a hard look. "Wouldn't you? Can you tell me you don't feel it when I touch you?"

"That's just lust, Ethan. I still have priorities and you still live somewhere else."

"Details, Dana. In the grand scheme of life, your business and my residency are just details." She said nothing and he sighed. "It's late and we're both tired. Why don't we just . . . see where this goes? Meet me for breakfast and we'll talk some more." He slid his fingertip down her cheek. "Look at the bright side," he said huskily. "Maybe you'll get to know me better and find I really am a bastard and find your way clear to have a fling with me."

Dana found her lips curving. "Breakfast is only a few hours away."

"So use it to get some sleep. Meet me at the coffee shop tomorrow at seven-thirty. You can go on to work from there." He bent at the knees, catching her gaze. "Well?"

She blew out a sigh. "All right."

Relief was clear in his green eyes. "Good." He hesitated, then grasped her jaws gently and pressed a kiss to her forehead. "Good night. Lock the door behind me."

"I will." She did, then fell against the door, her pulse thrumming through her body. What had she done? Agreeing to meet him again. It would only make it harder to say good-bye.

But what if she didn't have to say good-bye? Caroline's words still echoed in her mind. What if she wasn't the director of Hanover House anymore? Didn't she deserve a life, too?

She glanced at the floor of her living room, with its carpet purposefully set askew. Then looked at her hands. And remembered. Ethan still felt his guilt after two years. She felt hers after twelve. This was her life. And there was no place for Ethan Buchanan in it.

She waited fifteen minutes, then left her apartment, locking the three deadbolts behind her. She hated sleeping in her apartment where dreams were a sure occurrence. She'd sleep at Hanover House tonight. Besides, she had a new client to see to.

# Chapter Eight

*Chicago,*
*Monday, August 2, 7:25 a.m.*

Sitting in the booth at Betty's coffee shop, Ethan was both weary and energized at the same time. The hours between leaving Dana's apartment until seven that morning had finally yielded some results. He'd returned to the security office, refreshed and ready to go again, and after more hours of tape, he'd spotted Alec, just for an instant.

Clay answered on the first ring of his cell phone. "Did you find him on the tape?"

"Yeah. Alec wasn't on the Thursday night bus from Indy to Chicago, which is where I'd been looking, but I found him getting off the Friday morning bus."

Clay blew out a sigh. "Thank God. It was a long night here. Randi needs to talk to you."

"Ethan, you saw him?" Randi's voice was shaky. "Please say he's all right."

Ethan visualized Randi sitting next to

Clay all night, waiting for his cell to ring, and his heart clenched for her. "Randi, I only caught a glimpse of them on the platform camera getting off the bus last Friday. Alec was groggy, but he didn't appear to be hurt."

There was a tortured sob. "Ethan, promise me you'll keep looking until you find him."

Her heartache broke his own heart. "Go rest, Randi. I'll keep looking for your son."

Clay took the phone. "Hold on, I need to move." A minute later he was back. "I went outside so we can talk," he said. "Randi followed me all night. She's a wreck."

"I saw him for just a few seconds, Clay. He looked like he'd been drugged."

"You'd think someone would find a twelve-year-old staggering around suspicious."

Ethan sighed. "Hell, three-quarters of the people walking around the bus terminal look drugged. Especially after the all-night routes. Alec didn't stand out all that much. Now the bad news is that after I caught them on the platform getting off the bus, they disappeared into the crowd. I checked the lobby and terminal tapes, but can't find them."

"How long have you been watching tape, Ethan?"

Ethan shrugged, glanced at his watch. It was just a few minutes till seven-thirty. He let his eyes settle on the door. She'd be here any minute. "Probably fourteen of the last eighteen. I did sleep a few hours, so don't ask." And he had taken a few hours to rest his eyes and eat dinner with Dana Dupinsky. Those hours had been more refreshing than sleep.

"I need to come out and help you look at those tapes."

"I'm getting ready to let you. I can't watch more than a few hours at a time without a break. My eyes start to twitch. I watched from two-thirty to seven, but I had to break again. And until she sends another e-mail, this is the only lead we've got."

"I could get a flight out and be there by lunch."

"You could, but somebody needs to be there to run a trace in case this woman calls."

"All right." Clay didn't sound too happy about the prospect. "Oh, I dug a little on your security guy, Bush. He was a good cop. He might make a good local ally."

"Good. I thought as much." Ethan

straightened when the bell on the coffee shop door jingled. His heart got its second wind when Dana walked through the door, perfectly punctual. Perfectly . . . perfect. "I need to go now. Call me if you need me."

"Ethan, wait. I'm not done yet. Are you okay?"

"I'm fine." He was. He was better than fine, just seeing her, just being under the same roof. Once again he felt rejuvenated, his blood rushing harder, his head clearer. She was scanning the coffeehouse, looking for him, her body tall and straight and strong and for a crazy moment he was reminded of the scene in *The Natural* when seeing Glenn Close stand up in the crowd gave Robert Redford the magic he needed to hit the ball out of the park. Dana was that for him now, and right now, he thought he could do anything. Right now, even finding Alec seemed a little more possible.

Mindlessly he was on his feet. "My breakfast is here, Clay." *And my lunch and my dinner,* he thought. She was like . . . sustenance. "I have to go."

"You can talk to me while you eat," Clay said, exasperated.

Ethan could tell the very moment she saw him. "Is whatever you have to say about Alec?" he asked as she started toward him, her eyes now locked on his. His lungs paused midbreath, like an elevator stuck between floors. Like last night when he'd seen her across the terminal. Like the morning before when she'd first looked into his eyes.

"No, it's about Stetson." Their newest client. "We have to decide what we're going to tell them if you don't finish their network this week. We could be in breach of contract."

"Clay, I promise I'll call you back later and we'll talk about all the clients. In an hour. Let me know if anything happens with Alec. Bye." He cut off Clay's frustrated shout, dropped his cell phone in his pocket, and stretched his hand toward her, waiting. She was dressed much as she had been six hours before, a fresh sleeveless polo shirt hugging breasts any man would consider a gift, yet another simple cotton skirt showing off legs that seemed to go on forever. Ethan's mouth very nearly watered at the sight of her. His body had responded at the first jingle of the doorbell. It was Pavlovian, but he didn't care.

Heads turned as she passed, but she didn't notice. Her brown eyes were on his and she didn't falter. Without hesitation she took his hand and it was the same as before. The jolt, the flash of awareness. Her other hand lifted to his face, her fingertips brushing against the stubble of his cheek. Her eyes narrowed, not in suspicion, but in concern.

"What's wrong?" she asked and once again they'd achieved that connection, that sense that they'd been together always. "You didn't go back to your hotel and sleep, did you?"

The denial on his lips disappeared. "I've had some bad news from home."

"I'm sorry."

He lifted the hand he held to his lips, pressed a kiss to her palm. Watched her concerned eyes heat, the pulse at the hollow of her throat quicken, her breasts rise and fall at the rapid intake of her breath. Then glanced over at the counter to where Betty stood, once again agog. "We'd better sit down. I wouldn't want to be responsible for Betty's fourth commitment of the year."

"I'm sure she'd go with a smile on her face."

They sat, their hands joining across the table. Ethan ran his thumbs over her knuckles, wishing he'd done more than kiss her forehead the night before, but at the same time was glad he had not. He was learning her, a little at a time. Giving her time to learn him.

She lifted a russet brow. "So are you going to buy me breakfast or not?"

"I don't know. Does it win me more nice guy points?"

"And if it does?"

"Then you're on your own. I can't afford any more points in the nice guy column."

She grinned at that and Ethan shifted on the bench seat. He'd been aroused the moment she walked through the door, but seeing that lush mouth smile got him harder than a spike. "Duly noted, Mr. Buchanan." She waved Betty over and ordered eggs and bacon for them both, then grew serious once they were alone again. "This bad news from home . . . is it your family?"

"Close enough. It's Richard's family actually. They're all I have left now."

"You said you grew up with your grandmother. She's no longer alive?"

"No. She died a year after I got out of the Academy."

"So why were you living with your grandmother? Where were your parents?"

"My mother died when I was seven. My dad was on a submarine somewhere in the

North Atlantic. It was more than a month before he could get home so Gran took me in."

Her eyes widened again, this time with horror as she thought about a small boy dealing with the grief of losing his mother all alone. "That's terrible."

Again the shrug, more defensive this time. "My dad did the best he could. He was on a nuclear sub and it was the Cold War. They couldn't just pop up and let him off at the nearest bus stop." He'd become annoyed, which wasn't her intent.

"I didn't mean to make you upset," she said quietly. "I wasn't referring to the military or your father. Just you as a little boy. You must have been so scared and alone."

He drew a deep breath that visibly strained the buttons of his shirt. "I didn't mean to get upset." His eyes focused on her face in speculation. "I never have before."

"Never?"

Ethan considered the question carefully. "Well, not about my father."

Betty appeared and slid their breakfasts to the table. "You need anything else, just shout," she said and walked away, looking over her shoulder all the while.

Dana waited until she was gone. "So

your father never made you angry." She said it like she didn't quite believe it. "And other things? What things *do* make you angry?"

It was a heavy question, one that deserved a thoughtful answer. He looked up from his eggs. "You're sure you don't want to know my sign, phone number, or my favorite color?"

Her lips curved. "Not really, but if that's what you'd like to tell me, that's what I'll take."

His gaze dropped to those full lips and once again wondered how they would feel against his. Then he lifted his eyes to find hers warm and aware and suddenly her question didn't seem so hard after all. "Leo, 202-555-8943, and blue. People who drive slow in the fast lane, people who don't stand for the flag, and people who hurt little kids."

She drew in a breath. Let it out with a nod. "Fair enough. Will the bad news from home take you back there?"

"At some point. Whenever they call."

"Can't I help you, Ethan?"

He shook his head again, touched. "No, not with this. But thank you for asking. Do you always do that?"

"Do what?"

"Help people you barely know? First the old lady yesterday, now me."

Her smile was oddly self-deprecating. "You're not the only Good Samaritan lurking about. Besides, I thought I was getting to know you better." She patted his palm lightly before pulling her hand away. "How long has it been since you slept, Ethan? And I'm not talking about a nap on the El."

He grimaced. "For a whole night? I think it was Thursday."

"Then go get some sleep." She regarded him steadily. "I know this hot dog vendor down in Wrigleyville, next to where we ate last night. Best dogs in town."

He smiled at that. "Are you asking me out on a date? Without Caroline's help?"

She smiled back and his heart did a little end zone dance in his chest. "I guess I am. How about seven tonight? If you're not there, I'll understand."

"If I get tied up, how can I reach you?"

Her expression grew pained, wary. "If I tell you to call Betty, would you be angry?"

"No," he said, and saw her relief. And wondered who had become so angry with her in the past that she'd asked about his temper twice in five minutes. He pulled a business card from his pocket. "That number I gave you is my cell number. Call me if you need to."

"All right." She glanced at her watch. "I've got to be getting back to work now."

"I'll walk you to your car."

Outside the coffee shop he caught her hand and they walked to her car in easy silence, but once there she turned to him, her eyes cautious. "I'm surprised you haven't asked me any questions or checked up on me. Why?" She looked like the notion troubled her.

"Last night I didn't have time."

"And today? Will you check up on me today?"

He knew how easy it would be. But he shook his head. "No. Because for now I know what I need to know."

"For now," she repeated. "All right. Seven then. Unless you get tied up."

"Dana, wait." He put his hands on her shoulders and gently turned her to face him. "Actually, there is something I need to know."

Her eyes flickered, wary once more. "What?"

"Just this." And without further warning he dropped his head and took her lips in a kiss that was intended to be one of gentle exploration, but with a husky little whimper she changed everything, opening up to him, taking the kiss from a chaste peck to openmouthed and wholly sexual. He took a step forward, crowding her body against her car and she lifted her arms around his neck and her body on her toes, instantly perfecting their fit. He thrust and she pressed and before he knew it his palms cupped her breasts, his thumbs brushed against her nipples, and she'd gone stiff in his arms.

This wasn't how he'd planned it. It was just going to be a kiss, but the feel of her body molding itself to his had taken him to the limit of his control. In less than a minute all he could think of was sinking deep into her body, feeling her warm and tight, surrounding him. But dammit, they were standing on a busy street in the daylight. And he didn't care.

Grabbing on to his control, Ethan stepped back. Dropped his hands to his sides. Waited for his heart to start beating somewhat normally again, for the painful ache in his groin to subside. Watched her test her lip with the tip of her tongue as her breasts rose and fell inside the simple sleeveless polo shirt that had felt so soft against his hands. "I'm sorry," he murmured.

Her eyes were wide and turbulent, but she met his gaze without apology. "I'm not."

He lifted his fingertips to her damp lips, traced their shape. He'd wanted to know what it would be like to kiss her. Now he knew. He also knew he could never be satisfied with a simple kiss. Hell, there had been nothing simple about it. He drew a deep breath. "Dana?"

"Yes?"

"I really, really wanted to do that last night. I really, really want to do that again."

"So do I."

The breath he held came out on a hiss. "But I don't have enough time right now."

"Me, either." She slipped into her car, then turned her face up to look at him and the hot need in her eyes had him clenching his fists. "I'll see you at seven."

He stood there, rooted to the asphalt, watching as she pulled her car out of the lot and onto the street. She'd just disappeared from view when his cell phone rang.

"Are you done with breakfast?" Clay asked acidly.

Ethan blew out a breath. "Yeah."

"Then perhaps you'd care to get back to work."

Something in Clay's tone lifted the hairs on his neck. "You got a call?"

"Another e-mail. I need you to get someplace where you can trace it for me."

Ethan set off for his car at a fast jog, his heart beating harder than it had just minutes before when he'd held Dana Dupinsky in his arms. "Give me fifteen minutes to get to my hotel room. What does it say?"

"Alec is still alive."

"I didn't think they'd say he was dead. Was there an attachment?"

"Alec lying on a twin bed. The bedspread pattern was baseballs and footballs."

Ethan frowned hard. "No hotel I've ever stayed in has bedspreads like that. It's like she's got him stashed in somebody's house."

"That's what I was thinking. Right under Alec's hand is a piece of newspaper — yesterday's date. The top part with the city name is cut off."

As of yesterday Alec was still alive. Ethan's blood rushed to his head. "Could it have been cut and pasted into the picture?"

"You'll have to be the judge of that. I forwarded you the e-mail. She also complimented the Vaughns on not going to the cops and laid out the terms of the ransom. If they want to see him again, they need to pony up five million. Details to follow."

Ethan stopped abruptly at his car. "Stan doesn't have that much money."

Clay hesitated. "Yeah, buddy, he does."

"Do I want to know how he got it?"

"I'm still working on it, but I think the answer is no."

"Damn."

*Chicago,*
*Monday, August 2, 7:30 a.m.*

The e-mail had gone well. She didn't even need Rickman's laptop. It had been damn easy to open a Yahoo! mail account on the public computer at the copy store where the clerk was too boggled by the sight of her breasts jiggling in a tiny tank top to adequately check her ID. Good thing because not only was Alicia Samson five inches shorter than Sue, according to a search of an online Morgantown newspaper, as of yesterday she'd been declared a missing person. Her ID was useless from here on out.

Now she stood outside Leroy Vickers's place of business, waiting for him to come

214

out. It would be Vickers's second round of deliveries for the morning. Sue knew this because she'd made it a point to track the movements of every person on her "to-do" list. She'd found them all on her own, except for Vaughn. To find Vaughn, she'd needed James's help. He'd tracked down the old woman in Florida and Sue had been able to take it from there. She'd needed him no longer and now wished she'd been as thorough killing him as she'd been with the old woman. *Because now James will stop at nothing to stop me.*

Nervously she glanced around, then cursed her paranoia. James had been in Chicago, trying to pay her old cohorts for her whereabouts. But Donnie Marsden hadn't heard anything from him since the day he'd been at Earl and Lucy's. And Sue didn't intend to let Donnie or the others know where she was anyway. Just in case they got greedy.

Well, she amended. She'd let Leroy Vickers know where she was. Soon. Making sure the coast was clear, she slipped into the back of the laundry delivery van Vickers drove. His job was a small source of comfort. When he'd gotten out of prison he hadn't been able to get a decent legit job and nobody in the drug business would touch him with a ten-foot pole. Because he'd squealed. Turned against one of his own. Had he turned on Donnie, he might have been dead in jail. Sue didn't have that much power in those days.

She did now.

He finally came out and flopped behind the wheel, muttering something foul about his boss. He'd let himself go over the years. Flabby arms and legs. She, on the other hand, had been pumping iron in preparation for this moment and the others that would follow. Sue waited until he'd pulled into a back access road before slipping her arms around the seat and pressing the tip of her knife to his throat. Her right hand held a knife, her left, a length of duct tape. The duct tape she slapped against his mouth, silencing him.

"Keep driving," she said, enjoying the way his body tensed. "Both hands on the wheel." He swallowed and the sharp end of her blade bit into his skin. "I'm back, Vickers," she purred. "Aren't you glad to see me?" His only response was to press back into his seat, away from the knife. Sue just pressed harder and with her left hand pulled her gun from the waistband of her jeans and shoved it against his temple.

"Pull into that alley over there." He did,

his body now shaking like he had palsy. "What do you think you deserve, Vickers? What do you think five years of my life is worth?" She asked it calmly even though her heart was racing in anticipation. "What do you think you owe me, Leroy? Don't worry. I'm here to collect. With interest. Put the van in park."

And in a move she'd practiced for just this moment, she shot both his wrists, first one, then the other. He yelped in pain, but this alley was behind an elementary school, deserted this time of year. No one would hear him. He hugged his arms close to his chest, his hands now useless. Blood poured from his wrists. If she'd had more time she would have sat here until he became weak from blood loss. But she didn't have time. She had to get back to the shelter before Dupinsky realized she was gone. Before the kid woke up.

"Now listen carefully, you little chicken-shit," she muttered over his moans. "I'm going to take the knife away. I want you to roll off this seat to your knees." There was just enough space between the two front seats for him to obey her order. "Then I want you to crawl back here, on your knees." She shoved the gun against his temple. "Now do it."

He rolled and landed like a trout between the two seats. She backed up into the rear recesses of the van. "Now crawl, Vickers. Like the damn dog you are."

He looked up, his eyes wild with pain and hopeless fear. And he crawled. "Lie down." She pointed at a pile of laundry with her gun. "It's good you got yourself fired from the deli and the corner grocery," Sue said, amused. "This laundry van is so much more convenient. I'll be able to clean up right here." His eyes widened and he shrank back against the bags, his arms cradled against his chest. "Yes, I've been watching you for the last six months, just waiting for this moment. You were the only one of us to break, Vickers. The only one of us to take the easy way out. I'm surprised the others haven't snuffed you out before now. But then, nobody else served as many years as I did."

Quickly she pumped a shot into his thighs, then his knees. He couldn't run and his hands were useless. He lay on his back, writhing, his muffled moans of agony pure music to her ears. She put the gun aside and held the knife for him to see. "You sat in that courtroom and told them everything. *Everything,*" she hissed. "You're a ball-less worm. Figuratively speaking of course." She ran her finger down the blade. "Now you'll be one in the literal sense as well." She gave him a minute to understand, then when the horror filled his eyes she moved, plunging the blade into his groin. He screamed, the sound muffled. She wished she dared rip the tape off. To hear him scream. Instead she withdrew the blade and plunged again. And again. The sensation rolled through her, the power. It was headier than orgasm and twice as strong.

He was silent now, his eyes rolled back in his head. But he wasn't dead. Not yet. After leaving James half done, she wasn't about to make the same mistake again. She wiped her knife on the fluffy white towels he'd been set to deliver and emptied the rest of the magazine of the nine mil into his head. *Now* he was dead.

She had just enough time to clean up and get back to the shelter. Maybe she'd even buy a pack of cigarettes. One down, four to go. With Vaughn as the grand finale.

*Wight's Landing,*
*Monday, August 2, 9:00 a.m. Eastern*
*(8:00 a.m. Central)*

Sheriff Louisa Moore paused outside the door of the coroner's office. Kehoe sat hunched over a microscope. She tapped lightly on the glass and he motioned her in.

"You were right, Lou," Kehoe said. "Your John Doe on the beach was no suicide."

Lou leaned one hip on his desk, unsurprised. "It didn't make sense that a man would go to a stranger's shed in his boxers to commit suicide. What did you find in the autopsy?"

"Subdermal bruising around the wrists and ankles. You couldn't see it on the skin's surface because the body was too bloated, but the slides don't lie."

"So somebody tied him up before they blew his brains out."

Kehoe looked at her over his glasses. "Looks that way."

"Could you get a better fix on the time of death?"

"Wednesday morning, between one and four a.m."

Lou bent her mouth in an impressed

frown. "That's a pretty specific time interval."

"I sent samples of the bugs to a forensic entomologist I know at Georgetown University. Based on the larval development cycles, that's the time frame we're looking at."

"Stan and Randi Vaughn were still in Annapolis Wednesday morning," Lou mused. "Their hotel confirmed they checked out late Friday morning, around eleven."

Kehoe blinked, his eyes owlish behind his thick lenses. "You think they're involved?"

She shrugged. "They were twitchy yesterday morning when I took their statements."

"You might be twitchy too if you were on vacation and came back from a side trip to find this guy in your shed," Kehoe said mildly. "I seem to recall two of your own deputies heaving up their breakfasts off the side of the Vaughns' dock yesterday morning."

"It was a hell of a discovery, I'll give you that," she said, "but I still have a feeling that Mr. and Mrs. Vaughn knew a hell of a lot more than they were saying."

"Well, that's your bailiwick, Sheriff. I

will tell you that Stan Vaughn's parents are salt of the earth. I've known them for years."

"Huxley said the parents come down for the summer." Huxley was Lou's head deputy, a veritable walking encyclopedia on the town and its inhabitants. Lou had been farther underwater than Huxley had been away from Wight's Landing, but then, that was pretty much par for the course in this small Rockwellian town.

"Past few years that's been true. Lately they've taken to traveling, now that Stan's bought the business."

"What business is Stan Vaughn in?" It was more than curiosity on her part. Now that this suicide was a murder, her gut instincts about the younger Vaughns were significant.

"Dick had an electronics store in Baltimore, but in the last few years Stan's grown it to, oh, I don't know, twenty stores or more, all up and down the coast from Virginia to New York. Anyway, the business has been so successful, Dick retired and he and Edna have been traveling the world. I just got a postcard from London, in fact."

"John, did you get anything else from the autopsy that might help us identify the body?"

"Other than the bruising, the autopsy didn't show anything else regarding his death. Cause of death was most certainly the shotgun blast. Mr. Doe was about twenty-five years old. His prints aren't in the system and his mouth was destroyed by the blast, so dental records are out. If we can match him to a missing person, I can match DNA of course. But without something to compare to, I can't help you with an ID."

"I went through missing persons yesterday and again this morning. Nobody matches."

"Well, if he was on vacation, he might not be missed until after he was supposed to return home." The phone rang and he reached over his desk to pick it up. "Coroner's office. Kehoe speaking . . . Yes, she's here." He handed Lou the phone. "It's for you."

"This is Sheriff Moore."

"Good morning, Sheriff. My name is Detective Janson and I'm with the Homicide Division in Morgantown, West Virginia. I hope I'm not interrupting anything important."

"I was meeting with our coroner, but we were almost done. How can I help you?"

"Well, I'm investigating a case and was

hoping you could help."

Lou sat on the arm of one of Kehoe's chairs, the hairs on her neck stirring. "Of course."

"We found the body of a young woman in some woods off our main highway Friday morning. Time of death was between midnight and six a.m. Thursday, the day before."

"Cause of death?" Lou asked tersely.

"Nine millimeter to the head. Why?"

"Because I've got a John Doe of my own, shot about twenty-four hours before yours. Can I put you on speakerphone? It's just me and our coroner, John Kehoe."

"Sure." Janson waited until she'd hit the speaker to continue. "My Jane Doe has a name now, Sheriff. That's why I called you. We were able to match her prints to a Cheryl Rickman. Miss Rickman's fingerprints were on file in the Baltimore school district. She'd been a speech therapist in an elementary school there. When we informed her parents they said she was supposed to have been on vacation in Wight's Landing this week."

Kehoe stiffened when Janson said "speech therapist." "On vacation?" he asked.

"Yeah. She took a job as a private therapist and her employers asked her to join them at their beach house. She worked for a family named Vaughn. Can you help us find them?"

"Yeah, we can." Lou turned to Kehoe who looked shaken. "Why would the Vaughns hire a speech therapist, John? Neither of them has a speech impediment."

Kehoe drew a breath. "No, the therapist was for their son, Alec. He's deaf."

Lou narrowed her eyes. "There wasn't any child in that house yesterday, John."

"Maybe they left him back in Baltimore with friends or took a vacation just themselves."

"Then why invite the speech therapist to come?"

Kehoe shook his head. "I don't know."

"We just found out our John Doe was murdered, Janson. Whoever did it set it up to look like a suicide. We found the body in a shed on the Vaughns' property. I was just getting ready to go out there. Do you want me to talk to them about Cheryl Rickman?"

"Are they suspects in your John Doe?"

"They have alibis for both Wednesday and Thursday," she said, "so not directly, no."

Lou could hear paper rustling on Janson's end. "We may be able to help each other, Sheriff. Cheryl Rickman's parents said she had a fiancé. Name's Paul Mc-Millan. I've been trying to track him down to question him on Miss Rickman's disappearance."

"Let me guess," Lou said. "White male, twenty-five, five-eleven, one-seventy-five?"

Janson sighed. "Meet John Doe. Yeah, talk to the Vaughns. Maybe they can shed some light on anything this couple was involved in that might have gotten them killed."

"I'll keep in touch." Lou disconnected the line, then turned to Kehoe. "I'm sorry, John."

Kehoe's jaw clenched. "I've known Stan since he was a boy. He's no murderer."

Since Vaughn's alibi was tight, she wouldn't argue. For now.

*Chicago,*
*Monday, August 2, 9:45 a.m.*

Ethan sank down into his car seat, yanking at his tie, his phone to his ear. "*Dammit.* I missed her by two hours. Might as well have been two days."

"You saw her face this time?" Clay asked, his voice hard.

"No, same damn cap. Copy store clerk gave me a description, but he wasn't looking at her face." Ethan started the engine and cranked up the AC. "She sauntered in, wearing shorts and a tiny shirt. Made sure the poor geek behind the counter saw every little jiggle."

"Blinded him with her headlights, huh?"

"Hell. She could have been wearing a rubber Nixon mask and the guy wouldn't have noticed. He could only say she was under forty. The security video played like a porn flick."

"I take it none of that exposed skin had any tattoos or any other identifying features."

"Maybe. There was something on her shoulder. I almost didn't notice it at first because she'd covered it with makeup, but when she leaned across the counter to put her cash in his hand the strap of her shirt slipped and I noticed it picked up a stain."

Clay's tone was approving. "Good eye."

"Thanks." Ethan grimaced. "My eyes feel like they've been scrubbed with sand."

"Well, hold 'em open a little longer. Did this new e-mail come from Rickman's laptop?"

"No, she opened a Yahoo! mail account. She didn't have the laptop with her."

"I wonder why. What about ID?"

"She used Alicia Samson's again. The clerk said she didn't want him to run the card, said she was too close to her limit. He just held it while she used the computer, then she paid cash. She did the same thing in Morgantown."

"So if the card's reported stolen, nobody will link it to her. Can we get fingerprints?"

"She wiped the keyboard before and after. Didn't touch anything else."

"Shit. So, what's next?"

"I'm on my way to an electronics store to buy some video duping equipment. I slipped the kid a hundred bucks to loan me the tape long enough to make a copy. I'm going to try to enhance it, to see if what she was trying to hide pops out."

"No pun intended."

Ethan huffed a weary chuckle. "I'm too tired for your junior high jokes. I'm going to buy the damn equipment, copy the damn tape, return the original to the clerk who will probably replay it until he has hair on his palms, then I'm going back to my hotel and go to sleep."

Clay was quiet for a minute. "That's the best plan. Call me when you wake up."

There was more. Dread settled over

Ethan, thick and suffocating. "What, Clay?"

Clay sighed. "Cheryl Rickman is dead, Ethan."

Regret sliced through him. The woman had given her life protecting Alec. "I knew it was coming. Still, I'd hoped . . . How do you know?"

"Right after you finished tracing this last e-mail, the new sheriff showed up. Sheriff Louisa J. Moore. She heard from the police up in Morgantown who found Cheryl's body Friday. So now she knows the body she took from the shed is Paul McMillan."

"You were there?"

"Yeah. She surprised us. I didn't get a chance to leave. I said I was a friend but she didn't buy it. She knew a cop. And she knows Stan and Randi are hiding something."

"She said something?"

"No, but I could tell. She asked why Cheryl hadn't been here, with Paul. Stan told her they'd given Cheryl the week off because they'd sent Alec to stay with his parents. The sheriff just got this look in her eye and said, 'London is a great experience for a boy his age.' "

Ethan felt ill. "Stan's parents are in England? Shit. Stan never told us that."

Clay's chuckle was entirely without

humor. "Stan hasn't told us a lot of things, E, but we'll get to that later. Moore looked straight at me then. Said her coroner was good friends with the Vaughns, that he'd gotten a postcard just last week. She wanted me to know she knew Stan was lying. Which he did very well by the way. Never broke a sweat."

Ethan pressed his thumbs into his eye sockets. "Wonderful."

"It was quite a performance. Then Moore calmly said she had evidence McMillan was not a suicide. Stan acted astonished, but Randi went pale. And then Moore looked me right in the eye and asked if she could search the house."

It was what they'd wanted when they insisted Stan report finding McMillan's body. They'd wanted the local police to find something to lead them to the killer. And yet the thought of a flock of uniforms descending on the beach house itself made Ethan's stomach churn. He could only imagine what it had done to Randi's. "And you said?"

"I said I was a guest. That it was up to the home owners, the Vaughns. But *then*, Randi asked, very calmly I thought, if Moore had a warrant. Surprised the hell out of me. Moore just said no, but that she could get one. Randi graciously showed her to the door."

Ethan wasn't sure what to say. "I didn't know Randi had that in her."

"She didn't for long. After Moore drove away, Randi ran for the bathroom and threw up. Stan ranted that by forcing him to report McMillan's body I was going to get Alec killed."

"God, I hope not," Ethan murmured.

"I don't think so, E. After Moore left I did a quick background search. She worked Special Victims in Boston before she came down here. It's likely she's worked at least a child abduction or two. I think it's time we dealt her in."

"Clay, this woman who has Alec knows we haven't been to the police. She said so in the e-mail this morning. She could have somebody watching the house right now. We know she's capable of killing. Two people are dead. I sure as hell couldn't live with my conscience if she killed Alec, too."

"She might have read the local paper on-line to know the police weren't involved," Clay challenged. "Or maybe it was just a good guess. Either way, we don't know that she won't kill him anyway."

Ethan pondered the question, searched his soul. They should tell the police. They should. Then in his mind he saw Alec as the woman had dragged him off that bus. He'd been groggy, quite possibly drugged, but still alive. And today's attachment showed that scrap of yesterday's paper. As of yesterday he was still alive. The fact remained that Alec was *still alive*. Ethan needed to keep him that way. "Are you willing to risk Alec's life?"

A long, long pause hung between them, then Clay sighed. "No."

"If anybody tells, it has to be Randi and Stan. I don't want any more dead Vaughns on my conscience."

"Richard wasn't your fault, Ethan," Clay said harshly. "If the tables had been turned, it would be you that was dead."

"I know that," Ethan said bitterly, then thought of Dana's words just a few hours before. *Sometimes it's hard to be the one that survives.* "I know that," he repeated wearily now.

"You're tired. Go get your duping equipment, then sleep. Take a pill if you have to."

*Pills.* A thought popped into Ethan's mind. "Can you find out how many Phenobarbital pills it would take to drug Alec up? Without asking Randi. I don't want to scare her."

Ethan could almost hear Clay sit

232

straighter. "Randi said the bottle had just a few more than he'd need for their vacation. If the Hooter's girl's been doping him up, she'll need a refill soon."

"That's what I was thinking. I'll canvass the pharmacies in the vicinity of the place she used this morning. Maybe she went in for a refill."

"That sounds like the first proactive plan we've had since this whole nightmare started."

"I agree. I'll call you after I've had a chance to analyze this tape."

"*Wait.* I'm not going to let you hang up. Breakfast, buddy. What was that all about?"

Ethan drew a breath, and his heart eased. Just the thought of Dana Dupinsky's sincere brown eyes was enough to chase away his mood. "Eggs and bacon."

"Don't insult me. Are you going to tell me about her?"

"How do you know it's a her?"

"Because I know you, Ethan. Well?" Clay's voice had an unpleasant edge.

"Why are you so interested in my *breakfast* all of a sudden?"

"Because you've never allowed your *breakfast* to distract you from your *priorities*."

233

"I know my *priorities,* Clay," Ethan said sharply. "Alec is my priority."

A frustrated huff. "It's just been a long, long time since you had breakfast, pal."

Ethan scowled. He knew exactly how long it had been since he'd had *breakfast.* To the damn minute. The knowledge had become especially acute when he'd found himself pressed up against the warmth of Dana Dupinsky's ripe body mere hours before.

Ethan still said nothing and after a pained silence, Clay trudged on. "You had a pretty steady diet of women after Jill. Then you came home from the desert and . . . Became a hermit, I guess. You have to admit, Ethan, you go two years without a relationship and suddenly you meet someone at a time you most need to focus. It's hard to understand."

Ethan sucked in both cheeks. "My relationships are not your business to understand."

"You're my friend, Ethan. I just don't want to see you get hurt."

"She wouldn't hurt me."

"Not intentionally. But if she distracted you from finding Alec, you'd hate yourself."

That stripped the wind from his sails.

"Clay, it's complicated. She's . . ." He searched his mind for a parallel. "Were you ever caught in a really bad squall when you were out at sea? So bad you weren't sure you were going to come out of it right side up?"

"A time or two."

"Did you ever have the sea just go calm on you? Like the storm never was?"

"No."

"Neither had I until yesterday morning." He pulled his car from the copy store's lot. "I have to go. The electronics store will be opening soon."

# Chapter Nine

*Chicago,*
*Monday, August 2, 10:00 a.m.*

"You wanted to see me?"

Dana looked up from her computer and found a warm smile for Jane Smith. "Have a seat." Jane sat, her eyes fixed on the carpet. "I wanted to give you a day or two to settle in before we talked. I'd like to understand where you came from, where you'd like to go."

"Go? Go where? I . . . I just got here."

Jane's voice held tremulous fear, her hands clasped tightly between her knees, her back hunched over. "Well, not today, Jane. But at some point you'll want to leave and build a life for you and Erik. Have you thought about the kind of life you'd like to have?"

One shoulder lifted. "Don't wanna get beat up no more."

It was a common refrain. "That's a good start. Can you tell me about your life before?"

"My husband drank. Beat me if I did anything he didn't like, which was about every day."

"What about Erik?"

"What about him?" she mumbled.

*What about him?* What a question. "He's a very troubled young boy."

She looked up, her odd eyes bleak. "His daddy . . . hurt him."

That Dana could believe. The child hadn't made eye contact in the two days he'd been here. Every time she'd checked up on him she'd found him curled up in a ball on his bed. The one time she tried to touch him, he flinched as if she'd burned him. And someone had. Recently. "How, Jane? How did his father hurt him?"

"Beat him sometimes. Burned his face. That's what made me leave."

"I'd like to talk to Erik."

"No." It was said quickly and with heat. "He's been through enough."

Dana sat back in her chair, studied the woman's huddled form. "I understand your not wanting to hurt him further, Jane, but Erik needs help. Maybe more than I can give him."

She looked up and it took every nerve Dana had not to flinch when Jane's eyes filled with tears, her pupils stark against nothing but white. "Leave him be. Please."

Disturbed, Dana nodded. "All right. I won't talk to him just yet. But he does need to be seen by a doctor, Jane. If his father hurt him, we need to check him out."

Jane's eyes flared. "Nobody touches my kid." It was almost a snarl and she started, as if she'd surprised herself as much as Dana. The woman's eyes dropped back to the floor. "Erik's never been . . . right," she continued, her voice calmer now. "He has seizures."

*It's Erik's mother who isn't exactly right,* Dana thought. "What kind of seizures, Jane?"

"Epileptic. He's on medicine. I need some more soon. Keppra and Phenobarbital."

"Do you have the bottles?"

"No. I left the bottles so my husband wouldn't see it missing and know we were gone."

"Well, I'll talk to Dr. Lee about a refill. What did you do before you came here, Jane?"

Jane's jaw tightened fractionally. "What do you mean?"

"I mean, did you have a job outside your home, have you had any job training?"

"Why?"

Dana walked around her desk and perched on the edge, trying to lessen any feelings of intimidation. "Jane, Hanover House isn't a place you can stay forever. Women come, get their bearings, then they leave. We have a policy of a three-week maximum stay." Which they routinely broke, of course. Somehow Dana felt loath to mention that fact.

"But I'm afraid to leave," she whispered. "He'll find me and make me go back."

*Me.* Not *us. Me.* "Back to where, Jane?" she asked and the woman stiffened.

"You don't understand. You're the only one I can trust. This is the only place I'll be safe."

*I'll* be safe. Not *we'll.* Not *my son. Me. I.* There was a pattern here Dana didn't like. "Back where, Jane?" she repeated.

Her brows bunched stubbornly. "It don't matter. I'm never going back there anyways."

"That's good for you and Erik. But Erik needs a stable home. To make that happen, we need to find you a job. Did you have a job before Erik was born?"

"I was seventeen." It was said defensively, Jane's arms coming up to cross over her chest. And it was in that movement that Dana saw Jane's scars. Small and light, they crisscrossed the inside of her arms wrist to elbow. It was just a glimpse. But it told Dana a great deal about the woman sitting before her.

At one time Jane had cut herself. Not as an attempt at suicide, but an initial cry for attention. Later to exert control over the only thing she'd had control of at the time. Her own body. Dana had seen this more than once over her years as a therapist. Now Jane's world was upside down again. Stress often caused people to fall back to familiar ways of coping. They'd need to watch both Jane and Erik more closely.

Dana focused on the present. Jane did not want to think about a job, which was not unusual. Most women needed some time to process all the things they needed to do now that they were truly alone in the world, many for the first time in their lives.

"Tell you what. Why don't you go through the want ads in the paper, then later this afternoon, join us for our group therapy session? Jane, you took the biggest step in walking away from your husband. That was braver than what most people do in a lifetime. It's my job to help you make the most of the second chance you've given yourself."

Jane's nod was brief. "Can I go back

now? I hate to leave Erik for so long."

"Certainly." Dana handed her the newspaper, fighting the urge to shove it in her hand when Jane just sat looking at it. Finally Jane took the paper, stood up, walked out.

Dana stared after her, instinct screaming that something was very wrong. But she'd also learned that no two women responded to abuse the same way. She sat down and finished making her notes, deep in thought when she was jerked back to reality.

"Good morning," Caroline said from the doorway. "Can I come in?"

"Could I stop you?" Dana asked dryly.

Closing the door, Caroline chuckled. "Probably not." She sank into a chair. "So what happened last night?" she asked with no further preamble.

Dana gave her best bland look. "You could have just called and asked."

Caroline grinned. "And miss the way you're blushing right now? No way."

"I'm not blushing."

Caroline raised her eyes to the ceiling. "First stage is denial."

Dana shrugged, trying for careless, knowing she couldn't pull it off. "You're right."

Caroline narrowed her eyes. "Did he do

something wrong?"

"No, nothing like that. He was a perfect gentleman." *Except when his hands covered my breasts. And it was the most incredible thrill.* Dana propped her elbows on her desk, her chin on her fists. "We had dinner and he told me about his accident. His friend died and he's still grieving, but talking seemed to help. We had hot wings. I ate vegetables."

Caroline arched a brow. "One sad little celery stalk doesn't count, Dana. Then what?"

"He wanted to take me home, but I said no."

"Prudent," Caroline said.

"But he didn't give up, so I had to let him walk me to my apartment."

Caroline grimaced. "I bet that was a real eye-opener."

"He was less than impressed. We chatted a bit more. Then he left."

"He left." Caroline ran her tongue over her teeth. "You're going to make me pull every little detail out of you with a crochet hook, aren't you?"

Dana dragged her fingers through her hair. "Dammit, Caroline. We talked. He kissed my forehead. That's it. No rabid romance." *No hot sweaty sex to top off my tank.* "I'm sorry to disappoint you." *You have no idea how much.*

"Okay. So when do you see him again?"

Dana looked at the ceiling. "Two hours ago."

Caroline's grin lit up the room. "Now we're cookin', Dupinsky. So what happened then?"

Dana had to laugh at her friend's glee. "We talked some more. Then he walked me to my car. And he kissed me. On the lips."

"And?"

Dana closed her eyes, her cheeks burning, her heart pounding at the memory of that kiss, her lips still tingling hours later. "Oh, my God."

"So he really *didn't* lose anything he couldn't live without," Caroline said wryly.

Dana thought about that hard ridge, pulsing just where she'd needed it. "Oh, no."

"So when do you see him again?"

"Tonight at seven. If Evie's busy, can you spend an hour or two here?"

"For you, for this? Absolutely. Now, I did have another reason for coming this morning besides the Buchanan report." She glanced at the door and dropped her voice. "Jane."

Dana frowned down at her notes. "What about her?"

"She really worries me, Dana. Yesterday, I caught her smoking in the bathroom. I wasn't angry, I just asked her not to do it again. But she was furious. Had this controlled little explosion. I could tell she hadn't meant to do it, and that she was fighting to calm herself back down." Caroline frowned. "For just a second, she reminded me of Rob."

Dana blinked. Caroline's ex-husband had been a monster. "Oh, Caroline, really."

"I'm serious. Then later, when David came to fix the roof? She'd gone out back to smoke and I saw her staring at David."

"David's a handsome man. Most women stare at him."

"Not like this. This was nasty. Lascivious. Calculating." She shivered. "I didn't like it."

Dana sighed. Her own instinct was one thing, but Caroline's concurrence was something she couldn't just ignore. "What do you think we should do, Caroline? Those bruises she came here wearing were real. Erik's been through some serious trauma."

"I don't know what to do. Her boy breaks my heart. Just . . . watch her for now, okay?"

"I will."

244

Sue shut the door to her room, breathless, having skipped up the stairs an instant before Caroline opened the door to Dupinsky's office. She eyed the kid sitting up on the bed, groggy but aware. Dupinsky better come through soon with the refill. She needed to keep the boy uncommunicative, as she had no doubt that Dupinsky would try to talk to him. It was a typical social worker response — talk, talk, talk. That Dupinsky was forcing her to look for a job so soon had been a bit of a shock. She'd expected some pampering, a little kindness. She threw the newspaper, barely missing the kid's head, watched him flinch.

At least she could use the job search to her advantage. This morning she'd sneaked out to get her latest e-mail to the Vaughns and to kill good old Leroy Vickers. But if she were out looking for work, well, she wouldn't have to sneak around anymore. She'd still have to be careful, still need to be sure she stayed far away from old haunts, from where anyone could recognize her. James was still out there, hovering. Of that she had no doubt.

She'd forced the kid to take another of his pills and was chasing it with Benadryl when a movement caught her eye, out the

245

window, down on the street. It was Caroline, walking to her car. That woman was dangerous. Sue had heard every word they'd said. Sooner or later Dupinsky would listen to those disturbing observations, and lack of pampering or not, this was a pretty good place to hide. Caroline needed to be dealt with.

She pulled her cell from her backpack. Fred answered on the third ring. "I was getting a little concerned, SusieQ. I didn't think you'd call me back."

"Well, I did. Look, I'll do what you want me to do, but I have another favor for you."

"Stackin' up the favors, Susie? I don't know."

"Trust me. This one you'll enjoy."


*Chicago,*
*Monday, August 2, 4:30 p.m.*


*She was hot and wet and constant fluid motion, rising to meet him like a wave of the sea. Her long, long legs wrapped around him, her husky voice whispered his name, her brown eyes filled with lust. He pushed deeper and she moaned and —*

Ethan jerked awake, instantly lifting his head from the pillow. The clock was beeping obnoxiously. He dropped his face back into the pillow with a groan. His head still ached, but his body ached worse, certain vicinities more than others. It had been a dream. Just a dream. But so damn real and so damn good. He was rock-hard and ready to go from just a dream. What would it be like when he touched her for real? Because he would. He'd thought it when she first looked up at him in the bus station yesterday morning, but knew it after that kiss up against her car. She'd come alive in his arms and it had been like . . . *Like she was made just for me. And I'll see her again in a few hours.* His stomach rumbled, but he wouldn't eat. Not until he met her at the hot dog stand. He had to eat. He had to see her. Doing both at the same time was the only way to satisfy his conscience because as he'd told Clay, he did understand his priorities.

Which now included assembling the equipment he'd bought and checking out that copy store surveillance video. Dragging himself out of bed, he flipped on ESPN to catch the tail end of the Orioles game while he opened boxes and connected cords, wondering if Dana was listening to the Cubs play while she took pictures of mothers and babies.

The O's were up by two when he'd finished converting the copy store's video to digital and he switched his concentration to the image on his computer screen, magnifying the woman's shoulder, playing with contrast and color, trying to see what the makeup covered.

A half hour later he sat back. Her left shoulder had a tattoo, but all he could see was an uppercase *A*, stylized similar to the first letter of a medieval hand-drawn text. The rest stubbornly remained hidden beneath the thick makeup. "Better than we had this morning, but still not enough," he muttered, dragging his hands down his face. He needed a shower and a shave. And food. But food would have to wait for the best dogs in town. And Dana.

He still had work to do before he met her tonight. He'd only stay a few minutes, because he did know his priorities and right now his priority was a twelve-year-old boy who needed every waking moment he could give.

*Mom.* Alec was home. His mom was stroking his hair and he was home. It had all been an awful, awful dream. He'd tell her about it, make it into a joke. But she'd stay with him anyway, stroking his hair until he went back to sleep. She always did.

He'd tell her all about it, when he opened his eyes. But it was hard to do. Hard to open his eyes. He fought, so hard. He wanted to see her, needed to see her. She was stroking his hair and nothing had ever felt so good.

He struggled with his eyelids, felt them flutter. Lifted them enough to see her face. Blurry pictures ran together, then apart, then slowly together again. *Mom.*

The scream caught in his throat. It wasn't her. Wasn't his mother. His mother's face was smooth and beautiful. This face . . . A long red scar ran down this face. The mouth didn't smile. He fought to breathe. *Mom.*

But the hand continued to stroke his hair and he drew a breath. *Not his mom. Not a dream.* Who was she? Her unsmiling mouth moved strangely and he knew she was talking to him. Still her hand soothed.

His eyes fluttered back down. He fought hard, fought the current that pulled him under. It was black and dark. *No. Not again. Mom.*

Evie looked up when a shadow fell over the boy. "He's asleep again," she murmured.

Jane's eyes narrowed, then she relaxed when she saw all was well with her son. "He woke up?" she whispered hopefully.

"No, not really. He was thrashing around in his sleep." Evie had been sitting with Erik for a full hour, stroking his hair, hoping he'd give her some indication that he was all right. He'd opened his eyes at one point, and there'd almost been a spark of recognition, an indication that he knew where he was. She gave a final parting stroke to Erik's hair and stood up. "I just wanted to be sure he was all right. So how was group?"

Jane shrugged tightly. "It was okay."

Evie patted her arm. "Don't worry, it'll all come together for you and Erik."

"That's what Dana said in group, just now." The woman braved a smile that tore at Evie's heart. "It's hard to believe people can be so nice, after . . ."

"I know. I remember when I first came

here. You wonder when the other shoe's going to fall. But here it doesn't. There's nothing to fear here. Look, if you want me to come sit with Erik, to give you a break, just let me know."

"You're very kind," Jane murmured, dropping her eyes to the floor. "Thank you."

Evie hesitated, then put her arm around Jane for a short, hard hug. "You're welcome."

From beneath her lashes, Sue watched the scarred woman's bare feet pad out of the room. These women had better learn to leave well enough alone. Dupinsky with her constant talking, Caroline with her damn rules, and now Scarface who had way too much interest in the kid. Sue closed the door to her room, then took the two steps to the bed and grabbed the kid's shoulders, lifting him off the bed. She shook him savagely, and for a moment his eyes opened. But there was no spark, no defiance. Just stupor. Which was exactly what she wanted him to have. She'd planted the seeds of the kid's mental deficiency with Dupinsky several times now. Erik was epileptic and autistic. No one had seemed to doubt her and if they did, well, then, hell, she wasn't a doctor, just a poor country woman running from her bastard husband. Here, the story rang true.

She dropped the kid back on the bed. Still no response. Good. For just a moment she stood and looked at him. Waited for a flicker of compassion for the boy she'd taken from his bed, drugged out of his mind for days.

Then gave a brisk nod when the flicker never materialized. She'd been a little worried that all this bleeding heart shit would rub off. She shouldn't have been. Because retribution was within her grasp and the kid was the carrot. The lure. The prize.

The sound of voices down in the alley behind the shelter caught her ear. Caroline and Dana were getting into separate cars. Dana apparently was off to her date. Caroline was planning to make her fashion worthy. Then Dupinsky would go off to her date and Caroline would go off to meet Fred. But she wouldn't know it. Not until it was too late.

# Chapter Ten

*Chicago,*
*Monday, August 2, 6:15 p.m.*

With a curse Ethan jumped out of the shower. The hotel phone was ringing. "Yeah."

"I called your cell and you didn't answer," Clay complained.

"I was in the shower. What's happened?" Ethan asked, toweling off.

"No new e-mails, but I have some info on Stan. I've been going through his books."

"What books? Stan's never kept the books. That was always Randi's job at the store."

"Not anymore. Stan hired an accountant . . . and started keeping his own books."

"Hell."

"Oh, yeah. It's all on his laptop, which he initially wouldn't let me see."

Ethan pulled a pair of boxers from the dresser. "So what's on his laptop?"

"Appears to be classic money-laundering. Looks like Stan is just a go-between. He makes a sale to one client, takes in a whole lot of cash, then turns around and buys from another. I need you to tap into the legit books on his company's server to confirm."

Ethan shrugged into a shirt. "Can't Randi get you in?"

"I don't want to ask her until I know for sure. Besides, she's kind of . . . tranq'd."

Ethan sighed. "Let me get dressed and change phones. Then I'll tap in."

Ten minutes later Ethan was in Stan's company server courtesy of the file Clay had found on Stan's laptop listing his account log-ons and passwords. Apparently Stan didn't trust his memory. It was appalling, but all too common. Ethan saw CEOs of major corporations writing their passwords down so they wouldn't forget them. When that happened, security was compromised. Like this moment as Ethan easily breached Stan's company's computer system. "I'm in. Give me transaction dates from Stan's records."

Clay did, but not one of Stan's dealings matched the official company books. Ethan sighed. "How long has this been going on?"

"It started right about the time he opened the third store in Philly three years ago."

"When Alec had his surgery. Dammit. Now we know where he got the money."

"It doesn't appear to have become a habit until he expanded into New York State."

"Which is when he became so successful," Ethan said grimly. "I guess he liked having the cash even after the surgery was paid for. This will kill Randi, with Alec missing, not knowing if Stan had a part in it. He's going to jail." Ethan pressed his knuckles into his eye sockets. "Is it possible Stan wanted out and this is a ploy to convince him otherwise?"

"If it is, he's not saying. But I think it's pretty obvious now why he didn't want us going to the police. This all would have come out and he didn't want that to happen."

Ethan blew out a breath. "I'd still like to think that was secondary. That his primary intent was to keep Alec safe. I can't believe he knows anything about Alec's kidnapping."

"I know, E, but we can't afford to ignore this. All his transactions are with people in the New York/New Jersey area. He does have a few contacts in Chicago, but no money's changed hands with them. I'll keep looking. Any progress on the Hooter's girl?"

"I got some good shots of her body, but not her face. I've printed that list of pharmacies we talked about. I'll canvass them and the other businesses around the copy store in the morning, closer to the time she would have been there. Not many of the places would have been open then, so hopefully the ones that were saw something."

"It would be a hell of a lot better if you could show them her face," Clay said doubtfully.

"I'm planning on going back to the bus station tonight to look at more tapes. If I see her face I'll have even more to show tomorrow. But first I'll grab something to eat. I'm starving."


*Wight's Landing,*
*Monday, August 2, 7:50 p.m. Eastern*
*(6:50 p.m. Central)*


Lou sank into her chair, massaging her temples. Coroner John Kehoe gave her back a brusque pat.

"I always hated identifications," he said. She supposed he'd done enough of them in his thirty-year career as a medical examiner. She'd done too many herself. One was too many.

"Me, too. John, why don't you call it a day, go down to the pier?"

He stood, unsteadily. "I think I might. What about you?"

"I've got a little paperwork yet. I'll see you tomorrow."

She'd put no more than a superficial dent in the stack when the phone rang. Dora appeared in the doorway. "Sheriff, Detective Janson from Morgantown is on line one."

"Thanks." Lou picked up the phone. "Janson, this is Moore. My body was officially ID'd as Paul McMillan by his parents." Ironically, by a scar from the appendectomy that saved his life the year before. "The Vaughns don't know what he was doing in their shed. They said they gave Rickman time off because their son went to Europe with his grandparents."

"You believe them?"

"No. I know the grandparents are in Europe and I tried to contact them, but Vaughn claimed he didn't know exactly where they were. I sent a request to the customs department to find out if the kid really did leave the country, but that'll take a few days. Stan Vaughn and his wife know something, but their alibi is tight."

Unfortunately, their alibi was so tight she'd been unable to convince the judge to give her a warrant. It still stuck in her craw. In Boston, the DA would have issued her a warrant in an hour. But this wasn't Boston and apparently the judge had known Stan Vaughn's father for years, and had as much trouble believing Stan was involved as John Kehoe had. One call from Stan had railroaded her attempt at a warrant before she'd even petitioned.

"They had room service delivered to their hotel the night McMillan was killed," she told Janson. "They were both seen over the next two days by a number of the staff. It would have been hard for them to drive up to Morgantown and back. It's twelve hours round-trip."

"Well, that was my next question because I'll be making the drive tomorrow morning."

Lou straightened in her chair. "What do you have?"

"Rickman's parents called. They got a call from the sheriff in Ocean City. My MapQuest tells me that's about an hour from you. They have a seventeen-year-old punk in custody for armed robbery of a convenience store at about midnight on Wednesday."

"Between our murders. He could have done McMillan, but not Rickman."

"True, but it gets better. Punk has in his backpack a laptop power cord covered with Cheryl Rickman's prints. The Ocean City sheriff called Rickman's parents to ask about the power cord and the parents called me. I just got off the phone with the Ocean City sheriff. Punk's clammed up tight. I'll be down there by ten a.m. Want to meet me at the jail?"

Lou sat back, a satisfied smile curling her lips. "Thanks. I appreciate you including me."

"We both want to catch whoever killed this young couple. I'll see you tomorrow."

Lou hung up. "Hey, Dora, has Huxley gone home yet?"

"No, he's out on patrol and I already called him. He's on his way in to talk to you."

Lou would have Huxley set up a watch on the Vaughns' beach house. And while she waited, she'd do some checking on the man visiting the Vaughns. Everything about the man had screamed cop. She typed his name into the search screen. *Clay Maynard.*

That Maynard was in Wight's Landing on vacation was an outright lie and it was obvious that he didn't like Stan Vaughn one little bit. Lou couldn't blame Maynard for that. Slimy sonofabitch had an answer for everything. She lifted her brows as Maynard's results came through. Thirty-eight years old, D.C. resident. Former cop. No surprise. DCPD, eight years, decorated. Former Marine. Made sense. Currently ran his own business with an Ethan Buchanan. Security consulting.

Now, why would the Vaughns need a security consultant? It was a good question. No doubt Stan Vaughn would have a damn good answer. Trouble was, she wanted the truth.

*Chicago,*
*Monday, August 2, 7:10 p.m.*

Ethan's nose located the hot dog stand before his eyes did. A line of about twenty people waited for the best dogs in town. He searched the clusters of people, looking for the one he prayed was still waiting for him. Expelled a huge sigh of relief when he

260

saw that she was. And stood, stock still, just looking. Drinking in the sight of her.

She stood in the middle of the crowd, but apart from it somehow. Watching the way everyone else had fun. She'd dressed up for him and the knowledge made his heart knock hard in his chest even as he felt frustrated that the simple black dress and the killer high heels would be wasted. The dress hit her legs midthigh, making them look even longer. Hugged her body in all the right places, making his hands itch to run over every inch, every curve. From fifty feet away he could feel the way the very air crackled around her. She simply took his breath away.

He spied a group of teenagers on skateboards. "You guys want to make ten bucks?"

They eyed one another warily. "What do we have to do?"

"Stand in this line and get me some hot dogs and fries and Cokes."

One of the kids gave him a suspicious look. "Why don't you just stand in line yourself?"

Ethan pointed to Dana. "See that lady over there? I've got about twenty minutes to have dinner with her, and I don't want to spend it standing in a damn line. You get it?"

The boys followed his pointing finger and slow grins took over their faces. "Guess so," said the first kid. He stuck out his hand. "Gimme the money first."

Ethan pulled a few bills out of his pocket. "This'll cover the dogs. You get paid when I get my dinner. Now pull your tongues back in your mouths and go."

Dana felt him coming before she saw him. She'd thought herself prepared this time, but the slam of awareness once again stole her breath as she watched him approach with single-minded determination. Head and shoulders over most men in the crowd, his hair glinted golden in the rays of the evening sun. Broad-shouldered and lean-hipped, he stood out from those he passed, his suit and tie to their shorts and T-shirts. It was a different suit from the one he'd worn that morning. He'd slept, she thought. His eyes no longer held the shadows of exhaustion. Instead they were bright and arresting. *And focused on me.*

The words she'd practiced were pushed from her mind when he reached her and in one smooth movement took her face between his palms and took her lips with his, a simple kiss of welcome. The chatter of the crowd faded away, replaced by the thunder of blood in her head. Automatically her hands came up to grasp his wrists and she held on. He ended it with a chaste little nudge of his lips that said there was more to come.

He lifted his head and took a step back, his eyes taking a quick trip up and down her body. "You look incredible." He smiled. "But I guess you knew that."

She'd hoped so. Still she felt her cheeks heat. "Caroline insisted I clean up a little." Dana thought of how Caroline had commandeered her closet an hour before. This dress was the only decent thing she owned. "She can be very persuasive."

"Tell her I said thank you." He glanced over his shoulder at the people lined up to buy hot dogs, then turned back to her with a frown. "I hate to tell you this, but I can't stay long."

Disappointment speared, but she lifted her chin and pasted on a smile. "I understand." Visions of an evening of conversation followed by more of what had happened against her car that morning drained away. At least he'd had the decency to tell her himself.

He brought their joined hands to her lips and pressed gently. "No, you don't. I got some more news from home. That family thing I told you about."

Another time, with another person, she might have probed, but there was distress in his eyes and a hardness to his jaw that said the topic was off-limits, so she didn't. "I'm glad you came, even if you can't stay."

"I needed to see you."

It was simply said and touched her heart. "I thought about you all day," she murmured. She lifted her fingers to his face, brushed her thumb under his eye where this morning there had been dark circles. "You got some sleep. Good."

His eyes flashed then, a burst of heat she felt down to her toes. "I dreamed of you."

The husky timbre of his voice had her swallowing hard and she suddenly found herself without any words to reply. She could only stare up at him, fascinated and charmed. And unspeakably aroused. If it was a line, it was a hell of a line for sure. But his eyes were clear and honest and sincere and she so wanted to believe it was true.

His lips curved. "So I finally caught you unaware."

His smile made her heart thump crazily in her chest. "I suppose you did at that."

He took her hands, kissed her palms. "Sorry I was late. I couldn't find a parking place."

"I should have warned you about that. I took the El."

"I'm just glad you stayed."

Again she searched for words. "It's . . . it's a nice night. I like to watch the people."

"I know." It was said with a teasing little grin that lit up his whole face, made him look years younger. Carefree.

"You were watching me," she accused, flustered because she was . . . flustered. It was a new sensation for Dana Dupinsky and she decided she liked it. She was flirting and flustered and found she, too, felt much younger. Carefree even.

"Just for a minute. I couldn't help it. I came around the corner and there you were, pretty as a picture." He let go of one of her hands and toyed with the hair just above the bandage on her head, holding her captive with his searching eyes. "Is it healing?"

"I'm fine." But she was so much better than fine. Her heart was pounding to beat all hell and every last nerve ending was on fire. "But I think I need to sit down." Her knees were weak. "These shoes are killing me."

His eyes flicked down her legs, lingered for a moment before coming back up to rest on her face. "I wish I could say you shouldn't have worn them, but I'm damn glad you did." He grinned then and she knew her face had pinked up. "You're cute when you blush."

Dana rolled her eyes, a little relieved that the moment was broken. She didn't think her heart could have taken too much more of that intense green stare. "Let's find a bench."

They did, and sat facing each other, his arm casually draped across the back of the bench, his hand holding on to hers. And once again his eyes were focused. *On me.*

"Tell me about your business partner," she said suddenly.

His eyes widened, surprised. "Why?"

"Because your work is important to you, so your business partner must be as well." She dropped her gaze to their joined hands, then forced herself to look at him. "And I'm trying to get to know you better."

He was quiet for a moment, just looking at her, and she got the uncomfortable feeling he was trying to see inside her head. The discomfort intensified when she thought he just might be able to. "I did all the talking last night, telling you about Richard." His head tilted. "You're a good listener. Tell me about yourself, Dana, and let me be a good listener, too."

She'd never found it easy to talk about herself, even with Caroline. But now, she found herself wishing she could. Wishing she could tell her worst secrets to a man who was little more than a stranger. And because she did so want to, she knew she should not. "That's not very easy for me," she murmured and he dipped his head closer to catch her words. For a moment he hung there, their faces just inches apart, and she thought he'd kiss her. She'd all but closed her eyes in anticipation when he spoke. So quietly. Gently.

"My partner's name is Clay. I met him on my first deployment right out of the Naval Academy. Richard and I had put in to go together, and I was glad we did, because Clay made my life a living hell those first few weeks. I was glad Richard was there."

He'd understood. Stunned she could only stare as he maintained the short distance between them and continued. "Clay gave us all nicknames. I was Goldilocks."

Dana moistened her lips. "Hell on your tough-guy image."

His gorgeous mouth curved. "You could say that. But Clay and I became friends.

He quit the Corps after his tour in Somalia, became a cop. We kept in touch though and when I came home from Afghanistan, he came to the hospital. Made things a hell of a lot better those first weeks home. I hadn't seen myself as leaving the Corps, ever. He helped me see that my life wasn't over because I couldn't be an active Marine anymore."

"Thank you for telling me." She bit her lower lip, conscious of his eyes on hers, too close and yet not close enough. "Next time I'll tell you."

He moved closer and she held her breath. "I'll hold you to it." Then his mouth was on hers, warm and mobile and once again the crowd faded away and there were just the two of them, kissing on a warm summer night. Like a normal couple. The hand that had rested on the back of the bench threaded through her hair, bringing her closer, harder against him, and when the tip of his tongue touched her lips, she opened for him. The hand that held hers squeezed hard, then let go, running up her arm, leaving a trail of fire in its wake. His fingertips found her shoulder under the fabric of her dress. Caressed her there. Dana felt the hum deep in her throat, felt his fingers tighten in response.

Heard the impatient clearing of a throat above them. Smelled onions and fried potatoes. The throat cleared again. "Jeeze, man. Get a grip or get a room."

Ethan jerked away and looked up with a scowl. Dana could hear the pounding of his breath in her ear and it was another moment before she had the presence of mind to turn her own eyes upward to where a teenager stood holding a shallow box filled with cans of soda, fries, and the best dogs in town, heaped high with everything.

"Now give me my ten bucks."

Ethan leaned forward, wincing, and pulled his wallet from his back pocket. "I ought to deduct for your mouth, kid. Here's your ten. Now go."

Dana had to chuckle as the kid walked away examining his ten-dollar bill. "You just can't find good help anymore." She took one of the hot dogs and settled back against the bench, happy when Ethan's arm came around her shoulders. Happy. Content. Sitting on a bench eating a hot dog with a man's arm around her. It happened every day to all kinds of people, she was certain. *But it's been such a long time since it's happened to me.* All too soon Ethan crumpled up the empty box.

"I hate to say this, but I have to be going. Can you meet me —" Ethan jumped, then reached behind his back where her little black purse had become wedged. "It buzzed."

"My pager. I usually carry it in my pocket." She checked the message and Ethan felt her whole body tense. She looked up with a frown. "I need to find a phone."

Ethan squeezed her shoulder, but she was already standing up, tugging at the hem of her dress. "Dana, wait. Don't you have a cell phone?"

She was scanning for a phone booth, her face tight. "Can't afford one. Dammit."

Ethan stood up, grasped her upper arm gently but firmly. "Use mine."

She did, stepping a few feet away to dial, her face turned discreetly away. "It's me," he heard her say, then, "A cell phone that belongs to a friend. What's wrong?" Her shoulders jerked with a swift indrawn breath. "Oh, no. Oh, God, no. Max." Her voice shook and her hand flew up to cover her mouth. "The baby?"

Ethan walked up behind her, covered her shoulders with his hands, and tugged until she leaned into him. She was trembling so he smoothed his hands over her upper arms.

"I am calm," she said into the phone. "Tell me where you are and I'm on my way." When she'd finished she took a few deep breaths before handing him his phone over her shoulder. "I'm all right," she said, but her voice was still shaky. She turned and managed a smile that came off looking haunted. "Thanks for holding me up."

"Caroline?" he murmured and she nodded.

"I have to go to the hospital. She's hurt."

She was paler than when she'd hurt her head the morning before. "What happened?"

"She went grocery shopping when she left my apartment. She was pushing her cart to her car when some idiot came speeding through the parking lot and . . . hit her."

"How bad is she?"

"They don't know yet. Dammit, the asshole didn't even stop." She closed her eyes and he could see her fighting to concentrate. "I need to get to my apartment and get my car."

"I'll drive you," he said, guiding her back to his car.

She hadn't said a word since he'd buckled her in the passenger side of his car, just staring out the window and biting her lips. Every few minutes she'd murmur something under her breath. A prayer he thought. He murmured one as well for the spunky little woman who'd all but forced Dana to have dinner with him the night before. He thought he owed Caroline Hunter a great deal. He took her hand, and her grip was shattering.

"I know you're upset," Ethan said quietly, "but if you're this tense, you'll only upset her."

"You're right. I'll calm down." Dana felt like she'd swallowed a brick. She hadn't experienced this kind of raw fear since she discovered Evie's broken body two years before, strangled and stabbed. Left for dead. And now Caroline had been struck by a car, left for dead. The day after Lillian's funeral.

Dana's blood ran cold. Hit-and-run. It could have been Goodman. He could have followed Caroline from Dana's apartment. *But he doesn't know where I live,* she thought desperately. Unless . . . *He fol-*

*lowed me from Lillian's funeral yesterday after I'd picked up Evie. Damn that girl.* Rage sluiced through her, leaving her shaken. But rage would help no one, and neither would her fear. She took one of her own fear management lessons and visualized herself sweeping the fears into a box. Locking it tightly. And walking away.

*Think of something else. Someone else.* "So did you get any business with Bill Bush?"

Ethan slanted her a look from the corner of his eye. "Not yet. I haven't given up, though. You're looking a little better."

She was feeling calmer. "Thanks. I need to call Evie about Caroline. I didn't want to call her when I was so upset."

"Who's Evie?"

"She's my . . ." What? What had her relationship with Evie become? "I'm her guardian." They were nearing their exit. "You want to exit here."

He acknowledged with a nod. "Why are you her guardian? What relation is she to you?"

Dana considered her answer. Telling him the truth wouldn't be too dangerous. It might even come in handy should she ever tell him the whole truth. *If.* "Evie was a runaway. Now she's family."

Ethan fished his cell phone from his pocket. "Call her. Let her know about Caroline."

Dana didn't have to consider anything there. She would not call Hanover House from Ethan's cell phone. "That's okay. I'll just wait till I get to the hospital."

*Chicago,*
*Monday, August 2, 8:15 p.m.*

"It's done."

Sitting on her bed, holding the cell against her shoulder as she painted her toenails, Sue smiled. "I know." The news had come through Evie, who was white-faced and trembling. And mad enough to spit nails. Apparently she'd been all ready to go to the hospital when Dana called and commanded her to stay put. Ruby had overheard Evie's end of the phone conversation and Ruby liked to make sure everyone was well informed.

"You didn't tell me she was pregnant." Fred sounded disgusted.

"Yes, I did."

"Okay, fine, but you didn't say she was ready to pop the kid any second."

Sue was amused. "You have some kind

274

of Madonna complex, Fred?"

There was a moment of petulant silence. "Don't push me, Susie," he warned. "I did your favor. Now it's your turn."

"You did half my favor, Fred. She's still alive. But I'll be nice and do your favor for you anyway. I know what to do. I'll take care of it tomorrow." While she was out "job hunting." She twisted the top on the nail polish and tossed it in her backpack. "I'll meet you at noon."

Her smile grew. By noon she would have completed several more of the items on her to-do list. She dialed Donnie Marsden's number. Time to start setting the stage for the finale. "Donnie. It's me."

"I was beginning to think I'd imagined you. Are you ready to tell me about this plan?"

"Not just yet, but I will." *I'll be ready when I'm ready.* "Have you called the boys?"

"Yeah, everybody but Vickers. I couldn't find him." *Not surprising,* Sue thought with a smile. The van holding Vickers's body was parked in the woods behind an elementary school. Someone would find him — eventually. "The guys all want more info," Donnie went on. "They don't want to walk into a trap. I don't blame them."

"Tell them the only person that will be lured into a cage will be our little bird."

"How?"

"I have something our bird wants to get back."

"And then?"

Sue wiggled her newly painted toes. Revenge, she thought, was such an individual, personal thing. "Then you each get a half hour to do your worst. Be as creative as you wish. I had ten years to think about my revenge. You have four days to consider yours."

There was a moment of silence. "Up to and including what?"

"I get to finish the job," Sue said simply. "And our bird needs to know it's me finishing the job, so no loss of consciousness is allowed. Anything else is your call. If you plan ahead, you can make thirty minutes last a very long time."

"What do you get out of all this, Suze?" Donnie's voice was soft.

Sue thought about every day of every one of the ten years she spent behind bars. Every birthday she grew older, every day she was trapped into a routine of someone else's making. She grimaced. Every time Fred forced her into the supply closet for a "heart-to-heart." The fire that simmered in her gut fanned into a raging flame.

"I get to watch."

*Chicago,*
*Monday, August 2, 8:15 p.m.*

Dana focused on the elevator display. "You don't have to come with me. I'm fine now."

"I don't think so, but I'm not going to argue with you," Ethan replied smoothly and watched a worry line form across her brow. She wasn't fine, Ethan thought. She was still trembling from the argument she'd had with Evie from a pay phone in the hospital lobby. She'd tersely ordered Evie to stay put before hanging the phone up with a slam. Another day he might have pressed for information, but he knew this wasn't the time. Besides, she had promised to talk about herself next time and he planned to hold her to it.

The elevator dinged and the doors slid open, exposing the nurses' desk of the maternity ward. A nurse pointed to a waiting room in response to Dana's request for Caroline.

Ethan caught her arm before she could charge away. "I'm going to go now. I didn't want to intrude, I just wanted to be sure you were all right." He leaned forward and kissed her cheek, and had stepped back to go when her hand shot out and clutched his lapel.

"Stay," she murmured. "I know you have to go, but if you could stay for just another minute or two, I'd appreciate it."

Her voice was totally calm, but there was an underlying thread of yearning that was impossible to refuse. Ethan drew her into his arms and let her hold on. She did, silently, her grip on his back almost bruising. Finally she let go with a shaky breath and looked up to meet his eyes. "Thank you. I didn't hurt you, did I?"

Ethan smiled down at her. "I'm sure I'll live." He brushed a lock of hair away from her face, cupped her cheek in his palm. "How can I help you, Dana?"

Her lips trembled and for a split second he thought her eyes would fill, but she quickly controlled herself and forced her lips to curve. "Meet me for breakfast tomorrow?"

"It's a date." He'd lowered his head to kiss her good-bye when a sharp voice calling Dana's name had him jerking his chin up. A tall dark man approached, looking grim.

"We've been looking everywhere for you."

Beside Ethan, Dana tensed. "Is she all right?"

"She's asleep. The baby's stable now." The man cast a harsh look Ethan's way. "We need to talk, Dana. Privately."

"All right. Ethan, meet Caroline's brother-in-law, David Hunter. David, Ethan Buchanan."

Ethan nodded at David. Jaw clenched, David nodded back. The possessiveness in the man's eyes was unmistakable and Ethan gave in to the adolescent urge to stake his claim, slipping his arm around Dana's waist. "We'll just be a minute," Ethan said.

Hunter jutted his jaw to one side. "I'll be in the waiting room with the others."

Ethan waited until he was gone before lifting a brow. "The others?"

"The family," Dana murmured. "They come together when there's a crisis. Please forgive David. He's upset about Caroline. He's not normally so rude."

Hunter was upset, Ethan could agree with that. About what, he might disagree. But because Hunter had just had a shock, Ethan let it go. "I have some appointments early tomorrow." He wanted to start canvassing the area of this morning's e-mail at about the time Alec's kidnapper had sent it. "Can you meet me at six? At the coffee shop?" It would be convenient to the bus station as he planned to view videos all night if he had to.

"I'll be there. Ethan, thank you. For everything." She lifted on her toes, wound one arm around his neck, and kissed him softly. "I'm glad you were with me." And with that she headed to the waiting room, leaving him wanting a hell of a lot more. He hit the elevator button, brooding a bit. The elevator door dinged when a thought struck him.

In the car she'd asked him if he'd gotten any business from Bill Bush. Now why would she know the name of the security manager at the bus station? He looked back over his shoulder as he stepped into the elevator, but she was gone. He'd known the first time he'd met her that there was a great deal more to Dana Dupinsky than met the eye. It was time to start figuring out exactly what that "more" was.

David emerged from the waiting room before Dana stepped through the door. "We need to talk," he said tightly. "But not around the others." He led her to a play area, deserted at this time of night. "She's fine for now," he said before she could ask. "She fractured her leg and there's a small tear in the placenta. The baby's vitals were unstable when they first brought her in, but they were able to get them both stable. The doctor says with rest and no additional stress she could still go to term."

Could. Dana shuddered. "Thank God." But he made no murmur of assent and she looked up to find his gray eyes dark and hard.

"The driver never tried to stop, Dana. No skid marks, no tires squealing."

"You think it was Goodman."

His eyes flashed. "Don't you?"

"I thought it, in the car over. We should tell Mia."

He gritted his teeth. "Dammit, Dana, did it cross your mind this could have been you?"

She met his gaze without flinching. "It did. I've been careful."

"Careful. Yeah. So where did you meet that guy?"

Dana narrowed her eyes at even the notion of comparing Ethan Buchanan to Lillian's husband. "Bus station, Sunday night."

"You were out in the middle of the night, hours after Detective Mitchell told you to keep your doors locked, and you call that *careful?*"

Temper started to bubble. "I call it doing my job, David."

"Your *job* is the reason Caroline is lying in there and my brother is scared to death."

His words stabbed deep. She wanted to fling back words of her own, but he was right. *Caroline is hurt because an irate husband is furious with me.* Guilt welled, and with it the fear of what Goodman might try next. The fear she could handle, could push into the little box in her mind, but the guilt lay in her gut, making her feel sick. She sighed, suddenly tired. "David, we've both had a scare. Let's just step back and call Mia and figure out where to go from there."

David looked away. "Fine. Call."

*Wight's Landing,*
*Monday, August 2, 9:45 p.m. Eastern*
*(8:45 p.m. Central)*

Wight's Landing advertised its scenic views and James Lorenzano had to admit that they didn't lie. From where he sat enjoying his beer and crabcakes, he could

282

watch scenic bartender Pattie in a little white tank top shaking both martinis and breasts that actually might be real. There'd been a time when he thought he might never again enjoy the simple pleasure of watching a woman's questionably real breasts in a little white tank top. That time had been recently as he'd lain in a pool of his own blood while the paramedics responded to the 911 placed by the bystander that had by pure chance come along in time to scare Sue away before she could finish the job.

He had been stupid not to see it coming, but he'd been too busy enjoying Sue's very real breasts. He made it a policy never to do clients, but Sue had been so tempting. She'd tricked him that night, slowed him down by putting something in his drink. Which, ironically enough, had been celebratory champagne. Her treat. A celebration picnic. He'd tracked down her mystery woman in Florida and she'd been ever so grateful.

They'd see how grateful she was when he caught up to her.

Tracking Sue to Wight's Landing had been a royal pain in the ass. He'd come out of the hospital looking for her, his first stop being her apartment. Empty. His second stop had been her aunt and uncle's house. He didn't expect to find her there, but had hoped her brother might have an idea of where she was. Her brother had called his uncle from his little road trip with Sue, as it turned out. They were heading east, was all Sue had told Bryce and all Bryce had told his uncle. James got that much out of the old man before he'd breathed his last. James got more from his contact at the phone company — the address of the pay phone Bryce had used to make the call. From that little town he'd moved slowly east through more little towns until he'd heard the news of a grisly suicide on a beach.

It was Sue's work, he knew it. Because it was a technique she'd learned from him. One of those damn pillow talk moments he now regretted. She'd been here. Trouble was, he couldn't find her or her brother. So here he sat, trying to glean information the old-fashioned way. Spying on the men in blue lifting a mug at the end of a long day.

Behind him sat a table of Wight's Landing's finest, fresh off shift. Apparently the town's police force was on the small side, so when one deputy got pulled away from patrol, another had to cover him. Such was the dilemma of Deputy Billy, who was complaining that he had to give up his day off to cover some guy named Huxley because the sheriff was going to meet some detective from West Virginia at the jail up in Ocean City. And it apparently had to do with that corpse in the shed. Which had everything to do with Sue.

James would follow the sheriff, find out who in the jail had so piqued their interest. As if he couldn't guess. It explained why Sue's trail had so abruptly stopped here at Wight's Landing. What it didn't explain was why? Why this place? What was the connection between the old woman she'd killed in Florida and this little beach front town? He'd find out. Then he'd get Sue.

# Chapter Eleven

*Chicago,*
*Monday, August 2, 8:45 p.m.*

Mia held up her badge for the nurse
standing inside the curved station only to
have the woman frown. "Mrs. Hunter has
already given a statement. She's resting
now."

"I won't bother her, Nurse Simmons," she
said. "I'm here to see Dana, her friend."

Nurse Simmons pointed to an area at
the end of the hall. "That way."

"That way" was a play area. David
Hunter and Dana sat alone, David in an
adult-sized chair, his face grim. Dana sat
on a kiddie chair at a plastic table wearing
a drop-dead black dress and heels. She was
building a tower, nervously manipulating a
multicolored pile of Legos. Even if she
hadn't known about Caroline, Mia
would've known Dana was scared. Dana
could never keep her hands still when she
was scared. "Nice dress, kid."

Dana looked up and Mia sighed. Guilt filled her friend's brown eyes and Mia knew there was no power on earth strong enough to wipe it away. Dana soothed other people's fears, helped other people deal with their guilt and shame. Her own just got stuffed deep down.

"Well?" Dana asked, moving the Legos as if they were a shell game.

"I talked to the officer who responded to the scene on my way over. No skid marks, witnesses heard no tires squealing. The make and model of the car don't match the one Goodman owns, but he could have stolen one. How could he have found her?"

"Caroline was at my apartment." She plucked at her dress. "Helping me pick this out."

Mia looked over at Hunter. "Hot date?"

"No." His single word had the impact of a freight train. With refrigerated cars.

Dana pressed her fingertips to her temple. "I was with Ethan Buchanan."

Realization dawned. "The background check Caroline had me run yesterday."

"We had a date tonight." Dana had separated a pile of red blocks and was building a new tower, her fingers twitchy. "I took Evie by my place after the funeral yesterday. If Goodman followed us, he knows where I live. If he was watching tonight, he saw Caroline and me leave in her car. She dropped me at the El station."

"Well, that connects the dots at least." Mia sat down in one of the kiddie chairs and put her hands over Dana's when she started on a blue tower. "Stop. You're making me nuts."

Dana's hands stilled and her shoulders shook in a long shudder. "Sorry."

"It's okay. We'll find him, Dana. Until then, you're just going to have to be careful."

"Well, that's constructive," Hunter said acidly and Mia shot him a cool look.

"We've put out an APB on him. My partner and I will check the list of his haunts again."

"It's been four days." Hunter lurched to his feet. "Why haven't you found him?"

"David," Dana said wearily. "They're doing the best they can."

Hunter turned, showing them a very muscular, tense back. "Well, it's not good enough."

Mia sighed. "You're right. It's not. But it's all we can do, Mr. Hunter. Unless you have another suggestion." Hunter's shoulders sagged and he turned, apology in his gray eyes.

"I'm sorry, Detective. I was out of line. Can you at least tell her to shut down that damn shelter? Or tell her to stop going to the damn bus station in the middle of the night?"

She met his eyes. Saw what Dana had obviously never seen and wondered how long Hunter had been in love with her. She felt sorry for any man who loved a woman tied to her work by chains stronger than mere humanity. Guilt-ridden social workers and cops. What a pair she and Dupinsky made. "I could. She wouldn't listen to me any more than she listens to you."

He must have detected something in her tone, a compassion he didn't want, because he turned away with a jerk. "None of this would have happened if she hadn't had that damn shelter. Caroline would be fine and there wouldn't be some maniac after them."

Dana looked up, her face pale. "David, that's not fair."

It wasn't, but Mia couldn't blame him for feeling it. Saying it, maybe. Feeling it, no. "I think Caroline would take exception to that," she murmured. "Get some sleep, both of you. Dana, don't go home tonight. Give me a key and I'll check out your apartment."

"Make sure you step over the drunks and junkies," Hunter said bitterly.

Because she agreed with Hunter's sentiment but ultimately understood why Dana kept that apartment, Mia stood up and laid a hand on his arm. "Mr. Hunter, let it go."

He shrugged her hand away. "I'm taking my mother home, Dana. I'll be back later."

Dana went back to stacking blocks. "He's angry with me," she said when he was gone. "He has a right to be. Goodman never would have gone after Caroline if it weren't for me."

Dana didn't see the real reason for Hunter's anger. "So tell me about Ethan Buchanan."

Dana's lips curved into a smile that totally filled her eyes. "He's a really nice guy, Mia."

Poor David Hunter didn't have a chance. Mia pulled Dana to her feet. "Abe will be here soon, but until he does, let's go to the cafeteria, get some fries, and you will dish all, girl."

Dana shot her a calculating look. "I'll dish if you get me in to see Lillian's kids. Soon."

Mia scowled. "Soon. Now, I want some juicy gossip. My well is low."

It was dark, but a light burned in the bathroom down the hall. Alec lifted his head from the pillow, careful not to wake her. Her, the woman with the eyes that he now knew weren't white at all. They were blue, but so light they were almost invisible. He drew a deep breath, let it out. Testing. But she didn't wake up.

He was so hungry and thirsty. She gave him a little water — just enough to keep him from dying. How many days had he been gone? It was hard to keep track. She'd made him take twice as much medicine as the doctor prescribed. She'd kept him drugged out of his head. But she was running out of pills. And he was developing a tolerance. That's what his doctor called it. When the same amount of medicine didn't do the job anymore.

But he'd pretended to sleep tonight, pretended that he was drugged. He'd lain here on the bed, wondering who she was and why she was doing this. It was money, he knew. His parents had it. She could have it all, he thought. He just wanted to go home, back to his parents.

*If they were still alive.* The thought

made his breath hitch and he sternly controlled it. He couldn't make a sound. Which was frustrating because he had no idea when he did. He thought about all those times he'd fought Cheryl, not wanting to put on the speech processor, not wanting that ocean of loud, loud sound. He'd been afraid, he thought. Afraid of the sound. Afraid of looking stupid. Sounding stupid. He wished to God he had that little speech processor now. He'd use it to be able to figure out what was happening.

But he didn't have it so he'd have to find another way. But first, he needed some food. She'd brought food to the room for herself. A few times she'd given him a slice of bread. One piece of cheese. If he didn't eat soon, he *would* die.

Alec slid off the bed. And waited. She didn't wake up.

He was alive. And he was starving. He could only hope his stomach wasn't growling so loud it woke her up like it used to wake Cheryl. *Cheryl.* His chest hurt and part of him wished he were still dopey from the medicine. Then he wouldn't have to think about Cheryl. To see her in his head. Cheryl was dead. He'd seen her body. She'd dumped Cheryl on the side of the road like she was a bag of trash. He'd been so . . . so damn mad. His eyes stung now, thinking about it. About how he hadn't been able to do anything to stop her.

He had to do something to stop her. He had to do something. Anything.

But first he had to eat or he'd pass out again. Softly he stepped. Waited. He knew that floors creaked in old houses, but he didn't know if this one did. He'd find out fast enough if she woke up, he supposed. But she didn't, so he took another step, and another, until he was in the hall, past the bathroom, and on the stairs.

Holding tight to the rail he made his way down, step by step. His head was dizzy and once he almost fell, but he made it to the bottom and let himself cheer inside his head. It was dark down here, too, but there was a light at the end of the hall. Not a lightbulb.

It was a computer. Somebody had a computer and it was on. He could at least find out what day it was. Trying to be light on his feet he walked down the hall and peeked inside.

It was the kitchen. There was a laptop computer on the table. And somebody was using it. Damn. He must have made a sound because the person looked up.

He sucked in a breath. It was her, the lady from his dreams. Or nightmares. He wasn't sure which. He'd woken a few times to find her sitting next to him, stroking his hair. The first time he'd screamed. Long and loud in his head where only he could hear. She had a scar. An ugly, red, scary scar. But she'd smiled. Kind of. And she'd stroked his hair, just like his mom did. So the next time he woke up, he'd been a little less scared and the time after that, a little less. She might be working with the crazy lady, but she had nicer eyes.

She smiled now, that weird half smile, and put her finger to her lips, pointed to her lap. Alec looked at her, looked at the refrigerator. He needed food and soon. And she didn't look mad, so he crept in, keeping to the edge of the cabinets until he could see what she was pointing to. A baby. She had a baby. He looked up, met her eyes. Saw her lips move. She was talking to him, but he couldn't understand anything she said.

He hated that. Hated not knowing what people were saying to him. About him.

Cheryl said he was too paranoid, that people didn't talk about him. He didn't believe her, but he didn't have that problem anymore, did he? Cheryl was gone and if he didn't get food, he would be, too. Alec pointed at the refrigerator and the scarred lady nodded. It was full of little plastic bowls. And a plate of chicken legs. He thought he could eat them all. He took one, glancing her way. She wasn't looking at him, just at the computer. So he wolfed down the chicken leg and took another. And another. Then he felt really sick.

It was too much food, too fast. He needed some water. Now. Oh, no. *No.*

Evie focused on the screen, trying not to spook him. Trying not to watch the way he devoured three chicken legs like he hadn't eaten in days and didn't know when he'd eat again. It was a feeling she remembered well. She gave him his privacy, carefully not looking at him until he started to breathe heavily, choking sounds coming from his throat. Then she looked around just in time to see the three chicken legs come flying back out of his mouth. White-faced, Erik crumpled into a heap.

*Chicago,*
*Tuesday, August 3, 2:00 a.m.*

Ethan started when the cell phone in his shirt pocket buzzed against his chest. He'd only slept for a few minutes, so there wouldn't be much bus station videotape to rewind. The caller was Clay and nerves grabbed his gut. "It's two a.m. What's happened?"

"It's three here," Clay replied, his voice weary. "They found Alicia Samson."

Ethan's heart sank. The ID used at the copy store in Morgantown. "She's dead?"

"Yes. Damn, I was hoping she'd just been on vacation. I called the restaurant where she worked to see if she'd come in. Her boss had just heard and was almost hysterical. A group of kids found Samson in some woods. She'd been dead since Thursday morning."

"When our girl used Samson's ID to send the first e-mail. Cause?"

"Shot in the head, same as Cheryl Rickman. Ethan, we have to bring the authorities in."

"I know." Ethan pressed his thumb into his throbbing temple, weighing the options. Three people were dead because of a woman who seemed to be able to disappear at will. A woman who still had Alec. "We don't know where she is, or even who she is. It sure as hell would be better to walk into the cops with a picture or some kind of ID."

"How close are we to finding her on the bus video?"

"I've been watching video for hours. I still haven't found them."

"They couldn't just disappear."

The pain behind Ethan's eyes was growing. Rapidly. He could feel it coming on and desperately patted his pocket, searching for the little packet of pills he never left home without. He hadn't had an episode in months. Dammit. "That's what we keep saying." He found the packet, fumbled with the clasp as everything went dark. "Dammit all. Hold on." Ethan placed the pill on the back of his tongue and waited.

*"Ethan?"* There was fear in Clay's voice, raw and undisguised.

The pill had dissolved. "Just wait, Clay. I'll be fine. Just a headache."

"Can you see?"

"I will be able to in a minute." He knew it, yet still the panic clawed, and with it, the helpless rage. These blackouts were the reason he'd been medically discharged. The reason he wasn't on a mission in the desert somewhere. The reason he was here. Here, looking for Alec. He was Alec's only hope right now. The thought was both humbling and terrifying. *Right place, right time or wrong place, wrong time?* he wondered, remembering the way Dana had neatly flipped the two the night before. It depended on your perspective. And perspective was attitude. And attitude . . . it could make all the difference between success and failure.

"I didn't hear the sound of grinding metal so I assume you weren't driving at the time."

"No, I wasn't." Twinkling lights started to appear at the end of a dark tunnel and Ethan finally started to relax. "I'm sitting here in the damn bus station security office."

"You seeing now?" Clay asked gruffly.

"Clay, I'm fine. Look, I need to get back to these tapes."

Clay sighed. "Just be careful."

"I will." Ethan hung up, well aware that they'd solved nothing. A man and two women were dead and Alec was still missing. He should go to the police. And he would. He just needed a little more time.


*Chicago,*
*Tuesday, August 3, 2:30 a.m.*

Viciously Sue pulled the clean shirt over

the kid's head, pushed his arms through the sleeves, shoved him to the bed. Held the note before his eyes. *That was most unwise.*

The boy nodded at the words of the note, his body drawn up in a ball, still sweaty and trembling. She'd had to clean him up. Had to wipe the vomit from his face. Furious, Sue scrawled another sentence on the paper and made him look at it. Saw him go even paler. Clench his eyes tight. Watched the tears trickle down his face. *Your mother will pay.*

The boy was obviously not as affected by the medicine as she'd thought. And she was down to only two pills. She'd have to wait until morning to give it to him so that he'd sleep while she was gone doing her errand for Fred. She'd chase it with more Benadryl. That seemed to have more effect. But the boy couldn't be kept drugged twenty-four/seven anymore. Not when Scarface had seen him lucid. Dammit.

She'd have to find another way to keep him in line. She thought about tomorrow. About her plans for Fred. For the Vaughns. About the little package that would ensure the Vaughns' compliance. It would make the boy fall into line as well.

*Adopt, adapt, and improve.* It was a damn good motto.

Ethan rubbed his eyes, frustrated. He'd replayed the same footage again and again to no avail. Hours of video and there'd been no sign of Alec. Alec and the woman arrived Friday morning and had for all intents disappeared into the crowd. Ethan neatly stacked the videos he'd spent all night viewing. A twelve-year-old boy just didn't disappear into thin air, so there must be another explanation. Alec was somewhere on these videos. *I just haven't found the right place to look.* He'd be back to look again once he'd finished canvassing the area around the copy store Alec's kidnapper had used yesterday.

For now he needed a break. A long jog would clear his head. But he needed to leave in less than an hour to meet Dana, so a jog would have to wait.

Dana. Ethan eyed his laptop, sitting next to the video monitor, its case closed. Bush had wireless Internet in here, so Ethan could plug into the Web anytime he wanted to. Dana knew Bush. She'd called the security manager by name last night. She ate at Betty's coffee shop often enough to have the owner remember her favorite meal.

300

She apparently spent a lot of time at this bus station. More than he'd think she'd need just to pick up a flaky friend. His brows furrowed, Ethan opened his laptop and launched his Internet browser. He'd been putting this off most of the night, a little afraid of what he'd find, if he was honest with himself. Ethan got into the people database he used most often for background checks and stopped, his hands poised over the keyboard. Once he did this, there would be no going back if he didn't like what he found. But then he thought of Dana's eyes, so comfortable and wise. She couldn't be doing anything wrong, of that he was certain. So he typed in her name and waited.

And blinked when information began to appear in the results screen. She was a photographer, it seemed. Sort of. She'd declared only $2,867 income last year on her Schedule C. As a photographer, she sucked. Good thing photography seemed to be a secondary concern. Her name appeared as the director of a nonprofit business. A shelter for runaways. Ethan remembered what she'd said about Evie the night before. *She was a runaway. Now, she's family.* Now her poverty made sense. She put her money back into her business, she'd said. That meant she drew little to no salary, leaving more for the runaways she sheltered.

He'd been right. She did listen too well for it not to be a key part of who she was. A sense of relief washed over him and with it a distinct pride. She was exactly who he thought she'd be. A woman who put the needs of others before her own.

The last item of interest was a head turner. It seemed Dana Dupinsky also had a criminal record. One conviction for attempted grand theft auto. More than thirteen years before. Looked like she had turned her life around. And then some.

He thought about the way she lived, her lack of funds, the place she called home. He couldn't change any of that in the next thirty minutes. But he could make her life a little safer by making sure she had a way to call for help should one of those junkies come a little too close before she was able to close the three deadbolts on her apartment door.

He had just enough time to buy her a preloaded cell phone from a corner convenience store before meeting her for breakfast. Ethan slid his laptop into its bag. He'd stow it in the trunk of his car, along with the gun he'd been keeping in the back of his waistband. That way if she decided to run her hands all over him, she'd be touching him and not the weapon he still wasn't ready to explain.

# Chapter Twelve

*Chicago,*
*Tuesday, August 3, 6:00 a.m.*

Ethan was waiting for her on the sidewalk
this time. The sight of him there surprised
her, left her unguarded. He was still wearing
his clothes from the night before.

So was she.

He straightened when she approached,
studying her face as she got closer. He
must have seen what she'd tried so hard to
hide. That she was scared and mad and
guilty. He opened his arms and she walked
straight into them, felt them close around
her. Slid her arms under the jacket of his
suit, splaying her hands flat against the
taut muscles of his back. Felt the first measure of peace since . . . since the last time
she'd been in his arms.

"What happened?" he murmured. Laid
his cheek on top of her head. Cocooned
her.

"She kept having contractions all night."

Ethan pressed his lips to her temple and made her sigh. "How early would she be?"

"Six weeks."

"Not optimal, but manageable." His voice rumbled, the vibrations tickling her cheek.

"You said you weren't a doctor," she said and felt his silent laugh.

"Richard went through this once." He cleared his throat. "With his middle daughter."

Richard who had died when he had not. She held on a little tighter. "Was she all right?"

"Not at first. Brenda's blood pressure went crazy and they had to take the baby seven weeks early. The baby was in NICU for a few weeks, then they let them all go home. But she's fine now. Healthy and . . . Well, healthy."

His voice had roughened at the end, pulling at her already bruised heart. She leaned back, looked up into his face. "How many kids did Richard have?"

"Three. All girls." He changed the subject abruptly. "You haven't slept, have you?"

"A little. On the sofa in the waiting room. I'll catch a few hours when I get back to — home." Dana stopped, caught herself. Nearly bit her tongue. She'd almost said Hanover House. She must be more tired than she'd thought. "I haven't had a bite since those hot dogs last night. Why don't we go in?" She tried to tug free, but his arms held firm.

"In a minute." One big hand threaded through her hair to cradle the back of her head while the other brought her even closer, her thighs brushing against his. She could feel him against her abdomen, hard and pulsing. Fully aroused. He wanted her. It was a heady thought. "Just another minute." His voice had softened, pitched lower. Caressed. Her heart took a quick tumble and her knees wobbled and her hands came up to frame his face. His impossibly handsome face. "I thought about you," he murmured. "All night."

Everything inside her went liquid. "I thought about you, too. It was a long night."

He brushed her lips with his and she wanted to whimper. To beg. "I thought about kissing you up against your car yesterday," he said and a shudder raced down her back. "How you felt against me. How I wanted to feel you against me again."

He was seducing her with words and whispers. Making her want so much more.

She slid her arms around his neck and lifted on her toes. She could feel him now, thick and hard. No longer pulsing against her abdomen, but against her core where it did so much more good. Determined to hold her own, she caught his gaze and held it. Challenging him. "So do."

His eyes flashed and his fingers tightened against the small of her back. He sucked in a breath. "Not here. I can't do what I want here."

*Oh, God.* The very words brought a host of images to her mind, each one more erotic than the last. "What do you want?" It was a whisper, a husky, throaty whisper.

He stared, hard. Seemed to consider his answer for a long moment. Then he dropped his head so that his lips just brushed her ear. "I want to make you forget your own name."

She did whimper then, her hips arching, bringing her even more solidly against him. Every nerve ending she possessed was on fire. Her heart was beating harder than if she'd actually had sex. And he'd used nothing more than words. He straightened, let his eyes drop to where her breasts rapidly rose and fell in the little black dress. Then raised them to meet her eyes. And cocked one blond brow. It was her turn.

*So this is foreplay,* she thought. She'd never experienced it before. Not in a bedroom and certainly not on the street. But she could be taught. She leaned up, licked the corner of his mouth. Made him groan, a deep, wonderful, throaty sound that made her tingle down to her toes. "It's a short name." She licked the other side of his mouth and his hand left her hair and closed over her butt, kneading convulsively. She could feel him trembling. Trembling. "Only four letters. You'll have to work hard to make me forget."

His eyes glittered. Dangerously, she thought. But she wasn't the least bit afraid. "Oh, I think I'm up to the task," he said silkily.

Her lips curved. "Oh, I think you are, too."

Then he smiled and completely took her breath away. "Good morning, Dana."

"Good morning, Ethan. How are you?"

"Better now that I'm with you." He kissed her then, deep and rich and full and when he lifted his head, she sighed. He kissed the tip of her nose. "And you?"

"You make me feel better, too," she said. "I don't know how you do it, but you do."

"I'm glad. Are you ready for breakfast?"

"I am. And I'm really hungry. Those hot

dogs were a long time ago."

That they were, Ethan thought as he opened the door for her. His heart was finally coming back to a normal pace. He'd thought it would bang right out of his chest when she asked him what he wanted. He'd kept it light, because he'd thought what he really wanted might scare her to death, but now he wasn't so sure. When he found Alec, returned him to Randi safe and sound, he sure as hell planned to find out.

Betty eyed them curiously as they slid into their booth. "You two go out on the town?"

Dana smiled and once again sent his heart hammering in his chest. "Nothing so exciting, I'm afraid. Ethan has to run soon, so can you make his breakfast fast?" She waited until Betty was gone, then leaned forward. "Let's not mention Caroline being in the hospital. It would just make Betty worry and Caro has enough people worrying from Max and his family right now."

"That I understand. Clay — you know, my partner — he's the same way with me."

She lifted a brow, studying him. "You seem pretty healthy to me."

His eyes flickered. "I am now. I wasn't always though."

After a beat of hesitation, she asked, "What *did* you hurt in Afghanistan, Ethan?"

"Richard and I were thrown from our vehicle when it hit that land mine. I hit my head." He shrugged. "Blacked out. Woke up in the hospital with brain swelling. It was a long time before I could string three words together coherently. The words were there, just out of my reach. That was . . . frustrating."

He was such an intelligent, articulate man. "I imagine so," she said, holding his gaze.

"I still get headaches sometimes. Migraines with visual aura, the doctors called them."

"You can't see for a little while. I had a client with those. Not optimal, but manageable."

It hadn't been so hard telling her about his headaches at all. She seemed to take it in stride. He could respect that. He leaned back and just looked at her for the pleasure of doing so. She was rumpled and had long ago worn away all traces of makeup, yet he still found her beautiful and fascinating. More so now that he knew who she truly was. He wondered why she'd kept it secret. "Was it a client in your photography business?"

She blinked. One long blink. "That client? No."

He waited, but she said no more. Betty came with coffee and when she was gone Dana sighed. "You asked about me last night. I said I would tell you and I will. Maybe not all at one time, because it's hard for me to talk about some of it. You'll just have to be patient."

"I've been known to exhibit that quality occasionally," Ethan returned dryly. "Go."

She drew a deep breath as if fortifying herself. "I was born here in Chicago. I've never been out of Illinois."

Ethan's eyes widened. "You mean you've never seen the ocean?"

"Not even once." She sipped at her coffee thoughtfully. "I never really missed . . . what I'd missed. Not until recently. I'm not sure why I seem to lately." She brooded a moment, then abruptly charged forward. "My father was an alcoholic and my mother worked as a hotel maid to keep food on the table." She raised a brow. "Does that make you think badly of me?"

She wanted to appear as if she didn't give a damn if he did or not, but Ethan could see his answer was important. "No."

"All right. My dad died when I was ten. My mother married again when I was twelve. He was worse than my father."

Ethan got a sick feeling in his stomach that must have shown on his face because she waved her hand and shook her head. "No, it wasn't like that. He didn't molest us. He just beat the shit out of us. And her. My mother. I hated him and he hated me. I got rebellious and when I was fourteen I quit school and ran away."

"Us?"

"I have a sister." From the set of her mouth it was clear that was the end of that topic.

"But you didn't leave Chicago."

She laughed. "Hell, I didn't even leave the South Side. I met up with a rough crowd and . . ." She paused. Considered. Lifted a shoulder. "And I got pulled in for some petty theft. Did a stretch in juvie. Now do you think badly of me?"

That wasn't in the information he'd found, then again, being juvie it wouldn't be. "No."

"Okay. I got out of juvie and they sent me home. My stepfather whaled the tar out of me for a few weeks, then one day I'd had enough. I'd learned a little on the street. How to do some damage with a blade."

Ethan's eyes widened again. "You

stabbed him?" *Go girl. Good for you.*

"Only a little. I should have waited until I'd learned how to do a little more damage with a blade. I got him, but not like I wanted to. He probably should have had stitches." She smiled as if genuinely amused. "But he was afraid of needles, too. Kind of ironic, isn't it?"

"You say *was*. Is he dead?"

Her eyes flickered. "Not yet. I expect it soon. He's sick and old and dug his hole so deep nobody will pull him out. Especially not me. Does *that* make you think badly of me?"

He was becoming annoyed at the question. "No. Is your mother still living?"

Now her eyes didn't just flicker. They flashed with a pain so intense it left him breathless. Then she dropped her eyes and sipped her coffee. "No. My mother died."

"I'm sorry."

Her mouth drooped. "Me, too." She squared her shoulders. "But back to me."

He held up one finger. "Wait." Betty was coming out of the kitchen with their food and he suspected Dana wouldn't appreciate her listening. She waited until Betty was gone again before she picked up the salt shaker and salted her eggs.

"After I stabbed him, I ran away again,

313

because I wasn't going back to juvie. This time I knew how not to get arrested for picking pockets. I could be taught, you see."

He said nothing because he had no idea of what to say. His own childhood, although lonely, had been idyllic in comparison to hers.

"I learned a little here, a little there. Things a law-abiding citizen probably shouldn't know. Ran some scams. Never did drugs, I can say that. Well, maybe a little pot, but I never inhaled and that's the story I'm sticking to. Luckily I never saw the seedier side of the runaway strip either. But one day I got caught trying to steal a car. I never did get the hang of that hot-wiring thing. I guess I would have made a lousy electrical engineer. Unfortunately I was eighteen by then. Now I've got a felony record. Do you think badly of me?"

Ethan shook his head, so incredibly touched that she'd shared this with him and knowing full well he'd never tell that he'd known already. "Not yet. You'll have to do better than that, Dana."

"I met a guy waiting for my appointment with my parole officer. Charlie was his name. The guy. Not the PO. Charlie had a Harley." Now her brown eyes twinkled, again in what seemed like genuine amusement. "I was a biker chick for about a year. Even got me a tattoo," she added in an affected drawl. "Eat, Ethan."

He did need to eat quickly. He was chasing a woman with a tattoo, ironically enough. "So where is it?" he asked, then gulped down eggs that wanted to stick in his throat like kindergarten paste. "Your tattoo."

She waggled her brows. "Maybe someday you'll find out." Then she sobered. "That's why I told you. If you were to check on me like I checked on you, you'd see my record."

"So? Did you pay your debt to society?"

"I copped a plea. Thirty days served, two years probation. Was barely in long enough to get head lice."

"You were a kid."

"I was an eighteen-year-old with more bravado than brains. If it makes a difference I went back later and apologized to the person whose car I tried to steal." Her lips quirked mirthlessly. "She told me to go to hell, but I tried. To make amends, not to go to hell."

"I guessed that," Ethan said dryly. "What happened to Charlie?"

She swallowed a bite of eggs with a

shrug. "I married him. It went about as well as you'd think a marriage made in a parole office would. Charlie, as it turned out, had a lot in common with my father and stepfather. When he got drunk, he got violent. One day I ended up in the ER getting poked with needles and thought, *This sucks.* So I left him."

There was a great deal she'd left unsaid, but he didn't press. Not today anyway. "That's why he's so ex he's way past Z."

She smiled ruefully. "You got it."

"Well, I still don't think badly of you and I *really* want to see your tattoo."

Her grin was quick. "You are a nice man, Ethan. I'll try not to hold it against you."

He pushed their plates out of the way and reached for her hand across the table. "I think you're a nice woman, Dana. I think you're a lot harder on yourself than you are on everyone else."

Her eyes went just a little bit sad. "It's late, Ethan. You need to go."

"Wait." He'd nearly forgotten about the cell phone he'd bought her. "It's got five hundred minutes preloaded."

She lifted one brow at his outstretched hand but made no move to take the phone. "I don't take what I haven't earned, Ethan."

Which he might not have understood before today. "You let me buy you breakfast. Take the damn phone, Dana."

"Breakfast costs $6.95. A phone costs a hell of a lot more." She shook her head. "I wouldn't let Caroline buy me a phone, why should I let you?"

"Because Caroline doesn't want to see your tattoo," he retorted and made her laugh. "There. Take it. It's the only way I know how to get in touch with you. My numbers are programmed in, both my cell number and the hotel where I'm staying. I don't know when I'll be free today and I want to see you later. For dinner." He slid the phone across the table and watched her look at it. "You don't have to hot-wire it, Dana. Just press the pretty numbers, listen with the top part and talk into the bottom part. You don't need to be an electrical engineer. I promise." He stood up and straightened his tie.

She looked up at him with a wry expression. "You think you're so funny. Okay, I'll take the damn phone for now, but when you go back to D.C., it's going back with you."

His heart slammed up into his throat. When he went back to D.C. She said it like she didn't care if he went back or not. But he was going back. On that she was right. When he found Alec, he'd go back and resume his old life. Which seemed even emptier than it had before. Shoving his confusion aside, he bent down to press a hard kiss on her lips. "Go home and get some sleep. Call me if you need me. I'll see you for dinner tonight."

*Chicago,*
*Tuesday, August 3, 6:45 a.m.*

Sue didn't have a lot of time. Dupinsky had called the shelter from the hospital saying she'd be back by seven-thirty. That left Sue less than an hour to get a new ID and get back to the shelter. It would be easier to find prey this time of the morning, before the population of the city flooded the streets. Especially if the ID bearer was just getting off work and too tired to be careful. She picked up her pace when an acceptable candidate stepped off the El.

Sue matched her stride. "Excuse me." The woman was young, a little overweight, dressed in Winnie the Pooh scrubs lightly spattered in blood. How apropos. She glanced over her shoulder with a wary

318

frown, then took off at a brisk walk. Sue paced the woman, timing her attack. "I'm from out of town, miss. Can you help me find my address?"

"Sorry," the woman mumbled and kept moving. Good instincts, Sue thought. But ultimately not good enough. With a shoulder check that would have done any hockey player proud, she shoved the woman into the next alley, pulling her pistol from her waistband to the woman's temple in one fluid motion. Like a damn ballet, it was.

"Don't say a word," Sue muttered and watched the woman's eyes widen in terror.

"Take my purse," the woman begged in a hoarse whisper. "Just don't hurt me."

Sue rolled her eyes. They never listened. They always said a word. Sometimes a whole string of words. One little squeeze of the trigger, the pop of a bullet making contact with bone, and *alacazam,* the blood splatter on the woman's Winnie the Pooh scrubs was greatly increased. The silencer had really been a smart buy. Quietly, the woman slumped to the ground and Sue picked up her purse, found her wallet.

Today she was Kristie Sikorski, pediatric nurse, mother of three.

Dana still felt the tingle on her lips when she pulled into the alley behind Hanover House an hour later. Even the short kisses left her senses reeling. But more astonishing than even the kiss itself had been the look on his face right before he'd kissed her. She'd made herself say it, "When you go back to D.C." She'd made herself acknowledge once again that he was not a permanent fixture. The cell phone gesture had been so kind . . . so domestic . . . She'd had to remind herself that whatever they had would last only as long as they were in the same city. And as soon as his business was done, he'd be gone.

She'd expected him to chuckle. She hadn't expected him to look like she'd punched him in the gut. As if he'd forgotten he'd return. As if he wasn't thinking what they had was temporary after all. And just thinking he'd thought it made her heart tremble.

The trembling was replaced by annoyance when she pushed on the back door and found it unlocked. Evie always forgot to lock the damn door. With a frown she pushed it shut and snapped the three deadbolts shut. The top one didn't creak. David had greased it for her when he fixed the roof on Sunday.

David. The frown became a scowl. He'd pushed too far last night. But he had been right about one thing. She'd placed Caroline and everyone else at risk.

"You never came back last night." This quiet observation from beside the coffee-pot came from Beverly, their resident who was ready to leave the nest. Tomorrow was her good-bye date, in fact. Today would be her last day at Hanover House.

"No. I stayed at the hospital all night."

"How is Caroline?" Beverly poured Dana a cup of coffee and handed it to her.

"All right for now. Thanks." The coffee was strong, the way Evie made it. "Evie's here?"

"She's upstairs with the new kids."

Shauna Lincoln, the mother Caroline had picked up on Sunday night. Shauna had finally arrived, toting two toddlers with infected tonsils who had cried all day yesterday.

Beverly closed her eyes on a faint shudder. "Those kids cried all night."

Dana patted her shoulder. "You'll probably get a screaming baby on the bus with you all the way to California." And laughed when Beverly grimaced. "You ready, Beverly?"

"As ready as I'll ever be. Dana, thank you. I'd probably be dead today if it weren't for you. I'll miss you." Quickly Beverly hugged her, then overcome, rushed out of the kitchen and up to her room. It was a much-needed affirmation. Dana knew her work was vital. Critical. But she also knew it was dangerous. Something had to change.

But for now, Dana had to smooth things over with Evie. Their phone conversation last night had been anything but cordial. Dana found her in her bedroom, sitting on the edge of her bed, rocking one of the sick babies. Evie's dark brows rose. "Caro?"

"Better this morning."

"Good."

"She has a ripped placenta." Dana watched Evie pale, but her rocking didn't falter. "They may need to take the baby early if she doesn't stabilize."

"Hmm," was all she said. Then, "Erik came down for food at about two in the morning."

Dana's eyes widened. "Erik? That's wonderful!"

"No, not really." Evie continued to rock, her voice cold as ice. "He was lucid. Extremely lucid. Eyes bright, movements steady. Until he wolfed down three chicken legs in the space of two minutes. Then he threw up all over the kitchen floor."

Dana drew in a breath, let it out on a sigh. "Jane's been taking him his meals in their room. Apparently he hasn't been getting enough of them."

"Apparently not. Anyway, I was holding this little guy at the time and he let out a shriek. Jane came bolting down the stairs like the house was on fire. And she was very angry with Erik. Very, very angry."

Dana's eyes narrowed. "Did she strike him?"

"No. Just cleaned him up. None too gently. I tried to check on him later, but she said he was asleep."

"Dr. Lee's coming later today. We'll need to tell him what happened."

"I recorded it in the log." Evie stood up, the sleeping toddler in the crook of her arm. Reached for the doorknob with her free hand. An effective dismissal.

"I'll check on him now," Dana said. "And, Evie? Goodman's out there. Please don't leave the door unlocked. Please."

Evie's dark eyes stilled. "I'll note that as well." And the door closed in Dana's face.

With another sigh, Dana knocked on

Jane's door. Jane appeared, her translucent eyes widening at the sight of Dana in the doorway. Braless in a skimpy tank top and short shorts, Jane looked more like an exotic dancer than an abused mother of a ten-year-old boy. Dana chided herself for the thought. A woman had a right to dress the way she wanted in the privacy of her own room. And it was unbearably hot outside. "Hi, Jane. I was just checking to make sure everything was all right. From last night."

Jane turned to look over at Erik, giving Dana a quick glimpse of a shoulder tattoo. A stylized capital *A* peeked out from the shoulder strap of the tank top. "He's sleeping," she murmured. "I guess the chicken didn't agree with him last night."

"Or his stomach couldn't take being full after being hungry for a while," Dana said quietly. The scars on Jane's arms, the tattoo . . . They seemed at odds with the defeated woman standing before her. "Did you get enough to eat before you came here, Jane?"

Jane dropped her eyes. "Not always. Sometimes we went without. I tried to stretch the food we had as far as I could. But sometimes Erik's medicine takes his appetite. I've been trying to get him to eat since we got here."

"You were angry last night. Why?" Dana watched her carefully. Very carefully. And had she not been, she might have missed the way Jane's teeth clenched. Because it was gone, faster than it had appeared, and in its place was resolved despair.

"I was embarrassed. Not angry."

"Sometimes stress can make us do things we wouldn't normally do," Dana said, still watching. "Sometimes we strike out at those closest to us without meaning to."

"I . . . I don't know what you're talking about."

Dana gently grasped one of Jane's arms and just as gently ran her fingers over the faint little scars. "Sometimes when we're stressed we strike out at ourselves. Hurt ourselves. Sometimes we hurt those we love."

And then Dana saw what Caroline had meant. A controlled little explosion went off in Jane's eyes and for a split second hate flared, pure virulent rage. Dana took an unplanned step back just as Jane jerked her arm away and crossed her arms over her chest. "I would never hurt my son." The words were hissed.

"I'm sure you wouldn't," Dana soothed.

Her eyes were drawn to Jane's hands reflexively digging into her bare upper arms. And then she saw the smaller tattoo, just under the knuckle on her left ring finger. A little cross. A prison tattoo. She looked up. Saw that Jane knew what she'd been staring at.

"What did you do?" Dana asked quietly.

Jane's chest was pumping like a bellows. "None of your damn business."

Dana cast a glance over her shoulder at the sleeping boy. She'd need to talk to Dr. Lee about this. Find out if they needed to involve Children's Services to remove Erik from his mother. But that needed to be based on the behavior she saw now. Not the behavior that came before. People made mistakes. Paid their debts. Went on with their lives. Dana had. She wished she could believe Jane Smith was one of those people, too.

"You're right. What is important is the well-being of your son. Are we clear, Jane?"

Jane jerked a nod. "Yeah." Then for the second time in ten minutes, a door was carefully closed in Dana's face.

"Hell," Dana muttered, then glanced at her watch. Still fourteen hours until dinner.

Then the phone rang and Evie appeared in her doorway, her face like stone. "That was Max. The baby's monitors just went nuts and Caroline's asking you to come."

*Chicago,*
*Tuesday, August 3, 9:00 a.m.*

Evie sat down next to Erik with a worried frown. Jane had taken the Sunday want ads and was out looking for a job. She stroked the boy's hair, feeling the dirt and oil on her fingers. Not every woman who came through Hanover House was an attentive mother, but Jane Smith was one of the most neglectful. Also one of the most antisocial. Rarely did they see her. Rarely did she eat meals with the others, usually stating she was taking hers and Erik's up to their room. Evie remembered the way he'd wolfed down the chicken legs — like he hadn't eaten in days. And she wondered how much food Erik was really getting.

Someone needed to take care of this child. "And it might as well be me," she murmured. She got some towels. She'd wash this child's hair as he lay here on the bed if she had to. He was still sweaty and dirty from throwing up the chicken last night, for God's sake.

Which worried her more than anything else. His eyes had been so bright, so alert. Nothing like they'd been before. Nothing like they were now. She'd seen his file, knew he was waiting for Dr. Lee to come by with a refill for his epilepsy meds. She wondered if Jane was giving him the right dose. He was so thin. Maybe she was giving him too much.

That it wasn't an accident had occurred to Evie, but that wasn't something one voiced without good proof. Getting the dose right would be one of the things she'd work on with Dr. Lee this afternoon. Erik's extreme hunger and nausea the night before would be another.

She lifted his head to pile the towels beneath him, but when she brought her hand away it was red and sticky. She jolted, just for a second. Then realized it wasn't blood. It was sweet and candy-sticky. Gingerly she lifted her fingers to her nose.

No, it wasn't blood. It was Benadryl. She remembered Jane asking for the bottle on Sunday, just before she went to Lillian's funeral. Normally Evie dispensed a single dose at a time, but she'd been distracted that day. Jane had quite obviously kept the bottle. Gently she bathed Erik's face and his neck and he stirred, opening his eyes.

"Please talk to me, Erik," she said softly. "You don't need to be afraid of me."

But Erik just looked at her blankly, closed his eyes, and went back to sleep.

With a sigh Evie called Dana's pager. Although she hated to admit it, she needed some help.

*Ocean City, Maryland,
Tuesday, August 3, 10:00 a.m. Eastern
(9:00 a.m. Central)*

Lou Moore approached the counter at the Ocean City jail just in time to see Janson signing in, flexing his shoulders after his long drive. "Detective Janson, I'm Sheriff Moore."

"Nice to meet you, Sheriff," Janson said, shaking her hand. "Our robber's name is Bryce Lewis. His driver's license says he's seventeen and from Chicago. Also we found Cheryl Rickman's car early this morning. Someone had switched the plates which was why we overlooked it at first. They found it about two blocks from the bus terminal."

"So maybe whoever killed Rickman took

a bus out of town."

"I thought that, too. We'll be checking with the bus company, but since we don't know who we're looking for, I don't expect to get much at this point."

She saw an officer leading a young man in shackles. "Is Lewis considered violent?"

Janson shrugged. "He pulled a twenty-two on the convenience store owner who in turn pulled a Saturday Night Special from behind the counter. Lewis apparently got the deer in the headlights look and the store owner ended up bashing him on the head with a sack of quarters he had sitting next to the register."

"Has he said how he came to have Rickman's laptop power cord in his backpack?"

"No. He hasn't said a word except for one phone call. He said he'd called a relative, but no one came to bail him out. He was arraigned for the attempted robbery on Friday."

They went into the small interview room and sat across the table from the sullen young man and his young attorney. It was Janson's interview, so Lou sat back and listened.

"I'm Detective Janson with the Morgantown, West Virginia, Police Department," he said. "I investigate homicides." He let the statement hover but Lewis looked bored. "This is Sheriff Moore. She's the sheriff in Wight's Landing."

For a split second, Lewis's shoulders tensed. To his credit, his attorney didn't bat an eye. "I'm Stuart Fletcher, public defender's office. Let's make this quick, shall we?"

Janson shrugged. "I have a body in my morgue. Female, twenty-six years old."

"Killed when?" Fletcher asked.

Janson sucked in one cheek. "Thursday morning last week, between midnight and six."

The defender's laugh was derisive. "My client was arrested *here at* midnight, six hours by car from your body. I think we have a pretty airtight alibi, Detective."

Janson remained unruffled. "Your client was in possession of one of my victim's belongings at the time of his arrest."

"And this belonging would be — ?"

"A power cord for her laptop computer."

Fletcher snorted. "Tell me you came all the way from West Virginia with more than that."

There was a very long pause during which Janson and the defender didn't break eye contact. Lou knew Fletcher knew something. *Privilege my Aunt Fannie*. The boy had told him something and Fletcher didn't plan to reveal a damn thing.

"Paul McMillan," Lou said and once again saw the boy flinch. "Vaughn," she added, and the kid nearly jumped from his chair. She looked at Janson and he nodded, pleased. "I also have a body," she said, "for which your client's alibi won't hold. My body is the fiancé of Detective Janson's body. An interesting coincidence, you'll allow."

"Time of death?" Fletcher asked impatiently.

"This past Wednesday morning, between one and four a.m."

Fletcher tilted his head, eyes narrowed. "Precise."

"My ME analyzed the bugs eating what was left of Paul McMillan's head."

Lewis jumped up and tripped on his ankle shackles, fell to his knees, and threw up.

Fletcher didn't bat an eye. "The food here sucks," he said calmly. "And this interview is over. Guard, please take Mr. Lewis back to his cell." He leaned over, whispered in Lewis's ear, then straightened and presented them with a smile. "I hope you have a pleasant drive back to West Virginia, Detective."

When they'd gone, Lou frowned. "He had to have been working with someone."

"It's the only way to explain Rickman's murder," Janson agreed. "I'll let you know if anything turns up from Rickman's car. If we can put Bryce Lewis in the car, that may be enough for an indictment, which might shake him up enough into revealing his partner. As long as he's only facing the robbery, he has nothing to lose by keeping his mouth shut."

Lou shook his hand good-bye. "Nobody's bailed him out yet, so at least we don't have to worry about him going anywhere. It buys us some time."


*Ocean City, Maryland,*
*Tuesday, August 3, 11:30 a.m. Eastern*
*(10:30 a.m. Central)*


James Lorenzano sat on the other side of the visitation glass, waiting patiently. Sue wasn't here, but her brother was. Got himself arrested for knocking off a convenience store. James had to smile, picturing Sue's reaction to that news. Whatever her plan had been, her brother had taken it the opposite direction. He hoped she was adopting, adapting, and improving. Wherever the hell she was.

James knew that when compared to his own skills, Moore and her detective were mere amateurs. The boy would talk. Maybe not today, but definitely tomorrow.

Bryce Lewis sat down on the other side of the glass and just looked at him.

"I came from your uncle's house," James said, forgoing formal introduction. He saw a little spark of hope, which he would squash like a bug. "He's dead."

Shock. A little grief. Mostly fear. "Why?"

James smiled. "I think you already know. Where is she, Bryce?"

Bryce licked his lips. "Where is who? I don't know what you're talking about."

James stood up. "Fine. We'll play this your way today. I'll be back tomorrow and we'll play it mine."


*Chicago,*
*Tuesday, August 3, 11:00 a.m.*

Dana sank onto the old sofa in the waiting room, drained. Physically. Emotionally.

David sat down on the cushion next to her. Stiffly. He looked as weary as she was sure she did. He still wore the clothes he'd had on last night. At least she'd been able to get a shower and a fresh set of clothes at Hanover House before Max had called. By the time she'd arrived, the worst of the crisis was again over and Caroline was resting. The tense smile Caroline had managed when Dana barreled through the doorway broke her heart more than the sight of Max's gaunt face, streaked with tears. All Dana had been able to think was that this was all her fault. *All my fault.* Because it was.

Bent over, his balled fists pressing into his eyes, David sighed. "I'm sorry, Dana."

She glanced over in surprise. "Why?"

His hands fell limply between his spread knees, but his back stayed bowed. "Everything, I guess. I was out of line last night. You didn't cause this. I was just mad and scared."

Dana leaned into him, rested her forehead on his shoulder. "I'm sorry, too. You were right. This isn't a game and I've put Caroline and Evie and everyone else in danger. I want you to know I've been doing some serious thinking about it. I'm not sure what I'll do about it, but I'll be making some changes." She had been thinking about it, all through the night. All through the last three hours of hell.

Her work was important. Vital. Caroline believed it as much as she did. And Dana knew Caroline would never voluntarily walk away. Caroline had received too much from Hanover House. It was a debt Caroline would try to repay until the day she died.

Dana swallowed hard. Bad choice of words. Or maybe not. Her best friend might have died yesterday and if she had, Dana would have lost something bigger than herself. Therefore, sometime in the last few hours, she'd decided that the only way to keep Caroline from the work was to move the work away from Caroline.

*I'll leave Chicago.* It was a terrifying thought, leaving behind all she knew. Now she knew how her clients felt. It was a humbling realization.

David had been silent for a long stretch. "Did you hear me?" she said. "I'll be making changes. Caroline and Evie won't be in danger anymore."

David turned then, his eyes sad. "I heard you," he said quietly. "I know what you've done for Caroline and for women like her. And for my brother and my family I'm grateful. But not enough to see you get hurt, or worse. One of these days it's going to be me or Evie or, God forbid, Caroline, who finds *you* beaten to death on your living-room floor."

Dana flinched, the image he'd purposely conjured hitting way too close to home. "You cross the line, David."

"I'm your friend, Dana. I'm allowed to cross the line."

"Not that one."

He stood up, jaw taut. "Well, now I know where I stand, at least."

"David, wait." But he gestured for her to be quiet and headed for the door.

"No, it's all right, Dana. I'm going home for a while. Tell Max if he comes looking for me."

And he was gone, leaving her alone in the deserted waiting room. Her pager buzzed again on her hip and wearily she checked the number. It was Evie, again. She'd buzzed five times in the last three hours, but never with their emergency 911 code, so Dana had waited until Caroline's crisis was over.

With a sigh she pulled Ethan's cell phone from her pocket. Stared at the pretty numbers. Punched in the number for Hanover House. Listened in the top and talked in the bottom. And remembering, smiled wistfully. "Evie, it's Dana."

"What number are you calling from?"

Caller ID. At least Evie would have the number now. "My . . . my new cell phone."

Evie laughed in disbelief. "Where did you get a cell phone, Miss Skinflint?"

The taunt was not in jest. She and Evie had some things to work out. "It was a gift. You can use it from now on if you want to get in touch with me."

"Is Caro okay?"

"She is. So is the baby." For now. "What's up?"

"It's Jane and Erik."

Dana sighed. "What about them?" And she listened as Evie explained her concerns. Then frowned as Evie related the latest. The missing Benadryl.

"I should have just dispensed a dose, but I was upset over Lillian. It's not an excuse."

"It's okay. It's not like we don't all make mistakes. Is he awake now?"

"Not really. Just groggy and he stares like I'm not getting through. I have no idea how much she gave him. His heartbeat seems normal though."

Dana checked her watch. "Dr. Lee is coming over this afternoon. Where is Jane now?"

"Job hunting."

"Call Dr. Lee and ask if he can come a bit earlier. I'd like him to take a look at Erik without Jane around. He should be bringing Erik some new epilepsy medicine. Maybe that's why Jane was using the Benadryl — because she was out of his meds."

Evie was silent for a second. "Do you really think so?"

Dana sighed again. Thought about the little scars on Jane's arms, the hostile, explosive glare that had hardened in her translucent eyes when she'd realized Dana had seen them. They were three for three on Jane. She, Caroline, and now Evie. "No. Tell Dr. Lee that, too. Oh, and, Evie? Nice work. Really, really nice work."

Another silence, one of surprise this time. "Thanks. I needed to hear that. Dana, you sound tired. I can handle this here. Why don't you go to your place and get some sleep?"

"Mia doesn't want me to go back to my place in case Goodman's there. I'll sleep here."

"Um . . . Dana, did you take my makeup? It's not in my room and I can't leave without it."

The makeup Evie never left the house without. Her shield. Dana supposed they all had their shields. Evie's just came in a plastic case. "Evie, you know I wouldn't touch your makeup. But I can pick you up some more. Go check on Erik. I'll see you later."

Dana hung up and laid her head against the sofa. Slept. And dreamed.

# Chapter Thirteen

*Chicago,*
*Tuesday, August 3, 12:40 p.m.*

It was fair to say he'd never seen it coming. Because Fred was a fucking moron. Now she had him where she wanted him *and* his pretty quarter kilo of coke to boot.

Where she wanted him was gagged with his own smelly socks, handcuffed to a bed with his own cuffs, spread-eagled and ready for her worst. Her worst would be very bad indeed. He'd extorted, black-mailed. Treated her like a whore. Like his little slave.

Sue was nobody's slave. A fact Fred was about to learn.

She'd met him at the motel room he'd designated promptly at noon, the quarter kilo she'd picked up for him in her back-pack along with her weapons, the paper-work for the offshore bank accounts she'd just opened, as well as several other goodies that were part of her plan. It had been a very productive morning.

She'd also brought the last little bit of the powder she'd bought to make James sleep at that celebration picnic all those weeks ago. She'd given James enough to knock him out cold. She'd only given Fred enough to make him sleep for a little while. She wanted Fred awake, lucid. She wanted him to know exactly what was going to happen to him. She wanted him to feel every little cut, every little frisson of pain.

She'd seen the lascivious pleasure in Fred's eyes when she'd pulled a little lace teddy from her backpack. Seen his eyes sparkle when she drew a small bottle of sparkling wine and two cold flutes from the cooler she'd bought especially for this occasion. They were celebrating, she'd said. The beginning of what would be a fruitful business relationship.

He'd bought it, lock, stock, and barrel. After two glasses of cheap, twist-top wine, he started to weave on his feet. Before he'd been able to protest, she'd had him on the bed, his hands cuffed to the headboard with the plastic flex-cuffs she'd taken from his own pockets. From experience she knew he always carried at least a half dozen of the flex-cuffs that looked like trash bag ties, but were ultra strong. Fred had used them on her more than once during those Hillsboro "heart-to-hearts." Just because he could.

Well now, *she* could. And she did. One of the advertised benefits of the flex-cuffs was that they wouldn't cut the skin like conventional metal cuffs. Sue grinned as she stripped the shoes and socks from his feet, then pulled his ankles over the bottom edge of the bed and firmly secured them to the legs of the bed frame with very strong twine. The flex-cuffs wouldn't cut his skin, but she sure planned to.

She hadn't originally planned to include Fred in her retribution, but hell. *Adopt, adapt, and improve.* She couldn't think of a more deserving recipient of retribution and knew there were hundreds of women at Hillsboro who would pay to be in her shoes right now.

Because right now Fred was waking up and he was pissed. He pulled at the cuffs but they were way too strong and he was way too weak from the spiked wine. He lifted his head and glared at her first, then lifted his brows in speculation. She stood before him nude. Fred, the sorry fucker, thought he was about to get lucky. Sue didn't want to ruin her clothing with his blood. She'd shower when she was finished.

Sue drew her knife from her backpack and showed it to him, knowing the exact moment he realized his plight. The lecherous look in his eyes became stark terror.

She laughed, unable to contain the rush of sheer joy, then flipped the TV on to a noisy channel. "Let's have a heart-to-heart, Fred." She sat on the bed and unbuckled his belt. "You know, you used to make us do this, back at Hillsboro." She pulled the belt from his pants. "Unbuckle your belt, that is. I figured that in some sick way you were able to convince yourself that if we unbuckled you, unsnapped you" — she unsnapped and unzipped him — "and unzipped you that somehow that made this a consensual act. Well, today you'll be happy to know I consent at last." She slid the knife down his pants, cutting the fabric from his body. "I guess you don't." He was bucking like a bronco, trying to get away.

Fucking moron. He couldn't get away. "Hold still, Fred. You wouldn't want to lose anything important there, now would you?" He stopped the frantic bucking as if he'd been unplugged. "Didn't think so. Of course you're going to anyway. But business before pleasure." On the nightstand she put the cooler she'd bought especially for this purpose. "I need your fingers, Fred. Don't worry, it's for a really good cause." His eyes widened and he pulled his hands, but went nowhere of course. Sue grabbed his first finger and sliced it off. His howl of pain was twice muffled, once by the socks in his mouth and again by the noise of the TV. Focused on her task, Sue repeated the action nine more times, until Fred lay quivering and shaking and moaning and crying.

And bleeding. He was doing a hell of a lot of bleeding. Sue dropped the severed digits in a plastic bag, and put the bag in the cooler. The fingers would be a nice incentive for the Vaughns to do her bidding. What parent wouldn't pay to keep a similar fate from happening to their kid? It was bloody brilliant, if she did say so herself.

She had to hurry though, because Fred was going into shock and she didn't want him to miss the final cut. So to speak. "That was business, Fred." He just looked at her, his eyes dull with pain. "Now for pleasure. You've had your pleasure. Ninety-eight times over ten years according to my count. That includes last Friday, of course. Now it's my turn, Fred." She took his flaccid cock in her hand, sliced, and was rewarded by a low moan. She looked at his member with disdain. And tossed it in the garbage.

With care she showered and cleaned the bathroom, making sure she wiped every surface clean. She dressed, watching him lie there on the bloody bed, still. But not dead. She put a bullet through his skull. Now he was dead.

Gathering the cooler, her backpack, and his wallet, she stopped for one last look back. Then turned off the TV, hung the DO NOT DISTURB CARD on the doorknob, and drove Fred's car back into the city. She'd had a productive morning, all in all. Opening the bank accounts, sending another e-mail to the Vaughns. Picking up Fred's quarter kilo before whacking his various appendages. She was tired, but she still had one more stop to make.

She had a package that absolutely, positively had to get to Wight's Landing overnight. Next stop, FedEx, then back to the shelter before Dupinsky's doctor arrived to examine Erik. Dr. Lee was due to arrive at three, Scarface had told her before she'd left this morning, want ads in hand. Sue might even have time for a nap before he got there.

Detective Mia Mitchell looked up when a shadow fell over the dead woman's body. From her position on one knee she had to look pretty far up. Her partner was a big man. "Gunshot wound to the head, just behind the ear, Abe. Exit wound at the temple. Her purse is gone, no ID. Based on the scrubs, I say she's a nurse."

Abe Reagan crouched down, his eyes sharp, his hands gloved just as hers were. "Pediatric," he said. "Winnie the Pooh scrubs." He looked up. "The nurse in Kara's pediatrician's office wears the same ones."

Kara was Abe's seven-month-old daughter. "Do you know this nurse?"

"Nope." He shot a glance over to the guy from the ME's office who was waiting with the body bag. "How long has she been here?"

"Not more than seven or eight hours," the ME said. "You ready for me to take her?"

"In another minute or two." She pulled out her cell, dialed missing persons, and in a minute they had their answer. "She's Kristie Sikorski," she told Abe. "Husband reported her missing this morning when she didn't come home from work." She slid her phone in her pocket. "He'll meet us as soon as his parents arrive to watch their three kids."

Abe was examining her hands. "No sign of a fight here."

"No, but there are cuts on her face where it looks like she got smashed against this wall."

"She's still wearing her diamond ring."

Mia frowned. "I saw that. Whoever mugged her took her wallet, but left her jewelry."

Abe stood up, brushed at his slacks. "I don't know that it's a mugging. I've seen a lot of execution-style murders that look just like this."

From his days as an undercover narcotics cop, Mia knew. "Well, let's go talk to the husband. Maybe he can help us out."

*Chicago,*
*Tuesday, August 3, 1:30 p.m.*

Ethan flopped into his car seat and jacked up the AC. Nothing. Six hours of combing every shop and alley in a one-mile radius around yesterday's copy store had turned up absofuckinlutely nothing. No one had seen her. He'd hit a dead end and had nowhere else to go. Not until *she* chose to contact them again. They were at her mercy. So was Alec.

He groaned when his cell phone buzzed in his pocket. It couldn't be good news.

"Another e-mail," Clay said tightly.

Ethan pulled the car into traffic. "I'm on my way back to the hotel. What did it say?"

"She wants a good faith deposit of twenty-five grand by tomorrow noon. It's an offshore account. We have the number."

"Then that's all we have. I don't have anything from my search today."

"Hell," Clay grumbled. "But I do have other news on that slug we pulled out of the wall. There weren't any matches locally, but my old pal has a pal at the Bureau and they ran a trace. It matches a slug pulled from an elderly woman shot during a home burglary in Florida about six weeks ago."

Ethan rubbed his head. "That doesn't make any sense."

"I know," Clay said. "But guns change hands. There may be no connection."

Ethan sighed. "I'm so damn tired of having no connections. I'll call you when I get to the hotel."

*Dupinsky would be next.* That's all Sue could think when she walked back to Hanover House and saw a strange car parked in the alley with a pile of mail on the front passenger seat identifying the driver as Dr. George Lee. He wasn't supposed to be here until three o'clock. But he was early and Sue had no doubt about how or why.

Dupinsky. Meddling bitch. Calling the doctor in early to check the kid when she'd *explicitly* told them not to. When this was over, Dupinsky would pay. Getting Caroline out of the way had been business. Teaching Dupinsky not to meddle would be purely personal. The scent of Fred's blood was still in her nostrils and for a moment she allowed herself to entertain fantasies of Dupinsky tied and gagged and bleeding. Gagging her would be the only way to get the damn woman to shut up. But for now she had bigger problems. Even now the good doctor could be discovering that little Erik had no bruises. No signs of physical abuse. Oh, the good doctor would be discovering all kinds of things about Erik if she didn't stop him.

Sue crept around to the back and slipped in the kitchen door which only Dupinsky remembered to lock. And there was the doctor examining Erik. Evie and Dupinsky were nowhere to be seen. Somebody's kid was wailing to beat all hell upstairs, so Sue bet Evie was up there, too. Dupinsky was probably still at the hospital with darling Caroline.

Dr. George Lee was a small man. No more than five feet six. Perhaps a hundred thirty pounds. He was very old, at least seventy. She could take him down. Easily.

Her gun drawn, Sue cleared her throat. The doctor looked up and in an instant she could tell he'd accurately evaluated the situation. Slowly he pulled his stethoscope from his ears. "You must be Jane."

She smiled. "Let's go, Doc," she said. "Get your bag."

"I could scream."

"And I'd kill you and the kid and be gone before anybody came." She held the pistol at an angle. "Nice silencer. It really does the job. Now come, before I finish the kid off."

Lee looked down at the boy. "You've been poisoning this child. Starving him."

"Oh, just a little." She took a step closer and grabbed the doctor by his shirtfront and placed the pistol at the boy's temple. From the corner of her eye she watched the kid's eyes go glassy with terror in his thin face. "I have killed six people this week, Dr. Lee. Unless you want the kid to be number seven, you will move. *Now*."

His hands shaking, the doctor took his bag. "I'm going. You won't —"

"Get away with it, I know, I know. That's what everybody says. Wait. On second thought, take a letter, Doc. Right there on your little notepad." With his hands shaking badly, he picked up his pen. "Smart man. Write that you got an emergency call and you had to go. That the boy is just suffering from post-traumatic stress. *Write it*." He started to scrawl, his handwriting barely legible. "Did you bring the kid's epilepsy medication?"

The doctor drew in a breath. "I did."

"Then put it on top of the note. Now *move*." She moved the end of the silencer to the good doctor's temple as he shuffled to the door, then paused and looked the kid straight in the eye. Performed the three signs she'd learned from the American Sign Language book she'd perused in the bookstore that doubled as an Internet café that morning. She could send his parents a ransom note and learn how to threaten their kid all under one roof. And drink a damn good double mocha latte while she did it. Talk about one-stop shopping. *Mom . . . will . . . die.*

The kid went pale and she figured she'd done the signs well enough.

She walked the good doctor to his car, urged him to take the wheel, checked the address on his mail, and forced him to drive a few blocks from his home, then had him pull into an alley where she forced him out and up against the wall. She took his wallet, his car keys, and on a lark pulled his spectacles from his face. Then she turned him around to face the wall and shot him in the back of the head. Kicked at his bag until it opened and dumped the contents on the ground. Picked up the few bottles of medicine he carried. It would look like a drug-motivated theft. All too common, she imagined.

In an hour or so she'd return to the shelter, seemingly exhausted from her job search. She was, actually. Exhausted. She hadn't had such a busy day since she'd taken the kid.

"I hate identifications," Mia muttered, leaning against the morgue's viewing window. Her eyes stung and she rubbed them hard. "They never get any easier."

Abe sighed, his shoulders hunched. "I need to go home and kiss my wife and play with my baby." He cast a glance down at Sikorski's young husband, who sat on a bench alone, his head in his hands, quietly weeping. "I'll make sure he gets home all right. You go home, too, understand?"

"I will. I promise," she insisted when he shot her a disbelieving look. "I've got a date tonight, so there's no way I'm sticking around to do paperwork." She leaned her head back and closed her eyes. "I just need a few minutes, though."

Abe squeezed her shoulder. "Have fun on your date."

She forced a grin. "He's a fireman. How could I not?" She watched him walk away, help Mr. Sikorski to his feet, and support him as the two men walked away from the morgue. From Kristie Sikorski's lifeless body. Three little girls didn't have a mommy anymore and it was Mia's job to make somebody pay.

Some days, though, it was just too much. Too much suffering and grief. There was a tapping on the glass behind her and Mia jumped and spun, startled. Then scowled at Julia VanderBeck, the ME, who stood looking at her through the window with a perplexed frown. Julia motioned her to come inside the morgue, and biting her lip, Mia obeyed.

"Did Abe go home?"

"Yeah, why?"

"Because I have something I wanted the two of you to see," Julia said, leading her past Sikorski's body to another sheet-covered body. "This guy came in a half hour ago. He was found in an alley."

The hairs rose on the back of Mia's neck. "Nine mil to the head?"

"Yeah. You know the silencer pattern I showed you on Sikorski's skull? The way the skin ripples away from the entrance wound?" She pulled the sheet back, exposing an elderly Asian man. "Same pattern, same place. I lay you odds that ballistics will say it was the same gun."

Mia flipped the toe tag and frowned. There was something familiar about him. "Lee."

"Dr. George Lee," Julia said. "His wallet

355

was gone, but he has a Medic Alert bracelet."

Mia let the toe tag drop. "Oh, hell. I know this man. He does pro bono work for a friend of mine that manages a shelter." She looked at Lee, trying to put the pieces together. "This is the second person that works with my friend to be assaulted in two days."

"Too much coincidence," Julia murmured. "Was the other person shot?"

"No, vehicular. Hit-and-run. You remember Lillian Goodman, the domestic DOA from last week?"

Julia grimaced. "Not one I'll soon forget. These are all related?"

"Maybe. But Sikorski's shooting doesn't make a bit of sense. Damn, I'll have to tell Dana about Dr. Lee. This is going to kill her."

*Chicago,*
*Tuesday, August 3, 6:00 p.m.*

"Dana. Dana, wake up."

Dana came awake with a start, scrambled to sit up, staring at her hands. *There'd been so much blood. Everywhere. Blood on her hands. God.* But her hands were

356

clean and Max Hunter was staring down at her with compassion. He was one of the few that knew the content of her dreams. Still stunned, she stared back up at him.

Max squeezed her upper arm. "Caroline's fine, but you were dreaming." Translated, she was saying things in her sleep she wouldn't want others to hear. "It's dinnertime."

She checked her watch and yelped. "It's six o'clock." Ethan said he'd call about dinner. All the thoughts were starting to reassemble in her mind. From her pocket she pulled the small cell phone and pushed buttons until she reached the call log. He hadn't called. Disappointment swamped. But he had said he didn't know when he'd be free.

Max was staring at the phone. "Where did you get that?"

She felt her cheeks heat. "It was kind of a gift. Yeah. How is Caro?"

"Awake and demanding a chili dog. Go talk to her. She could use the company."

Caroline was flat on her back, staring at the ceiling.

"Hello, darlin'," Dana twanged and Caroline huffed a chuckle. Dana sat down on the edge of the bed. "So are they going to do the C-section?"

"Doesn't look like it. We've been stable since that little scare this morning, but they said they'd keep me another day. They may let me go home tomorrow, but I'll still be on bed rest until the baby's born." She shrugged. "So we wait and see. I will tell you I'm tired of lying in this bed. I sent Max out for a chili dog. He may have to hide it, so cover for me."

"I heard that," said Mia from the doorway. "Conspiracy to smuggle dietary contraband into a hospital." She tossed them a saucy grin. "How are you, Caroline?"

"Hungry, bored. My butt hurts. Oh, and I did all my Christmas shopping from QVC today. My charge cards are loaded, but I'm set for December. How about you, Mia?"

"Not too bad." She came into the room, a package under her arm. "I brought you something I hope you'll like. Dana, you want to open it?"

Dana ripped the paper off the flat parcel, revealing an oil painting of flowers dripping off a balcony. Sunshine was everywhere. It nearly made her feel better. "It's wonderful."

"My partner's wife paints in her spare time. I'm hiding her birthday present to him in exchange for a few paintings, so my

Christmas shopping's pretty well done, too."

"This painting is like having a window," Caroline said. "What's your partner's present?"

"She's just fixed up their basement so she bought him a pool table. Fills up my whole damn apartment." She squeezed Caroline's hand. "I don't have much news for you. We found the car that hit you. It had been stolen. We've got forensics checking it out."

Caroline's voice was small. "So you haven't found Lillian's husband?"

Mia shook her head. "There's a rumor that he's in Detroit. We'll look till we find him. Until then, you ladies be careful." She walked out but stood in the hallway, gesturing Dana to come with her. There was more then. More Mia didn't want Caroline to know.

Dana pulled her cell phone out of her pocket as an excuse to leave the room. "Caro, I need to give Ethan a call. Find out if we have plans for dinner."

Caroline's eyes had widened. "You let him give you that? It must be serious."

"Oh, hush. I'll be back in a few." Rapidly she walked back to the waiting room where Mia paced. Her gut clenched. "What?"

"I couldn't tell you in there. I don't want to stress her out. Dana, sit down."

Dana sat down, dread a palpable thing. "Who now?"

Mia sighed. "Dr. Lee. He's dead."

"Oh, God." Her startled cry was followed by a breath that physically hurt. "Please, Mia. He was sweet and old. Who would hurt him?"

"I'm sorry, Dana. Dr. Lee was found in an alley about two blocks from his house."

"Evie said he was at the House today, but that he left a note saying he'd gotten a call and had to leave."

Mia's eyes were sharp. "It looks like he may have had some car trouble on his way home from your place and when he got out to check, he was robbed. But under the circumstances, we can't ignore Goodman."

Dana's mind was reeling, picturing the scene. "Did he suffer?"

Mia shook her head. "No. The ME said he died instantly."

A thought struck, stealing her breath. "Mia, if it was Goodman, he followed Dr. Lee from the shelter. He knows where we are. I should evacuate. Where will I put them all?"

Mia sat down next to her. "Now don't panic. It may be this is totally unrelated to you and the shelter at all. And, anyway, if Goodman caught him coming out of your place, he would have killed him closer to the shelter, then gone looking for you. He didn't. Dr. Lee was killed a block or two from his house. If Goodman was involved, it's more likely he tracked Lee separately. Was there any way Goodman could tie Lillian to Dr. Lee?"

Dana's pulse was thundering in her head. "Yeah. Dr. Lee had to relocate Naomi's shoulder when she first arrived. Damn asshole father pulled Naomi's arm out of its socket. He gave her something to help her sleep. Dr. Lee always paid for the prescriptions out of his own pocket, and the labels had his name on them." And now that generous man was dead. Because he'd helped her. "If one of the bottles was in Lillian's apartment . . ."

"Then that's most likely how Goodman found him." Mia grimaced. "Look on the bright side. If Goodman's gunning for anyone, it'll be you and you're not near the shelter right now. It's unlikely he would come into a hospital, so maybe you should stay here tonight."

Dana just looked at her. "You're kidding, right?"

Mia shrugged. "No, I'm not. I've set up

drive-bys at your apartment and at the shelter, just in case. And I'll stop by there on my way home to make sure Evie's got everything all locked up. You stay somewhere else tonight." Mia gave her a hug, then left.

Dana sat for a while, brooding. Dr. Lee was dead. Which may or may not be her fault. Caroline was hurt. Likely her fault. She felt unsettled, grim. Detached. Displaced. And she was alone. She didn't want to be alone. She wanted Ethan. Wanted the way he could settle her with just a look. The way he could tempt her with a different look. Just thinking about him made her pulse throb. Everywhere. But he hadn't called.

She could call him. He'd programmed his hotel into her cell phone. Summoning her courage she pressed the pretty numbers and heard the operator announce the Chicago Sheraton then hung up abruptly. She didn't want to talk to him. She wanted to see him. Hold him. *Have him hold me.* She walked back to Caroline's room to say good night and found her friend asleep, so she left a note. And made herself leave before she could change her mind.

The kid was awake and alert. And cowering in the corner like a trapped animal. Sue held out a plate of chicken and a glass of water and a note. *Eat slowly.*

He eyed the dinner for a long moment, then took it, proceeding to eat in small slow bites. All the while he looked at her and in between the cowering, Sue saw flashes of contempt so she pulled out the good doctor's spectacles from her backpack and with great drama slid them on her face. She could see he understood right away.

Smart kid. Sure as hell didn't get it from his old man. The contempt in his eyes disappeared as if it had never been there. She took the note back and added a line. *Leave this room tonight and I will kill you tomorrow.* Another midnight stroll could ruin everything.

She was safe here for the time being. Caroline and her suspicions had been taken care of. Dr. Lee's death was being attributed to robbery. Vaughn had the account number and would be depositing a practice deposit of twenty-five thousand dollars in the next twenty-four hours, another five million in the next forty-eight. And the ID she'd use to get out of the country was sitting in the top drawer of Dupinsky's desk.

Things were going pretty well, all things considered.

*Chicago,*
*Tuesday, August 3, 7:15 p.m.*

*Another one.* It was all Ethan could think as he sat at the little table in the front room of his hotel suite, looking at the video he'd obtained from the site of the latest e-mail, a combination Internet café and bookstore. He'd digitally remastered the video, analyzed it frame by frame, until he could clearly see the credit card she'd given the clerk to hold as she used the Internet café's computer. Ethan picked up the photo, stared at the name on the charge card with growing despair. It belonged to Kristie Sikorski.

He'd found that Kristie Sikorski was a pediatric nurse with three kids. Ethan didn't have much hope that they'd find her alive. He didn't have much hope period. The bitch still wore that damn hat so they still couldn't see her face. Once, she'd actually glanced up, enough to see the bottom half of her face, but the frame enlargements just showed a heavy layer of pancake makeup and dark red lipstick that all but hid the true shape of her mouth. They were no closer to finding Alec than before.

She'd been bolder this time. Sitting, enjoying a cup of coffee before she sent her e-mail. She'd been reading a sign language book. The sight of it made his hair stand up on end. Ethan took the picture, stared at the book in the woman's hands. She'd been studying sign language just minutes before sending a ransom note. *How cold.*

The photo she'd attached to the ransom note showed Alec, lying on the same bed, curled into a ball. He had to be sleeping, Ethan told himself. But he looked dead and Ethan suspected their woman knew it. That she used it to manipulate the fears of a terrified mother. Ethan wished he could soothe Randi's fear. Dana would be able to. Dana could tell Randi that it wasn't her fault that her son was kidnapped and make her believe it, because in the short time he was with her, Dana made him believe things, too.

He needed her, he thought. Needed the sustenance he got from just being with her. He'd call her. See if she was free for just an hour. An hour would be all he needed to build him back up enough to go out and look some more. For a child that could literally be anywhere in a city of three million people. Weary, Ethan rested his elbows on the table, his forehead on his clenched fists.

The knock at the door startled him. Quickly he scooped the pictures into a stack, slid them under the large book that detailed the hotel's services before opening the door.

And he could only stare. Dana looked up at him, her normally calm brown eyes wide and turbulent, her lips firmly pressed together, her hands clenched at her sides. And inside his mind, his thoughts simply folded, like a house of cards.

Dana could only stare. He stood there with red-rimmed eyes and tousled hair, his shirt hanging open, exposing yards of muscles and all that golden hair. Her eyes traveled down to the pair of faded jeans snug on his hips. Zipped, but unsnapped. His feet were bare. And everything inside her went liquid with longing. She licked her lips, tried to bring words from her throat. They came out rusty. "I woke you. I'm sorry."

He shook his head. "I wasn't asleep." In a civilized move, he stepped back, allowing

366

her to enter. In a civilized move she did so.

But the soft click of the door closing ended all civilization as she knew it and she was in his arms, her hands in his hair, her aching breasts pushed hard against all those muscles, desperate for relief. He took two steps and she was flat against the door, his body thrusting against her. Then she was pulled closer as his hands closed over her butt, lifting her into him and she could feel him. Oh, God, she could feel him. Hard and throbbing.

Greedily she met his mouth halfway and they devoured, consuming each other, and on some level she understood he needed this as much as she did. His lips were hot on hers, came perilously close to punishing in their intensity, then as if realizing his strength, he pulled back, ran his open mouth down the side of her neck, his breath coming hard and heavy, like he'd run a mile. Gently, he kissed the hollow of her throat. And pressing his face into the curve of her shoulder, he shuddered.

"I needed you," he whispered and sent her heart tumbling. "How did you know?"

With trembling hands she stroked his hair. "I didn't. I just knew I didn't want to be alone tonight. That I wanted to be with you."

"Did I hurt you?"

"Sshh. No." She could feel his sadness, stronger than at any time before. But not just sadness. It was desperation. Whatever had brought him here had become worse. Much worse. "What's wrong, Ethan? Can't you let me help you?"

He straightened, pulled her away from the door and into him. Ran one hand up her back, cradled her neck. Pulled her closer so that her cheek pressed against his bare chest, the coarse hair tickling her skin. "Just be with me. Only for a little while."

*Only for a little while?* Dana wondered if that would be enough. For either of them. "All right." So she stood there, brushing her cheek against his chest, her arms around his neck. Imperceptibly rocking. Slow dancing to no music. She pulled back a little so she could see his face. Saw the pain in his eyes, in the grim set of his mouth. And knew any physical release she'd hoped for would have to wait. "Have you eaten?"

"No." As he looked at her the intensity in his green eyes shifted. The pain was still there, but it was joined by the same awareness she'd seen every time they'd been together and deep down she felt the flutterings of a thrill. "I was planning to call you, take you out. Now I'm planning on ordering room service."

"We could just stay here until it arrived, couldn't we?"

"We could." One corner of his mouth moved. It didn't really curve, so it wasn't really a smile. But the grimness softened. Dana leaned up and kissed the corner of his mouth.

"That's a little better."

He sighed. "You don't look like your day was any better than mine. Is Caroline worse?"

"Not really. But . . ."

"But what?"

She found she wanted to tell him so badly. To just let it all out, then put her head on his shoulder and have him tell her it would be all right. To not have to be the one to worry this time. But she couldn't. Not everything anyway. It was funny, actually, and someday she might even be amused. She'd come here tonight with the full intention of pushing him into bed. She'd share her body before her secrets. *I am one screwed-up woman.*

She sighed and told what she could. "One of my friends was killed tonight. Looks like he may have been robbed." She hoped he'd just been robbed. She really hoped so.

His hands instantly came up to bracket her jaws, his thumbs stroking her cheeks. "Oh, Dana, I'm sorry. Who was it?"

"A doctor friend of mine. He was a good man. He didn't deserve to die that way."

He led her to the sofa, sat down, and pulled her on his lap. "Tell me about your friend. The one that was killed. How did you come to know him?"

The whole story of her life was poised on the tip of her tongue. But that would put the secrets of others at risk and after only three days, that was not something she could do. So she found a tenable compromise. "I volunteer with runaways." True in every sense of the word. It had been so long since she'd drawn a full paycheck she was more like a volunteer than an employee and every one of her clients was running away from someone. "Dr. Lee volunteered medical services."

"I am sorry."

She laid her head on his shoulder. Sighed deeply. "Me, too."

He kissed her hair. "I didn't think you were really a photographer."

Her head snapped back, her eyes wide, her spine straight as a board. "I told you I only volunteered with the runaways. Taking pictures of babies is how I make my living."

Ethan let his head fall back to look up at her face, once again humbled and touched. She'd shared another piece of her life that he sensed was intensely private, although he wasn't sure why. Her work with runaways was something she should be proud of. "You might make a living taking pictures." *Not much of one,* he thought. "But which gives you the most ongoing satisfaction? Snapping pictures or helping runaway kids?"

She never hesitated. "The second one."

"Then that's the one you really are. It doesn't matter how you make your money." Lazily he trailed his fingertips across her stomach, felt her muscles quiver and flinch in response. Watched her breasts rise and fall in the sleeveless polo shirt that seemed to be her stock uniform. Watched the expression in her eyes go far away.

"What an insightful thing to say," she murmured. "What about you? What are you?"

He considered her question. It was a good one. He considered his answer, because it was an important one. "I suppose I don't mind being a security consultant, but I'll always be a Marine, because that's where my heart is."

Her eyes were changing, warming. He thought he could sit and look at her eyes all day long. "You miss it," she murmured. "The Marines."

"Every damn day."

"It must have killed you to walk away."

"It was the hardest thing I ever had to do. At first, when I was in Walter Reed I pretended to myself that I'd get better. Go back." He closed his eyes, remembering.

"But it got easier? Not doing what you love?"

"Over time. I still wake up sometimes and think I'm in the desert. That it's time to wake up and shoulder my pack and head out. Of course, the ceiling fan and the AC is always the first clue I'm in civilization." He smiled. "And the lack of sand. Some of the guys filled little bottles of sand to take home with them, but I figured I had enough sand in my mouth and other vital orifices to last me the rest of my life."

She made a face. "Thank you for painting that picture for me."

His fingertips moved to the silk of her bare arm. He could feel her shiver where he touched her skin. "I really do *not* miss the sand. But the rest of it . . . the challenge, the excitement . . ."

She met his gaze. "The accomplishment?" she asked quietly and he knew she understood. Just as he'd known she would from the moment she looked up at him from the bus station floor with her brown eyes, first assessing, then filled with calm acceptance.

"I think that's the biggest thing. I was part of something bigger than just me. I was doing something important. Using everything I'd learned to protect my country. To make a difference in the world. Some people think that's old-fashioned and corny."

She swallowed hard, but didn't break eye contact. "I don't."

"I didn't think you would."

"So what makes you feel important now?"

He drew in a breath that seemed to burn his lungs. *Not much,* he thought. *Certainly not finding Alec.* "I don't know."

She said nothing for a long minute. Then leaned over and kissed his lips. "Thank you."

She was close. So close that if he moved his head he'd be kissing her again. "For?"

"For telling me. I'm so glad I came tonight. You make me feel better, Ethan."

Something had changed. "I could make you feel even better."

Her generous mouth curved against his. Butterfly kisses. "I seem to recall a certain someone promising to make a certain other someone forget her own name."

He raised his brows. "And?"

"Da-na. D-A-N-A. Dana Danielle Dupinsky. I remember all my names."

His hands skimmed up, pausing at the sides of her breasts. From this distance he could see her eyes darken. Could hear her heart beat harder. And his teasing threat now became so much more. She'd come here to feel better and she wouldn't leave until she did. Until they both did. He trailed the backs of his fingers along the underside of her full breasts, let his thumbs flick over her nipples, just once. And heard her breath catch.

"Good old triple-D," he murmured.

Her swallow was audible in the quiet room, her answer husky. Aroused. "In your dreams, Buchanan."

"You're right. They have been. But I'm damn tired of dreaming."

A flash of her eyes was the only warning she gave before abruptly shifting, throwing her leg across his lap so that she straddled him. "So wake up." And when she crushed

374

her mouth to his, every last nerve in his body did.

With a groan he lurched forward, grabbed her butt, and pulled her down on him, pushing her skirt out of the way so that there was nothing between them but denim and slick, wet nylon. It was still way too much. Her hands were on his chest, on his shoulders, tearing at his shirt, and he jerked his arms out of his sleeves. She pulled her shirt over her head and sent it sailing as his fingers fumbled with the hooks of her bra. Then it was gone and her breasts were pressed against him, her nipples hard as diamond bits. She froze at that first delicious contact, her eyes closed, her head tilted back, as if absorbing the feel of them together. As if it had been an eternity since she'd done so.

"Dana," he rasped and in slow motion her chin dropped and her eyes opened, slumberous and smoldering. "How long has it been?"

"Five years." Not taking her eyes from his, she wriggled her hips, grinding against him, and he groaned again. "Five very long years."

His heart gave one hard slam against his ribs and he threaded his fingers through her copper hair and pulled her mouth back to his. His other hand filled itself with one glorious breast and he kissed her and kissed her.

And he kissed her. It was more than she'd hoped, more than she'd expected. More than she'd dreamed. She pulled her lips from his and kissed her way across his face as she lifted to her knees. He muttered a protest at the loss of contact until she tunneled her fingers through his hair and pulled his mouth to her breast and once again closed her eyes as he feasted and suckled and tongued. Sharp currents arced down her body, straight to the place that wept for him and she pressed against the hard plane of his chest, trying to find relief from the awesome need that only this man had awakened in her.

Then his hands were pulling at her panties and his fingers found her, plunged deep inside, and sent her gasping over the edge. She cried out as she came and Ethan went stiff beneath her, sucking her other breast with a ferocity just short of pain, his thumb continuing to stroke her inside, pushing her higher until she arched her back, his name on her lips when the world shattered into a million pieces. Spent, she collapsed against him, panting, her heart a wild thing in her breast.

With a growl he came to his feet, holding her in his arms as her legs still straddled his waist. Without a word he crossed the small suite to the bedroom and in a smooth movement dropped her on the bed and pulled her panties down her legs. And they were gone. With difficulty she opened her eyes, watched him ease his zipper down with a grimace. Watched his erection spring free.

Drew a deep breath, part appreciation, part apprehension. He was a mountain of a man. In every way. He jerked his jeans down his hips, then bent over to retrieve a condom from his pocket. "Take off your skirt."

Not taking her eyes from him, she complied, lifting herself on her heels so she could unbutton the waistband, unzip the zipper. Impatient, he yanked and the skirt joined his jeans on the floor. Then he was above her, his hands level with her head, one knee bracketing her hip, one foot on the floor. "Is this what you want?" he gritted and wordlessly she nodded. He put the condom in her hand. "Then you put it on."

Hands trembling she complied, feeling his whole body jerk when she touched him for the first time. His breath expelled on a hiss. "Dammit, Dana, hurry." She did and lifted her eyes to his. Felt her heart skip a full beat. He was hot. Ready. For her.

He slowly lowered himself between her thighs. And groaned. Even more slowly he entered, grimacing when she winced. "I'm sorry," he muttered, sweat beading on his brow.

She held his gaze with those calm brown eyes. "I'm not."

It was what she'd said the first time he'd kissed her. He kissed her now, voracious, openmouthed. Needing everything she'd willingly give him and some things she might not. He nudged and rolled his hips until he was in her as deep as he could get, then groaned again when she lifted her knees and took him deeper. "You feel so damn good."

She hummed in pleasure. "My middle name's becoming fuzzy, Ethan, but my first name is still crystal clear."

With a hoarse laugh he began to move, then his voice broke when she clenched her internal muscles and stroked him. "More." He didn't care that he begged. "Please."

So she did, and he did, setting a rhythmic pace. She was tight and she was wet and she was his and he wished he could stay inside her just like this forever. But then her face changed, her breath hitched. Her hands clutched at his shoulders and she started to whimper. "Ethan."

The sound of her voice dragged him under and his hips plunged, taking everything she had to give. Her hands were on his ass, her nails scoring deep. She was bucking under him and then she was arching again, crying his name, pulling him into the current, the dark blessed current, and he let go.

Fell. Arms straining, lungs burning, teeth bared, he came so hard he saw white lights twinkling before his eyes. But there was no darkness. No panic. Just peace.

He dropped his head to her shoulder, his heart thundering as if it would burst. Her hands went limp, her arms slid bonelessly to the bed. For a full minute there was nothing but the sound of strident breathing.

"Ethan?"

"Hmm?"

"Who am I?"

The laugh on his lips fizzled as realization struck him. *Mine. You're mine.* He raised up on his elbows to look down at her. Any and all little quips had fled his mind. He could only stare into those brown eyes and watch them stare back. Her curving lips went sober and she traced his mouth with her fingertips.

"What are we going to do now?" he murmured.

The tip of her tongue stole out to moisten her lips. "I have no idea."

His body did, though, stirring back to life and her eyes widened and her breath caught. "Maybe I do," she whispered, arching against him.

"That's not what I meant, Dana."

Her hips stilled. "I know. But for now, can it be?"

He hung there, still buried inside her. And tried not to let her words hurt. She'd told him at the beginning she wasn't looking for a relationship. Well, hell. She'd found one, whether she liked it or not. She'd just lost a friend. The doctor. And gained another. *Me*. He pressed a kiss to her forehead. "For now, we sleep."

# Chapter Fourteen

*Chicago,*
*Tuesday, August 3, 10:15 p.m*

Ethan woke with a jolt when her back slammed into his chest, her feet skidding over the sheets as she tried to back away. She was dreaming, he realized. A nightmare.

He tightened his arm around her waist. "Dana."

She went abruptly still, her body covered in a thin sheen of sweat for the second time that evening. Her heart thudded like hell under his palm. He kissed her ear. "Sshh. It was just a dream. You want to talk about it?"

"No." It was a wispy sound and he pushed up on his elbow to look down at her face. She was pale in the light coming in the window. "I'm sorry. I didn't mean to wake you."

"It's all right, Dana." He kissed her temple. "I'm starving. I never did call room service."

Her smile was shaky. "I'm hungry, too."

He leaned back and switched on the light, picked up the phone and called for room service. "They said it would be at least forty-five minutes. Can you think of anything we can do for forty-five minutes to keep ourselves occupied so we don't fall back asleep?"

Color was returning to her face. "I might be able to think of a thing or two."

"Hmm." Was all he said. Then without warning he stripped the sheet, making her gasp.

"Ethan!"

"Roll over, Dupinsky." He gave her a little shove. "Right now."

She was looking up at him like he'd lost every marble he owned. "What?"

"I want to see the tattoo."

"Oh, that." Obligingly she rolled over and he laughed out loud.

"So passé, Dana. On your butt." One on each cheek, to be exact.

She glared up at him. "What, you think I'm going to put them on my shoulder?"

He blinked, thinking of the video woman. "No, that would be a bad place for a tattoo."

She dropped her forehead to the pillow. "Besides . . . I couldn't look at the needle."

He scooted down, getting close to her curvy rear end. "You've got to be kidding."

She blew out a breath. "Charlie played in a band. Called themselves Born2Kill."

He smacked a kiss next to the skull with the knife in its teeth. "The butterfly's cute."

"The butterfly is a symbol of life." She rolled over and pulled at the sheet, rolling her eyes when he held it out of her grasp. "I'm cold."

He flopped to his side, pulled her close until they were nose to nose. "Symbol of life?"

Her eyes shifted, sobered. "I got it the day I filed for divorce."

"Then I like the butterfly best." He kissed her, felt her relax in his arms.

"You only have forty minutes, Ethan," she murmured against his lips. "Get busy."


*Chicago,*
*Wednesday, August 4, 8:15 a.m.*


Dana reached out and hit an empty pillow. She drew in a deep, heady breath, unwilling to open her eyes. But the day was wasting. She could feel the sun on her face already.

She lifted her head, wincing when her body informed her she wasn't a young woman any longer. But even young she would have been sore after a night like they'd shared. She opened her eyes to a clock that read 8:15 a.m. and an empty pillow bearing a note and remembered him telling her he'd have to leave early for more appointments.

Stiffly she sat up and grabbed the note and chuckled. *Dear Dana,* he'd written, *I hope by morning the memory of your name has returned. If not, you're Dana Danielle Dupinsky and you're not a photographer. As to the "Born2Kill" tattoo on your left cheek, I have only to ask, "What were you thinking?" I'll call you later. Sweet dreams. Ethan.*

She slid from the bed. She'd dreamed the same old nightmare, but after that one bad one, she'd dreamed sweet dreams for the first time in years. One of the last dreams was Ethan filling her, but she'd woken to find it reality and for a third time he'd brought her to a climax so powerful the only name she could remember was his.

But now it was time to work. She'd lost a full day away from the House. She'd call Dr. Lee's family today, she thought soberly. Offer to help with the funeral arrangements. And Beverly was leaving today, for California. She was supposed to drive Beverly to the bus station this morning. It was one of her favorite things, seeing women off to start a new life.

Mia had told her not to go near the shelter, just in case she was followed, but Dana refused to give up the one activity she most enjoyed. Beverly would need to meet her close to the bus station. Dana picked up the hotel phone on the nightstand. "Evie?"

"Where have you been?" Evie exploded. "We have been looking all over for you. You had me scared to death."

"Oh, I'm sorry." She was. She'd never considered someone would be looking for her. Given Dr. Lee and Caroline and Goodman, she should have. "Evie, that was thoughtless of me. I didn't mean to scare you. I'm fine."

"I called that cell phone number you gave me and it just rang."

Dana frowned, then remembered Ethan pulling her skirt to her waist on the sofa in the other room. Her cell phone had probably fallen out of her pocket. "I must have left it in another room. I stayed with a friend last night."

"Which one?" Evie asked suspiciously. "Mia says you didn't stay with her."

So they'd been beating the bushes. "A friend you haven't met yet."

Stunned silence. "You have a *boyfriend* and you haven't introduced him yet?"

"You and I have not exactly been on the best of terms this last week," Dana said wryly.

"I suppose not." Evie's tone was equally wry. "Well, when we get off the phone you need to call David. He's worried sick and he's been lying to Caroline all night telling her he's talked to you so she wouldn't worry. You really had us whipped into a frenzy."

Dana sighed. He would have been worried. "I will. Evie, Mia doesn't want me coming near the shelter, just in case Goodman comes looking for me next. I don't want you leaving either and keep the doors locked, especially the kitchen door. You always forget."

"I won't forget today. What about Beverly? She's packed and ready to go."

"Have her meet me at Betty's coffee shop in an hour. I'll walk her to the bus from there. Her papers are locked in my desk. You know where to find the key. Give them to her."

"I will. Dana, about Dr. Lee . . . I'm sorry."

Sorrow welled and Dana swallowed it back. "I know. Me, too. Evie, I'm sorry about a lot of things. I know I don't say it often enough, but I love you."

Dana heard Evie clear her throat. "I love you, too."


*Chicago,*
*Wednesday, August 4, 9:00 a.m.*

Security Manager Bill Bush placed a cup of coffee next to the monitor Ethan had been staring at for hours. "You're the most persistent P.I. I've had come through in a while."

"Thank you." Ethan took the coffee with significant gratitude. "I decided the laws of physics preclude this woman I'm looking for from simply disappearing, so she must have boarded another bus because she didn't exit the station Friday morning."

"Fair assumption." Bush sat down in his creaky chair.

"I know she was in Chicago on Monday morning, because she sent an e-mail to the kid's father." Ethan had his story carefully catalogued in his head. They'd told Bush they were looking for a mother who'd violated a custody agreement. Ostensibly they would not be searching for the woman's face. They'd know what she looked like and Bush was smart enough to pick up on that. "I want to get tape of her leaving with the kid so we can have it when we take her to court for violating the terms of the custody agreement. Then maybe the boy's dad can get full custody."

Bush studied him carefully. "You so sure the mom's not the better parent?"

"Oh, yeah. Anyway, knowing she was in Chicago on Monday, I figure she had to have come through here sometime between Friday morning and Monday morning. I've been watching only the exits. I'm up to Friday night at nine-fifteen."

"You should take a break. You're looking twitchy." He shot Ethan a long look that it didn't take a genius to read. Bush knew something wasn't kosher. "One of the things I learned in twenty-five years on the force is that it's not a bad thing to need help every now and again. That it doesn't make you less of a . . ." He let the thought trail. "Cop."

"I'm not a cop," Ethan said.

"That you're not," Bush agreed. "Soldier maybe, cop not."

"Not a soldier, either." It was a reflexive snap. Marines were not soldiers. Marines were Marines. From Bush's reaction, it was exactly what he'd expected Ethan to say. He'd played right into the old man's hands.

Bush chuckled. "Where'd you serve, Buchanan?"

"Afghanistan."

Bush grimaced. "Sand."

Ethan nodded grimly. "Hell, yes."

"You quit the Corps?"

Ethan shook his head. "Med-down. Land mine followed by a sniper attack."

"I was in 'Nam. Government discharged most of us in the seventies. Became a cop."

"So did my partner. Became a cop, that is. I probably couldn't pass the eye test now."

"Hell, boy. I couldn't pass any of the Academy's tests now. I'm too damn old. But I served as long as I could and I'm proud of what I did. So did you and so should you."

Ethan hesitated, then went with his gut. "I'm looking for this woman, but she manages to stay a few steps ahead of me. I've got pictures from the neck down, but never her face."

"Kid's daddy didn't have any pictures of her face?"

Ethan met Bush's gaze unflinchingly. "She looks different now."

Bush grunted. "Women are good at that. You sure she's the bad apple, Buchanan?"

"Very sure."

"You got those pictures with you?"

Ethan patted his briefcase. "Right here."

Bush rolled his eyes. "Do you need an engraved invitation, boy? Let's have 'em." He wiped his hands clean and took the photos. Gave a low wolf whistle.

"Yeah, modesty does not seem to be her strong suit."

"Hiding in broad daylight," Bush said. "She's got a tattoo."

"I know. I've gotten a few shots of it. Starts with *A*."

"I'm not talking about that one. I'm talking about this one." Bush squinted and held one of the close-ups of her hands up to the light. "Prison tattoo, right here on her ring finger. See the little cross just below her knuckle? Means she did time."

Ethan wasn't looking at her knuckles. He was looking at her hands. Holding the sign language book that reflected the light off its glossy surface. She wasn't wearing gloves. The book was very glossy. There would be prints. And if she'd served time, her prints would be in the system. He'd been so intent on seeing her face, he'd neglected her hands.

They might finally have something for the cops. He needed to talk to Clay.

*Chicago,*
*Wednesday, August 4, 9:00 a.m.*

Well, Ruby was wrong this time, Sue thought as she looked out the window to the street in front of the shelter. Evie was hugging Beverly, the woman due to go to California today. Ruby had assured her that Dupinsky always drove the departing client away from Hanover House in a grand ceremony, but it would seem Dupinsky had become busy with a new boyfriend. How sweet.

But Beverly would not be singing "California, Here I Come" today. She turned to look at the kid who lay sleeping. Satisfied she'd sufficiently frightened him the day before, she grabbed her backpack and slipped from the shelter.

Alec waited a long time after the smell of stale cigarettes had lessened. Then opened his eyes a slit. She was gone. And she'd taken her backpack with her. He shuddered once again, remembering what he'd found inside. He struggled not to throw up, taking deep breaths until he felt steady again. She'd been asleep last night and he'd needed to know what she kept inside that backpack. Besides the doctor's glasses.

Now he knew. Besides the doctor's glasses he'd found a little cooler, the plastic kind his mom used when they went to the beach. It was cold. Alec swallowed back the bile that burned at his throat. It was filled with three plastic bags of ice. And one plastic bag of fingers. They'd looked like Halloween props, but they'd been very, very real. Alec drew a deep breath, gagging. Controlling it.

She'd killed that doctor. And he'd seemed so nice. She'd killed him and cut off his . . . Again he shuddered. Took great gasps of air. He was sweating, soaking wet. Had been all night. He looked down at his hands, made his fingers work if for no other reason than to assure himself they still did.

She'd killed Paul, and Cheryl, and now that doctor. And she would kill him. He was certain of it. He'd done nothing but think about it all night long. She said she'd kill his mother. Alec filled his lungs until they hurt. He couldn't be sure that she hadn't already. His mom could be dead, right now. But his mom wouldn't want him to die, too.

He had to do something or he'd die. Alec flexed his fingers. Or worse. He didn't even want to think about his life without fingers. He'd rather be dead. But he didn't want to be dead. *So do something. Do it now.*

Carefully he removed the one other thing he'd found inside the backpack, the thing he'd hidden under the covers. A plastic bag of white powder. He knew what this was. He'd read enough on the Internet to know exactly what he held in his hands. Cocaine. More than one person could use in a week, he thought. This was cocaine for selling. The bitch who'd stolen him was a drug dealer.

Alec knew his mother didn't like the word *bitch*. But his mother wasn't here. He was all alone. Well, maybe not all alone. There was the red-haired lady and the girl with the scar.

The girl with the scar was nice. She'd cried so hard last night and he'd known it was because the doctor was dead. Alec had read the note the doctor left behind. The doctor had cooperated with the white-eyed lady to save Alec's life. The girl with the scar didn't suspect the bitch of killing her doctor friend.

But she'd smiled at him through her tears. She'd washed his face yesterday morning, had stroked his hair the days before. He'd trust her. He flexed his fingers again, thinking of the cooler, of the fingers. He didn't have much of a choice.

Summoning the courage he hoped would make his parents proud, he took the bag of white powder and went in search of the girl with the scar. When she saw the powder, she'd call the police. When the police came, Alec would get a pencil and paper and tell them what he knew. The police he knew he could trust. His mother had told him so.

And if the girl with the scar didn't call the police and kept the white powder for herself . . . Well, then he'd know he couldn't trust her after all.


*Ocean City, Maryland,*
*Wednesday, August 4, 10:00 a.m. Eastern*
*(9:00 a.m. Central)*


James sat on the other side of the glass, waiting patiently. Today he'd know where Sue was. What her game was. Her brother should be very ready to talk right about now.

He tilted his head to one side as Bryce Lewis stumbled into the visitation room, his face one massive bruise. James imagined he had bruises other places as well. He hadn't really been specific after all. He wanted him hurt, but not so that he ended up in the clinic.

Lewis sat in the chair across from him, his body stiff, his face a study in stoic acceptance. "She's in Chicago," the boy said without preamble.

"Why?"

"She's taken a kid with her. His name is Alexander Vaughn."

A connection. The Vaughns owned the beach house where the body had been found. She'd kidnapped their child. Now he had to figure out how the Vaughns connected to the woman he'd tracked to Florida. The woman Sue had killed. "How much is the ransom?"

"A million dollars."

"And your share?"

"Half."

James laughed. "She'd never give you half. Where is she hiding in Chicago?"

"She was going to hide in my uncle's house."

"Impossible. Their house burned to the ground. Bad habit they had, smoking in bed."

"They were innocent old people," Lewis said hoarsely. "Why?"

Lewis's eyes glazed with tears and James stood up. "Same reason your sister did an old woman in Florida and that guy in the shed. Because she could, and so can I."

Sue was in Chicago with a kid. She'd go stir crazy if she hid too long. And when she popped her head from her hidey-hole, he'd be there. He checked his watch. He could be in Chicago before dinnertime.

*Chicago,*
*Wednesday, August 4, 10:00 a.m.*

Evie sat staring at the bag of coke on the kitchen table. Erik had brought it to her, saying absolutely nothing, his eyes solemn, but alert. So watchful. As if he was just waiting for what she'd do next. She'd called Dana right away. On that new cell phone that had been a gift. But once again it rang and rang. She'd tried again with no success, only getting the canned message that came with the phone. She'd left messages for Dana. Three times. She'd called

Dana's pager three more times.

She'd called Mia, but Mia was off-duty and not on-call. Would she like to leave a message? the police operator had asked. No, she would not. She couldn't call Caroline. Nobody was supposed to stress Caroline right now and Evie imagined this qualified as major stress. The most important thing was getting Erik out of Hanover House and somewhere safe. She rubbed her head. Wished she knew what to do.

Then she remembered the woman who worked with Dana when they needed to go through Department of Children's Services. Dana trusted her. Her name was Sandra Stone.

Evie got through the first time and thought it must be kismet. "Miss Stone, my name is Evie Wilson. I work with Dana Dupinsky."

There was a guarded pause, then, "What can I do for you, Miss Wilson?"

Evie looked at Erik with his big solemn eyes in that pinched, thin face. She gave him what she hoped was a reassuring smile as he munched on the peanut butter and jelly sandwich she'd made him. "I've got a problem, Miss Stone, and I'm hoping you can help me."

Ethan was switching to the next surveillance tape when his cell phone buzzed in his pocket. He'd called Clay right after seeing the sign language book in the woman's hand, but just got voice mail. Clay was finally calling him back.

Bypassing salutations, Ethan snapped, "Where have you been?"

"A little busy." Clay's voice was drawn. Tight. "So we finally got something?"

"Finally, yeah. Yesterday at the bookstore, she touched the book she was reading without gloves. I think we should buy every copy of the sign language book the bookstore had on the shelves. We can get prints. And now we know she's in the system."

"How do you know?" Clay asked, strangely. Almost detached.

Ethan frowned. Something was very wrong. "She has a prison tattoo on her finger."

Clay was quiet for a moment. "Let the police gather that evidence."

Ethan frowned as he set the VCR to play. "Why?"

"Because we have to bring them in now.

398

Sheriff Moore knows Alec's gone."

Ethan slumped back in the chair. "How?"

"She's a damn good cop, that's how," Clay snapped. "She didn't believe Stan's story about Alec being with his grandparents in Europe. She had her office check with the Customs Office and found out this morning that no passport was issued to Alec Vaughn. Therefore Alec can't be in England with his grandparents. Therefore *we lied*."

"Oh, shit," Ethan murmured. "What happened?"

"Stan clammed up. Randi went pale and I stood there and looked at her as if I had no idea what she was talking about. What was I supposed to do? Then Stan got nasty and asked if he needed a lawyer. Moore said no, but that she'd appreciate it if he didn't leave town. Then on her way out she asked me if I knew a guy named Johnson. He was my captain in DCPD."

"So she knows a great deal," Ethan murmured. "Well, hell." He sat in silence watching the gray figures move silently across the monitor on the tape from last Friday night. A group had just arrived on the Friday ten-thirty p.m. bus from someplace south. Hillsboro, he thought absently.

They had four known dead. Kristie Sikorski had been found yesterday in an alley. They had kidnapping, which was a felony in its own right. Transport over state lines, which would have brought in the FBI. And after four days of miserable searching, they finally had something to go on. He'd have to march into the local police department and confess. And hope he hadn't done too little, too late.

Ethan sighed. "I'll go report it now, Clay. Tell Stan and Randi."

"It's the right thing to do, Ethan."

"I suppose it was the right thing to do Friday night." Ironic, he thought. The tape he was looking at was made right about the time he and Clay had traced the first e-mail.

"You did what you thought was right. I agreed with you. I'm in this as deep as you are."

"I'm sorry."

"Don't be. Just go report all this to CPD before anybody else gets killed."

Ethan watched the crowd on Friday night's tape disperse, then froze. "Wait."

"Ethan —"

Ethan was on his feet. "No, I mean it. Here they are. I see them. It's Alec."

It was the woman, holding Alec by the

upper arm, dragging him across the terminal. Practically lifting him to his feet when he stumbled. She was still wearing the damn hat, but he could see Alec. "She's heading toward the east exit," Ethan said tightly. Then watched the pair pause.

And his heart simply stopped.

For out of the shadows came a woman in a sleeveless polo shirt and a cotton skirt. She went down on one knee in front of Alec, tried to get the boy to look up, brushed at his hair when he didn't. Ethan tried to breathe.

He couldn't.

"Ethan? Are you still there?"

"Yes." He made himself say the word, forced it from his throat.

"Dammit, Ethan, what the hell's wrong with you?"

Ethan blindly sank into the chair. Watched Dana put her arm around the woman that had kidnapped a child and killed four people that they knew about. He watched her tip up the woman's chin and he blinked at the first glimpse of their kidnapper's face. It was bruised and battered, unrecognizable. He watched the pain cross Dana's face as her eyes catalogued every bruise.

That she could be involved in something so heinous was unthinkable. Impossible.

Runaways. Dana volunteered with runaways. Runaway *women,* not teenagers as he'd assumed. The bruises on the woman's face looked real. Dana sheltered battered women.

*"Ethan,"* Clay all but snarled. "What's happened?"

Ethan paused the video, freezing the frame as Dana bestowed one of her warm smiles on the woman who'd stolen his godson. The same smile she'd given him just hours before, curled up in his arms. In his bed. "I know where Alec is."

*Chicago,*
*Wednesday, August 4, 12:00 p.m.*

She should have showered at the Sheraton, Dana thought, toweling her hair. It had to have had better water pressure than the little trickle in her shower. Critically she looked at her reflection in the bathroom mirror, tilted her head to one side. Saw on her neck the shadows of a small bruise put there by Ethan's mouth. She swallowed hard. What a mouth that man had. Just the thought of his mouth

402

made her want him all over again.

She'd come straight to her apartment after dropping Beverly off at the bus station. She couldn't go to the shelter and she really needed some clean clothes, so she'd chanced a trip to her apartment, looking over her shoulder all the time. Her gun sat on the back of the toilet, just in case. But, she realized as she pushed her skirt into an overflowing hamper, she'd left both her pager and her new cell phone in Ethan's room. So she'd called the hotel and left a message with the front desk. *Call me at home.* She left her home phone number — not something she'd ever done with a man before.

Now she rummaged through the basket under her sink, found the bottle of perfume Caroline had given her for Christmas. She'd never used it. She'd use it today, hoping to please Ethan.

With a sigh she again regarded her image in the mirror. "What will you do when he's ready to go home?" she murmured. While under a load of guilt and fear and shock, she'd decided yesterday to leave Chicago. Today, she knew it was still the right decision. She could do her work anywhere. Even Washington, D.C.

She could live near Ethan. It was a heady

thought. Unless . . . She bit her lip. Unless he wouldn't want her there. What if this was just a fling for him? Was it any more for her? It wasn't supposed to have been, but it was. Unquestionably. And Dana didn't lie to herself.

A brisk knock at her front door made her frown. Nobody knocked on her door in the daytime. Goodman? She shrugged into her robe and slid her gun in its pocket. Walking resolutely to the door, she checked the peephole and gaped for a full five seconds before slowly opening the door.

Ethan stood before her, his face grim. "Dana, we need to talk."

*Chicago,*
*Wednesday, August 4, 12:00 p.m.*

"I came as soon as I could get away." Sandy Stone was a fortyish woman with graying hair and thick glasses. But her eyes were kind and Evie knew Dana trusted her.

"Thank you. I didn't know what else to do. I called Dana's cell phone and her pager and even her phone at her apartment, but it just rang. So I called you."

Evie led her back to the kitchen where Erik sat silently, his large eyes still watching. "This is Erik. His mother goes by Jane Smith."

Sandy sighed. "Original."

"We get a lot of them," Evie said. She ran her hand over Erik's hair, smiled down at him. "Erik's mother is less attentive than some mothers we get here. I've worried that Erik's not getting enough nutrition and that she might be improperly medicating him. But this morning Erik brought me this." Evie tapped the table next to the bag of white powder. She'd been loath to even touch it, avoiding it as if it were a snake poised to strike.

Sandy drew a very deep breath. "This belonged to your mother, Erik?"

Erik just looked at them, his eyes darting from Evie's face to Sandy's. And said nothing.

"If his mother has brought drugs into his environment, I can take him now and come back for her later." Sandy tapped the bag with her pen and Erik's eyes followed the movement. Then Sandy asked again. "Does this belong to your mother?"

"Yes, as a matter of fact it does."

With a gasp Evie spun. Standing in the kitchen doorway was Jane. But not the

Jane who arrived a few days before broken-spirited and bowed over. This Jane stood tall and strong. And wore Evie's makeup.

And this Jane held a gun.

"You meddling women just can't leave well enough alone," Jane said. Her creepy light blue eyes narrowed. She pointed the gun at Evie and for a moment Evie was transported back. Two years. She'd been at the mercy of a man with that same cold, dead look in his eyes. He'd hurt her. She'd never be the same again. She couldn't fight back that day. Today . . . Evie's hand tightened on Erik's thin shoulder, felt the bite of his bone as he pressed closer to her chest. Today there was a great deal more at stake. She thought about what Dana would do and felt her mind settle. Coldly, Evie met Jane's reptilian stare.

"I don't consider it a failing. Who are you?"

Jane just smiled, and Evie's blood ran cold. "Get paper and a pen," she said. *Now.*

Evie looked at Sandy, who looked shaken. "You should do what she says, Evie," Sandy murmured. Evie looked down at Erik who was pale and trembling. But there was a resolute tightness to his lips as he stared at the woman with the gun.

Evie found a piece of paper and pen in

the junk drawer, wishing with all her might that Dana kept her gun here at Hanover House. "I have paper and pen."

"Then write this down. 'We're leaving. If you behave Evie will live.' *Write it.*"

Evie looked at Erik and comprehension dawned. "He's deaf. That's why . . ."

Jane looked amused. "Kewpie doll for you. Now hurry up, I want to get out of here."

Evie wrote the words, then pointed to her written name, then to herself.

Erik's eyes flashed and his jaw set and he suddenly looked much older than ten. And Evie knew he knew the same thing she did. There was no way Jane was planning to let any of them live. She made her mouth curve and didn't care that it was only half a smile. "It'll be okay," Evie said and hoped Erik could understand.

"I wouldn't get my hopes up if I were you," Jane said. "Who called the social worker, you or Dupinsky?"

Evie lifted her chin. "I did. I didn't need Dana for this." It was a lie, but the only way she knew to keep Dana safe. "Besides, she and I have been fighting all week."

Jane considered it, then nodded. "That you have. You, social worker, I suppose you left word with your office as to where you were going."

Sandy hesitated, unsure of what Jane wanted to hear. "It's procedure," she whispered.

Jane laughed. "Of course it is. Well, just to make you feel better, you would have picked the same prize whichever door you opened. Either way, I can't stay here anymore, which pisses me off. The bed is hard as a rock, but the beef stew was really tasty. On the floor, on your stomach. I really, really hate social workers by the way," she added companionably. "Just thought you'd like to know."

Evie didn't think she'd ever forget the look in Sandy's eyes as she struggled to the floor. The woman knew what was going to happen and Evie knew there wasn't anything either of them could do to stop it. All she could do was pull Erik's face to her chest to keep him from watching Sandy die.

# Chapter Fifteen

*Chicago,*
*Wednesday, August 4, 12:15 p.m.*

Dana met his eyes and her stomach went queasy. "Why are you here, Ethan?"

He didn't relax his gaze. "I need to talk to you."

"No, I mean why are you in Chicago?"

He flinched, then reached into his pocket for his phone, his eyes still focused on hers. "Yeah," he said into the phone. "I'm here."

Dana took a physical step back and he took a step forward, maintaining their distance, and in that moment she actually considered drawing her gun from her pocket.

"No, not yet. Tell her to be patient." He listened, then his eyes grew wide, horrified, and Dana watched every drop of color drain from his face. "Dear God." It was a whisper. A horrible one. Ethan's lips trembled and he firmed them. "His?" He ex-

409

pelled a hard breath. "Yeah. Tell them to come. . . . The Sheraton . . . Yeah, call me when you get here." He snapped his phone closed. "You have a gun in your pocket, Dana. Why?"

Dana swallowed. He was different, this Ethan. Brooding and dangerous. Nothing like the man who had loved her so tenderly the night before. "Dangerous neighborhood." She lifted her chin. "Why are you in my apartment and who is the *she* that should be patient?"

"Her name is Randi Vaughn. She's Stan's wife."

"Richard's brother."

"Yes. Randi's son Alec was kidnapped a week ago."

Dana didn't flinch, although every muscle in her body wanted to do so. "What does that have to do with me?"

Temper crackled in his eyes. "I tracked Alec here, to Chicago. I've been watching surveillance video in every major bus station between Maryland and Chicago. That's what I was doing on Sunday. What were you doing in the bus station on Sunday, Dana?"

Her throat threatened to close. *He knew.* "I told you. I was meeting a friend."

His eyes flashed. "Why won't you tell

me? Dana, don't you understand? I know who you are and what you do."

Her heart was beating too fast. "Why are you here, Ethan?"

He leaned a little closer. "Dammit, Dana. Friday night at ten forty-five you met a woman and a twelve-year-old boy. She kidnapped that child and you have been hiding them."

Her heart was hammering. Jane. Erik. She'd known something was wrong with that woman. With the boy. *But not this. Not this. There must be some mistake. He must be mistaken. I can't have missed that. Not that.* She looked away, unable to take his stare any longer. "Ten," she murmured. "He's ten."

Ethan's lips firmed. "He's twelve. I ought to know. He's my godson." Abruptly he pulled her to her toes until their eyes were inches apart. *"Is he alive?"*

Dana nodded. Slowly. His godson. He wasn't mistaken. *Dear God.* "Yes. He's weak, nonresponsive at times, but he's alive."

"What do you mean nonresponsive? Unconscious?"

"He sleeps a lot. And when you talk to him he doesn't respond."

"That's because *he's deaf,* dammit. *Where is he?*" He gave her shoulders a

411

desperate little shake. "Dammit, tell me where he is."

She winced now as his fingers bit into the flesh of her arms. *Erik is deaf.* That explained a great deal. "He's in my shelter. He's safe there. Ethan, you're hurting me."

Ethan dropped his hands and she rubbed her upper arms. "Where is your shelter?"

Her eyes flew up, wide and wary. "No. That I won't tell you."

Ethan drew a slow breath, controlled the fury that made him want to shake her again, just to make her *understand.* "You still don't *get it.* The woman you're hiding kidnapped a child and is holding him for five million dollars' ransom. The woman you're hiding just sent Alec's parents a severed finger in the mail."

She stood staring at him with a face so pale he thought she'd pass out. He grabbed her arms when she sagged. Hauled her up on her toes again. Made her look in his eyes. "The woman you're hiding has murdered four people, Dana. *Nobody in your shelter is safe.*"

She dropped like a marionette with sliced strings and sat on her sofa staring up at him in absolute horror. "Oh, my God." Then horror gave way to shocked panic as the truth sank in and she jolted forward. "Evie is there." She grabbed his arm and pulled herself to her feet. "I'll get dressed. Wait." She flew back to her bedroom, stumbling as she went. Ethan followed her back and watched as she dropped the robe, yanked on underwear. "I didn't know. I didn't know." She chanted it under her breath, as if the words gave her momentum to move. Her hands fumbled with the bra and managed it. Ethan had a shirt ready and pulled it over her head.

"Hurry, Dana. Please hurry."

She dragged on a skirt and looked up at him her brown eyes terrified and filled with terrible soul-wrenching guilt. "Ethan, I didn't know. I swear it."

He pulled her close for a fast, hard hug. "I know, baby. Let's go."


*Wight's Landing, Maryland,*
*Wednesday, August 4, 2:00 p.m. Eastern*
*(1:00 p.m. Central)*

Dora stuck her head in the office. "Sheriff, you have a Sheriff Eastman from up in Ocean City on line two."

"This is Sheriff Moore. What can I do for you?"

"I have some information for you," Eastman said. "Your boy Lewis got a visitor yesterday, right after you and Janson left. Name of the guy was James Lorenzano. They talked for a few minutes, then Lorenzano left. He was back today."

"Oh?" Lou was writing down the name. "Lorenzano?"

"Yes. I had my office run a check on his ID. Minor mob ties in New York. In between Lorenzano's two visits Lewis was beaten."

"Does Janson know?"

"I called him. I tried to talk to the kid but he's not saying a word. I'll keep you informed."

"Thanks." Lou hung up the phone with a frown. D.C. security consultants, New York mobsters? An engaged couple murdered three hundred miles apart? And the Vaughns. She couldn't forget about them. They'd lied about the whereabouts of their son.

"Sheriff," Dora called. "Janson on three."

When it rained. "Hey, Janson. I just talked to Eastman from Ocean City."

"He called me, too. I wanted you to know something new."

"Forensics on Rickman's car?"

"Not back yet. But I questioned the clerks in the bus terminal today and they told me there was a guy asking a lot of questions Friday night. He asked to see the surveillance video. Gave some story about investigating a child custody matter. Ethan Buchanan."

Lou wrote it down next to Lorenzano's name. "Thanks." Lou knew exactly where she'd seen Buchanan's name before. She hung up the phone and pulled up Clay Maynard's company Website. Sure enough, there was Buchanan, just as she'd remembered.

"He used to play baseball with my kid," Huxley said, coming in to look over her shoulder. "Grandmother was Lucinda Banks. Raised that boy right. Went into the Marine Corps."

Huxley was her main source of information, usually whether she wanted it or not. Today they were both happy. "He's not in the Marines anymore."

"Combat injury in Afghanistan. He was with Richard Vaughn. Vaughn didn't make it."

"That would be Stan Vaughn's older brother?"

Huxley's lips thinned. "Older and better. Stan couldn't come close to filling his brother's shoes. Big disappointment to Dick and Edna. Those boys used to run all summer. My Zach would play with 'em from time to time. But Ethan and Richard were tight, best friends, and eventually Zach got tired of playing third wheel. You know how it is with kids."

So Mr. Buchanan was old friends with the Vaughns. And he'd been asking questions in Morgantown. "I think it's time to pay another visit to the Vaughns."

"Can't," said Huxley.

Lou looked up at him with a frown. "Why not?"

"Just took off in Stan Vaughn's private plane. I checked with the control tower. Flight plan says they're going to Chicago. You said they weren't under arrest, so I didn't detain them. All of 'em went up. Stan and Randi and that houseguest of theirs."

Lou huffed a frustrated sigh. "I wonder if the budget would cover a ticket to Chicago."

Dora appeared at the door. "You leave out of Reagan National at five. With the time difference, you'll be there at six. I got you a hotel out in the suburbs to save some money. You'll be needing a rental car. You comfortable driving in Chicago, Sheriff?"

Lou had to laugh. "I'm not sure how I managed in Boston PD without you two."

Dora just beamed. "Thank you, Sheriff."

"Now, if you can tell me where the Vaughns are staying, I'll have everything I need."

"Chicago Sheraton," Huxley said, then looked sheepish. "The guy who handled their suitcases remembers Miss Randi mentioning it."

Lou grinned up at him. "Huxley, why aren't you the sheriff?"

"Because he wouldn't have enough time for fishing," Dora stated.

Huxley's face had reddened charmingly. But his mouth tightened and his expression grew sober. "One other thing, Sheriff. When I got back to my desk, there was a package waiting for me. It was addressed to you."

Lou stood up, now as sober as he. "Where is it?"

"Still there. I didn't touch it."

Lou was already through the door. "Why didn't you tell me that first?"

She heard Huxley's sigh behind her. "That's why I'm not the sheriff."

Dana slid her key in the lock. Felt her heart stop when the door gave even before she turned the key. "It's unlocked. Evie promised me she'd keep it locked." Pictures rushed to the front of her mind, bile rising in her throat as she remembered Evie two years before, lying slashed and bloody with a length of twine twisted deep into her neck. A maniac had once left her friend for dead. *This time I brought the maniac here myself.*

She was trembling now, so hard she could barely hold the doorknob. *Pull yourself together, Dupinsky.* Maybe she just forgot to lock the door again. But even as she pushed the door open, she knew it wasn't so. Then she saw the sprawled figure on the floor and hissed out an oath, instantly recognizing her.

In two steps she was on her knees next to the woman lying in a pool of blood. Turning her over. It was surreal. It was her worst nightmare.

But Dana was awake. Ethan dropped to his knees beside her.

"Evie?" he asked tersely.

Dana shook her head, trying to hold her

thoughts together. To keep calm. "No." It was Sandy Stone. *Evie must have called her,* was all Dana could think as she pressed shaking fingers to Sandy's throat. And felt nothing. Sandy was dead. Something had gone wrong and Evie had called Sandy to take Erik away from Jane. *Where are Evie and Erik? Where is Jane?*

Then from the doorway a voice asked, "Who is she, Dana?"

Dana looked up with a start to find Mia standing there, a frown on her face and a gun in her hand. Over Mia's shoulder loomed David, looking grim. Beside Dana, Ethan tensed, taut as a bow, his eyes fixed on Mia's gun. "It's Sandy Stone," she said to Mia, her voice shaking. "She's a social worker with Children's Services."

Shrewdly Mia assessed Ethan Buchanan, then lowered her weapon to her side. "Well, at least the note makes sense."

"Note?" Dana tried to focus on Mia's face.

"The note signed by Goodman saying how much he hated social workers and that the next dead social worker would be you. Various expletives deleted. But Goodman didn't do this, Dana. Detroit PD has him in custody as of this morning. So why is a social worker lying dead on your floor?"

Dana looked back to Sandy's body, then to her own bloody hands, her stomach roiling. Sandy was dead. "Where is Evie?" she asked, her voice hoarse and shaking.

"She's not here," David answered from behind Mia. "Ruby got home and Dylan was screaming, but nobody else was here. Ruby found my number on the refrigerator and called me and I called Detective Mitchell." Beside her Ethan went completely still.

"Where's Alec?" Ethan asked tightly.

David frowned. "Who?"

Dana forced herself to stand up. Forced her legs to hold her steady. "He means Erik."

Mia's gaze focused on Ethan when he lurched to his feet. "Is this Buchanan?"

Dana jerked a look back. Ethan was pale. "Ethan, this is Detective Mia Mitchell. She's with CPD. She's also my friend. Mia, Ethan's been looking for a missing little boy. A woman who called herself Jane Smith arrived Friday night. I picked her up at the bus station. She had a boy with her she called Erik. He's the same little boy Ethan's been looking for. Jane said Erik was her son, but he's not."

Mia pulled her notepad from her pocket, alert. "She kidnapped the boy? Why?"

"For the money," Ethan answered through his teeth. "She's demanded five million dollars in ransom."

Mia flicked him a look. "P.I.?"

"Yeah," Ethan said bitterly.

"And the boy? Who is he?"

"The boy is Alec Vaughn. He's my godson."

"Mia, Erik was the boy Dr. Lee came to examine yesterday."

Ethan grasped Dana's shoulder and pulled her around to look at him. "The man who was killed yesterday?" he demanded.

Dana nodded, fully aware now of what had happened.

"You think this Jane killed Dr. Lee?" Mia asked.

Dana looked up at Ethan and he shut his eyes. "She's killed four people that we know of," he said heavily. "Dr. Lee makes five. This social worker is six. I didn't know she was here until a few hours ago."

Mia looked drained. "Six murders. Do *any* law enforcement agencies know about this?"

Ethan shook his head. "She threatened to kill Alec if the police were contacted."

Mia sucked in her cheeks, her jaw taut, eyes flaring with unspoken recrimination.

"Well, let's hope we're not too late," she snapped. "Looks like she took the boy because he's certainly not here. I've checked the house, top to bottom. Was Evie here, too?"

Dana's stomach heaved as she finally allowed herself to think the words. *Jane had Evie.* Jane, who had killed so many already. Jane, who all Dana's instincts screamed was a problem. *I brought her here. Put everyone I loved in danger.* "Yes." Her own voice sounded like a stranger's. "Evie wouldn't have left Erik." Evie, who'd been through so much herself. *Please don't let Evie be dead. Please.*

"Detective," Ethan said slowly, a grimace on his face. "Did Dr. Lee have all his fingers when you found him?"

Dana pressed her hand to her mouth as her stomach violently churned.

Mia looked repulsed. "Yes. Please don't tell me . . ."

"Alec's parents received a severed finger today, a man's finger. They're on their way to Chicago as we speak."

Mia blew out a breath. "Oh, hell. I have to call this in and get my partner over here. Dana, sit down. You look like you're going to faint. Mr. Buchanan, we're going to have to talk and it's not going to be pleasant."

Ethan pulled out a chair and gently pushed Dana into it. Her eyes were glassy, staring at the dead woman on the floor. "I know," he said grimly. "And I have to call Alec's parents and tell them I lost him." He grabbed a towel from the counter and cleaned Dana's bloody hands. "Trust me, Detective, I'd much rather talk to you."

*Chicago,*
*Wednesday, August 4, 4:30 p.m.*

Detective Mia Mitchell paced the room while her partner sat at the scarred table in the interview room. Detective Abe Reagan had said little up until this point, just watched him with piercing blue eyes that made Ethan want to squirm like a recalcitrant child.

Dana sat at Ethan's side, her hands hugging her upper arms, her eyes closed as he related the events once again, flinching when he told them about Paul McMillan, Cheryl Rickman, and Alicia Samson. She seemed terribly fragile and he was afraid to touch her lest she simply shatter into pieces. So he kept his hands to himself even though all he wanted to do was hold her and give her some comfort. And maybe take some himself.

Two of her friends were dead, her friend Evie was missing.

And Alec was gone. They'd been an hour too late. He'd tried to reach Clay and Randi, but got cell phone voice mails. They were still in the air. When they landed, he'd have to tell them the truth. The monster that had Alec had eluded them once more.

"So what happened when you got to Chicago, Mr. Buchanan?" Detective Reagan prompted when Mitchell just continued to pace.

Ethan sighed and went on with his story. "I went to the bus station, just like I'd done in all the other cities. Told security I was looking for a child taken in a custodial fight."

Reagan lifted a dark brow. "In other words, you lied."

Ethan met his eyes. "I lied. I searched the security tapes in bits at a time. Then the Vaughns got another e-mail Monday morning."

Dana's eyes opened and she flashed him a confused look.

"It was right after we'd had breakfast," he told her in a soft murmur, then straightened in his chair and went on. "It said Alec

424

was still alive and that we'd done well not to call the police. That the ransom would be five million dollars. Details to follow. I traced it to a copy store. It was the same woman I'd seen on the tapes in Indianapolis and Columbus."

Mia stopped pacing. Turned to face him with utter contempt. "And to tell the police at this point never crossed your mind?"

"Of course it did," Ethan said harshly. "Every damn minute of the day. But this woman had Alec and knew we hadn't gone to the police. Dammit, I saw what she'd done. I saw that man's body in the shed. She threatened to kill Alec and I believed her."

"When did you plan to come to us, Mr. Buchanan?" Reagan asked quietly.

Ethan's laugh was completely void of humor. "When I had something to give you. Which looked less and less likely with each day. I'd decided to call you anyway. This morning. Then I saw Dana on the tape and all I could think of was getting to Alec."

Mitchell grabbed one of the chairs and abruptly straddled it with a snarl. "What other e-mails did you receive, Mr. Buchanan?"

Good cop and bad cop, Ethan understood. Mitchell and Reagan had their harmony down pat. "The next day, yesterday, we got another one. This time it was sent from an Internet café in a bookstore. This one had the specifics of the accounts the Vaughns should use when they paid the ransom. Gave them until today to make a practice deposit or the next package would be smaller. We didn't know what that meant until the Vaughns got the package this afternoon — a bloody finger that belonged to a grown man." He swallowed. A picture flashed in his mind. Alec's hands. His whole, untouched hands. And Ethan's stomach heaved, even the possibility too obscene to imagine. "I can't even . . . God."

Ethan lurched to his feet, bile burning at his throat. He shuddered and braced his hands on the table. Lifted his head and met Mitchell's clear blue eyes with defiance born of desperation. "She has my godson, Detective. Do you know what his life will be like if she damages his hands? He's deaf. He uses his hands to communicate. I should have come to you. Yes, I should have, but all I could think about was Alec, terrified and helpless."

There was no sound in the room as he

and Mitchell stared at each other, the tension thick enough to slice. Then from beside him, a flash of motion as Dana's hand slid over his. She said nothing, just held his hand where he still gripped the table. With another shudder he dropped his chin to his chest, his knees weak. Such a simple gesture, yet he was the one who felt shattered now. It was another minute before he realized how cold her hand was. She was shivering, hugging herself with her free arm. Goose bumps marred the surface of her bare arms. Abruptly Ethan shrugged out of his suit coat and draped it over her shoulders. This time the shudder was hers as her eyes slid closed and she absorbed the warmth of his body from his coat.

"Are you all right?" he murmured and she jerked a nod.

"Whose ID did she use this time, Mr. Buchanan?" Mitchell asked, her voice quiet now.

Ethan met Mitchell's eyes again, finding the contempt nearly gone. "The name on the ID she used at the bookstore yesterday was Kristie Sikorski."

Mitchell and Reagan exchanged a look. "We found her yesterday afternoon," Reagan said quietly. "She's dead."

Ethan's shoulders sagged. "I know. I'd

decided to come to see you this morning. And then I found her on the bus station's tapes with Alec, meeting Dana. I drove straight to Dana's apartment and from there we went to the shelter. The rest you know."

Reagan tilted his head, considering. "And you have no idea who this woman is?"

"If I did, I'd have come to you days ago. I don't know who she is or why she's done this other than for five million dollars."

Reagan shrugged. "That much money could be reason enough."

Mitchell turned to Dana who'd said nothing during the entire interview. She'd just sat there and listened, growing paler with each revelation. "Dana, tell us about Jane."

Dana drew in a breath, visibly gathering her composure. "When I picked her up, her face was battered. Someone had beaten her badly, sometime within the past few days."

Reagan looked over at Mitchell. "I've known of people to injure themselves to throw off an investigation, but it's been rare."

Dana's hand slipped out from under his coat and pressed her fingertips to her temple on a quiet sigh. "I saw evidence that she'd cut herself sometime in the past. Long ago, long enough that the scars were barely noticeable. But to beat her own face? Those bruises were brutal. I don't know if she could have done that to herself."

Mitchell frowned. "Could she have an accomplice, Buchanan?"

"Her e-mails always said 'we.' I had trouble believing she could overpower Paul McMillan so easily, but I never saw anyone else on the tapes except Jane and Alec."

"Was Alec bruised, too?" Reagan asked.

Dana shook her head. "Not where I could see. Later Evie checked his back when he was asleep and Jane was out smoking, and she didn't see any bruises, either. Jane would never let us look more closely."

Reagan's dark brows went up. "And this didn't make you suspicious?"

Dana's eyes flashed. "Not at first. Our clients have trouble trusting anyone, even us."

Reagan appeared unruffled. "But later? You were suspicious later?"

Dana's shoulders sagged. "Yeah. By Sunday we were. Caroline was the first to be suspicious. Jane got angry with her when Caroline told her not to smoke in the bathroom. Caroline said Jane reminded her of her ex-husband."

Mitchell's brows rose. "Really? When was this?"

"Sunday afternoon, when Evie was at Lillian's funeral."

Mitchell and Reagan shared a look. "The timing's interesting," Mitchell murmured.

Dana's eyes widened. "Oh, no, Mia. You don't think that Jane . . . but Goodman . . ."

"Detroit PD says he's been up there since the night he killed his wife."

Dana shook her head. "But Jane was there at Hanover House when I called Evie Monday night. I know it. I specifically asked if everyone was accounted for. I was worried about Goodman coming after the residents."

Ethan remembered the phone call she'd made from the hospital lobby, how Dana had chided the girl, telling her to stay put and watch the house. Now the conversation made more sense. "Who is Goodman?"

Dana shot him a short look, pulling his coat more tightly around her. "One of my former clients was killed by her husband last week. We thought Caroline's accident might have been his revenge. We thought he might have even killed Dr. Lee."

He remembered the turbulence in her eyes the night before, when he'd opened his hotel door to find her standing there. Now that made sense as well. That her work put her in such danger didn't seem to faze her. That her friends were affected did. That alone pissed him off, that she could be so ambivalent to her own safety. Yet he kept his voice level. "But Goodman didn't."

"No," she whispered. "Jane did. And I brought her here."

Mitchell leaned against the table next to Dana. "Did you suspect Jane was a killer?"

Dana shook her head. "No. I thought she might be dangerous to herself. Evie thought that maybe she was giving her son too much medicine. But the idea that she could kill? It never entered my mind."

"Then this is not your fault. Caroline would be the first to tell you that. So would Evie."

"Caroline can't hear about this, Mia. Please." Stricken, Dana looked from Mitchell to Reagan. "She's got to stay un-stressed. There isn't anything she can do for Evie."

"I'll do my best to keep it from her." Mitchell squeezed Dana's hand with an encouraging smile. "We'd better tell Max to keep her tuned into QVC and not let her watch the news in case this gets out." She slid off the edge of the table and her expression turned stern once more as she looked back at Ethan. "Do not even consider leaving town and as soon as the Vaughns get here, you let me know."

"Will you bring in the FBI?" Dana asked, her voice just a bit stronger.

"Our lieutenant will make the call," Reagan answered. "It's possible as the boy was transported over state lines. But this is also a murder investigation now, and within our jurisdiction. We'll let you know as soon as we know."

Ethan rose to his feet. Unsteadily. His head was throbbing and he was coming up on eighteen waking hours on just the few hours' sleep he'd had the night before. While Dana slept beside him. It seemed like a lifetime ago now. "Can we go?"

"Yes." Mitchell frowned. "Are you all right, Mr. Buchanan?"

"I'm fine. Just tired." It was just a matter of time before his vision started to black. He didn't want to have to pop one of his pills in a police station when it did. He pulled Dana to her feet, put his arm around her shoulders, felt her sag against him. "We'll take a cab to my hotel, Detectives. I'll call you when the Vaughns arrive from Maryland."

*Chicago,*
*Wednesday, August 4, 5:30 p.m.*

"This is a nightmare," Dana whispered, her eyes on the elevator lights as they rose to the fortieth floor where the Vaughns had a suite. Twenty floors higher than she'd gone last night when she'd come to Ethan, needing him. She needed him now.

Something had changed in the cab ride over. His cell phone had buzzed, it had been his partner, Clay. And Ethan had forced out the words, "I lost him. Tell Randi I'm sorry." There'd been a pause, then he'd grimaced. "Not yet," he'd said. "But the night is still young." He'd flipped his phone shut and stared straight ahead, his jaw tight.

"What?" Dana had asked, afraid to know the answer. "Not yet what?"

"Clay wanted to know if the police planned to press charges," he'd said grimly, not sparing her a glance. Neither of them

433

had said a word after that, but the closer the cab came to the hotel, the more pronounced the silence had become, the angrier *he* had become. He'd gone very still at one point, grappling for a packet of pills in his pocket.

He had ocular migraines, he'd said. He'd had one right there in the cab. He sat there, his eyes clenched, his fists clenched, his whole body clenched. Retreating, deep into himself. Even when his vision returned, he said nothing. Now he stood alone in the elevator, a warrior whose armor was invisible, but there. Definitely there. *Keeping me out.*

Ethan still said nothing. Just stood there until the elevator bell dinged and the doors slid open. Then, ever the gentleman, he waited for her to exit first.

"They're in Suite 4006," he said, starting down the hall.

Dana stood still, now, and watched him walk away until he'd gotten about fifteen feet and turned. "Are you coming?"

Dana swallowed hard. "I said I would. I said I'd face Erik's mother."

A muscle twitched in Ethan's cheek. "*Alec.* His name is Alec."

"I said I'd face Alec's mother," she corrected, wishing she felt as calm as she sounded. "I know they'll be angry with me. I know they have a right to be. But I need to know if you plan to be angry along with them. If you are, I need to . . ." To what? To run away? To sink into a sobbing heap? That certainly wouldn't help anyone, least of all Evie and Alec.

"To better prepare myself," she finally said. "Ethan, I understand that these people are your friends, that you've known them most of your life. I don't expect your protection at their expense. But if I'm going to be standing alone in there, I need to know it now."

Ethan seemed to sag then and although Dana longed to run to him, she kept the fifteen-foot gap between them. "I'm sorry," he said hoarsely. Unsteadily he took a step forward. Dana started moving and met him halfway and then once again she was in his arms and there was comfort. "I'm so sorry." His voice was shaking. "I've fucked everything up."

Dana drew a breath, took in his scent. Felt it soothe. Just enough. "I'd say we both did. For two people who only wanted to do the right thing . . ."

"If the police press charges . . ." He laid his cheek on the top of her head. "I've already involved Clay. I don't want to bring

435

you down with me, too."

She let out the breath as a sigh of relief. She knew in that moment she'd tell him the truth. Soon. "You won't. You can't." *I'll do that on my own.* "What have I done, Ethan?"

His face went desolate. Stark. "No worse than anything I've done. Randi knows we lost Alec. She knows the police are involved now. Let's just get this over with."

*Gary, Indiana,*
*Wednesday, August 4, 5:30 p.m.*

Alec had seen that chicken place before. It was hard to miss a fifteen-foot rooster dressed in a baseball uniform on top of a restaurant roof. They were driving in circles. Had been for what seemed like hours since they'd left the scarred lady's house in the dead lady's car. He'd seen some papers in the car, letters that said Children's Protective Services across the top. The scarred girl hadn't called the cops. She'd called a social worker.

Who was now dead.

Shot in the head. He hadn't seen it happen. She'd hidden his face, the scarred girl. Her name was Evie. It had said so on

436

the note she'd written. Now he knew he could trust her. Now it was too late. They were trapped with the white-eyed lady whose name he still didn't know. Whose reasons were as big a mystery now as they'd been the night he'd seen her from the beach house closet. Seven days ago. He knew because he'd seen a newspaper that morning on the kitchen table. *The Chicago Tribune.* It was Wednesday. He'd been gone for seven days and he didn't know if his mother was alive or dead.

They'd driven around for a while, him in the front seat and Evie in the back. He'd stolen a look back at her and she'd looked scared. But she'd smiled that weird half smile at him and mouthed for him not to worry. He could guess *w* words well when hearing people said them, even though Evie's mouth shaped the words crooked.

He drew a deep breath, tried to stay calm, but his heart was knocking right out of his chest. He'd been kidnapped by a killer. He'd thought he was next when she'd followed an old lady's car into an alley and made him get out. He was glad he hadn't drunk any water in a while because if he had, he would have wet himself, he'd been so scared. But she hadn't shot him. She'd forced the old lady out of her car and hit her on the head. Then she pushed him into the front seat and locked Evie in the trunk.

Alec watched the roof-top chicken disappear in the side mirror, then focused his eyes on the next familiar building, an old high school. He read the sign as they drove past, tucked it away in his mind. He'd memorize every last building because he'd need to know how to get away once he escaped. And he would. He didn't know how, but he would.

He'd been saying he had to do something for days now, but he'd been so tired, too tired to move. Now, he was alert, his mind was clear. He hadn't had a Pheno pill since that morning and that one he'd managed to spit out after White Eyes had left in such a hurry. He was worried about the Keppra though. If he didn't get enough of that he would seize. Which would be very bad. But he'd worry about that later.

Now he had to find a way to escape and get help for Evie. He had to do something.

*Chicago,*
*Wednesday, August 4, 5:35 p.m.*

Ethan would have gladly faced a firing

squad rather than knock on the door of Suite 4006. He stood there looking at the door for long minutes, before Dana's arm slid around his waist, hugging him. Then she knocked for him.

Clay opened the door and without a word looked Dana up and down before meeting Ethan's eyes. "You told the police?"

Ethan nodded. "Everything. I tried to keep you out of it as much as possible."

Clay shrugged. "Not much chance of that now." He extended his hand to Dana. "I'm Clay Maynard. Ethan's partner."

"I'm Dana Dupinsky." Ethan watched as her chin lifted a fraction of an inch as she shook Clay's hand, and felt a stirring of pride thread through the dread that had nearly closed his throat. "I run a women's shelter."

"Come in. We've been waiting for you."

Randi sat on the sofa, Stan in a chair. All eyes were on Dana. Ethan could feel Dana's body trembling against his, but she stood tall, her arm still tight around him. It was as if she kept herself rigid through sheer will.

Clay pulled out a chair but Dana shook her head. "No thank you. I'll stand."

"Dana," Ethan murmured. "Sit down

before you fall down. Please." So she sat and Ethan stood behind her, both figuratively and literally. He covered her shoulders with his hands and squeezed lightly. "Randi, this is Dana Dupinsky. Alec was in her shelter from Friday night until this afternoon."

Dana wanted to flinch at the look the woman aimed her way. She'd expected anger, but she hadn't been prepared for the venom that filled the woman's eyes. "Mrs. Vaughn."

Randi Vaughn's face was like stone. "You *hid* that monster in your home. With my son."

"No, ma'am," Dana said quietly. "It's not my home, it's a shelter for women who have been battered. It's open to any woman with a need. The woman that called herself Jane appeared to have a need."

Ethan's hands squeezed. "She arrived all beaten up, Randi. I saw the bruises on her face on the bus station video. Dana had no reason to believe she wasn't telling the truth."

Randi flashed him a furious look. *"She let that monster hurt my son."*

Dana somehow found calm, reminding herself that this mother had been through

hell in the last week. "That monster murdered two of my friends and has taken my
friend hostage along with your son. I don't
know if Evie is alive or dead." Her throat
closed and she cleared it as Ethan's hands
stroked her shoulders. "I'm sorry all of this
happened, Mrs. Vaughn. You can't know
how sorry I am, but I never would have *let*
Jane hurt a child."

"She was drugging him," Randi cried,
her eyes filling with tears. "You're supposed to be a *professional*." She all but
spat the word. "Didn't you see it?"

Dana's lips trembled and she quickly
pursed them. Mrs. Vaughn had a talent for
hitting vulnerable spots. "I did. I called a
doctor I trusted to examine your son. Jane
came back early and now my doctor friend
is dead. My assistant called Children's Services to come and take your son, and now
my social worker friend is dead and my
friend is gone." Her voice shook and ruthlessly she controlled it until she could
speak steadily, Ethan's hands on her shoulders all the while. "We did all the normal
things we knew to do."

"But this is not a normal situation," Clay
finished for her, kindly, and Dana shot him
a look of appreciation. "Miss Dupinsky,
you're the only one who's seen her face.

Can you give us anything that would be useful?"

"I gave the police sketch artist a description. Ethan has it." She looked up and over her shoulder to find Ethan already pulling the sketch from his pocket and looked back at Clay. "She had a tattoo on her right shoulder, about four by three inches. I never saw all of it. She had little scars on her arms. She'd cut herself a long time ago, which was my first indication something was very wrong. But the thing that was most . . . ." Dana rubbed her hands up and down her arms as new chills prickled her skin. "She has these creepy eyes. Light, light blue. Almost transparent."

Ethan held the sketch out to Clay who glanced at it before passing it to Stan Vaughn who'd said not a word since she and Ethan had entered the room.

"Well?" Clay demanded but Stan just shook his head. Sadly, Dana thought.

"I've never seen her before," he declared quietly and passed the sketch to his wife.

Dana sighed. "She didn't call your son Alec. She called him —"

"Erik," Randi whispered. "She called him Erik."

Ethan's hands tightened on Dana's shoulders as all eyes swung to stare at

442

Randi Vaughn. The woman's face was so pale Dana thought she would faint. Her hands shook so hard the sketch trembled.

"How did you know that, Randi?" Ethan asked softly.

Randi Vaughn looked up now, her eyes wild and terrified. Every ounce of venom was gone. "Because that's his name."

Dana twisted to look up at Ethan, only to see that he appeared as shocked as everyone else. Randi carefully set the sketch aside and the room became deadly quiet.

Randi folded her hands in her lap. "Because she's his mother."

# Chapter Sixteen

*Chicago,*
*Wednesday, August 4, 6:15 p.m.*

Jane sat down on the edge of the motel bed, the black metal of her gun in stark contrast to the rust-colored bedspread. "I am extremely annoyed. Tie him tight or I'll kill you."

Evie spared a quick glance at Jane from the corner of her eye as she struggled to tie Erik's hands with twine. The woman did look extremely annoyed. It was an odd description to give a woman who'd gunned down a social worker before their eyes. "I'm tying him as hard as I can," Evie said levelly. "My hand is disabled."

"Oh, yes." Jane's mouth curved in what appeared to be genuine amusement. "Your run-in with that other killer a few years back. You seem to have very bad luck, Evie."

"That I do," Evie murmured. She ran her hand over Erik's hair. "I'm sorry," she mouthed to him, still hoping he could understand. He blinked. Two times, in slow succession. Erik appeared to understand a lot more than Evie had previously thought. She remembered the look on his face as she'd released him from the protective hold she'd taken when Jane was shooting Sandy. His expression was one of grim acceptance, as if Sandy wasn't the first body he'd seen, "Why, Jane?"

Jane lifted a brow. "Why did I kidnap you and the kid?"

Evie was calmer than she ever expected to be. Two years ago she'd pled for her life and it had gotten her nowhere. Rob Winters had cut her, raped her, choked her, and left her for dead. It was only Dana's frantic call to 911 that had saved her life.

This time she had no intention of pleading for her life. She'd spent the last few hours cowering in the trunk of a stranger's car in fear and it had gotten her nowhere. Jane still held her at gunpoint. Jane still had Erik, whoever he was.

Jane would kill her. *I've been through pain. I almost died at Winters's hands. Before all this is over, I will die at Jane's.* Somehow the knowledge was a comfort. It left her with nothing to fear. "No, I don't expect you to tell me why you've taken

Erik," Evie answered calmly. "I know you'll kill me. What I want to know is why didn't you kill me back at Hanover House, like you did Sandy?"

Jane considered her thoughtfully. "You're a cool one under pressure. I can respect that. When the time comes, I'll make it as painless as possible."

Evie inclined her head. "I appreciate that. Will you kill Erik?"

Jane looked amused at this. "Not directly, no."

Evie's hand stilled on Erik's head, her mind working, trying to think of a way to get this child to safety if nothing else. "Will you make it as painless as possible for him?"

Jane lifted a brow. "That depends on the actions of another person."

"So why am I still alive, Jane?"

"Because the only things that Dana Dupinsky cares about, besides that shelter of hers, is Caroline and you. Caroline's taken care of for now. Dupinsky is next."

Evie drew a breath. So it hadn't been Goodman after all. A burden of guilt rolled off her shoulders. For two days she'd agonized over being the one to lead Goodman to Caroline because she'd attended that funeral. "So I'll be the tool of your revenge."

Jane smiled. "One of them, yes. Now put out your hands so I can tie you. I've got to go out and I can't have you doing anything heroic while I'm gone. Then, I'll retie the kid. I learned a long time ago that if you want something done right, to do it yourself."

*Chicago,*
*Wednesday, August 4, 6:15 p.m.*

Stan slowly rose and turned to Randi, his face a mask of disbelief. "What did you say?"

Randi drew a breath. "Her name is Sue Conway. She is Alec's mother."

Ethan shook his head, not understanding. "You mean you adopted him?"

Randi's eyes closed. "No. I took him."

There was absolute silence in the room. Then Stan dropped into his chair. "Maybe you'd better explain, Randi," he said acidly. "So there's no question who's to blame here."

"Shut the hell up, Stan." Clay's tone brooked no argument. Stan shut up.

Ethan sank into the chair next to Dana's, utterly thrown. "Who is Sue Conway?"

Randi opened her eyes, locked them on

Ethan's as if he were her lifeline. "I grew up here, in Chicago. Not too far from Lincoln Park. My parents were nice people. We lived in a nice neighborhood. Our next-door neighbors were the Lewises. They didn't have kids of their own, until one day their niece and nephew came to live with them. Sue and Bryce. Sue was twelve or thirteen at the time. Bryce couldn't have been more than two or three. I was sixteen or so. I used to babysit when the Lewises went out on Saturdays. Sue and Bryce's parents had died. There was a rumor their father had been killed robbing a store."

"Spare us the details," Stan snarled. "Get on with it."

"Shut up, Stan," Clay murmured. "Please."

From the corner of his eye Ethan watched Dana look around the room, taking in every face. He could almost hear her mind assessing each participant, making her conclusions, and was suddenly, fiercely glad she was sitting at his side. At the moment he was feeling neither calm nor logical. At the moment it seemed his life was standing on end.

"Go on, Randi," Ethan said and Randi gave a little nod.

"A few months after Sue and Bryce

came, Mr. Lewis asked me to babysit for them after school every day, until he and Mrs. Lewis came home from work." Randi dropped her gaze to the hands she'd clenched in her lap. "I needed the money for college, so I agreed. I'd pick Bryce up from day care on my way home from school. He was such a sweet little boy. Sue was sullen and disobedient, but I thought all teenagers were."

"Most are, Mrs. Vaughn," Dana said and Randi looked up, startled by the kindness in Dana's tone. "But Sue was different from other teenagers, wasn't she?"

Randi nodded. "I used to wonder why they paid me to babysit when Sue was old enough to do it herself, then one day I saw Sue in the bathroom, cutting herself with a razor blade. Up and down her lower arms. There was blood everywhere." Randi ran her fingertips up her own forearm. "I'd never seen anything like it."

"What did you do, Mrs. Vaughn?" Dana asked, as if she expected that very detail.

Randi moved her shoulders restlessly, obviously still upset by the discovery. "I took the razor away and cleaned her up. She sobbed and made me promise not to tell her aunt and uncle. That her aunt hated her and wanted any excuse to send her away. That I was the closest thing to a mother she had. That I was the only one who loved her."

"That you were the only one she could trust," Dana murmured.

Randi shook her head in disgust. "She had my number, didn't she?"

"She had mine, too," Dana said softly. "She played on your unwillingness to be the cause of any more pain, hers or her aunt's. So you never told anyone, did you?"

Randi closed her eyes again. "No, I never told anyone. Sue got older and wilder. I couldn't control her. The Lewises adopted Bryce, changed his last name. They tried to adopt Sue, but she fought them and they gave up. She swore she'd keep her daddy's last name. I didn't understand it. The Lewises would have taken such good care of her."

"Sue must have been close to her father, then."

Randi nodded. "He was a criminal, but she idolized him. Then one day I came home from school to find her having sex with a . . . a man, *a grown man,* right there on the Lewises' sofa. I was only seventeen. Sue couldn't have been more than fourteen herself."

"And she cried, saying her aunt would throw her out on the streets if you told."

"She did. So of course, I didn't say a word." Randi pressed her fingertips to her forehead. "My God, what was I thinking?"

"You were seventeen," Dana said pragmatically. "You did the best you knew how. The adults in her life couldn't get through, how could you?"

Randi sighed. "Well, the Lewises couldn't make her behave. Sue did drugs and went to wild parties. They could never leave her alone. Ever. Bryce was a good boy, but Sue . . . She was just horrible. Then one day my mother's ring went missing. Mother wore it every day. The only time she ever took it off was when she was washing dishes and she had a special little dish she'd set it in until she was finished but that day she'd heard the doorbell ring. Nobody was at the door, but when Mother came back, the ring was gone. Mother was just devastated. I knew Sue had stolen it. I was so angry for my mom . . . I just didn't even think and marched over to the Lewises' house, barged into Sue's room and found the ring in her drawer. She came in and found me searching and went ballistic, scratching and clawing, screaming that she'd get me and my

451

mother someday. Her aunt and uncle called the police who took Sue to juvenile detention. When she got out, she ran away and never came back. The next year I went away to college."

"But you didn't go to college," Stan said, his tone now bewildered.

Randi's mouth bent sadly. "Oh, yes, I did. Got my CPA when I was twenty-two, before I ever met you. How do you think I did the books for you all those years, Stan? I walked away from an entire *life* because of Sue Conway. I had parents, a career. Friends."

"What happened, Mrs. Vaughn?" Dana asked and Randi took another deep breath.

"I was living in the city, when one day I get this knock at my apartment door."

"It was Sue," Dana said softly. "And she said she needed your help."

Randi jerked a painful nod. "She was eight months' pregnant with Alec. Told me how some man had forced her. She cried so pitifully. She couldn't go home to her aunt and uncle. I had to help her since it was all my fault anyway."

"Because you were the one to turn her into the police all those years before."

Randi's eyes slid closed. "Yeah. I was the cause of everything wrong in her life, but I

452

could make it up to her. She said she just needed a place to stay until the baby was born."

"But she didn't stay, did she?" Dana asked. "You bought her things for the baby and made sure she saw a doctor, but after a week or two she left?"

Randi's eyes opened and in them Ethan saw stunned respect. "Yeah, she did. I'd bought her vitamins and baby clothes. But I came home from work one day and she'd cleaned out my jewelry box and stolen three pairs of my shoes."

"And her feet weren't even your size," Dana mused.

Randi blinked. "How did you know?"

Dana's smile was gentle. "I am a professional, Mrs. Vaughn."

Randi blanched. "I'm sorry I said that."

"It's all right. I recognized the potential for this kind of behavior when I saw the scars on Sue's arms. It's a common behavior in borderline personality types. They make some of the best manipulators you'll ever meet. I'd planned to dig deeper into this aspect of her background, but everything happened so fast and . . ." She faltered and her shoulders, held so steady, now sagged. "I was distracted at the time."

"Sue's been pretty active this week at

Dana's shelter, Randi," Ethan said quietly and took Dana's hand. "The police believe Sue was responsible for hitting Dana's pregnant best friend with a car on Monday night."

Randi's gaze flicked from Ethan back to Dana. "Is she all right?"

"She was lucky. Both she and the baby will be fine."

Randi paled. "I'm sorry."

Dana shook her head. "You didn't do this. Sue did."

Randi sighed, so wearily. "I'm sorry, Miss Dupinsky. I was cruel and wrong about you."

Dana's grip on Ethan's hand was punishing, but her voice was even. "It's all right. So, back to your story. I'm guessing a few weeks went by and you worried about the baby and then Sue shows back up, sorry for stealing and crying about being desperate and scared."

Randi nodded. "That's exactly what happened. She begged me to help her with the baby — she was in labor. I took her to a clinic and stayed with her while Alec was born." She swallowed hard. "I was the first one to hold him. He was so precious."

"And you took care of him because Sue would come and go."

Again the nod. "I found someone to watch him during the day when I was at work and at night . . . At night it was like he was my baby. I loved him and he loved me. And I lived in fear that Sue would come and take him."

"Which she did."

"A time or two, for a few days at a time. She always brought him back when she got tired of playing house. Alec was always dirty or sick or hungry. Once she broke into my apartment and just left him there. I'm lucky I got home a little early that day. He was starving and had diaper rash and . . ." Her voice cracked and tears spilled from her eyes, down her cheeks. "Then Sue came back, a few weeks later. I told her I was going to call a social worker, that she was an unfit mother. As soon as I said social worker she went ballistic. She slapped me so hard I fell on the floor, then she threatened to take Alec away and never come back. I didn't know what to do."

Dana's grip on Ethan's hand had lessened and now she let go, reaching over to pat Randi's knee. "What was the straw that broke the camel's back, Mrs. Vaughn? Drugs?" Randi nodded and Dana leaned a little closer. "Using or selling?"

"Both." Randi's lips quivered and she bit

them sternly. "She'd bring these guys to my place. Dirty, scary men. I was afraid to sleep in my own bed. Then one night I overheard them talking. They were all high as kites. They were running drugs from outside the country, which would have been bad enough, but they were talking about using Alec."

Dana's eyes widened. "They planned to use an infant as a mule?"

Ethan's stomach turned over at the thought. *Poor Alec. Poor Randi.*

"They'd already done it at least one other time, one of the times Sue had disappeared with Alec for a few days. They filled baby formula cans with coke, strolled through Customs with Alec in their arms. Nobody thought twice about white powder in baby formula cans." Her jaw tightened. "Alec could have been killed."

"I've read about drug rings like that," Clay said. "They're big in New York."

"Well, they were alive and well in Chicago, too," Randi said bitterly. "I didn't know what to do. I thought about going to the police, but I didn't want Alec to end up in a foster home or back with Sue. I wasn't sure if Mrs. Lewis would take him. She really hated Sue. And I knew if the police came around that Sue would take Alec. I'd never know if he was safe."

"So you took him," Dana murmured. "And left your life behind."

Randi drew a deep, deep breath. "I took him and left my life behind."

Dana got up out of the chair and took the space on the sofa next to Randi. She took Randi's hand in hers. "I would have done the same thing."

Randi lifted her chin. "And I reported them all to the police."

Dana's mouth curved into a wry smile. "Anonymously, of course."

Randi's smile was equally wry, but fleeting. "Of course. I ran east until I hit ocean — Baltimore. Then I got a job waiting tables and followed the trial with Chicago newspapers I got at the library. Sue got fifteen years for drug running and child endangerment. They knew she had a kid, but she couldn't produce him. They assumed the child had been harmed, but couldn't prove the child was dead, of course, so they went for endangerment instead. I didn't think about her taking Alec now because she was still supposed to be in jail."

"She obviously got out early," Ethan said, still unable to believe it all.

"Obviously," Randi agreed dully. She

looked from Ethan to Clay, plaintive. "Now that we know who has Alec, what are our chances of finding him?"

Ethan exchanged a glance with Clay. His friend was thinking the same thing. Their chances sucked. "I don't know, Randi," Ethan said. "We do have to tell the police."

Abruptly Randi's eyes filled. "Oh, God, Ethan, she has my son."

Grimly Ethan pulled out his cell phone and handed it to Dana. "Would you call Detective Mitchell, Dana? You know her number."

Dana took the phone and stepped toward the window to make the call. Ethan squeezed Randi's knee. "Where do you think Sue will take them?" he asked.

Randi shook her head, her tears still rolling. "I don't know."

They were all quiet then, the only sound the murmur of Dana's voice.

A brisk knock at the door made them all jump. Clay went to get the door and there was more murmuring. Then Clay reappeared, a look of resignation on his face and a woman at his side. Her dark hair barely brushed her shoulders and she appeared to be in her early thirties. Her face was probably pretty when she wasn't glaring, as she was at the moment. She wore a well-tailored jacket that almost hid the bulge of her shoulder holster.

Clay sighed. "Ethan, this is Sheriff Louisa Moore. Sheriff Moore, Ethan Buchanan."

Ethan automatically stood up. "Sheriff Moore."

She nodded. "Mr. Buchanan." She took curious note of Dana on the phone by the window, then narrowed her eyes at Stan. "Mr. Vaughn." She turned to Clay. "I got the package. Leaving it with me may be the only thing that keeps your asses out of jail."

"I was kind of counting on that." Clay's voice was dry, very dry.

Ethan lifted his brows. "What's going on?"

Sheriff Moore sucked in one cheek. "Not pleasant to be kept out of the loop, is it, Mr. Buchanan?" Then back to Clay. "Now you'll tell me what the hell is going on here?"

Clay nodded. "If you'll tell me who it belonged to."

Moore considered it, then nodded. "Deal."

"Ethan, I left the severed finger with Sheriff Moore's deputy before I got on the plane. The finger was still fresh enough to get a print."

It was a detail Ethan had nearly forgotten. "It was the right thing to do."

"So glad you approve, Mr. Buchanan," Moore said archly.

Ethan just sighed. "And the victim, Sheriff Moore?"

"Fred Oscola. He was a prison guard at Hillsboro Women's Penitentiary."

Ethan looked down at Randi. "Is that where Sue was sentenced?"

Randi nodded. "It was."

"Well, that gives us some connection." Ethan saw Dana snap his phone closed.

She slipped the phone into his hand. "Mia said to give them thirty minutes to get here."

Ethan gestured to an empty chair. "Sheriff, have a seat. If you can be patient for just a little longer, we have detectives from CPD on their way. It would be better to share the whole story at once."

"If I can get some dinner up here, I can be patient another thirty minutes."

"I'll order some," Clay said.

"I'll pay for my own," Sheriff Moore inserted and Clay nodded, still grim.

"I understand," he said and Ethan knew they still weren't out of the woods yet in terms of their personal culpability, but he'd worry about that later. Now, all he could see was Dana growing paler by the moment. It was as if she'd used all her reserves supporting Randi through her story.

Dana's eyes slid shut. "None for me. I don't think I could choke down a bite."

Ethan slipped his arm around her shoulders, gently pulled her away from the others, toward the window where Chicago lay at their feet. He listened with half an ear as Clay's deep voice called in the room service order. Pressing his lips against her temple, he felt her sag in his arms. "You were wonderful with Randi." Another kiss to her temple brought a shudder that wracked her whole body. "I know how worried you are about Evie, but you did what needed to be done. Now you have to eat," he murmured. "Evie needs you sharp."

At her friend's name Dana's back went stiff. "This woman is desperate and . . . evil, Ethan. We may never see either Evie or Alec again." The last was barely audible, yet loud enough to send a shudder of dread down his own spine.

"We'll find them," he whispered fiercely. "We have to. You have to believe that."

He simply held her for a long moment, felt her body slowly gain back its strength. Felt his own reserves fill as hers did.

461

"Thank you, Ethan. I needed that." She stepped back and gently patted his cheek, her eyes now calm again. "You go eat. I have some phone calls to make before Mia and Abe get here. If you'll give me the key to your room, I'll go make them down there and you can stay with your friends."

Ethan caught her gently and brought her back into the circle of his arms. "Not so fast, Dana. If you leave this room, I'm going with you. I don't want to let you out of my sight."

Her eyes widened. "She wouldn't come so close to us, Ethan," Dana protested. Then her eyes narrowed. "And if she does, I'll kill her."

Ethan didn't doubt she meant every word. "There is the danger factor," he said evenly, "but more than that I need you here with me." He rested his forehead against hers. "I need you to help me through this and you can't do it if you're passed out from hunger. Please. I need you."

"You need me?"

Ethan nodded soberly. "Desperately. You're Glenn Close to my Robert Redford."

Her lips curved sadly. "*The Natural?* All right, I'll eat. But I refuse to wear all white."

As Glenn Close did just before Redford hit the ball out of the park. "Why not?"

"My tattoo shows through."

"Born2Kill." He brushed a light kiss against her lips. "Dana, what *were* you thinking?"

She rested her head against his shoulder and sighed. "Don't tell Mia, but a few times I did inhale. Born2Kill was one of those times."

Ethan smiled against her hair, amazed that he could do so. Amazed that just holding her made his outlook brighter. *Wrong place, wrong time,* she'd said Sunday morning as she'd lain on the bus station floor. He'd thought her mistaken then. He knew it now. "Dana, I'm so glad you tried to stop that mugger on Sunday."

She pressed a weary kiss to his jaw. "So am I."

*Chicago,*
*Wednesday, August 4, 7:30 p.m.*

David answered his cell phone on the first ring. "Where the hell are you?" he growled. "I've been worried out of my mind."

"I'm at Ethan's hotel. I've just met with

Alec's parents. I spent the afternoon at the police department, working with sketch artists and Mia." Her voice broke. "She's gone, David. Evie's gone. And Jane . . . Jane's killed . . ." She pressed her fingers to her lips, trying to remember them all. "Six people, David. Maybe more."

"My God." There was a moment of stunned silence. "Why?"

Dana tried to think of a way to succinctly tell the tale. There was none, so she blurted it out the best she could.

"We have to find Evie, Dana," David whispered harshly. "This will break her."

Dana's eyes filled. "I know that. Dammit, David, don't you think I know that? You were right. I took risks and now Evie is in danger."

"Dana, I'm not blaming you."

"No, I'm doing that myself."

"Well, stop it. Look, I wanted you to know, I cleaned out your desk drawer before I called Detective Mitchell. All your tools and driver's license and passport paper stock are in a box under the seat of my truck."

Gratitude hit her like a brick. "David, you didn't have to do that."

"Yeah, Dana, I did. The only records they'll find on your hard drive are digital photos."

"I hadn't even thought about that," she whispered.

"I know you didn't. So I thought of it for you. I told Caroline you got a new family in tonight that was taking all your attention. Max is making sure she doesn't see TV. I haven't heard it on the news, anyway. She says for you to get some rest. Bye."

And he was gone. Carefully she hung up the hotel phone and sat, numb until Ethan sat on the bed and pulled her into his arms. He settled her on his lap, cradling her against him.

"I messed up, Ethan. I trusted her, brought her into my house. And now Evie is gone."

"Dana, what could you have done differently? Asked for references? What would happen if you asked all your clients for proof they'd been beaten and battered?"

"They wouldn't come," Dana murmured.

"No, they wouldn't. How many women have you helped have happy lives?"

Dana sighed. "More than a hundred. Maybe."

"More than a hundred women with their children. Think of the lives you've changed. Dana, you took a risk. I can't say I'm happy that you put yourself in danger from men like this Goodman character, but you risked yourself for something you believe. That makes you pretty damn special in my book."

Dana felt a swell of pride such as she hadn't felt in a long time. He understood. This man who had given up so much himself understood. "You did, too. Risked yourself for something you believed in."

"Yes, I did. I believed in the defense of our country."

"And in saving Alec. You risked your livelihood."

His nod was sober. "A by-the-book cop could press charges. But what good would my livelihood be if Alec isn't safe? How could I have looked in the mirror, Dana? How could you, knowing you'd denied someone the hope of a better life? Sue is a bottom feeder. You said it yourself to Randi — she's a manipulator. That you brought her into your shelter isn't your failing. And from what you've told me about Evie — she's a survivor. She'll hang on until we get there. Wherever she is."

And sitting there on his lap, looking into his steady green eyes, she felt some of the pain ease. Not all. Not even most. But enough to get her through the next five minutes and perhaps the next five minutes after that. "Thank you. I needed to hear that."

His thumb swept across her lips in a gentle caress. "Let's go eat and sort out this mess with the cops." He stood up, still holding her in his arms, and gently lowered her legs until her toes touched the carpet. Until she stood in the circle of his arms, his lips a breath away from hers, his eyes asking for what his voice did not. She answered, closing the distance herself, raising on her toes, covering his mouth with hers. Offering him the same comfort he'd given her. His hands came up to bracket her jaws, so gently. This kiss was chaste, but warm. He ended it with a nudge and a second kiss placed on her forehead.

"I needed that," he confessed. "More than I realized."

"So did I." She let out a breath, squared her shoulders. "I'm ready now. Let's go."


*Chicago,*
*Wednesday, August 4, 7:15 p.m.*


James looked up from his meal when the man sat down. Nervously the man drummed his fingers against the table. "So," James said, "you work for Donnie

Marsden." Donnie Marsden had been arrested with Sue all those years ago. They'd been partners.

"For a year," the man confirmed. His eyes were twitchy, looking every direction at once.

"Your boss says he hasn't seen Sue Conway. Is he lying?"

"I don't know if he's seen her. But he's talked to her, a couple of times. I listened in on the extension, just like you said to do."

James wanted to smile. Everybody had a price. Marsden couldn't be bought for fifteen thousand. His runner was spilling his guts for five hundred. "So what have they said?"

Sweat was beading on the man's upper lip. "He's meeting her tonight. Something's going down because Donnie's been callin' all the boys. It'll be Friday night."

James smiled. "I'll double your pay if you can tell me exactly where and when."

The man stood up. "I'll do it. Thanks."

James watched him slouch from the restaurant. "No, thank you."

# Chapter Seventeen

*Chicago,*
*Wednesday, August 4, 8:30 p.m.*

Dana made an attempt to eat, managing to down a few bites of a sandwich before rising to pace in front of the big picture window. Randi sat on the sofa, rocking herself. Stan just sat, his expression one of dull disbelief. For all his brave words, Ethan couldn't choke down a bite. Fortunately the oppressive silence was short-lived. A sharp knock came from the door and Ethan opened it to find Mitchell and Reagan standing there, grim-faced.

"Let us in," Reagan said, "and we'll talk."

Randi came to her feet, a heartbreaking mix of bald hope and sheer terror on her face. "What's happened? Have you found Alec?"

Mia shook her head. "No, ma'am. I take it you're Alec's mother? Or the woman who's been acting as his mother for the last ten years."

"I told them that much," Dana said. "I didn't know if it would make a difference in involving the FBI." She shrugged uneasily. "Because it's not really a kidnapping."

Randi lifted her chin. "I'm Alec's mother." Her tone dared them to disagree.

Reagan stepped forward. "For now, that's what matters. Let's find Alec first and sort through the rest later. I'm Detective Reagan and this is my partner, Detective Mitchell. Please have a seat, Mrs. Vaughn, and tell us what you know."

Randi's courage seemed to melt away as she looked from Reagan to Mitchell to Moore. "She said she'd kill Alec if we went to the police or the FBI," she said, her voice uneven.

Reagan gently pushed her to the sofa and took the chair next to her. "This has gone way beyond Alec now, Mrs. Vaughn. This woman has ruthlessly murdered at least six people. Innocent people that had families that loved them. One woman was a mother of three small girls. She's never coming home to her children, Mrs. Vaughn. This is bigger than any fears you have of the police. We decided not to go to the FBI yet, but you need to tell us what you know. We might be your only hope of seeing your son alive again."

Randi's eyes filled, tears spilled down her cheeks. "You can't possibly understand."

"Of course we can't," Reagan said, still gently. "But I can tell you that I'm a father, too."

"Then you'd do anything to protect your child," Randi whispered fiercely.

"If, God forbid, anything like this happened to my baby girl, I'd want Detective Mitchell handling my case. She's good at her job. So am I. You have to trust us. Please."

Ethan crouched at her side, took her icy hands in his. "You know it's the right thing to do. We took this as far as we could, but Detective Reagan is right. Tell him everything."

Randi visibly wavered. "Just one little girl, Detective?"

He pulled out his wallet and opened it to a chubby little angel with bright red curls.

"She's pretty," Randi whispered.

"Like her mother. Mrs. Vaughn, please talk to me. I can get the facts from Ethan or Dana, but you have memories they don't. They could be critical to finding Alec in time." He dipped his head, looked directly at her. "And time is something we're running out of."

"All right." Randi sat back, and clutching Ethan's hands, told the same story she'd told earlier. "I never expected her to do something like this," she finished on a whisper. "I thought she'd be in prison for another five years. I'm not even sure how she found me."

Clay caught Ethan's eye and lifted his brows. Ethan nodded and Clay cleared his throat. "Randi, do you know anything about a woman named Leeds living in Florida?"

What little bit of color that remained in Randi's face drained. "Sun City, Florida?"

Clay and Ethan looked at each other. "Yeah," Ethan said. "Who was she?"

Randi closed her eyes. "My mother. She was murdered six weeks ago when she woke up and surprised a robber. It was no robber, was it?"

"Did you go to the funeral, Mrs. Vaughn?" Reagan asked her.

"I . . . Yes, I had to. I hadn't seen my mother in over eleven years. I told my parents about Alec, about what Sue had done, that she'd been arrested. I begged them to disappear and they did. But she must have found them. My father died three years ago and I never got to see him again. I couldn't miss Mom's funeral. I went to the graveside and stood far away. Nobody even saw me," she said, a little desperately, then she sagged. "It was a setup, wasn't it? My mother was killed to draw me out."

Ethan patted her knee. "It would seem so," he murmured.

"Maynard, how do you know about this woman?" Moore asked quietly.

"Will the disk cover this?" Clay asked.

"What disk?" Ethan asked.

"The one that was accompanied by several spreadsheets showing just how Mr. Vaughn made his fortune," Moore replied, not taking her eyes from Clay's face. "Came in the box with the finger. Most likely yes, but it will depend on what you've done."

"You sonofabitch," Stan snarled, jumping to his feet. "You turned me in."

"Sit down, Mr. Vaughn," Sheriff Moore commanded in a voice that seemed to echo off the walls of the hotel suite. "Or I'll cuff you here and now."

Randi's face dulled with shock as Stan sank down into his chair. "You turned him in?"

Clay lifted a brow. "Yes. Stan broke the law. I was legally bound to turn him in."

"But he'll go to jail," she whispered.

Clay's face hardened. "Better him than

Ethan and me. We've helped you at personal risk. I may lose my license over this. Ethan might, too, if these officers choose to press charges against us. We'll lose our business. We're not going to jail for Stan, too."

Detective Mitchell stepped into the middle of the room, her hands raised like a traffic cop. "We'll sort out personal culpability later," she said in a level voice. "For now, Mr. Maynard, assume whatever information you gave Sheriff Moore will protect you, because every minute you spend negotiating is time Conway is free."

"So how did you know, Maynard?" Moore asked again.

"Conway fired a warning shot in the beach house. I had a friend run the ballistics. It matched a slug used in a robbery in Florida a month ago in which a woman was killed."

Moore sighed. "Just to be straight, you removed evidence from the scene of a crime."

"I did." Clay leaned back, crossed his arms over his chest.

Moore sighed again. "I thought so. As long as we're connecting dots, I found Bryce Lewis, Sue's brother. He's in jail in Ocean City for attempted armed robbery."

She told them about the West Virginia detective and Rickman's prints on the missing power cord. "Lewis has an alibi for Rickman's murder, but not McMillan's."

"Has Bryce Lewis been charged, Sheriff?" Reagan asked.

"With the attempted armed robbery. We needed more evidence to charge him with McMillan's murder. But he knew about it." Moore nodded in satisfaction. "Anyway, right after Janson and I left, Bryce gets a visit from one James Lorenzano. He's got mob ties in New York. He visited Bryce again this morning. Between visits, Bryce was beaten badly."

"But why did Lorenzano visit Lewis?" Mia asked, her brow furrowed. "Unless he's looking for Sue. Buchanan, didn't you say you thought there was an accomplice?"

Ethan nodded. "She gave us the slip when she bought those tickets to St. Louis."

"Maybe," Clay said, "it was Lorenzano she was trying to lose."

Ethan stood up and walked over to the window where Dana stood, once again alone in a crowded room. He put his arm around her shoulders, felt her stiffen. "What I want to know is how did Sue find you, Dana? Out of all the shelters in Chicago, why yours?"

Dana frowned, afraid she knew both how and why. Afraid of what else Sue knew. "Somebody obviously told her about us. She was an inmate at Hillsboro. Mia, call the prison and ask about Conway's cell mates or any women she came in contact with that had histories of abuse." She chewed on her lower lip. "Ask if Sue knew a woman named Tammy Fields." If she did, that would be the link, right there.

"Who was Tammy Fields, Dana?" Ethan murmured.

She looked up at him, troubled. "A former client. She left Hanover House with big plans for herself and her kids, but got scared and went back to her husband. I saw on the news that she'd shot him. The defense tried battered wife syndrome, but the jury didn't buy it. She'd been gone a month. When she went back, her actions seemed premeditated."

"Did you testify, Miss Dupinsky?" Moore asked.

She turned to look at Moore. "No. Tammy never named Hanover House or me as part of her defense. I went to visit her in jail before her trial, even offered to testify as a character witness, but she said she'd done a terrible thing and she wasn't about to ruin it for all the other women." She looked away. "I have to admit I was relieved."

"So you picked Jane up on Friday night," Reagan prompted. "You told us at the station that her face was bruised. Perhaps this Lorenzano helped put the bruises there."

"Perhaps, but it doesn't explain how she got our number. If Tammy did tell her, Sue would have had to have a contact inside the prison. I think it's more likely that she contacted Fred Oscola to get the shelter's phone number from Tammy. Maybe Sue thought we'd believe her story better with the bruises."

"I'll get Oscola's schedule," Mia promised. "First thing tomorrow morning."

"When did Sue leave the shelter?" Abe asked. "Be as specific as possible."

"To my knowledge she didn't leave Hanover House until Tuesday morning. Yesterday," Dana clarified. "I told her she had to go look for a job. That's what she said she'd done."

"When did she come back to the shelter yesterday?" Reagan asked.

Dana faltered. "I don't know. I wasn't there — I was at the hospital with Caroline." And then later here, in bed with

Ethan. *I was here, having the night of my life while* . . . "I left Evie alone with her. All night."

Ethan's hand rested at the small of her back. "You didn't know, Dana," he insisted with quiet firmness. "You didn't know."

"I told her not to go back to the shelter, Abe," Mia murmured. "We thought Goodman was watching her. Dr. Lee had just been killed."

Dana nodded, her throat suddenly thick just thinking about Dr. Lee's last moments. "Evie said he left suddenly and didn't say good-bye. That he wrote a note saying he had another emergency and left some of Alec's epilepsy medicine on the kitchen table."

Mrs. Vaughn looked up at that, relief in her eyes. "So he does have his Keppra?"

"My doctor friend got him a new prescription." Dana's lips trembled and sternly she pursed them. "Now he's dead. And Sandy, too."

Ethan pulled her to him and she didn't pull away. She wasn't sure she could if she'd wanted to. And she didn't want to. "I'm sorry, baby," he whispered. "We'll find her before she can do any more harm."

"Dana." Mia's voice was soft and

warning bells went off in Dana's head. "A beat cop found Sandy's car about two hours ago."

Dana's head shot up, eyes wide, heart pounding. That Mia hadn't spilled whatever this was immediately meant it wasn't good news. "Tell me."

Mia looked pained. "The beat cop found a seventy-two-year-old woman in the backseat of Sandy's car. She'd been knocked unconscious but she's in stable condition now. The old woman's car is missing. He also found this in Sandy's backseat." She pulled a plastic bag from her jacket pocket and handed it to Dana. "Don't take it out of the plastic. I have to get it to the evidence room."

Dana took it, her hand shaking. "It's Evie's," she confirmed, her voice as unsteady as her hand. "It's the St. Luke medallion Caroline gave her for her birthday two years ago. Right after . . ." She swallowed hard. "Right after she got out of the hospital."

"After Winters attacked her," Mia said to Abe who just nodded silently. And wrote it all down.

There was something comforting in Abe Reagan's thoroughness, Dana thought as she gave the bag back to Mia. "She never took off that medallion, Mia. Never." She exhaled on a ragged breath. "She wanted us to know she'd been there."

Ethan tightened his hold on her shoulders. Tilted her chin up. There was something comforting in Ethan's steady eyes, too, and Dana looked her fill, taking comfort wherever she could. His eyes narrowed slightly as he focused on her face. "Dana, the way I see this, we know a hell of a lot more than she thinks we do at this point. We have to use that."

Dana looked up at him, her jaw set. "She thinks we'll blame Evie's disappearance on Goodman," she said, forcing her voice to be stronger and Ethan felt a surge of pride.

Mia started to pace. "Conway has no idea we know about the Vaughns."

"We need to get all the places she frequented before she went to prison," Reagan said. "We'll need the address of your old apartment, Mrs. Vaughn, and the house where you grew up. Plus we'll run checks on all the drug runners that were arrested with her."

Mia nodded, still pacing. "We need to figure out what she has in mind. It seems like she wouldn't go to all this trouble unless she had something really big planned."

"It will be symbolic," Dana said. "Something that will make Mrs. Vaughn suffer like she did. And I'm certain Sue sees herself as having suffered a great deal."

"She has my son," Randi cried. "Isn't that suffering enough?"

Dana shook her head. "I don't think so, Mrs. Vaughn. I think she took Alec to lure you here. Why else would she work so hard to get to Chicago, to find a safe place to hide here? This isn't about Alec as much as it's about you. You betrayed her. You sent her to juvie when she was a teenager and you sent her to jail when she was an adult. In her mind you are the cause of everything bad in her life. I think it's going to get worse for you before it gets better."

There was a beat of sober silence, then Ethan forced himself to say aloud what he'd been thinking. "For you, too, Dana," he said. "She took Alec to get to Randi. She took Evie to get to you."

Dana looked up, met his eyes, and Ethan's heart simply stopped. She knew that she was second only to Randi Vaughn on Sue's list. And characteristic of Dana Dupinsky, she didn't care that she was at risk.

"No way in hell," Ethan growled, sinking his fingers into her shoulders. "There's no way in hell you'll even consider it." He looked up, found Mitchell's gaze resting evenly on his face. "Tell her she can't. It's stupid to even consider it."

"Dana, you can't. Buchanan's right."

Dana shrugged out of his grasp. "You can't stop me. It's me she hates, not Evie. The words she wrote in the note she left next to Sandy's body were for me. I know that. I also know I'll do anything to get Evie back unharmed." She turned to Mia, brows lifted. "You got that, Mia? Anything. She wants to trade, you do it."

Mia shook her head. "No, Dana. No trades. She'll kill you."

Dana walked to the window, standing alone in the crowded room just as she'd stood alone in the crowded park Monday night. "Evie's innocent in all this. I won't have her suffer because of me. You make the trade, Mia. Or I'll do it for you."

On that somber note, everyone in the room fell silent and it was then a cell phone started ringing. Everyone reached for their phones at once. Dana cocked her head, listening. "It's in your pocket, Ethan."

He fished the phone out of his pocket, his face hard as a stone. "It's yours. I forgot I had it. You left it in my room this morning."

Dana stared at the phone as if it would hiss and strike. "Only Evie knew this number."

Mia sprang into action. "Everyone stay quiet. If it's Sue with Evie, try to keep her on the line as long as you can. Remember, she doesn't know you know about Alec. She's Jane and her kid is Erik. *And you will not trade yourself.* Answer it."


*Chicago,*
*Wednesday, August 4, 9:35 p.m.*

Sue leaned back against the concrete wall that housed the mall's multiplex theater and took a nice long drag on her cigarette, the receiver of the pay phone against her ear. Finally there was an answer. A shaky voice. Dupinsky had found the social worker then, and the note. Just the picture of it was enough to make Sue smile.

"Hello?"

Sue exhaled a long plume of smoke, then crunched her brows. "Dana, is that you?" she asked, as small as she could make it.

"Is this . . . Jane? My God, I've been worried sick! Where are you?"

"Dana . . ." Sue took an exaggerated breath. "I was so scared . . . I ran. But I

483

wanted you to know . . . I needed to tell you . . ."

"Jane, were you in the house this afternoon? Did you see what happened, honey?"

"Y-y-yes," she whispered. "I was sitting in the living room watching TV with Erik when that man crashed through the back door. I thought I'd locked it when I came back in from smoking, but . . . I hid, Dana. I'm sorry." Sue swallowed again and again, trying to make her voice sound thicker. "I wanted to call the police, but I was scared and I hid. He killed that woman and I hid. He shot her . . . Oh, God, he shot her right in the head."

"I know, Jane." Dupinsky's voice was soothing and it scratched at Sue deep inside. *I hate when they use that voice. Like I'm an animal and they have to calm me down.* "Try to calm down." Sue gritted her teeth, dug deep for calm, and made herself listen. There was a quaver underneath Dupinsky's calm. She could hear it. Dupinsky was terrified. "I — I found Sandy Stone, Jane. She's dead. I need to know exactly what you saw. You're the only witness. You have to help us catch the man that did this or nobody in the shelter will be safe. Will you tell the police what you saw?"

"No. I don't want to go near the police, but I'll tell you and you can tell them."

"All right, Jane. Tell me, but first, is Erik all right? Was he too frightened?"

Actually Erik handled the whole thing just fine, Sue thought, remembering. Maybe there was hope for the kid yet. *Too bad he wouldn't live long enough for her to find out exactly how much of her blood ran in his veins.* "Erik's not so good. He was scared to death and now he just sits rockin' himself again. He had a seizure, a bad one. I hid with him in the downstairs closet under some blankets when the man came in, but the man didn't even look. He wanted to find you and Evie. He was yelling and screaming. Evie told him you weren't home so he hit her hard. She was bleedin', Dana. Real bad. Then he dragged her out the back door. He kept screaming that if he couldn't find you, he'd make you come to him. That you'd pay. That's what he kept saying, screaming — that you'd pay."

She could hear Dupinsky's breath coming fast now. Frightened little pants. It was nearly arousing in its own right. "I need you to listen, Jane. And think hard. Was Evie alive when he took her away?"

Sue grinned, hearing the anguish and

fear in Dupinsky's voice. Then she wiped the grin from her face. It was hard to sound scared when you were grinning from ear to ear. "Yeah, but she was bleeding a lot. She kept calling for you. I wanted to come out, I really did, but I had to protect Erik."

"You did the right thing, Jane. Your first responsibility is to your son. Where are you now? I'll come get you and take you where you'll be safe."

Sue looked around the mall parking lot, crowded with teenagers hanging out at the movie theaters on a summer evening. She'd be safe enough here. "I'm not going back to the shelter." She said it on a little hiccup, like she'd been weeping. "I appreciate what you did for us, but too many people are getting hurt at your place. You said we'd be safe, that no one could hurt us, but it was more dangerous there than back with Erik's father. I'm going to another town now, but I wanted you to know about Evie. She was good to Erik."

"Jane, wait. If he saw you, you could be in danger, too."

"He didn't see me. He didn't even know I was there. Thank you. I'll never forget you."

And with that, Sue hung up the phone

and took a nice long satisfied drag on her cigarette while digging in her pocket for the long-distance calling card she'd purchased just a half hour before. *One down, one to go. Little birds beware. The cat is coming.*

Wearily, Dana handed the phone back to Ethan, her lips pursed in a tight line. "She told me Goodman kidnapped Evie, that she saw it all, but was hiding. That when Goodman was gone, she took Erik and ran."

"She doesn't know Detroit PD caught Goodman this morning," Mia commented from the bedroom doorway, sliding her own phone in her pocket. "CSU is working to get a trace, but it'll be harder with a cell phone. Why would she call you, Dana? What's in it for her?"

Dana's shrug was grim. "She wanted to hear me in pain, to know I was worried about Evie and powerless to do anything. She set it up that if Goodman couldn't find me, he'd use Evie to get me to come to him." She narrowed her eyes when Mia frowned. "I know. No trades. I heard you."

"But you never said you wouldn't pursue it," Ethan said, his jaw taut. He was still angry. It all but emanated from him in waves.

"She still thinks you only know her as Jane," Reagan inserted, probably as much to keep the peace as anything else. "Good work, Dana. You never slipped once."

Another time, the praise would have made her warm with pride. Now, it barely registered above the rage that bubbled just below the surface of her mind. "I want to kill her," Dana muttered. "Slowly and painfully." She looked over her shoulder at Randi Vaughn. "She said Alec had had a seizure, Mrs. Vaughn, but she could be lying. If he did, does that put him in physical danger?"

Randi took a deep breath and Dana had to be impressed with how she tried to stay calm. "Depends on how deep he went under and how long it lasted. Normally they only last a few minutes, but he'll be weak as a kitten for at least a day. If she calls again, can you find a way to make sure he takes his medicine?"

Dana found a small smile for the terrified mother. "I'll try. She also —"

Another cell phone began to chime and Sheriff Moore raised her brows. "Well, you may be able to do that yourself, Mrs. Vaughn. I had the phone at the beach

488

house forwarded to my cell. This could be for you. Remember, you don't want to let on that you know she's in Chicago. You're still in Maryland, remember that. Try to keep her talking." She put the phone in Mrs. Vaughn's visibly trembling hands. "Good luck."

Randi clutched it with both hands, her skin taking on a greenish tinge. Ethan moved to her side, put his arm around her shoulders. He took the phone from Randi's shaking hands, flipped it open, and held it to her ear so that he could hear it, too. He gave her a nudge and a nod. "Go," he mouthed.

"H-hello?" Randi stuttered. Her body was shaking so hard he thought she'd crumble.

"Hello, Mrs. Vaughn. Do you know who this is?"

Randi flashed frantic eyes to Ethan, terrified to say the wrong thing. Ethan shook his head. "You don't," he mouthed.

"No. Who is this?"

A low laugh sent a chill up Ethan's spine.

"You don't have any idea, Randi? What if I called you Miranda? Would that help?"

Randi's eyes slid shut. "Sue. So it is you."

"I'm hurt there would have been any doubt, Miranda. You've done well so far. You've stayed put and haven't called in the cops. I'm proud of you."

Randi stiffened, her eyes darting from Reagan to Mitchell to Moore. "No, I didn't call the police or the FBI." The knowledge that Sue thought she was still compliant seemed to bolster her and she sat straighter. "Where is Alec, Sue?"

"I bet you'd like to know. I wanted to know, too, when I was sitting in a jail cell while the DA tried to indict me for murder. You knew it and you took the kid. Made it look like I'd killed him. You wanted me to fry. You stupid little bitch."

"I never wanted that, Sue. I never told them you killed Alec."

"Erik, Miranda. His name is Erik. No, you never told them I killed the kid, but you arranged for him to disappear just the same. It looked like I did kill him. I was just lucky the DA was inept. I got stuck with reckless endangerment. Did you know that?"

There was raw fury in her voice. And people talking in the background. Lots of people. Then the blast of a car horn.

"No, I didn't know that. I'm sorry, Sue. I did what I thought was right all those years

490

ago. Sue, Alec is sick. He needs medicine. Please bring him home. I swear I won't say a word if you just bring him home. I'll give you whatever you want. The five million. I swear." Her voice faltered, broke. "Please just let him come home."

Sue chuckled. "I did bring him home. Now you'll have to come home, too, if you want to see him again. This is what you're going to do. Got a pen and paper?"

Ethan took out his pen and motioned Reagan to hand him his notebook. Nodded at Randi who drew a shaky breath. "Yes, I do."

"Then write this down. You're to come to Chicago, with your husband. Take American flight 672 out of National into O'Hare. Rent a car. Then go to the Excelsior Hotel. Your room is reserved already. Do not go to another hotel and do not try to get another room or you'll get another finger and this one will be much smaller. Understand?"

Trembling, Randi nodded. "Yes. Is Alec alive? Please, Sue, is he alive?"

"Yeah, he is. But he won't be if you don't do every little thing I say. Oh, and check your e-mail. You were so good about the practice deposit in my account, now we're ready for the real thing. Check-in time at the hotel tomorrow is three o'clock."

The phone clicked and she was gone. Randi sat for a moment, completely drained, then steeled her spine. "Can we check my e-mail from here?"

Ethan was already tapping keys. "We have a new one." His eyes tracked back and forth as he read, then he blanched. "Five million by Friday at five p.m. or she starts sending us Alec in pieces."

"Will you let us trace that e-mail?" Clay asked tightly. "It will save you some time."

Reagan gave a short nod. "Do it."


*Chicago,*
*Wednesday, August 4, 10:15 p.m.*

Donnie Marsden had put on a little weight, Sue thought as she watched him make his way across the movie theater parking lot. She gave Donnie a little smile when he bent down to look in the open passenger side window of her most recently acquired automobile.

"Suze." He looked annoyed. "You weren't where you said you'd be."

"Once burned, Donnie." She wasn't about to be a sitting duck in case he'd told someone where she'd be. "Get in. It's time

492

to talk some details."

"Not yet. You promised no traps, but you killed Leroy Vickers."

Sue smiled. They'd found the van then, with Vickers's body inside. "Did I?"

Donnie frowned. "Don't play games with me, Sue. You killed Leroy. You might kill me."

"You didn't testify against me, Donnie. Neither did the others. They're safe. Get in the damn car."

After another minute's hesitation, he climbed in and pulled the door shut, then froze, his eyes focusing on the nine mil she had cradled in her lap. "Why the piece?"

"Insurance, Donnie. It's not that I don't trust you, I just don't trust anybody." She reached beneath her seat and brought out an empty shoe box. "Empty your pockets into the box. One false move and you're dead."

Pale and grumbling, Donnie complied. Three prescription bottles went in first, followed by his knife, a P-11, and a well-used straw, cut to just the right length. Sue frowned. "You stay clean through the weekend, you understand?"

Donnie shot her a glare. "It's for testing the merchandise."

"Okay, fine, whatever you say. Just no

testing anybody's merchandise until Saturday. Then you can blow your nose full of holes. Lift your pants' legs." He scowled and pulled a Beretta from an ankle holster and dropped it in the box. "Damn, Donnie, you're a regular walking arsenal." She slid the box under her seat and started the car. "I get nervous just sitting. Relax. I need you too much to set you up."

Donnie's scowl deepened when she pulled out of the parking lot, leaving the partying teenagers behind. "Where are we going?"

"Down memory lane, my friend. Don't worry."

"So what the fuck's this all about, Suze? And at this point, it better be damn good."

Sue just smiled. "Or what?" She let the challenge pass unanswered. "Friday night, nine o'clock. One of the boys needs to go pick our bird up."

"From where?"

"Excelsior Hotel. Room 2021. Here's a passkey." She pulled the key card from her pocket and handed it to him. "Whoever picks up should wear a bellhop uniform."

"Where'd you get this?"

"Never mind. Which of the boys do you plan to send?"

Donnie slid the key card in his pocket.

"Gregory. He's worked hotels before. He should still have a uniform, or know where to steal one. Who's the bird, Suze?"

Time for the unveiling. "Do you remember that apartment I had on Central?"

"Yeah." He gave a slow grin. "That bed saw some good times, didn't it, Suze?"

"I'm surprised you remember any of them," Sue replied dryly. Donnie used to "test the merchandise" in the old days, too. Sue was certain there were entire blocks of the early nineties that Donnie could not recall. But he'd been a hell of a businessman when he was sober. They'd cleared nearly a hundred thousand dollars that first year, enough to make a girl think she was in love. By the end of the second year, they had another seventy-five. Of course, all the cash was converted into new material, which had been seized at the time of their unfortunate incarceration.

Donnie winked. "Sex I remember. The other details from that period are a bit fuzzy."

Unfortunately Sue remembered all the details. Donnie, for all his boyish charm, was a rough customer. More than once he'd left her bruised and bleeding, especially when he was high. But he'd run the show at the time, so she'd pretended to enjoy the ride. How the mighty are fallen, she thought. *I run the show now.* But she hoped Donnie was still rough. Or that he at least knew somebody who was. She had debts to pay and the interest had become quite considerable.

"Do you remember a girl named Miranda?"

He frowned. "Name doesn't sound familiar."

"She used to bring us beer," Sue said flatly and Donnie grinned again.

"Sex and beer I remember." He thought a moment. "Miranda. Wasn't she the one whose baby you used to run the junk?"

Like she'd thought, whole blocks of the early nineties were tofu in the stir-fry of Donnie's brain. "Something like that," she murmured, then said nothing more as she took the car onto the highway. She knew he didn't really remember the seven months she'd gone away after that first lucrative year. Busted for petty theft by a neighborhood beat cop, the DA'd tacked on a charge of possession when a cavity search turned up her private stash. But she hadn't squealed, even with the promise of probation if she revealed the source. She'd kept Donnie's secret then and he hadn't even been sober enough to appreciate it.

Then two weeks into her sentence she'd found out she was pregnant. Horror stories about prison abortions abounded and out of fear she carried the damn kid to term, which as bad luck would have it was a month after she'd been released. Huge and waddling like a duck, she knew Donnie would have no use for her, so she'd turned to the only person she'd thought was stupid enough to help her. How wrong she'd been.

Miranda Cook — now rich bitch Randi Vaughn. Not so stupid after all. *Just incredibly unlucky because now I have her exactly where I want her.*

Donnie shook his head. "You're saying the beer girl turned us in? That mousy thing?"

Some mental engines took a little longer to warm up than others. "That mousy thing stole ten Gs from me and hit 911 on her way out of town with the damn kid."

"Which is why they never turned the kid up."

"You get the Kewpie doll," Sue said sarcastically.

"Well," Donnie mused, settling back into his seat. "This paints a whole different picture of revenge. Our birdie being a female, that is."

"I was hoping it would."

"So, Suze, what's in this for you? You go to all the trouble to track this chickie down, then let us have all the fun?" He narrowed his eyes. "What's the catch?"

"No catch. You just have the ability to wreak a different kind of damage than I can."

Donnie's mouth curved. "I see your point."

Sue exited the highway, doubled back the direction she'd come. "I wonder if you do."

He turned to stare out the window. When he looked back, she caught a glimpse of his face from the corner of her eye and knew that he did. Exactly.

"What's your story?" she asked quietly.

"Big guys, showing the new guy who's boss. Hell, I thought I was tough. I didn't know what tough was. Spent a week in the infirmary. Only happened once. After that, I learned."

*Yeah, one learned many things inside.* "I can relate."

"You, too?"

"Multiply it by a coupla' hundred and I'd say you'd be close."

"Shit." He turned back to stare out the window. "Guys?"

"Mostly. There's one less left in the world though."

"Good for you, Suze. I didn't have the nerve. I just wanted to forget it and go on."

She cleared her throat. "At any rate, Miranda will be arriving in Chicago tomorrow."

"Then why not tomorrow?" He was revving now. She could hear it in his voice. "Why do we have to wait till Friday?"

"Because she's got something else I want. When I get it, you'll get her."

The rest of the drive was completed in silence until she pulled into the drop-off lane of the El station closest to the mall where he'd left his car. "This is where I say good night," Sue said. "I'm not going near the mall again. You can take the El or a cab back. I'll call you Friday morning with the final location for our little party Friday night." She took the box out from beneath her seat and handed it to him. "No hard feelings on the search?"

"No. I guess I understand." He replaced his weapons, then grabbed the three pharmacy bottles from the shoe box. "I understand a lot better than you think."

She realized he was holding one of the bottles so that she could read the label. And when she did, she knew Donnie had one more reason to kill Randi Vaughn. "How long have you had it?" she asked him quietly.

"Diagnosed five years ago. Big guys, big-time AIDS. I got quite a score to settle with our little bird, Suze. Quite a score."

# Chapter Eighteen

*Chicago,*
*Wednesday, August 4, 11:30 p.m.*

Three pairs of eyes looked up when Dana emerged from Ethan's bathroom in a cloud of steam. Her eyes widened and instinctively she pulled her robe in a little tighter.

"We're showing Sheriff Moore our surveillance shots," Clay said, gesturing to the coffee table piled with paper. "There's coffee in the pot and Chinese takeout in the little fridge."

Sheriff Moore smiled kindly. "I put a pair of my sweats on the bed in there for you."

From his seat behind the small desk, Ethan just looked away. He was still angry with her for offering to take Evie's place. *Let him be angry,* she thought. But still, it hurt.

Dana decided to deal with Sheriff Moore first. "Where are my clothes?"

"Mitchell sent an officer by to pick them

501

up. You had Miss Stone's blood on your skirt. They thought they might need it as evidence."

Dana jerked a nod. That she'd had blood on her skirt was no real surprise. Her hands had been covered in Sandy's blood. She looked down at her hands now. They were clean, her fingertips pruny from the long bath Mia had pushed her to take.

But she had blood on her hands just the same. Evie's most certainly. Alec's to a certain degree. She lifted her eyes to find Moore and Clay exchanging worried frowns.

"I'm all right," she said. "I'm just . . ." *What? Just what?* "I'll just be a minute."

Clay's voice rolled through the room. "Dana, if you need to rest, please do."

Dana paused in the doorway. "No. I've had enough time alone, thank you. I need to help or I'll go insane."

Moore's sweatpants were just a little too short in the leg and the Boston PD sweatshirt was tight through the shoulders, but it was better than wearing nothing more than the hotel's terry robe when everyone else was dressed. Sheriff Moore pushed a cup of coffee in her hand when she reappeared a minute later.

"We were about to send divers in there,"

she murmured with a smile.

Dana's cheeks heated. "I'm sorry. I fell asleep in the bathtub." She looked at the clock on the television with surprise. "Wow. I didn't realize I'd been so long."

"Don't be sorry," Moore chided. "You needed the rest."

Dana's eyes flicked to Ethan who steadfastly refused to look up. "You should sleep, too, Ethan. You've been going twenty-four hours."

"I'll sleep when we're done," he said tightly. "You go to bed. We'll finish here soon."

It was a blatant dismissal and seemed to catch everyone by surprise. Dana ignored him and sat down. "Did Mia and Abe find the place she used to send the last e-mail?"

"Yeah, but the place is closed," Clay said. "They're trying to locate the owner."

"To see if she used another woman's credit card," Dana said grimly. "Which would mean another dead woman. Have we had any more calls?"

Clay shook his head. "No. But they were able to trace the call to a pay phone near the Camden Road movie theaters."

"She was at the mall," Dana murmured, thinking of the place. "That's why there was so much background noise. That

503

mall's near the neighborhood where Randi grew up."

"That's what Mitchell said." Sheriff Moore leaned back against the sofa cushions. "She also said they drove by Randi's old neighborhood. Sue's aunt and uncle are dead, their house burned to the ground."

Dana frowned. "Sue?"

"No," Clay said. "The Lewises' house burned down just before dawn on Thursday morning. Sue was just getting on the Morgantown bus then and Bryce was in jail in Maryland. It had to have been somebody else. We're thinking this Lorenzano character."

"He's been in Wight's Landing," Moore added. "After I found out about his visits to Bryce Lewis in jail, I had my deputies flash his picture around. The bouncer at the local bar remembers him making time with our resident bad girl bartender. Pattie's not talking."

Dana sipped at her coffee, tried to stay focused. "Sue might have planned to stay with her aunt and uncle when she got back to Chicago with Alec, whether they wanted her to or not. Finding their house burned down would have put quite a kink in her plans."

Clay looked up, impressed. "Could very well be."

Dana lifted a shoulder. "If she knew Tammy from prison, that's *how* she ended up at Hanover House. I've been racking my brain trying to figure out *why*. It would only make sense if there was absolutely no other place to hide. It was so much trouble, finding us, getting herself bruised. Even for Sue this seems like a lot of trouble just to pay back some social workers. But if her first plan was the Lewises' and if she was afraid enough of Lorenzano . . . It might have been reason enough."

"Was she tentative about going out in public?" Moore asked.

"They all are at first. But our goal is independence, so I insisted Sue look for a job, like I do with all new residents. She said she was afraid her husband would find her. But they're all afraid of that, too." Dana sighed. "Most of them have good reason to fear." She stood up, suddenly nervous all over again, and paced the floor. "I teach them to manage their fear, to tell themselves every day that they have nothing to fear. Chant it in their minds when they have panic attacks."

"Does it work?" Moore asked, her smile still kind.

"Sometimes." Dana stopped pacing. "Except when I bring killers into the house."

505

Ethan looked up. Finally. "You didn't know, Dana." He looked her square in the eyes, his gaze full of challenge. "But now you do. What you did before, all those women you welcomed into your shelter before, you did with calculated risk. The men who battered them were more dangerous than the women. Now you know differently. You know the danger. You know what Sue Conway will do."

Tears rose in her throat. "I know she'll kill Evie and Alec if I do nothing."

Ethan shook his head. "You know better, Dana," he said quietly. "She has no earthly reason to let Alec and Evie go. They've seen her. If she's caught, they can identify her. She won't let them go, no matter what you do. Something, nothing, it won't matter."

Moore stood up, met Dana's eyes. "He's right, Dana. I've worked with too many abductions in my career. You never give the abductor any power."

"We have to stay focused on finding Conway alive so she can lead us to Alec and Evie," Clay added. "We can't do that if we're wondering what you're going to do. If she's going to have yet another hostage because you gave yourself up."

"We need you with us," Moore stated.

"You've spent time with her. We need you to help us understand how she thinks. Evie and Alec need you here, helping us."

They were right. She'd already come to the same conclusion during her time in the tub, questioning herself, second-guessing her judgment. Always second-guessing. But this group was totally confident in their judgment. She found herself envying them even as their solidarity touched something deep inside her. They cared. Genuinely.

"You all practiced this," Dana said unsteadily, looking from Moore to Clay. Then to Ethan, who just sat there, his green eyes turbulent, his lips firmly pursed, and she wondered what he wasn't allowing himself to say.

Moore was sober. "Promise us you won't do anything resembling trading yourself or Detective Mitchell will put you in protective custody."

Dana knew Mia would do it, too. "You have my word." She could feel their collective tension lessen. They'd been waiting for her to come out of the bathroom to convince her not to do something criminally stupid. "I understand that I'd just make things worse if I did."

Clay looked over at Ethan. "That was a

hell of a lot easier than you said it would be."

Dana's eyes flew to Ethan. "Excuse me?"

Moore rolled her eyes. "Maynard, don't you know discretion is the better part of valor?"

Ethan's glare was sharp. "Thank you, Clay."

Clay's lips twitched. "You're welcome." He patted the empty chair at his side. "Now come have a seat, Dana. I want to know if you've seen this tattoo on Sue's shoulder."

"I already told Mia and Abe that I saw the tattoo on her ring finger and just a glimpse of the one on her shoulder, but let's take a look at those pictures. It might jog something out of my memory." Dana sorted through them, shaking her head. "She's covered this tattoo up with makeup, hasn't she? Makeup she stole from Evie. Evie couldn't leave the house because her makeup was gone." She swallowed hard. "Evie thought I'd taken it."

"Why would she think that?" Ethan asked, his voice gentle, and Dana wished he'd get up and put his arms around her as he'd done earlier in the Vaughns' suite. Tell her it would be all right. Lie if he had to. But he kept his seat, the desk effectively separating them.

"I told her not to leave the house, because I thought Goodman was out there. Instead, the threat was inside, where I forced her to stay." She looked down at her hands again. Wrong place, wrong time. Bad decision. *My bad decision.* For which Evie would pay.

"Dana, look at me." She did, finding his eyes on her, softer. Not angry anymore. The knowledge sent relief shimmering through her. "Does Evie know you love her?"

Dana's throat closed. "Yes. I told her. This morning, the last time I talked to her."

"Then that will be enough to sustain her until we find her."

Clay cleared his throat and Dana realized she and Ethan had been staring at each other across the room. Ethan looked away and Dana felt her cheeks heat again.

"I think we're done for now," Clay said. "We all need to sleep."

"This is where I say good-bye," Moore said. "I fly back to Maryland tomorrow."

Dana plucked at the Boston PD sweatshirt. "Your clothes."

"Send them back with Maynard. He'll visit the DA with me when he comes back."

Clay looked absolutely thrilled by the prospect.

Dana frowned. "They're not going to be charged, are they?"

"Well, that's up to the DA, but I kind of doubt it. I plan to pay another visit to Bryce Lewis tomorrow. Now that I know the right questions to ask, he should be a little more compliant." She paused, her hand on the doorknob, sober. "When this is all over, come down to the bay. There's something about listening to the waves that soothes pain."

Clay stood up when the door closed behind Moore. "I'm calling it a night," Clay said. "Ethan, can you toss me a carton of that *lo mein* from the fridge?"

Ethan looked at the fridge, two arm spans away. Then looked at Clay with narrowed eyes. "Get it yourself, Maynard."

Smiling, Clay did. A look at Dana's puzzled face had him chuckling out loud. "Good night." He went to the adjoining room and she and Ethan were finally alone.

Dana felt awkward as a teenager as she turned to where Ethan still sat, his hands folded on top of the desk, his jaw taut. "Go to bed, Dana. I'll sleep out here."

Dana took a step forward. "Ethan, if

you're still angry with me —"

"I'm not," he interrupted. "I just have a lot on my mind. I'll see you in the morning."

He didn't look tired. He looked mad. But he was an adult and she'd leave him with whatever thoughts were so important that he needed to be alone. "Fine." She was gratified to at least see him wince as she said it. "Good night." She went into the bedroom and closed the door, half expecting him to come rushing in, apologizing for his mood. But long minutes passed and he did not, so she gave up and went to bed alone.

*Chicago,*
*Thursday, August 5, 12:15 a.m.*

Sue crept up the stairs in the old apartment building. The old woman must be in good shape, she thought, being able to manage a three-flight walkup at her age. Her name was Jackie Williams and she'd been Randi Vaughn's neighbor eleven years ago. She was also the one who'd told the police where to find Sue eleven years ago. Randi Vaughn had called the cops initially and Sue had hidden while Donnie and the boys were arrested. For two days Sue had hidden. But when she came out, Jackie Williams was watching. Just waiting to squeal to the cops. And she had.

She was next on Sue's list. The revenge would fit the woman's crime. Jackie Williams had watched, then talked. In an hour's time she'd be doing neither of those things again.


*Chicago,*
*Thursday, August 5, 12:15 a.m.*

Alec had no idea what time it was. It might still be Wednesday. If it was Thursday already, morning was still a long way away. It was still dark. He'd been alone under the bed for a long time. She'd put him here after retying the ropes that Evie had tied too loosely. There was something wrong with Evie's hand, he thought. The way she'd fumbled had made the Bitch angry. She'd tied her and forced her into the bathroom. Then the Bitch had returned, that evil smile on her face. And Alec knew that she'd killed Evie, too. She'd dug his medicine from her bag. Let him see it, then just smiled and tossed it back. He needed that Keppra, he knew it.

512

Without it he'd be seizing in a few days.

He had to get away before then.

She'd taped his mouth so he couldn't scream and rolled him under the bed. It was a whole lot mustier than the life jackets in the closet Cheryl had tried to hide him under. *Cheryl.* He had to stop thinking about her. He couldn't cry. With all this dust he was already stuffed up enough. Any more and he'd suffocate.

He was afraid. Afraid under the bed and more afraid to roll out. If she was there . . . She'd killed that woman, that friend of Evie's. Just like she'd killed Cheryl. Just like she killed the doctor. He shuddered as he did every time he thought of the old doctor and the fingers in the cooler. *She'll kill me, too.* It was easier to stop there, to not think about what else she could do with that knife. The knife was scarier than the gun.

A spider crawled over his face. It was the third, he thought. Maybe the fourth. He'd gritted his teeth against the need to scream and made himself remember that stupid flash card with the dopey-looking cartoon spider Cheryl had used to make him practice the word. *Spy-dur.* Again and again. *Say nothing,* Cheryl had said and now he thought he knew why. The Bitch knew he was deaf. But she didn't know he could speak. His mom didn't really know. Nobody had known but Cheryl. They'd made progress, she'd said. They'd been practicing "Big Mac, fries, and a Coke," so he could walk into McDonald's and surprise his mom by ordering his own meal.

But he'd never tried it with anyone else. Never tried to use his words. He didn't know what they really sounded like. Cheryl said progress, but she could have been lying. He could sound stupid and nobody would ever understand him. But Cheryl didn't lie. She'd been brave. She'd tried to protect him. And now she was dead. *I owe her better than lying afraid under this bed,* Alec thought and prepared for the worst.

He rolled out from under the bed, half expecting the Bitch to be standing there, looking down, like she'd stood there and looked down at him in the closet. But nobody was there.

The air was better here, but he still couldn't breathe. He could see the bathroom door from where he lay. He knew Evie was behind it. Alive or dead, he wasn't sure. He'd be able to get away better with her, though. And she'd protected him, too. He couldn't just leave her here if she was alive. If he could stand up against that door, he'd be able to twist the doorknob and see. He breathed through his nose, drawing as much air into his lungs as he could. And started to scrunch his way toward the bathroom door.

*Chicago,*
*Thursday, August 5, 12:30 a.m.*

Dana didn't want sex. She wanted intimacy. Last night there had been someone there to hold her when the nightmares came. Today, she'd been able to hold the nightmares at bay for close to twelve hours now by staying awake, staying busy. She'd kept herself from thinking about where they were. If they were unharmed. *Please let them be unharmed.*

Now in the quiet of the night, the dreams would come. They always did and tonight she had new ones to add to the queue. She rolled to her back. Stared at her hands. She'd had blood on her hands today. Sandy's blood. When she dreamed, she'd have blood on her hands again. And she'd wake up, breathing hard, crying inside.

And she'd hoped tonight she wouldn't have to be alone when she did.

But Ethan had a right to be alone, if

515

that's what he wanted. He'd been through a lot today. Finding Alec, losing him again. Facing the despair of his friends and confessing his sins to two cops and a . . . What was she? Girlfriend? *Maybe.* Fling? *Probably.* Lover?

*Definitely.* And her lover was planning to sleep alone with no pillows or blanket. At least she could give him that. Gathering up two pillows and the extra blanket in the armoire, she opened the bedroom door.

And stood there, stunned at the sight of Ethan Buchanan standing rigid in the middle of the room, stripped down to his shorts, eyes clenched shut, jaw so taut a muscle twitched in his cheek. *He's in pain,* she thought, then her eyes slid down his perfect body and widened in shocked awe. No, not in pain. *In boxers.* That didn't come close to containing him. Only one word came to mind. *Mercy.*

His eyes closed, Ethan smelled the soap she'd used in the tub, just as he'd smelled it when she'd emerged from the bathroom in a cloud of fragrant steam. He heard her quick indrawn breath. And knew it was way too late to hide behind the desk again.

"I'm sorry," he said, turning to where she stood holding a pillow and a blanket. A second pillow lay at her feet. Her eyes were wide, her breathing uneven, and he was disgusted with himself. He'd startled her, on top of everything else she'd been through.

She swallowed hard. "Why?" Her voice was husky and deep and sent fire licking across his skin. Made him want to shove her up against the wall and take her where she stood. Just as he had the entire damn time she'd been in that damn bathroom, soaking naked in that damn tub. Then naked under that damn terry robe. Then naked under Moore's too-small sweats that showed off every damn curve.

"I . . . I didn't want you to feel pressured."

She nodded slowly, her eyes still wide. "I see." She visibly collected herself and bent over to retrieve the pillow from the floor. "I brought you these. The sofa is uncomfortable."

"Thank you." He took the blanket from her hands and held it up against himself. Gritted his teeth. "Dana, go to bed." *Before I take you there myself.*

She stepped back. Stopped. Her tongue came out to wet her lips and he gritted his teeth in response. "You . . ." She pointed at the desk. "All that time?"

His teeth grinding, he nodded. "I'm

sorry, Dana. I know this isn't the time, but I'm a guy. I'm just wired this way. I can't see you in the bathtub without wanting you." He took a step back. Clutched the blanket a little tighter. "Please, go to bed. I'll be fine. Just go."

Silently she did and he exhaled the huge breath he'd been holding. Let his hands holding the blanket sag. It had been a hell of a day. No relief. Then the door opened and up went the blanket again, a piss-poor shield.

"Ethan, I have a confession to make."

Wary, he only tilted his head and waited.

"Last night, when I came here, it was for two reasons. One, Mia had told me not to go back to Hanover House, that it wasn't safe. But mostly, I needed to be with someone. I'd just found out about Dr. Lee and I needed . . ." She looked away. "I came here looking for physical contact. I wanted you to hold me. I wanted you." She gave an awkward shrug. "When I woke up last night, I was having a nightmare."

He remembered the little cries, the way she'd thrashed in her sleep. "I know."

Her eyes shot up to his, suddenly panicked. "You do? How? What did I say?"

The notion that she'd talked in her sleep disturbed her. "You didn't say anything."

518

The little slivers of panic in her eyes eased. "Well, anyway, I woke up and you were there. You made me forget my nightmares. I wanted you to know how much I appreciated it." She put the pillows on a chair. "Good night, Ethan."

"Dana, if you have nightmares tonight . . ."

Her smile was brief and tight, her eyes now shadowed. "Why should tonight be different from any other night? Different theater, same movie. Good night, Ethan."

He'd meant to let her go. He really did. He watched her close the door, even threw the pillows on the sofa. She hadn't said, *Ethan, I want you. Ethan, come to bed with me. Ethan, come inside me until neither of us hurts anymore.* He tossed the blanket to the sofa with a sigh. No, she'd thanked him for holding her last night. He'd done a hell of lot more than hold her and they both knew it. He'd licked and sucked and caressed every inch of her beautiful body until she'd cried out again and again.

But tonight that wasn't what she needed. He opened the bedroom door, found her standing at the window, looking out at the night. Looking so very alone. And scared. She didn't turn when he came in, didn't say a word when he stopped behind her.

But her body shuddered when he wrapped his arms around her waist. He kissed the side of her neck and rocked her gently, careful to keep their bodies separated below the waist. He had only so much control. "We'll find her. Don't stop believing it."

"She'll be scared," she whispered. "Like before. I don't want her to be afraid, Ethan."

"What happened before, Dana?"

"It was Caroline's ex-husband. He wanted to get to Caroline and Tom and used Evie. She was needy and he exploited it. But she figured out who he was. So he . . ." Another massive shudder shook her. She was holding herself so rigid he thought she'd crumble.

"It's all right. You don't have to tell me."

"He raped her, Ethan. Horribly. Then he cut up her hands and her face, strangled her, and left her for dead."

"Who found her?" he murmured, although he thought he knew the answer.

"I did. She was living with me then. She was on the bed . . . There was so much blood."

He thought of the way she'd stared at her hands covered in Sandy Stone's blood that afternoon. Detached horror he'd thought then. Now he understood. "But you saved Evie."

Her laugh was brittle. "Sure. I called 911 and the paramedics came. She almost died twice on the way to the hospital, but they brought her back."

"They caught him, Winters?" *Please say they caught him.*

"Yes." There was a wealth of information in that one satisfied word, he knew. But there would be time for that later. "He went to jail and somebody stabbed him to death."

"So justice was done."

"Sure it was," she said bitterly. "He died and Evie had to go on. She's had plastic surgery on her face, reconstructive surgery on her hand. Therapy. Physical, emotional. Half her face is still paralyzed and she'll never have children."

"But she's gone on."

"Yeah, in the dark. In the house. She won't go out in the daytime, won't associate with people her own age. She takes classes online for a career she has no hope of achieving. She wants to counsel kids, but they're afraid of her. They see the scar on her face and cower." Her voice broke. "It's devastating, Ethan. And now, she's with Sue. Another maniac with a knife.

Can you blame me for being willing to do anything to protect her from that?"

He brushed his lips across the top of her head, his heart breaking for her. "No, I can't."

"I know it was stupid to want to trade. I know it won't do any good. But I think of Evie and Alec and . . ." A sob broke free, her shoulders started to shake. "I just can't stand it."

He turned her in his arms. "I know. I know." Her tears were flowing freely now, somehow made more devastating because she'd been so strong.

"I know I'm being selfish, that you're just as worried about Alec." Her hands were fisted against his chest. "Ethan, he's just a little boy. If I'd done something sooner —"

"She would have killed you," he interrupted firmly. "She is intent on whatever this plan of hers is. You could not have stopped her."

One fist pounded weakly against his chest. *I could have tried.*

"Then you would have died," he said flatly and she went still. And said nothing. His heart froze at the meaning he read into the gesture. "Is that what you wanted, Dana?"

Wearily she pushed away. Wiped her face with her sleeve. Rubbed her forehead. "No. I may be stupid, but I'm not suicidal."

No, not in the traditional sense, he thought. "Do you know why I was angry earlier?"

She sighed. "Because I told Mia to arrange a trade. I got it, Ethan. Dots connected."

"No, that wasn't it. Offering yourself as a trade might have been a brave thing to do, a sacrifice even. If you perceived there to be a downside."

She looked up through her lashes, the motion not the least bit coy. "What?"

"You offered yourself automatically. As if there had never been any doubt in your mind."

"There wasn't," she said between her teeth. He was making her angry. So be it.

"Why not?"

She turned on her heel and went into the bathroom. He followed, watched her splash her face with cold water. "Is your life worth so little that you offer it without a thought?"

Her hands paused under the water, then shaking, turned off the faucet and grabbed a towel. "You've known me four days, Ethan. You're hardly qualified to judge."

He grasped her shoulders. "Look at me. I've known you four days that in my life feels like four years. The first minute I met you, you were hurt defending a stranger. Then I find that's what you do, protect women from violent men. You put yourself in danger daily and I have to ask myself why. You live in poverty and I have to ask myself why. Anyone can see you believe in what you do. But, Dana, you didn't see the look in your eyes when you told Mia to make the trade. There was no sadness, no fear. Just surprise that anyone even objected. It scared me and that's what made me mad."

She closed her eyes. "I'm tired, Ethan. I'm going to bed now. You can sleep wherever you're most comfortable." She slipped beneath his hands and crawled into bed. After a half minute he followed, muttering an oath.

"Move over." He got into bed and pulled her against him so they lay spooned together. He would torture himself, feeling the softness of her butt against his groin, but if she could stand it, so could he. "You know what else?" he bit out. "It made me mad that you only agreed not to trade yourself because of the trouble it would cause everyone else."

"Go to sleep, Ethan." The words hissed between her teeth.

"Not until you tell me why. Why do you do this? Why is your life one big penance?"

"It's. Not."

"The hell it's not." He raised up on his elbow and flipped her on her back. Ignored the look of pure fury that kindled in those brown eyes so normally calm. "Honey, I was raised Catholic. I know a penance when I see one. Is it because you made a few bad decisions when you were a kid? Dammit, don't you think you've paid for that a million times over?"

The fire in her eyes blazed higher. "You" — her finger bored into his chest — "are not a board-certified therapist. And you" — she jabbed again — "don't know what you're talking about. So you" — a third jab that would surely leave a bruise — "shut up."

He was close to the truth now. He grabbed her hand, clamped it above her head. Grabbed the other hand when she tried to free herself. Rolled on top of her when she tried to pull away. "I've met men who've killed in the line of duty and they don't feel this kind of guilt." She thrashed beneath him and he had to use all his weight to keep her from bolting. "You did some time. Smoked a little pot. It's not like you *killed* anyone."

Like a popped balloon she stopped fighting. Her body went lax and warily he waited for her to lurch away when he loosed his hold. But she didn't. She just lay there staring at his face. Like he'd slapped her. "My mother," she finally whispered. "I killed my mother. Are you happy now?" Then she rolled over, punched the pillow, and didn't say another word.

*Chicago,*
*Thursday, August 5, 2:00 a.m.*

As beds went, Evie thought, she'd had better. But she'd certainly had worse. The bathtub in this grimy little motel was cleaner than she'd expected and if she kept her limbs relaxed, she didn't feel too stiff. The ropes that bound her hands and feet were securely tied. There would be no breaking them. The duct tape that covered her mouth gave her incentive not to cry. Tears would clog her nose, then she'd suffocate.

She had managed to sit up, only to find that Jane had not only tied her hands and feet, but secured the ropes at her hands to the safety rail in the wall. Pulling hard hadn't budged it and she cursed herself for allowing herself to become so physically weak. Before Winters, she'd lifted weights, jogged. Since . . . she'd done nothing but hide in the dark, just like Dana said.

She tried not to worry about Erik, under the bed where Sue had left him. Gagged and bound as well. It was pretty clear the kid was not Jane's son after all. So Evie's instincts had been . . . not too bad. She'd thought that Jane was one step up from the hamster mothers that eat their own young. She hadn't been too far off.

She tried not to worry about Dana. She hoped that Dana knew she was also in danger so that she would keep herself safe. And she was suddenly, fiercely glad they'd begun to make amends this morning. Dana had a boyfriend. She deserved one, after all. Nobody Evie had ever met was more dedicated to her job. *Because it's more than a job,* Evie thought and frowned when tears threatened. No tears. *Breathing is good. Suffocation is bad.*

The thump on the door jerked her from her thoughts. Jane was back. She steeled herself to meet those lifeless, colorless eyes.

And could only blink when the door flew open and an exhausted Erik slid to the floor.

# Chapter Nineteen

*Chicago,*
*Thursday, August 5, 3:30 a.m.*

*There was blood everywhere.* Everywhere.
*Splattered on the walls, seeped deep into
the carpet. Her shoes squished as she ran.*
Ran. *Dropped to her knees beside her body.
She knew the woman was dead. She always knew the woman was dead. Yet still
she grabbed, her hands slipping as she lost
her grip. So much blood.* Slippery. *She
grabbed again, as she always did.* It's a
dream. It's just a dream. *She knew it. She
just couldn't stop it. Couldn't stop herself.
Couldn't make her heart stop racing in fear.
She turned the body and braced herself for
the face. Who would it be tonight?*

*The scream tore through her mind as
she stared at the face, horror freezing her
where she knelt. Then the ringing began.
She groped for the phone, but it slipped
from her hands. She held up her hands,
the scream building once again.* Blood.

*Her hands were covered in blood. And still the phone rang and rang.*

The ringing woke her up. Trembling, nauseous, Dana came to her knees, shaking her head to clear the dream from her mind. She squinted at the bedside clock and in a rush remembered where she was. And with whom. And exactly what she'd revealed to him. She reached for the phone next to the bed and frowned when she heard only a dial tone. Then remembered the cell phone she'd set on the nightstand before her shower last night.

*Evie.*

Beside her Ethan lifted himself on his elbow and switched on the lamp on his side of the bed. Next to the lamp was her cell phone and his gun. He kept his steady green eyes focused on her while he reached for the phone and she felt the tension ebb, just enough to take it from his hand. Answer it. "H-h-h-" *Breathe. Just breathe.* "Hello?"

"Miss Dupinsky?"

Dana blinked and shook her head at Ethan. "Yes, this is Dana Dupinsky."

"This is Nurse Simmons from Rush Memorial."

*Caroline.* Dana's heart was suddenly pounding, so loud she could barely hear.

"What's happened to Caroline?"

"She's . . . she's taken a bad turn, Miss Dupinsky." The nurse stumbled over the words awkwardly. "She's asking for you. Can you please come right away?"

Dana gulped in air. "Is the baby? Or Caroline?"

"It's . . . both. The baby died and Mrs. Hunter is asking for you."

"Oh, God, oh, God." Dana swung her legs over the bed. "Tell her I'll be there. Thirty minutes, tops. Thank you." With shaking hands she dropped the phone into the bedsheets and tried to stand up, only to find Ethan holding her back, his grasp gentle, but firm on her arm. "Let me go, Ethan. I have to get to Rush."

"Dana, wait." There was a calm note in his voice that penetrated her panic. "You told me only Evie knew this number. Did you give it to Caroline?"

Dana slowly turned. He was sober, his eyes grave. And she understood. "No. I meant to, but I never got a chance. And Caroline thought they'd let her go home tonight."

"Call Max. See for yourself that every-thing is all right." His voice was still calm, but there was a steely undertone that told her he was angry.

Hands still shaking, she called Max's cell phone, her stomach tied in knots.

"Dana, what's wrong?" Max sounded groggy. He'd been asleep. She let out a breath.

"I don't know yet. Tell me the truth, Max, is Caroline in danger? Did the baby die?"

There was a half beat of silence. "She's fine, Dana. She's here at Ma's house with me. The doctor said it would be better for her to go somewhere without stairs. Why?"

Dana shuddered out a breath. "Oh, Max. Thank God." Ethan's hand ran up her arm, squeezed her shoulder. She braved a smile. "I just got a terrible phone call from Nurse Simmons. She told me to come to the hospital, right away."

"She lied, Dana." Max's voice was tight. "It was the woman who has Evie, wasn't it?"

Her pulse, which had started to slow with relief, started to race again. Sue had tried to lure her out. "It might have been," she whispered. "What if it was really Nurse Simmons?"

"Are you with Buchanan?" Max bit out.

Dana looked at Ethan, fear clawing at her insides. *Please not another one.* "Yes."

"Put him on. Now."

She handed the phone to Ethan. "It's Max Hunter."

Ethan listened, his eyes fastened on Dana's face. "I won't. Don't worry . . . I didn't expect she'd buy it, but it was worth a try . . . Sure. Thanks." He ended the call. "Call Mia. Now."

Dana's hands shook worse than before. Mia answered on the third ring, her voice husky with sleep. "Mia, it's Dana."

Mia's response to the news was much as Max's had been. "I'm on it. I'll dump the LUDs from your cell and see if I can get a location of her call, but I'm betting she's watching the hospital entrance, waiting for you. I'll call Abe and we'll check it out ourselves. Are you with Buchanan?"

"Yes," Dana gritted through her teeth. "And I won't go anywhere by myself."

Mia sighed. "I'm sorry, Dana. I'm just worried about you. I'm your friend. I'm allowed."

"Just find her, Mia. And call me if you find Nurse Simmons. Please. I need to know."

"All right. Stay where you are. I'll order an hourly drive-by on Max's mother's street."

Dana's heart stopped. Just . . . stopped. "You think she'll try again?"

Mia hesitated. "How do you think she knew Simmons was Caroline's nurse?"

Dana covered her mouth, horrified. Helpless. "She was in the hospital. Near Caroline." One look at Ethan's grim face let her know he'd already come to the same conclusion.

"We'll check it out," Mia promised. "Do not go anywhere by yourself."

"I won't." Carefully she hung up the phone. "Simmons is dead, isn't she, Ethan?"

Ethan pulled her close, pressed her cheek into his chest where his heart beat steadily. "Maybe. Let's not borrow trouble. I need to be sure Randi hasn't received any calls." Not letting her go, he dialed the Vaughns' room, had a brief conversation with Stan Vaughn. Turning off the lamp he slid them both down to the pillows, holding her just a little too tight.

It didn't matter. She held on to him just as tightly. A fist of fear grabbed her by the throat. "She tried to lure me."

"I know, honey." The gentle words were at stark contrast to the tensing of his body. "But she won't get you."

"She was close to Caroline." Dana could hear the panic rising in her own voice.

One hand came up to cup her jaw. "She

won't get her, either."

*No, she won't. Max won't let her. Mia won't let her. Caro is safe.* "What did Max say?"

"That we didn't fool Caroline with the story of you being too busy to come over tonight. She knows something's wrong. Max told her the truth."

"Okay." She found herself breathing to the rhythm of his steady heartbeat.

"Do . . . Do you want to talk about it?" he asked quietly.

"It" needed no clarification. The big bomb. The one thing she'd never planned to reveal. Yet she had and it needed explanation. But the nightmare was still too fresh. The vision of the face too disturbing to contemplate in her current state. Dana had learned long ago to compartmentalize her fears. She did so now, knowing the lock on the box was a fragile one. "Not yet. Please don't be angry with me. I just . . . Not yet."

"I'm not angry, Dana." He sounded more sad and that was worse than anger. Still his sadness was better than his contempt. *Compartmentalize. Refocus. New subject.*

"Did Randi get another call?"

"No. Stan said he'd finally made her take a sleeping pill when she didn't fall asleep

534

on her own, but that he was keeping watch. He said Sheriff Moore had her deputy change the beach house phone to forward to Stan's cell phone instead of hers."

"I liked Sheriff Moore."

"I'll like her a hell of a lot more if Clay comes out of this with his license intact."

"Why did Clay stop being a cop?"

His little sigh told her he knew she was doing the avoidance dance, but that he'd go along with it. For now. "Claimed burnout. I think he did it partly for me. Said he'd been thinking about leaving the force and since I was at loose ends, why not go into business?"

Dana felt a sudden surge of gratitude to Clay Maynard. "I liked Clay, too."

"Most women do," Ethan said wryly and Dana lifted her head to see his face.

"That's not what I meant."

He locked his eyes on hers. "Good."

The single whispered syllable had her gaze dropping to his mouth. Inches from hers. She could have it. His mouth. She knew she could have every last inch of him if she chose. *Did she? Could she?* She didn't know. She only knew that in covering his mouth with hers she could put off the terrors that lurked at the fringes of her mind.

His hand slid across the back of her neck. Warm and strong. Sending a hard shiver pulsing down her spine. But not forcing her one way or the other. Which was exactly the push she needed to close the distance between them.

He jumped when her lips touched his, his whole body tensing, arching. His hand pulled her down into the kiss until together they'd taken it from sweet to sensual. Both his hands now gripped her face, positioning it one way, then another, each movement further perfecting their fit. Her heart was pounding in her ears, her blood rushing. The very core of her body throbbing. And he touched her nowhere but her lips and face.

She lifted her head, breathing hard. So was he. His eyes glittered in the darkness. But he didn't ask. He wouldn't. He'd made that clear. He wanted her. He was wired that way. *God help me, so am I.* She needed this. For just a little while. Then she'd face the world again. The threats inside her mind and out. Both were real. Both were hideous. She'd steal some peace. *Just for a little while.*

She splayed one hand on his chest, the golden hair tickling her palm and his eyes flashed. She moved her hand lower, the iron ridges of his abdomen flexing as his body tightened. His hand covered hers. "We don't have to do this."

He'd make her say it then. "Please, Ethan." She closed her eyes, rested her forehead against his chin. "I don't want to go back to sleep. I can't. Not yet."

He moved suddenly, quickly rolling her to her back. Looming over her. His breath driving his chest hard and fast. "Be sure."

"I'm sure."

Abruptly he straddled her hips, her sweatshirt fisted in his hands. "What do you want?"

Arousal swelled. Stunned. *Anything. Everything.* "You."

He jerked the shirt over her head. Threw it to the floor. And in a single movement slid down, prone against her, his mouth on her breast. Greedy. God, so greedy.

She cried out. Arched into him and he sucked harder, pain and pleasure all rolled into one moment in time. A moment he stretched out, then started all over again when he moved to her other breast. Her fingers dug through his hair, pulling him closer. Her heels dug into the mattress and she pushed her pelvis into the rock hardness of his chest. She throbbed, she ached. She needed him. "Ethan, please."

He released her breast, moved down her torso, kissing and licking and setting every little area of skin he touched on fire. Reached the elastic waistband of her sweats and in another of his graceful movements, rolled off her, yanked the pants down her legs, and rolled back between her thighs. And hovered there.

She could feel the heat of his breath just there . . . where she wanted him. "Ethan."

He lifted his head, stared up at her. His lips a fraction of an inch from where she wanted him. "I want you to forget everything," he said, his voice hoarse. "Everything but me." He kissed the tender flesh of her inner thigh and her muscles quivered from the strain of holding back. "Just remember me." He kissed the other thigh and she moaned.

Then flicked at her with the tip of his tongue and she gasped.

Then his mouth was on her and she forgot to breathe. The pleasure was . . . sharp, vicious, it had claws, digging deep. Unwavering, it drove her higher and higher until all she could hear was the sound of her own breath, sobbing, begging. Then the shimmer grew and grew until it was a blinding flash, and everything unraveled in a fury of sensation and light and pleasure.

She was gasping for air when the weight on her legs disappeared. She struggled to open her eyes to find him standing at the nightstand, yanking the drawer, a grimace of pain on his face as he pulled a condom out of the box. Her eyes dropped to the waistband of his boxers where she could see the tip of his erection straining for freedom.

In awe, she watched him shuck off his boxers and with shaking hands slide the condom into place. Then he was on all fours on the bed, hanging over her, his eyes burning into hers. "Look at me," he muttered. "Think of me. Just of me."

"I am. I will. Please, Ethan."

Then he was easing inside her, shuddering his relief. "Oh, God." He dragged in a breath, his shoulders sagging, his powerful biceps supporting his weight. "I needed this. I needed you." Then he was thrusting, going deeper when she raised her legs to flank his hips, drawing a guttural groan from deep within his chest. She gave a cry of surprised delight when he undulated, stroking her internal muscles with thorough precision.

His smile was razor sharp. "You like that?"

"Yes." Her voice was like a stranger's,

husky and deep. Then he did it again and she could only moan. Which seemed to catapult him into full throttle, his hips pistoning so hard she could only hang on to his shoulders helplessly as sensation once again layered, climbed . . . And shattered. Bracing her heels on his thighs she arched just as he thrust. And came. Soundlessly. Magnificently. His muscles straining. Teeth bared.

He collapsed onto his forearms, his face buried in the curve of her shoulder, his heart pounding to beat all hell, his chest heaving against her as he struggled to breathe. Minutes passed before he spoke and when he did it was in a voice that sounded like dry sandpaper. "My God."

Completely spent, she ran a hand down the hard plane of his back. Pressed a kiss to his shoulder, his jaw. Anything she could reach without moving. Guilt would come at some point, she thought. Guilt for enjoying such awesome pleasure while someone she loved suffered. But now, there was only exhaustion. Exhaustion and some measure of peace.

Eventually Ethan roused himself, disappeared into the bathroom. When he came back he tucked her up against him, his arm wrapped around her waist in a gesture that was purely proprietary. His hand slipped up to cup her breast and she sighed, replete.

"Go to sleep now." He kissed her shoulder. "No dreams. Tomorrow we'll find them."

She drifted off, praying he'd be right.

*Chicago,*
*Thursday, August 5, 4:30 a.m.*

Sue watched the hospital entrance from her car parked across the street, annoyance mounting with each minute that passed. Dupinsky hadn't shown up. The bitch knew she'd been set up. With a frown she saw a car drive through the parking lot outside the front entrance. The car had driven past before, she was sure of it. That kind of careful drive-by meant only one thing — cops. Not only had Dupinsky known, she'd called the damn cops.

With a snarl, Sue carefully pulled her car into traffic. She'd thought it unlikely Dupinsky would call the hospital before she rushed over from wherever she'd holed up. The woman seemed to live by her intuition, which should have been haywire hearing that sweet Caroline's baby was dead. Dammit. And she'd thought she sounded so convincing, too.

*Adopt, adapt, and improve.* She needed a different way to get to Dupinsky, that was all. By the time she was through, Dupinsky would know what it was like to be meddled with.


*Chicago,*
*Thursday, August 5, 5:15 a.m.*

The kid was damn resourceful, Evie thought. After falling through the door he'd sunk to the floor in a heap, and she'd thought he'd passed out. It would be no wonder if he had. That poor baby hadn't eaten properly in days, his only decent meal in at least a week the one she'd given him herself the morning before as they'd waited for Sandy. She'd watched him lie there on the floor, helpless to do anything for him. But Erik wasn't passed out, or if he had been, he'd come to.

Then she'd been treated to the greatest show of sheer determination she'd ever seen as he'd slowly, hands and feet bound, methodically worked his way to the sink where he'd managed to turn the faucets with his nose and chin. He'd been letting the water run over the tape covering his mouth for some time now, stopping for a minute to press his face to the edge of the counter and scrape. Over and over, he scraped until the tape began to give. A few times he'd fallen to the bathroom floor, but he would lie there for a moment, then roll to his knees and start inching his way back to his feet, back to the sink. Finally, he worked an opening in the tape big enough to breathe because she heard his lungs rasp and rattle. Then he drank, audible gulps that made her remember how long it had been since she'd had water.

He gave one last scrape against the counter's edge and his mouth was visible, the tape hanging off his chin. He turned to look at her and the fierce pride in his eyes made her want to smile. But the tape still held her lips firm, so she gave him a hard nod instead.

He dropped to his knees next to the tub, frowning in concentration. His teeth clamped his lower lip, biting hard. Then he opened his mouth.

And spoke. "E ɔie hut?"

Evie blinked, astonished. He spoke. After six days of silence, this child spoke. Hut? *Hurt.* Her eyes stung. After all he'd been through, his first words were to ask if she was hurt. She shook her head, then leaning forward, tilted it. *You?*

He smiled grimly, but with intense satisfaction. Then he shook his head. "No." That word was very clear and she wondered why he hadn't used it before. Bracing himself, he leaned over the side of the tub, sliding until the top half of his body rested on the tub's edge, then with a grunt, toppled himself over the edge. He lay next to her legs, breathing hard.

A moment later he was on his knees, his mouth on her cheek, his teeth scraping at the tape that covered her mouth. After a few seconds, he leaned back, his thin chest heaving. But his eyes were determined. She could only nod in encouragement, but that seemed enough. He set his teeth on the tape again and after a few more attempts was finally able to catch an edge. He whipped his head back, yanking at the tape.

And her mouth was free. The first big gulp of air stretched her lungs painfully, but she thought it was the best pain she'd ever felt.

"Hup," he said. Scream for help.

So she did, big loud screams. And they waited. But nothing happened. Evie shook her head sadly. "Nobody is here, Erik."

His sandy brows snapped together at that. "Al . . . Alec."

"Alec? Your name is Alec?"

His eyes were fastened on her mouth and when they rose, they glittered. He nodded.

"Alec, do you know where we are?" She'd been in the trunk as they'd driven around town for hours. She had no idea of where they were. But he hadn't been in the trunk.

Again his brows knit and his lips pursed. "Guh . . ." He jerked his head aside in frustration. Evie leaned, tilted until he could see her face, her smile warm.

"Try, Alec."

He closed his eyes. "Guh . . . ah . . . wee." He opened his eyes, tentatively.

Guh-ah-wee. Evie drew a quick breath. "Gary? Gary, Indiana?"

He nodded excitedly. "Ssss . . . sk-kool. Sh . . . sh . . ." He stopped, frustrated again.

Evie nodded calmly and he gathered himself up.

"Sh . . . shik."

Evie shook her head. "I'm sorry, Alec. Shik?"

He clamped his lips together. "Doo . . . doo . . . doo." He said it in a higher voice, the last syllable stretched, then petering out. Evie pondered frantically, then smiled as realization dawned. "Chicken. Cock-a-doodle-doo."

He drew a breath, smiling again. Then she jerked and he stilled as the motel door opened. Closed. She saw the look of terror leap back into his eyes just moments before Jane roared through the doorway, her gun drawn. Her face wild and furious.

She took a step forward and simply plucked Alec from the tub as if he weighed nothing. Holding him by the shirtfront, she cracked him back against the wall. Alec's shoulders sagged and a low moan rose from his throat.

"Don't hurt him," Evie snapped and Jane just looked at her with a mocking sneer.

"*I* don't plan to. But you . . . You're quite another story. You, I will enjoy hurting a great deal." She pulled another gun from her back waistband. "Recognize this?"

Evie shrank back against the bathroom wall. It wasn't the gun she'd used to kill Sandy Stone, black and sleek. It was silver and heavy. A revolver. Dana's.

The phone ringing woke him. Ethan lifted his head, quickly discerning the ring came from the hotel phone, not Dana's cell. He leaned over her warm sleeping body and picked up the receiver before it could ring twice. "Yes?"

"Mr. Buchanan, this is the front desk. We're sorry to wake you, but we have a package here for Miss Dana Dupinsky left by Detective Mitchell. The detective said it was important."

Ethan let his body relax. His first thought had been that Sue had sent Dana a package similar to the one she sent Stan and Randi yesterday, but realized Sue would have no reason to do so. She thought they still believed Goodman to be responsible. "Thank you. Can you have someone send it up, along with some coffee?"

"We'll have the package up to you in ten minutes. The coffee might take a little longer."

He hung up, but didn't lay back down. Instead stayed where he was, leaning over Dana, looking down into her face. She'd slept the rest of the night and if she'd had nightmares, they hadn't been enough to wake her up. She said she'd killed her mother. Ethan knew that was not true. But in Dana's own convoluted sense of accountability, she'd done something that made her take responsibility for her mother's death.

He'd made her pain stop for a little while last night. He made her forget the nightmares, forget her own name. Instead he'd made her cry out with pleasure. He shivered, the memory of what it felt like to be inside her still very much alive. As was he. But that was to be expected when a man woke up next to a beautiful naked woman.

"What am I going to do with you, Dana Danielle Dupinsky?" he murmured. When all this was over, would he go back to his life alone as if nothing had happened? Could he? He was pretty sure the answer was no, but this was not the time to be making such decisions. They could wait until Alec and Evie were back, safe and sound. He smoothed the hair back from her brow, pressed a kiss to her temple. "Then we'll talk."

He rolled out of bed and pulling on a pair of jeans, closed the bedroom door behind him quietly. His eyes fell on the stack of CDs on the desk. He'd transferred all the videos to CD and last night had made copies of everything for Mitchell and Reagan. The police would be going over the tapes down at their office with a fine-tooth comb. But still . . .

Something nagged at him as he picked up the top CD. It was the bookstore where Sue had enjoyed a cup of coffee before sending the Tuesday e-mail. He popped the CD into his computer and dropped into the chair. He started the file and sat back, watching once again as Sue read the sign language book, then sent the e-mail, carefully wiping the keyboard before and after touching it. There was nothing new here. Nothing at all.

There was a knock at the door and Ethan opened it to a bellboy who held a plastic bag from Wal-Mart. A peek inside showed neat bundles of polo shirts and cotton skirts.

"There's a note inside," the bellboy said as Ethan tipped him. "Thanks."

The note was sitting on top of the clothes, unsealed, so Ethan scanned it. Mitchell wanted them to meet her at the station at nine-thirty. Dana still had a little more time to sleep. Setting the bag of clothes aside, he went to shut down the video clip, then froze, his finger poised over his keyboard. He'd always stopped the video when Sue had exited the store.

He shouldn't have.

There was another knock, this one from the adjoining door to Clay's room. "Come in," Ethan said excitedly. The door opened a crack and Clay's head poked through.

"I heard a knock outside," Clay said. "I wanted to make sure everything was okay."

"It was just some clothes Mitchell sent over for Dana. Come over here and look at this." He set the video back a minute or two. "This is Conway in that bookstore."

"Where she read the sign language book," Clay said.

"Yeah. Now, she's leaving . . ." He pointed to the monitor. "Look at the stack of books on Conway's table." A waitress appeared to bus the table and picked up the stack.

Clay whistled as the top book was clearly captured by the store's security camera. "*Michelin's Guide to Paris*? Why is she — Shit. She's going to run to Paris?"

"Maybe. The EU has a standing policy of refusing to extradite Americans if there's a possibility of the death penalty."

"And both Maryland and Illinois have the death penalty," Clay said grimly. "We need to make sure Mitchell and Reagan know about this. If she's planning to flee the country, she'll need a passport. They can post notices at the airports, watching for her."

"Mitchell wants us to meet her at nine-thirty. We can tell her then. Those international flights leave in the early evening, so we have time to set up the check."

Clay's eyes searched the room, his brows going up at the sight of Ethan's shirt and pants in a heap on the floor next to the sofa still piled up with the pillows and blanket Dana had brought him the night before. He took another long look at Ethan and Ethan felt his cheeks heating. "Don't ask."

Clay grinned. "Okay, I won't." Instead he picked up Ethan's clothes and laid them across the sofa arm. Then bent down to retrieve something from the floor. When he straightened he wore a frown. "Your pills. They fell out of your pants pocket last night."

When Ethan had yanked them off, frustrated, aroused to a state of physical pain. He'd thrown the pants across the room. No wonder the packet dropped out. "Thanks."

Clay just held them. "There's another one missing, Ethan."

Ethan's brows rose along with his

temper. "You count my pills?"

"Yes, I do. Because you lie to me. Don't deny it. When did it happen yesterday?"

Ethan closed his eyes, counted to ten. "In the cab, coming back from the police station."

"So you weren't driving?"

"No." He opened his eyes, met Clay's pained stare head-on.

"Ethan, please, promise me you won't drive anymore. This is twice in three days."

The thought of giving up driving sent panic through him. "I've been under some stress."

"Yeah, and it's not going to let up until this is over. Ethan, your life is worth more than your independence. Every time we have this conversation you put me off. Not this time. If you'd been driving, you could have been killed."

"I feel them coming on, Clay." Ethan tried to be reasonable. "I can pull over and —"

"You could have killed someone else," Clay interrupted and at that Ethan closed his mouth. "How would you feel then, Ethan? How would I explain that to the family of the person you hurt? Please. Promise me."

Ethan stilled. Remembered his frustration with Dana's calloused disregard for her own life last night. And sighed deeply. He'd been wrong, but he could be taught. "I promise. No more driving until this is over and I've been episode clear for at least a week."

"A month," Clay challenged without a hint of a smile.

"We'll let the doctor decide. I'll abide by his recommendation, just as I did last time."

"Starting this morning. When we go to the police station, I drive."


*Chicago,*
*Thursday, August 5, 8:15 a.m.*

Evie raised her cheek off the cold, hard tub, the murmur of the television tickling her ears. Jane was awake in the bedroom. Where Erik was. She hadn't heard a sound from the boy since Jane had tossed him through the door as if he were a bag of garbage. It was hard to say how long she'd been gone, or how long she'd been back.

The door opened and Evie winced when the light came on. Then Jane appeared and, standing in front of the mirror, proceeded to apply color to her white-blond hair, not saying a word. She sat down on the toilet seat and flipped open the *Trib*. This morning's edition. Jane went page to page. Then her hands tightened on the paper, crushing it in her grip. She lowered it, her light eyes narrowed and angry.

"I'm going to take off the tape. If you make a sound I have not authorized, an answer I haven't specifically requested, I'll kill the boy and make you watch." Evie could not contain a shudder and Jane smiled. Cruelly. It was a terrifying sight to see. "You agree?"

Evie nodded and one-handed Jane hauled her to a sitting position. With the other hand she ripped off the tape. Evie sucked in a breath, swallowed what would have been a cry of pain. Jane looked reluctantly impressed. "So, you're wondering if I'm going to kill you."

Evie blinked. Said nothing. Jane grinned. "Are you wondering if I'm going to kill you?"

"No."

"Really? And why is that?"

"Because I know you will."

"Still cool. I can respect that. Are you wondering about the kid?"

Evie nodded once, understanding the game. "Yes."

"He's alive. For now. Where does Dupinsky live?"

Evie gritted her teeth. And gave the address. And once more Jane smiled that terrifying little smile. "I already knew, of course. That's how I got her gun. But you knew that, too. Real question. Who is Dana's new honey?"

"That I don't know." Jane narrowed her eyes. "I really don't," Evie insisted calmly. "She and I haven't been on the best of terms this week. I was quitting."

Long agonizing seconds ticked by. Then Jane stood up, disgruntled. "I believe you. Where else does she hang? I need addresses."

Dana had gone under then. Evie felt a rush of hope. Dana knew to be careful, that she was in danger, too. "At Caroline's house."

Jane shook her head in disgust. "Nobody there. I checked. They're all at her mother-in-law's house, guarding her like she was the goddamn Queen of England. Where else?"

"With Detective Mitchell sometimes. That address I don't know."

"What about the brother-in-law?"

"David?" Evie shook her head. Tried for bland. "He's interested, she's not."

Jane looked totally unconvinced. "What, is she gay?"

"Not to my knowledge," Evie replied evenly and Jane laughed out loud.

"You play a good game, Scarface." Jane chuckled at the flinch Evie couldn't control. "One more before I rinse this shit out. Did you know Goodman had been arrested?"

Evie jolted. "No."

"Yesterday morning. Says so on page twenty. You know, I think that's something Mitchell would tell Dupinsky, don't you?"

Evie swallowed. "Possibly."

"Dupinsky tried to make me think she was worried about me last night, all the while knowing Goodman hadn't left that note." Her lips thinned. "She tried to lure me back." She stood up and peeled off more tape. Pressed it to Evie's mouth. "We're done for now."

Chicago,
Thursday, August 5, 9:30 a.m.

"Thanks for coming down," Mia said, closing the door to the conference room where they'd been seated. It was certainly less intimidating than the interrogation

556

room they'd used the day before, Dana thought, sitting between Ethan and Clay. Randi sat next to Clay and Stan managed to sit as far away from them as possible and still be at the table. Abe Reagan sitting at the head of the table made their little gathering complete.

Mia looked at Dana. "I see you got the clothes."

"I did. Thanks. Mia, did you find Nurse Simmons?"

Mia smiled. "Yeah, we did, just a little while ago. She's fine. She'd taken the phone off the hook, trying to get some sleep after her shift. We finally broke the door down. Scared the poor woman to death. Hopefully her heart is back to normal by now."

Dana slumped in relief. "Then Sue must have called me herself."

"We watched the hospital for about two hours," Reagan said, "but if she was there, we didn't see her. She may have been watching from somewhere else."

Dana drew a breath. "Did you find she'd been in the hospital close to Caroline?"

"Yes," Mia answered honestly. "She brought a flower arrangement to the nurses' station, but the name on the card didn't exist on their patient chart. While the nurse on duty was trying to figure out which floor to send her to, she kept her eyes open. Saw Simmons talking to Max. It was all on the surveillance tape."

Dana's empty stomach churned, thinking of Sue that close to Caroline. Thinking of Evie in her hands right now. "She'd never met Max," she murmured.

Mia shrugged. "She'd met David. That was close enough. We also checked out your old neighborhood, Mrs. Vaughn. A gray Olds Eighty-eight was seen driving slowly past the wreckage of the Lewises' house. The car matched the one stolen from the old woman we found in Sandy Stone's car. The old woman is recovering, by the way. The Olds was found abandoned later."

"What about the Internet café she used to send yesterday's e-mail?" Ethan asked.

Mia glanced at Abe, then back at Dana, and Dana felt the hair on the back of her neck rise. "She used a prepaid credit card," Mia said. "The name on the card was Faith Joyce."

Dana felt every drop of blood drain from her face and could only stare up at Mia. Mia stared back down, deep regret in her round blue eyes. Dana shook her head, disbelieving what she thought she'd heard. "What?"

Mia bit her lip. "It was the same card used to reserve the Vaughns' room at the Excelsior Hotel, Dana. The reservation was made yesterday afternoon at about three."

Everything seemed to go silent and all Dana could hear was the pounding of her heart echoing in her head. It wasn't possible. It couldn't be. She felt Mia's hands pushing her head down, somebody else pulling her chair away from the table. Ethan. Ethan was kneeling beside her, his face worried. Then his face started to spin.

"Who is Faith Joyce?" she heard Clay ask, but Mia was pushing on her head again.

"Give her some space. Don't you dare faint on me, Dana. Abe, can you get her water?"

Dana drew huge gulping breaths and when she opened her eyes the room was stationary again. She struggled against Mia's hands. "Let go of me. You're going to break my damn neck." Instantly Mia released her hold.

"Then sit up slowly. When was the last time you ate?"

"Yesterday."

Mia scowled. "Shit, no more sense than a snot-nosed kid." She glared at Ethan who still knelt at her side. "You were supposed to make sure she ate, Buchanan."

Dana took the water Abe offered. "Leave him alone, Mia," she said wearily. "He tried. I just couldn't eat." She sipped at the water. Commanded her stomach to settle. "It was Beverly. I dropped her off at the bus station yesterday."

Mia swallowed hard. "Damn," she whispered. "I was afraid of that."

Clay stood up, his face one big frown. "Who is Faith Joyce?"

Ethan gently tugged her chin so that she looked at him, and without taking his eyes from hers, he answered, "Dana's mother." When she only stared at him, he brushed his thumb across her chin. "I couldn't sleep last night. So I checked."

"I don't understand," Randi said quietly. "Why would Sue use Dana's mother's card?"

Dana pressed her fingers to her trembling lips. Focused on Ethan's steady green eyes just as she had done so many times before. "When women leave Hanover House to go to other cities, we give them a prepaid credit card to use until they're settled. If they stay with us long enough, they can make money at a job to put toward the card. Like a savings plan. We use the name

Faith Joyce. Joyce was my mother's maiden name."

Ethan took her hands and held tight. "I read about it, Dana. I know what happened."

She squeezed his hands and lifted her eyes to Mia's, conscious that every eye in the room was on her. "Beverly earned almost nine hundred dollars." Dana's voice broke and she cleared her throat. "I dropped her off yesterday morning. She was going to California."

Mia gripped Dana's shoulder, hard. "What was Beverly carrying, Dana?"

Dana caught Ethan's puzzled frown from the corner of her eye. He hadn't figured this part, she thought, and looked up at Mia, who had. Who'd maybe known all along. "A driver's license. A social." She pursed her lips hard. "And a passport."

Mia's head dropped back and she groaned softly. "Shit, damn, fuck."

Dana blew out the breath she'd been holding, dropped her chin to her chest. "Mia, Beverly might be dead. Please send someone to the bus station to see. I hate to think of her lying there . . . like that."

There was silence around the table as Abe dialed the bus station. When he hung up, Dana raised her head. "Well?" *Please, not Beverly, too. She was going to have a life.*

"They found her this morning when the garbage truck came to empty the Dumpsters. She was pushed between the Dumpster and the wall." Abe looked so sad. "I'm sorry, Dana. They've taken her to the morgue, labeled her a Jane Doe. Can you identify her?"

Dana nodded numbly.

"What name was on the ID, Dana?" Mia asked in a low voice.

"Carla Fenton," she whispered.

Stan Vaughn stood up and leaned forward. "If I am to understand," he said coldly, "the woman who kidnapped Alec now has a passport so she can leave the country?"

Mia turned, a forbidding scowl twisting her face. "You gave her twenty-five thousand dollars, Mr. Vaughn. If she hadn't stolen Beverly's ID, that was plenty enough to buy another. Sit down, please, until we get this sorted out."

Jaw clenched, Stan sat.

Dana closed her eyes. "If she plans to use Beverly's ID, she'll have to dye her hair brown and get brown contact lenses. Check the optometrists."

"Do you know how many optometrists

562

there are in Chicago?" Mia growled, then swore. "Hell, at least it's a place that she hasn't been yet, instead of us showing up after the fact."

Abe stood up, walked around the table. Knelt on one knee in front of Dana. "I'll get a list so we can get started. But first, where did Beverly get the IDs, Dana?"

Dana shoved down the sob, locked it away. Looked Abe Reagan in the eye. And lied through her teeth. "I have no idea, Abe. I just take the pictures for the passports." *Thank you, David,* she thought fervently.

"Your photography business," Ethan murmured, and dropped into his chair.

She turned to look at him and saw he understood. "Yes."

Abe looked up at Mia, his tongue in his cheek. Mia shrugged. And said nothing more. "Let's start checking optometrists," he said. "We'll start with the ones in the mall she visited last night." He stood up. "But first, let's check our Jane Doe. We could be wrong."

Ethan helped Dana to her feet. "I'll come with you."

"You don't have to," she murmured.

He put his arm around her shoulders. "Yes, I do."

"So we just stay here?" Stan demanded.

Abe looked like he was losing his patience. "Unless you want to take a trip to the morgue, yes. When we're done, I'll take you to the airport so you can make it look like you've come in on that flight from D.C. Someone will be tailing you at every moment until you get to the hotel. We've had people in the room already this morning, posing as housekeeping, planting listening devices. I hope our preparations meet with your approval," he added sarcastically.

"Oh, there is one more thing," Ethan said, his arm tight around Dana's waist. "On one of the tapes I saw Conway reading books about Paris. If she has a passport . . ."

Abe gave Ethan an impressed nod. "We'll check it out. Now, Dana, let's go."

# Chapter Twenty

*Chicago,*
*Thursday, August 5, 10:30 a.m.*

She'd seen a lot of human suffering in her career, Mia thought. But very little matched the pain on Dana Dupinsky's face when Julia's assistant uncovered Beverly's face. But Dana never faltered. She just stood there at the viewing window and · nodded, Buchanan's hands on her shoulders. It wasn't until the assistant had pulled the sheet back up that Mia saw the crack in Dana's composure. Mia had taken a step forward when Buchanan turned Dana around and held her tight as the dam finally broke, rocking her as she sobbed.

"She'll be all right," Abe murmured beside her. "She's strong."

Mia swallowed at the sound of Dana's weeping, muffled by Buchanan's shoulder. "Nobody's that strong, Abe."

Abe said nothing for a moment, then

quietly asked, "How long have you known, Mia?"

Mia turned and looked up at him with a blank stare. "What, about Dana taking pictures for passports? Awhile. She even took mine."

He tilted his head closer. "You know what I mean."

He would have been intimidating if she hadn't known the kind of man he really was. "Abe, let it go. Please."

He narrowed his eyes. Then rolled them. "Fine. You owe me one, Mitchell."

Mia turned back to Dana, still weeping in Buchanan's arms. The sight made her own eyes sting. In all the years they'd known each other, Mia had never seen Dana cry. Not like this. "Fine." Mia straightened her spine when the head ME emerged from the morgue.

"Is your friend going to be all right?" Julia asked.

Mia jerked a nod. "Yeah. Well?"

Julia shrugged. "Your gal is nothing if not consistent. Looks like the same model as all the others, nine mil with a silencer. Did this woman have any family?"

"Just Dana. Can you hold the body for a little while, Julia? Just until all this is over? Dana will want to make the arrangements."

"I'll try, but I'm nearly at capacity." She

frowned. "You guys got to stop this."

"Thank you, Julia," Abe said dryly. "We'll keep that in mind."

Julia winced. "You know what I mean."

Abe squeezed her shoulder. "Yeah, I do. You've been busy."

"I haven't been home for more than ten hours in the past two days."

"But Jack's holding the fort at home, right?" Mia asked, watching Buchanan pull a handkerchief from his pocket and tenderly dab at Dana's eyes. Found herself unable to turn away when Buchanan tilted Dana's head up and pressed a kiss to her forehead. Perhaps something good might come out of all this.

Julia smiled. "Jack and I . . . we're good." Her smile faded. "I had a reporter call. I told him no comment. But it's only a matter of time before this leaks out. This is an abnormal level of GSWs, even for us."

Abe sighed. "We'll cross that bridge when we come to it."

Buchanan leaned down to murmur something in Dana's ear and she stiffened. Then turned her head to meet Mia's eyes and gave a shaky nod.

"She's all right now," Mia said. "Let's go. We need to get the Vaughns to the airport."

Abe lifted a dark brow. "And while we're there let's find out if 'Carla Fenton' purchased any tickets for Paris."

*Chicago,*
*Thursday, August 5, 10:15 a.m.*

"What now?" Clay asked from behind the wheel. Dana and Ethan sat in the back, her hand gripped hard in his. She leaned her head back against the seat and closed her eyes. Crying that hard had given her one hell of a headache and had solved nothing. Beverly was dead. Dr. Lee was dead. Sandy was dead. Evie might be dead this very moment.

"Stop thinking," Ethan said quietly. She opened her eyes to find his steady green gaze fixed on her face. To Clay he replied, "I need something to eat." Then he smiled, a mere baring of teeth. "Then we're going to that Internet café we tracked that e-mail to last night."

There was a grim resolution about him that felt oddly comforting. "What are you going to do?" Dana asked him.

"Something Mitchell said in there got me thinking. That Stan had given Sue twenty-five thousand dollars and that she

568

could've bought any ID she'd wanted."

"She didn't have to," Dana murmured. "I practically gave it to her."

Ethan took her chin firmly. "From here on out I do not want to hear any more *I should haves* or *should not haves*. You did not know. If you had, you never would have taken her in. You would have called the police to come and take Alec away. Am I understood?"

His grim resolution surrounded her, lifted her straighter. "Yes." Her lips quirked. "Sir."

He smiled back, brushed his thumb over her lips. "That's better. I'm tired of being Sue Conway's victim. The first thing we're going to do is take away her financial freedom."

"That money's long gone by now, Ethan," Clay protested. "It would take us days to get into her offshore accounts."

"Not days." Ethan eyed the fast food places that lined the road. "After lunch, I'm going to go find some cookies for dessert."

Dana frowned. "What are you talking about?"

Ethan sat back, a satisfied smile on his face. "Computer geek-speak. Every time you visit a Website, you leave behind information. It's called a cookie."

"I always wondered what that was," Dana murmured. "I set my computer to accept none because I was paranoid."

"I'm counting on the Internet café not being paranoid. Those rental computers are like well-used hookers. You have no idea where they've been or how many people have been on them. In last night's e-mail she said we'd done well with the practice deposit. That means she checked her account, and she might have done it online."

Dana processed the information, pushing the throbbing pain aside. "So when Sue typed in her offshore account numbers, they were saved on the computer in a cookie."

"But you'd still need her password," Clay objected, then shook his head. "Never mind."

Ethan shot him a patronizing look. "Child's play. If" — he glanced back at Dana — "I have some information about her background. Most people use passwords that have personal meaning although you should use random numbers. If you can get me Sue's background — more than Randi was able to tell us — I should be able to break into her account."

Dana watched as Clay pulled into a

burger place, feeling a grim determination of her own. "Get me a single with extra pickles. And a large order of fries."

Ethan pulled her close in a hard hug. "Good girl."

Dana leaned into the hug, realizing how much she'd come to depend on his strength in so short a time. When this was over and he went home . . . Brusquely, she pulled away. "Are we going to separate or stay together?"

Ethan's eyes narrowed. "If you think you're getting out of my sight, you're crazy."

He'd actually flinched when she'd pulled away. "I meant do you want to go to the computer place while Clay drives me to Social Services. I'm not stupid, Ethan. I promised I wouldn't go anywhere alone and I won't."

"Why don't we all stay together?" Clay inserted smoothly. "If Conway is keeping tabs on Dana, I can sit outside and watch for her while the two of you check things out at the computer place."

"Then we'll go down to Sandy's office," Dana added. "Sue hated social workers so much, she's got to have a file. If it's in Chicago, someone in Sandy's office will have it."

"You may want to let the detectives ask those questions," Clay said softly.

Dana shook her head. "If Sue's records are sealed, they won't be able to hand those records over to Mia without a court order. And after what happened to Sandy yesterday, somebody will be mad enough to talk to me without one."

Ethan looked troubled. "Clay, I'm just dragging you deeper. We can go ourselves."

"Shut up, Ethan," Clay said mildly, pulling up to the drive-thru. "I'm not searching for cookies on an empty stomach."

*Chicago,*
*Thursday, August 5, 12:10 p.m.*

"It's not perfect, but it'll do just fine," Sue murmured as she picked her way across the littered basement floor of the abandoned apartment house. It was identical to the basement two buildings down, which was the one she'd really wanted. Unfortunately people lived in the apartments in the building two buildings down. But nobody had lived here for a very long time. The lock on the door was broken and anyone could come and go as they pleased.

She kicked an empty beer can, one of many. Under some trash she saw used condoms. A few needles. This was good. It meant the neighbors were used to wild parties down here. Nobody would notice a little loud music. Maybe a scream or two.

She and Donnie and the boys — hell, they'd blend right in.

She moved some cardboard boxes, sending a pack of mice scurrying across the floor. She'd been pleasantly surprised that the light worked. This was good, too.

She kept moving until she reached the back wall, behind the storage cages. And frowned when the very bad memories came rolling back. It was here where she'd hid. She'd been out, doing a job, only to come back to cops crawling everywhere, raiding Randi's place, two buildings down. She'd run to Donnie's, but they were there, too. Donnie was being hauled away in cuffs. The cops took everything from Donnie's, all their merchandise. So she'd run. Back to Miranda's place, two buildings down. Where she'd stashed some emergency cash in a hole in the wall behind the stove. She'd held out for nearly two days with no food or water, until she thought the cops had gone away. She'd emerged, crept up to the apartment, only to find the money gone. And a cop waiting. *Where's your baby?* It was all about the damn kid. Or Miranda. *Where's Miranda? Did you kill her, too?* She could still hear it in her mind.

Ten years later she walked out of Hillsboro a free woman. Except that she really wasn't free. She wouldn't be until Randi Vaughn knew what it was like to hide in fear. To go without food or drink. To be forced to submit to the will of men whose only merit was that they were bigger and stronger.

Tomorrow night this basement would become Randi Vaughn's private hell.

For now, it would be an adequate place to hide the girl. There was no fucking way she was leaving those two together again. She turned and pinned her eyes on Scarface who sat on the floor, her hands and feet still bound. Her dark eyes were narrowed and defiant above the tape covering her mouth. Not to be outdone again, Sue had wrapped the tape all the way around the girl's head. Three times. It would be a good deal harder to remove this time. "I hope mice don't bother you," she said and had the pleasure of watching the girl's defiance flicker as her eyes darted. She forced the girl to her feet and dragged her behind what had once been the apartment's heating unit. "I'll be back for you later."

*Ocean City, Maryland,*
*Thursday, August 5, 2:45 p.m. Eastern*
*(1:45 p.m. Central)*

Detective Janson was waiting for Lou in the Ocean City sheriff's office and both he and Sheriff Eastman stood up when she entered. "You made good time," Eastman said without preamble. "We've got fifteen minutes before Lewis's lawyer gets here." He gave her a look of disbelief. "Do I understand that Chicago's got four bodies?"

Lou sat on the arm of a chair. "Yeah. In three days. All head shots, same gun."

"Same MO as my two," Janson said. "Rickman and Samson."

"But not the same as your guy in the shed," Eastman said. "How you planning to pin any of this on Lewis?"

"We're not." Lou rubbed the back of her neck, stiff from the long trip. "We're planning to use it to show him how cold his sister is. She's not coming for him. She's got a passport and plans to skip the country." A last-minute check with Mitchell had provided those last bits of information. "Chicago PD didn't find any purchased tickets, but they have reason to believe she's targeting France. She's going to let Lewis take the fall for a kidnapping."

"Her own kid," Eastman said with a frown. "Defender's going to jump all over that. Not a kidnapping, he'll say."

"I'm not planning to tell Lewis that the kid is his nephew until I need to. And Lewis believed he was committing a felony at the time. We can get him on intent."

Eastman shrugged. "Hell, nothing good's playing at the movies this afternoon. I'm in."

Lou gathered up her notes with a dry chuckle. "Let's go talk to Mr. Lewis."

Fifteen minutes later they sat at the table, Bryce Lewis and his public defender on one side, she and Janson at the other. Sheriff Eastman leaned against the wall. Lewis looked like he'd seen better days. The bruises had faded, but fatigue had set in. The constant vigilance required to fend off unwanted inmate advances was obviously taking its toll.

"Let's make this brief, shall we?" Lou said, before the defender could. Lou looked Lewis straight in the eye. "Mr. Lewis, we know about your sister, about the kidnapping, and the ransom." She took satisfaction in seeing Lewis pale. "We know about the man who visited you. We know that he burned your aunt and uncle's house, with them in it."

"Whoa," said the defender. "What fantasy books have you been reading, because I don't see a shred of evidence supporting any of these allegations."

Lou's lips curved. "Don't worry. You will. Mr. Lewis, you'll be interested to hear that your sister made it to Chicago where she has murdered four people since Monday. Add to that McMillan, Rickman, and one other murder in Morgantown, she's at seven."

Lewis flinched. But he made no move to deny a word.

"How much was your share of the ransom, Mr. Lewis?" Janson asked with sincere curiosity. "A million? Two million?"

Lewis's eyes flickered. Narrowed. Lou could see anger rising in his eyes. "Oh, so that's how it was," she said. "She promised you considerably less. I thought as much." She reached into her briefcase and pulled out a copy of the e-mail Conway had sent to the Vaughns, detailing the ransom. "Take a look, Mr. Lewis. Her asking price for the boy you two kidnapped is five million."

Lewis still said nothing, but his fingers gripped his upper arms, hard.

Lou leaned forward. "Sooner or later we'll be able to put you in that house, Mr. Lewis. If I have to dust every surface myself, I'll find your prints. But I have help. Kidnapping is a federal offense. Now that we know how it went down, we'll be calling in the FBI. And not only did you kidnap the boy, you kidnapped Cheryl Rickman. Who turned up dead."

"We've established my client has an alibi for Miss Rickman's murder," the defender said icily. "Now, unless you have an actual charge to discuss, we're done." He stood up and took Lewis's arm, led him to the door.

"Sue's got a passport and a ticket to France," Lou half lied just as Lewis's foot hit the open space of the doorway. He stopped. And turned. His eyes were very, very cold.

"She's going to let you take the fall, Mr. Lewis," Lou said softly. "Don't let her do this."

His lawyer whispered something in his ear. Lewis nodded.

"What are you offering?"

Lou shrugged. "Depends on what he has to say." She patted the table. "Talk to me, Bryce. We're your only hope, because we want her a hell of a lot more than we want you."

Lewis slumped into a chair. "It was her idea." He looked up, fatigue fighting the anger in his eyes, and suddenly he looked only seventeen. "Nobody was supposed to get hurt."

Lou took out her notepad. "We're listening."


*Chicago,*
*Thursday, August 5, 4:45 p.m.*

Dealing with Sandy's friends had been an emotional experience. They'd been overcome with grief and rage. But they'd helped, giving Dana access to Sue's file, which was quite thick, having dealt with a number of social workers in her youth. It was hard to read, knowing the woman who'd endured so much abuse now had Evie and Alec in her hands. The social workers had been helpful, but discreet. Only Dana was allowed in the room where the records were kept. Ethan stayed outside, pacing like a sentry.

Now, back in the hotel room, Ethan sat in front of his laptop. "Okay, I'm in Sue's bank's Website. I found two cookies on the computer she used last night. Two accounts. She'll deposit it in the first, then move it to the second account she thinks we don't know about."

"Now you have to figure out her password," Dana murmured.

"So, tell us what you found," Clay said.

When she'd come out of the records room Ethan started to grill her for information, but she must have looked so bad that he stopped. But her respite was over. Time to talk.

"Sue's mom was a junkie that managed to keep a few steps ahead of the court, but one day Children's Services came in and took Sue and Bryce. Bryce was just an infant. Her mom supported her habit through prostitution." She looked at Ethan. "Her mom sold Sue occasionally, gave her away when she'd misbehaved. Her punishment, as it were."

Ethan paled. "My God."

"So at an early age Sue came to equate power with sex."

"And punishment," Clay said quietly.

Dana nodded. "Yes. Her mother had drilled into her that social workers were

580

evil, just out to get them. They moved around to dodge the system. It's all consistent with the cuts I saw on her arms. Girls who cut themselves do it because their lives are so chaotic, it's a way to maintain control. As a child she had so little control."

"I'd say she's remedied that situation," Ethan said dryly.

"Yes," Dana agreed. "I'd say she has. Sue was just like Randi described her while in foster care. Self-destructive, rebellious, violent. She claimed her foster parents abused her, but there was no evidence to support her complaints and the foster family had a good reputation in the system. For Sue, sex was power and she tried to use it that way. Finally she ran away and found her father. He'd just been released from jail."

"I see a pattern here," Clay mused.

"There usually is. Dad petitioned the court for custody of Sue and got it, but not Bryce. She had visitation, so she knew where Bryce lived. One day, she just took him."

Clay whistled softly. "Shades of Randi."

"I know. It's damn spooky. Dad had Sue and the baby in his car, apparently on their way south, when Dad decided to rob a convenience store, which Bryce repeated later."

"Some apples don't fall far from the tree," Ethan said.

Dana sighed. "Dad gets gunned down by the store owner in the process. Sue sees him go down and at twelve years old panics, takes the wheel, tries to escape, and wrecks the car. Social workers take her and Bryce, but this time her aunt steps forward. Mom has died of an overdose and Sue's Aunt Lucy decides to try and do the right thing."

Ethan was tapping keys. "Okay, I've got her first account up. Give me some names."

"Her father's name was Walter," Dana said.

"Good. What year was Dad born? This password needs letters and numbers."

Dana grabbed her notebook from her purse. "1955."

A few taps and Ethan crowed. "Damn, this was too easy. Walter1955. No money in the first account. Let's see if the same password works for the second account." Tap, tap, tap. "Damn. I should've been so lucky. When did he die? Walter?"

Dana checked her notes. "1987."

"Bingo." Ethan drummed his fingers,

waiting. "And . . . the balance is nineteen thousand eight hundred. Recent transactions . . . Fifty-two hundred wired to Western Union." He tapped keys rapidly, then looked up. "Located in the mall she called from last night."

"We need to get this to Mia and Abe," Dana said. "What will you do with the money?"

Ethan blew out a breath. "I'd love to take the rest of it, just to piss her off, but then she'd know we were on to her. I'm going to let Mitchell and Reagan make the decision. Call them, Dana, tell them we need to talk."

# Chapter Twenty-one

*Chicago,*
*Thursday, August 5, 6:00 p.m.*

"So talk," Mia said, sinking into a chair in the CPD conference room.

Dana had been appointed spokesperson by the short straw, so she just blurted it out. "We have access to Sue's bank accounts."

Abe coughed. "Excuse me?"

Mia gave them all a dirty look. "Do I want to know how you came by this information?"

"We didn't do anything illegal," Dana insisted. "Ethan looked at the hard drive of the computer she used last night. Then he was able to guess at her passwords."

Mia rubbed her forehead, and when she spoke, it was with a barely controlled fury such as Dana had rarely seen. "He just *guessed* them? What is he, Miss Cleo or something? Maybe he can *just guess* where Conway is, because we sure as hell don't know."

Dana looked at Abe who was shaking his head. "What happened today?"

"We found the optometrist," Abe said with a sigh.

"Who?" Dana asked simply.

"Guy in Lincoln Park. His wife found him two and a half hours ago, dead on the floor of his examination room. An inventory check showed one pair of brown lenses missing."

Dana sat on the arm of Mia's chair and put her arm around her. "I'm sorry."

"So am I. And now the press is on the story." Mia shuddered.

Dana's heart skipped a beat. "Will you give them a picture of her?"

"Our LT is pressuring us to," Abe admitted. "We want to keep Conway's identity low-key so she doesn't freak out and hurt Evie or Alec, but this is too big now. He gave us until tomorrow at noon. If we don't have her by then, we go public. Until then, he's assigned two more detectives to this case and as many uniforms as we think we need."

Mia bit her lip. "There's more. We got some new bodies today. An old woman that lived in Randi Vaughn's old building from eleven years ago and one of her former partners. Our ME noted the same silencer pattern as we saw on Dr. Lee and Kristie Sikorski on both victims. The old lady was Jackie Williams."

Abe flipped open his notebook. "I found Williams in the old police reports from Conway's arrest. Sue had hidden from the police for a few days, but Williams was watching, saw when Sue came back to Randi's apartment, and reported her. This old lady was tortured before she died. Bleach was poured in her eyes, blinding her. Her tongue was also cut out."

"My God," Ethan murmured, horrified. "My God." He cleared his throat. "And the second one?"

Mia winced. "Leroy Vickers testified against Sue. Let's just say he won't be doing that again."

Abe sighed. "We put the other people involved in Conway's arrest in protective custody. The arresting officer and his family, the prosecutor."

There was quiet, then Clay cleared his throat. "Have you heard from Lou Moore?"

Mia nodded. "She called a few hours ago. Bryce Lewis spilled his guts. Sue contacted him out of the blue a few weeks ago. They hadn't spoken in years. The Lewises wouldn't let him visit her in prison and he'd thought she was still there. Sue said she needed money, gave him a sad story, so he wired her money from his uncle's credit card. She met him here in Chicago and together they drove to Maryland. He claims he didn't know about the kidnapping until right before they stormed the beach house. He claims she promised nobody would get hurt, that they'd get their money for the kid, then give him back."

"Moore said Bryce Lewis didn't seem like the brightest bulb in the chandelier," Abe said. "She suspected some kind of learning disability, maybe diminished capacity."

Dana nodded. "That's consistent with what I know about Sue's mother. She was a junkie and a drunk when she was carrying him. That he was affected is no surprise."

"He knew about the tattoo," Abe said. "Apparently Sue liked to quote their father who said *Adopt, Adapt, and Improve*. I couldn't place it."

Beside her, Ethan tensed. "The Motto of the Round Table," he murmured. "It's a joke."

Mia looked sick. *"A joke?"* She had trouble even saying the words.

"I'm afraid so. The Monty Python group

did this comedy skit in the seventies. A robber goes to rob a bank and realizes he's in a lingerie shop. He says 'Adopt, Adapt, and Improve, the Motto of the Round Table,' then steals underwear," Ethan said sadly. "Sue's done that often over the last week, adapting her plans to fit the situation."

"Hell." Mia stood up and paced. "We have eleven dead people and no idea where this woman is. She's setting the stage and all we can do is chase her after the fact."

Ethan held up his hand. "I thought we had ten. McMillan, Rickman, Samson, Sikorski, Dr. Lee, Beverly, Sandy, and the optometrist makes eight. Williams is nine, Vickers ten."

"We found Fred Oscola's body," Abe said with a grimace. "It was found in a hotel this afternoon. Apparently Sue left the DO NOT DISTURB sign on the door-knob when she left so housekeeping left the room alone."

"Until they started to smell him," Mia added. "We had to get dental records to make a positive ID. Sue didn't leave much else. Not only were his fingers gone, but she cut off his penis. Julia says he was alive at the time."

"She hated him especially," Dana said.

"I wouldn't be surprised to learn Mr. Oscola used his power as a prison guard to force sex from the female inmates. This is consistent with Sue's whole attitude on sex. Sex is power. There was serious sex abuse in her background." Dana slid a sheet from her notebook onto the table. "I went to talk to Sandy Stone's friends today. Yell at me later, but I knew they wouldn't talk to you without a court order. I got some addresses we can check."

Abe picked up the sheet. "We would have had that court order by tomorrow. We requested it today."

Dana shrugged. "You have this a day sooner then."

Abe blinked and focused and Dana wondered how much sleep he and Mia had gotten last night. "Her foster home, too."

Mia stopped pacing long enough to glance at the sheet over Abe's shoulder. "Why?"

"We were thinking that Sue might go back to a house where she felt alone and isolated to hide Evie and Alec," Dana said quietly. "This drama she's setting up, it's personal. So the setting should be personal, too. She may have planned to use her uncle's house. She hated that place. It stands to reason that the replacement site

589

will be every bit as hated."

Mia slumped in the chair next to Dana. "What else you been thinking, kid?"

Dana knew she was forgiven. "That this is all about revenge. Randi betrayed her, not once, but twice. She's had ten years to plan this. It's going to be symbolic and include all the pain she's experienced. I'd like to better understand what that pain was, real or perceived. Have you heard from the prison?"

"Yeah." Abe flipped a few pages in his notebook. "Sue roomed with Tammy Fields, that woman you were talking about, for five years."

Dana winced. "Then that's how she found us. Now we know about Fred Oscola."

"No surprise based on how we found him," Mia said. "Whacking his fingers was business. She needed them to scare the Vaughns."

"Whacking his business was personal," Dana finished wryly and every man in the room cringed. "So we know she was probably raped in prison. How long was Oscola there?"

"Her whole ten years," Abe said, still looking uncomfortable.

"Long time to have to bear that." Dana

looked at Mia with a frown. "Don't take this wrong, but if I'd been forced like that for ten years, I'd be looking to make the person who put me there suffer the same."

"Then she shouldn't have killed Oscola," Mia said.

"Maybe he got greedy," Dana replied. "We won't know until we find her, but I'd sure be watching Randi Vaughn closely. Whatever Sue's got planned for her, it won't be pretty."

"What about you, Dana?" Abe asked softly. "What does she have planned for you?"

Dana mentally pushed her thoughts in the box. The box lock was become more fragile each moment. "Not much better. I'm every social worker who ever took her from her parents or made her live where she didn't want to live, do what she didn't want to do."

Mia leveled a stare at Ethan. "Are you armed?"

Ethan nodded, his jaw tight. "Within the parameters of Illinois gun laws, yes."

Mia's eyes flickered. "Right. Dana, do you still have your .38?"

Dana thought about her gun, still in the pocket of her robe on her bed where she'd left it in the hurry to get to Evie the day before. Never had she been so careless, leaving her gun loaded, out of its usual hiding place. "In my apartment. Can I go there and get it?"

"I'll go instead," Ethan said firmly.

Mia glanced at Abe as if Ethan hadn't spoken. "Conway might be watching her place."

"I'll go instead," Ethan said through his teeth.

Abe hesitated. "If she's watching, seeing Dana might draw her out into the open."

Ethan lurched to his feet. "No. You won't use her as bait."

Dana tugged on his arm. "Sit down, Ethan. Please."

Ignoring her, he continued to stand, pointing at Mia. "Last night you were ready to put her in protective custody for offering herself as a trade. What are you thinking?"

"That I've got eight bodies in the morgue, Mr. Buchanan," Mia said evenly. "Dana is one of my best friends. Do you think I'd put her in any more danger than she's already in?"

Ethan's frown was menacing. "You will not make her bait."

"We'll be there," Abe said. "On the street watching."

Ethan shook his head. "And if Conway's waiting inside?"

Abe didn't budge. "Dana can wear a wire."

Twin bands of dark red had risen to Ethan's cheekbones. "So you can hear the pop when Conway comes up behind her and plugs a nine mil in her skull? With all due respect, *Detective,* no fucking way."

"Mr. Buchanan," Abe said calmly. "The woman has killed eleven people in the last week. She is holding two hostages. I've got the Vaughns sitting in a fishbowl at the Excelsior and so far, no bites. We'll send uniforms to all the addresses in this list to warn them, and maybe we'll catch her that way, maybe not. I see this as an acceptable —"

*"Acceptable?"* Ethan thundered.

"An acceptable, controlled risk," Abe continued, still calmly. "As long as Dana is willing."

"I am," Dana said quietly. She stood, framed Ethan's face between her palms. His eyes flashed and burned. She could feel him tremble. "Ethan, this is the right thing to do. Besides, it's not like she couldn't have killed me at any time today. She could have been waiting outside the police station, even. *I* can't go on like this much longer. Please understand that I have to do this, as much for me as anyone else."

Ethan pulled from her grasp and looked at Mia. "You go with her."

Mia shook her head. "Conway saw me, that first night at Hanover House. She knows I'm a cop. She sees a cop and she stays hidden. We're nowhere, then."

Ethan jerked his head toward Abe. "Him then."

Again Mia shook her head. "If she was waiting for Dana outside the hospital last night, she's seen us together. Same song, second verse."

Ethan's jaw twitched. His fists curled and uncurled. "Then I'm going with her."

Dana looked at Mia and Abe. "All right?"

He glared at Mia. "And she gets body armor."

Mia nodded once. "Agreed."

The room was completely silent as Ethan's labored breathing quieted. Then Clay cleared his throat. "There is the small matter of nineteen thousand dollars still in her bank account. What do you want to do with it?"

Grimly, Abe held out his hand. "Give me the accounts. I'll have one of our guys take the money. If we can't touch her, at least we can hinder her a little bit."

Ethan's eyes went hard and flat. "I was hoping you'd say that."

*Chicago,*
*Thursday, August 5, 7:30 p.m.*

"This is a goddamn stupid idea," Ethan muttered, climbing the dirty steps behind her.

"Sshh." Dana threw a frown over her shoulder. "Be quiet."

Because he saw fear in her eyes, he closed his mouth. She unlocked the door, pushed it open. And exhaled. "Looks clear, Mia," she murmured into the mike pinned to her shirt.

Ethan pushed past her. Her kitchen and bathroom were clear, as was the second bedroom that was empty of all furniture. He shot her a quick look, but she just shook her head. "This was Evie's room. Before her attack."

Her bedroom looked exactly the same as it had the day before when she'd dressed so hurriedly. When she'd been terrified for Evie. Clothes were strewn all over the bed.

"It looks clear," he said, but she was frowning.

She bent down and picked up her robe between two fingers. Silk, it draped on itself. He remembered it on her. How her pocket had bulged. It didn't bulge now.

"Mia," she said into the mike, her voice shaky. "My gun is gone."

In less than sixty seconds Mitchell and Reagan were there, breathing hard. "No tampering on the front door?"

"No. Evie had keys, so Sue has keys." Dana shook her head weakly. "I should have thought of that before."

Mia slid her arm around Dana's shoulders. "Did she take anything else? Looks like she did some major damage in here."

"No, Caroline did this." It was barely audible and Mitchell frowned.

"Caroline was helping her get dressed for our date Monday night," Ethan said. "It looked like this yesterday when I got here. She changed her clothes to get back to the shelter, because we thought Sue was still there. She left the gun in her robe pocket, on the bed. Is there a way to find out when Sue was here?"

"We'll ask if anyone saw anything," Reagan said, but he sounded doubtful.

"Ethan, go to the living room and make

her sit down," Mia ordered. "She looks faint."

Dana dropped the robe back on the floor where she'd found it. "I'm not going to faint. Why would she steal my gun, Mia? She's got one. We know that."

"Is your gun registered to you, Dana?" Reagan asked.

She faltered. "No."

Mitchell closed her eyes. "Shit."

Reagan tilted his head forward. "Then who is it registered to?"

Dana swallowed hard. "My mother."

Reagan lifted his brows. "She really gets around. Why do you have a gun registered to your deceased mother?"

Dana blew her bangs off her forehead. "Because I have a felony conviction for attempted auto theft. I couldn't get a gun on my own and I was afraid of my ex. My mother put her name on the registration."

Reagan rolled his eyes. "Mia, you're going to owe me so much when this is done."

"I'm good for it," she snapped. "Buchanan, take her into the living room. Don't touch anything. We'll call CSU."

He led her to the living room where Dana gingerly sat on the edge of the old sofa and bit her lip. "She's going to use my gun, isn't she? She's going to kill somebody with my gun." The rest of the color drained from her face. "She's going to kill Evie with my gun."

Ethan had thought that immediately, but didn't want to worry her any more than she already was. "You can't know that, honey. Maybe she just wanted to be sure you couldn't shoot her with it."

She looked at him through narrowed eyes. "Don't patronize me, Ethan."

He sat on the sofa next to her, took her hand. "All right. I thought the same thing."

She sat there, her eyes fixed on the middle of the floor. "This is worse than my dream."

"You want to talk about it now?" he asked gently, but still she shook her head, not taking her eyes from that same spot on the floor.

He followed her gaze to the middle of the ugly old throw rug that sat off center and sideways. But it had been off center and sideways yesterday and Sunday night, too. He had only a moment to wonder when Reagan appeared from the back and, also following her gaze, stopped at the edge of the rug. He bent down and started to roll it aside.

"Don't." Dana surged to her feet, but it was too late. Beneath the throw rug, the carpet bore a large dark brown stain the width of the rug and easily half its length. Reagan studied it for a moment, then rolled his head sideways to study Dana who just stared like a deer caught in the headlights.

Ethan's stomach turned over and he had to swallow back the bile, not for the sight of the large bloodstain, but for the understanding of what it represented.

"You never moved, did you?" he asked raggedly.

She wouldn't look at him. "No." Her lips just formed the word. No sound emerged.

She'd died here, Dana's mother. The old article he'd found said she was discovered by her daughter, horribly battered and bleeding. It never provided an address or a culprit. He'd remembered the look in her eyes the morning she'd told him about herself, the abuse at the hands of her father, then her stepfather. He'd read the article and assumed the stepfather was responsible. He'd confirmed it when he found the stepfather's name on the list of lifers at the state prison.

He'd assumed she'd moved. Most people would have moved. Dana Dupinsky was not most people. Somehow she'd transformed the scene of a senseless, vile crime into her own private, never-ending hell. Every time she came home, she had to see it again, walk it again. This place with its junkies and pushers was one big fucking penance.

"Hell, Abe," Mitchell said from behind them.

Reagan came to his feet. "Don't tell me. Her mother?"

Mitchell shot the very pale, shaken Dana a look of such intense caring that Ethan almost forgave her for putting Dana in jeopardy. "Yeah. Cover it back up, will you? Ethan, take her back to the hotel. Call me when you get there, okay?"

*Chicago,*
*Thursday, August 5, 11:00 p.m.*

Something was wrong. From a block away, Sue sat in her car staring through the houses at the little two-story that belonged to the officer that had arrested her eleven years ago. Taggart was his name. He lived alone, but she could see shadows of others moving around inside. Her instincts hummed. The cops were there, waiting. *Waiting for me.*

Well, they'd be disappointed, she

thought. Sue tapped the steering wheel thoughtfully. The only way the police would be here was if Randi tipped them off. There was no other logical way they'd even be suspicious. She'd thought the kid would have made a difference. That Randi Vaughn would have learned the consequences of ratting to the police. Obviously old habits died hard. So would Randi Vaughn.

Now that Randi Vaughn had alerted the police, they would be sure to be watching her hotel. This called for a change in tomorrow evening's logistics. Same party location, different pickup plan for the guest of honor. She'd give Donnie the heads-up tomorrow. She pulled into a gas station, thinking of the empty cans in the trunk that needed filling.

Tonight's logistics, however, were right on track.


*Chicago,*
*Thursday, August 5, 11:45 p.m.*


"Dana, you really need to eat," Ethan said from the bedroom doorway.

She could see Ethan's reflection in the window as she looked down on the bright lights of the city. He'd been trying to get her to eat ever since they'd returned from her apartment, but the very thought of food made her throat close up. "Ethan, I'm really not hungry," she replied in a testy tone designed to drive him back to the sitting room.

Instead she watched his reflection approach, shivered when he put his warm hands on her cold shoulders and pressed a gentle kiss to her temple.

"Don't give up, baby," he murmured, but his reflection showed the worry in his eyes.

"I haven't," she murmured back, but she could hear the lie in her voice. Sue had Evie and Sue had her gun. Sue had killed eleven people and nobody knew where she was.

He tugged on her shoulders. "You've been standing here looking out the window for two hours, Dana. Come to bed. You need to sleep."

She pulled away from his hands. "No. I don't want to sleep."

"Because you dream."

She gritted her teeth, anger simmering so close to the surface. Normally she could hold it down, keep it boxed up. Not tonight. "Y'think?" she asked acidly.

The man did not budge and she wanted to curse him for it. "Yes, I think. Are you ready to tell me about it now?" When she gritted her teeth harder, he just covered her shoulders with his hands again and began to massage. "Remember that first night at Wrigleyville? You got me to talk about Richard and I felt better. You need to start listening to yourself."

Her laugh was bitter. "Physician, heal thyself?"

"If the shoe fits, baby." His hands slid from her shoulders down her arms and locked around her waist and despite her efforts to resist, her body seemed to know how they fit best. She leaned into him, resting the back of her head against his shoulder.

"Why do you keep insisting I tell you about my mother?"

"Because you think it's the biggest part of you," he murmured.

Dana blinked and turned around to look up at him. "What?"

"Dana, everything you've made of yourself you attribute to one very bad event." He skimmed his thumb over her eyebrows and her eyelids drooped. "The night your mother was killed. Not by you," he added, "even though that's what you'd have yourself believe."

"You checked," she said wearily, leaning her forehead against his bare chest, his hair tickling her nose. "You must have thought there was some validity to it to have checked."

"No, I never thought there was validity to it. You could not kill another human being."

"I could kill Sue," she said viciously and his arms came around her back like a vise.

He hugged her hard. "Like I said, no other human being."

She drew a breath, inhaling his scent. "Point made."

"Dana, talk to me. Tell me what happened that night. I need to know, to help you."

She looked up then, searched his eyes. Those steady green eyes that always made her think of spring. Of new life. "Why?"

His eyes grew sad. "Is it so hard to believe that I could simply care about you?"

Her eyes stung. "Yes."

His fingers feathered the hair from her face. "Dana, do you have any friends that you haven't helped more than they've helped you? Any where you're the taker, not the giver?"

The question threw her off guard. "I don't know."

"Think about it." He kissed her mouth, so tenderly she wanted to weep. "Then think about being the taker for once. Letting people do for you. Without needing to pay them back in some way." He put his arm around her shoulders and led her to the bed. "Like right now. Let me help you sleep. No strings." His voice was deep and smooth and husky and his hands gentle as they pulled off her shoes, her shirt. He undressed her like a baby, then slipped one of his T-shirts over her head. "Go to sleep. We'll talk in the morning."

He tucked her in and turned out the lights and she could hear him taking off his own clothes. He slipped in behind her and gathered her close. She could feel his arousal pulsing against her, but it was more a comfort than a temptation. He was there. He'd be there when she woke in the night. Because she would wake in the night. She always did.

"Tomorrow, honey," he murmured in her ear. "We'll find them tomorrow."

"You said that last night."

"And I'll say it again tomorrow. Until it's true. Until this is over."

She was drifting now, secure in the circle of his arms. "And you go home."

His arms tensed, then relaxed. "And I go

home. What will you do? When it's over?"

She blinked, seeing only the darkness, feeling only him. "I don't know. I know whatever it is, I can't do it here."

He raised his head and she could feel more than see his frown. "Here?"

"In Chicago. It's too dangerous." She yawned, melted into him. "Caro and Evie . . . need to find a safer way."

"But not you," he said, too softly and too late she realized her mistake.

"No. Not me," she answered honestly.

"Where will you go?"

"Oh, I don't know," her voice wobbled. "New York, Atlanta . . . Philadelphia maybe."

A long pause. "But not D.C.?"

She said nothing, could say nothing.

His body stiffened, but his voice remained gentle. "I've gotten too close, haven't I?"

"Ethan —"

"Go to sleep, Dana."


*Chicago,*
*Friday, August 6, 3:00 a.m.*


"Wake up."

Evie's eyes flew open at the sudden pain

of Jane's hand cracking against her jaw. She blinked, focusing on the tall figure looming over her. Bit back a whimper when she was hauled to her feet. Closed her eyes again at the thrust of cold hard metal under her chin. It would be now. She'd kill her now. With Dana's gun.

Jane just chuckled. "Not yet, pet. You've got a bit more to do before I take you out. I'm going to cut the ropes at your feet and you're going to walk out of here. Hands stay tied, mouth stays taped. Try anything and I'll shoot you where you stand. Got it?"

Evie remained still and Jane jabbed the blunt barrel of the gun harder, cutting off her air. "Indicate you have heard," Jane said coldly. Evie jerked a nod and apparently that was enough because the pressure against her windpipe lessened. She drew a quick breath through her nose and Jane chuckled again. "Let's get this show on the road. I need to get back and catch some sleep before the second performance begins tonight."

*"No."*

Ethan's eyes blinked open at the pitiful moan and he twisted around to look at the clock on the nightstand. It was the middle of the night and Dana was dreaming. How could he have guessed? He turned on the lamp next to the clock and leaning up on his elbow, shook her shoulder gently. "Wake up. Dana, wake up." She did, with a jolt, her eyes becoming aware all at once.

"I'm sorry." It was a harsh whisper. Her breath was coming in sharp little surges, her body trembling. Her lips quivered as if she was about to cry. He wondered if she would have, had she been alone.

"You keep saying that," he murmured. "Tell me now. What's in your dream?"

She closed her eyes. "You already know."

"I know the bare facts, Dana. Why won't you trust me with the rest?"

Her eyes flew open at that. "It has nothing to do with trust, Ethan. For God's sake, I'm sleeping next to you. Doesn't that tell you I trust you?"

"You don't do a lot of sleeping," he shot back. "Do you dream like this every night?"

She seemed to shrink back into the pillows. "No. Only when I sleep normal hours."

"Which is how often?"

She lifted a shoulder. "A few times a week. Sometimes I'm at the bus station. Most of the time I'm up with a client or one of their kids."

"So you avoid sleep."

She sighed. "I suppose."

"That seems emotionally healthy," he said dryly. "And this works for you?"

Slowly she shook her head. "Obviously not."

"Well, at least we agree on something."

She bit her lip. "I don't know where to begin."

"I'll help you. Was your mother still alive when you married the biker dude?"

"Yes. I never brought Charlie home, although he and my stepfather would have had lots in common." Abruptly she rolled over, crunching the pillow beneath her head. "I hated him."

"Charlie or your stepfather?"

She was quiet for a moment. "Both. I especially hated my stepfather, I think." Sighed again. "But underneath it all, I think I hated my mother more."

He rubbed the flat of his hand down her

609

back, felt her tension begin to ease. "Why?"

"Because she stayed with him, stayed with my real father, too. I used to wish she'd take us and leave. Go somewhere safe, where our dad couldn't find us. Then he died and I was so glad. Do you know how guilty that makes a child, being happy her father is dead?"

"No," he answered simply, stroking her back. "But I can imagine."

"I don't think you'd come close," she said bitterly. "But I was happy. For a few months it was just the three of us, living with my grandmother."

"You had a sister?"

"Still do somewhere," she answered, still bitterly. "Although Maddie wouldn't say the same. She says she has no sister."

"So she also blames you for your mother's death."

"Yes."

"I don't understand. Your stepfather did it. He's serving a life sentence."

"You checked that, too, huh? Yeah, a life sentence. He's got cancer now, so he won't serve much more of it. I won't be sorry to see him go."

"So your mother just jumped out of the frying pan into the fire?"

"Pretty much. She brought this man into my grandmother's house, I remember. I didn't like him and I told him so. Next thing I knew I was on the floor."

Ethan frowned. "He knocked you down and your mother still married him?"

"He was a good provider," she said, her tone like acid. "We wouldn't have to live with Grandma anymore."

"I think I'm starting to get the picture," he murmured and moved his hand to her head, brushing at her hair with his fingers.

"When I left Charlie I wanted a real life," Dana said, changing direction abruptly. "I started waiting tables to earn money for college. Took as many classes as I could afford. One night on campus I saw this flyer about support groups for victims of abuse, so I went. The woman who led the group managed a shelter named Hanover House."

"I thought you started the shelter."

"No. That would have been Maria." Affection warmed her voice. "She was the first person I ever knew who really cared about me. She's the reason I went into psychology. I wanted to be like her. Plus I wanted to fix myself," she added wryly. "Anyway, I started to understand the cycle of domestic abuse. Hated my mother a little less. I tried to get my mother to go to Maria's support groups with me, but she wouldn't. I think that's when I began to understand that I resented Mother choosing the easy way over us. She would always see herself as having no choices. I just saw her as weak. Not loving us enough. I didn't give up. I kept trying to get her to come to the groups, to leave him. He kept beating her. Then one day he put her in the emergency room. She called me."

"And you went to get her."

"Of course. She was my mother. I took her back to my apartment. Told her she was staying there and I think she just gave up fighting me. My stepfather came to where I was waiting tables. Mad. And I think I just . . . snapped. I yelled at him, that he was an animal and a child abuser. I told him that my mother had finally chosen me over him."

"And he . . . ?"

"Went ballistic. The restaurant manager had to throw him out. Nearly got myself fired in the process. I thought he'd go off, nurse his wounds, and come after me again."

"But he went looking for your mother."

"He found her." There was a long, long pause. "I found her later."

His hand stilled on her back. "Was she alive?"

"No." She whispered it.

"I'm sorry."

She said nothing for a long time. When she did speak, her words were barely audible. "There was so much blood. Everywhere. I . . . It was splattered on the walls. Soaked into the carpet. I . . . I could hear it . . . squish. Under my feet." She shuddered. "I still hear it."

"In your dreams."

She nodded, then took a deep breath, as if bracing herself to go on. "She was all in a heap. He'd beaten her. And stabbed her with one of my kitchen knives. So much blood. I turned her over and screamed when I saw her face. I couldn't even recognize her face. I was screaming for someone to call 911, but nobody did. It was a bad place to live, even then. Nobody ventured out when they didn't have to."

He'd gone back to his soothing strokes. "So how did you get help?"

"I made myself get up and get the phone, but it kept slipping out of my hands and that's when I noticed my hands were covered in blood."

He remembered how she'd looked down at her hands when she'd come out of the shower the night before. He couldn't think of anything to say. So he said nothing. Just kept stroking her back.

"I called 911 and I waited what seemed like forever. They finally got there and I was . . . hysterical. They told me that later. I must have told them to call Maria, because she came and took care of me while they took my mother away." She flinched. "Maria made me go into the kitchen, and look away, but I can still hear them zipping the body bag. Maria started cleaning me up and that's when the phone rang."

She said nothing more and finally he asked, "Who was it?"

"My stepfather. I could hear his voice shaking. He was still caught up in his rage."

"What did he say?"

She seemed to stop breathing. And said nothing.

"Dana, honey. What did he say?"

She shuddered hard. Once. "He said, 'You killed your mother. Are you happy now?' "

Ethan's hand froze on her back. It was exactly what she'd said the night before. *I killed my mother. Are you happy now?* He had to work to make the words come. "You know you didn't kill her, Dana."

"Did I beat her with my fists?" She was speaking calmly now. Too calmly. "No. Did I stab her with my kitchen knife? No. Did I push her into a situation she wasn't equipped to handle? That I did. Then I made it worse by publicly humiliating him, pushing him into that frenzy. I didn't make him kill her, but I'm responsible. I set the events in motion."

"The events were set in motion before you were born, Dana. Your mother made choices. You were a child."

"I wasn't a child when I pushed her to make a choice." Still that eerie calm. "I acted like a child though. Me or him. Choose. If she'd chosen him, she might still be alive."

He didn't know what he could say to make her believe she was not responsible. "So what happened then?"

"Maria was there for me through the whole thing. She gave me the opportunity to work at Hanover House. Kept me at her side. I look back now and know it was to make sure I was all right. But it turned into . . ." She sighed. "My life. Maria died right before I graduated. She had a bad heart. I thought she was asleep at her desk. It was the way she would have wanted to go, I think. Working. I went on to get my master's those first few years as the director of Hanover House. Got certified as a therapist. And . . . that's it."

That was far from *it,* he knew. "When did you start . . . taking passport pictures?"

"A year or so before that. Maria dabbled in helping women find new identities." Abruptly she flipped to her back, looking up at him. Fiercely. "I do more than take the pictures, Ethan. I do it all. The passports, the driver's licenses . . . All."

"I thought as much." But that she'd told him squeezed his heart. "How many women have you helped this way?"

"Two dozen or so over ten years. It got a lot harder after 9/11. But the computer technology's gotten better, too."

He lifted his brows. "So you intend to continue?"

She frowned, uncertain. "I don't know. Probably not. I almost got caught this time."

His pulse spiked as he considered it. "God. If they search your house . . ."

"David took it all away. All my tools and the laminating equipment."

His heart slowed back to normal even as jealousy clawed at his gut at the note of sad affection in her voice. He remembered the look in the man's eyes the night they'd met and again yesterday when they'd found Sandy Stone's body. Hunter was in love with her. It didn't take a P.I. or a cop to see it. But he didn't think Dana did. "Decent of him."

She swallowed. "Yeah, it was."

He had to ask. "Dana, do . . . do you love him?"

"Yes, but not the way you're asking. He and Max and the Hunters, they took me in. Made me family. David's been like the brother I never had. He feels the same way."

Relief shimmered like a jewel even as he doubted her take on Hunter's emotions. "Good." He leaned down to brush a kiss across her lips. "What do you dream, Dana?"

Her eyes flashed from sensual awareness to annoyance. "You don't give up, do you?"

"I don't consider it a failing."

"It's . . . Dammit, Ethan." She shifted on the pillow, crossing her arms over her breasts under the blanket. "It's me, all right? Walking through the blood. Hearing my feet . . ." She grimaced. "Hearing them squish. I always turn her body, and my hands are always covered in blood. But it's not always her face. After Evie was attacked, it was hers, for a very long time. Sometimes it's the face of a woman who's just come through the shelter." She stopped. Closed her eyes. "Last night, for the first time . . . It was mine." She opened her eyes. Shrugged. "I . . . guess that freaked me out, seeing myself dead like that."

He moistened his suddenly dry lips. "I guess so. What about tonight?"

Her smile was grim. "Lucky me again. Now you know it all, Ethan. Every last insane quirk I possess. Now it's time for me to go to sleep. I'll try not to wake you again."

She tried to roll over and he stopped her, taking her mouth in a hard, fierce kiss, his heart stamping in his chest when she came up off the pillow, meeting him more than halfway. "I don't mind," he murmured, gratified when her arms released their death hold on herself and twined around his neck.

"I hate that I dream," she whispered. "That you see me this way."

Vulnerable, he thought. "Human?" he said instead.

"I always wanted someone to hold me when I dreamed. Thank you for being there for me this week. I don't know that I could have made it this far without you."

*And when this is over?* he wanted to ask. He opened his mouth to ask, then closed it, afraid of the answer. "You were here for me, too. Every time I was with you . . . I felt like I could go on, search for Alec a little more."

Her smile dimmed. "I'm scared."

"Me, too." He kissed her forehead. "Me, too."

"Tell me again. Please."

"Tomorrow, honey. We'll find them tomorrow."

# Chapter Twenty-two

*Chicago,*
*Friday, August 6, 4:15 a.m.*

Jane had said nothing for the last hour, just drove with that scary smile on her face. Evie chanced a glance at her from time to time, but mostly kept her eyes straight ahead. Cataloging their path, as Alec had.

Alec. Where was he? In the trunk? Not in the backseat. Evie had managed to check as Jane was forcing her into the front, retying her hands in front of her, instead of behind. She'd tied her ankles together hard, but had removed the gag and this time there was no blindfold. After doing an odd circle around town, Jane was heading west. The same way they went to Caroline's house.

Caroline. Was she all right? Was the baby alive? Safe?

The car slowed as Jane pulled into the exit lane. "I need to get some gas," she said. "If you make a fucking sound, you're dead. Got it?"

Jane stopped the car and got out to stretch, guzzling the last of the water from the bottle she'd kept in the cup holder between them. Close, but still so far away. Parched beyond anything she'd ever known, Evie licked her lips before she knew what she was doing. Jane laughed softly and threw the bottle in the trash can before pulling the nozzle from the gas pump. When she was finished she started to get in the car, then hesitated. She stood up and looked around. The road was deserted. They were the only car there.

"I need to pee," Jane announced. "I'll be in the shop for only a minute. You can't get far in a minute with your feet tied like that. I will find you and I will kill you. Got it? Oh, and if you try to get help from anyone, even the guy inside, he's dead, too. So stay put and nobody gets hurt." She locked all the doors and set off across the parking lot at a brisk walk. Evie looked around the car, searching for anything she could use to escape.

And froze. Stunned. On the seat was Jane's cell phone. She'd left it on the seat. Glancing quickly at the shop, Evie grabbed the phone and dialed.

The phone woke her. Ethan was already reaching for the light and a second later the phone was in her hand, his arm around her shoulders. Hands shaking, Dana answered.

"Yes?"

A broken sob. "Dana, it's me."

*Oh, God, oh, God.* Dana's heart started to pound. "Evie. Baby, where are you?"

Ethan was already reaching for the hotel phone. Dialing Mia's number.

"Dana, she's got me. Jane's got me."

"I know. Where are you?"

"At a gas station. It's the one three exits from the exit we take to Caroline's."

"Where is she, Evie?"

"Using the bathroom inside. Dana, listen. She's got Erik, too. His name is Alec, though. I don't know where he is now, but this morning he was at a motel in Gary. Alec said he saw a chicken and a school. That's all he had time to say. Go find him, Dana. She's OD'd him on his pills and hid him under the bed. Shit. She's coming. I have to go. She's got your gun. I love you."

The line went dead. "Evie!" Nothing more. Dana grabbed the receiver from Ethan. "Mia, it was Evie. She's at a gas station about ten miles from Caroline's house."

"Calm down, Dana. I'm on it."

"*Wait!* She knows where Alec is." Ethan's head snapped to stare at her, hope painful in his eyes. She nodded at him. "Something about a motel in Gary and a chicken and a school. She said Alec told her. I didn't know he could talk."

Ethan shook his head. "Neither did I."

"I'm on it," Mia repeated.

"*Wait!* Send paramedics to the motel. Sue OD'd Alec on his meds."

"Got it." There was a click as Mia hung up.

Dana hung up and jumped from the bed. "Sue's taking her to Caroline's house."

Ethan grabbed her arm. "Which is why you're staying here."

Dana pulled away, shaking her head savagely. "I have listened to you tell me for two damn days that we'd find them. Now we've found them. I will not sit here. You can stay or you can come, but you're not stopping me, Ethan."

He hesitated for a moment, then rolled out of bed, grabbing his pants. A moment later he was pounding on the adjoining door to Clay's room. Dana came out of the bedroom, pulling her shirt over her head. She took one glance at Clay in his jockey shorts.

"Hurry up. We roll in thirty seconds

with you or without you."

Clay pulled on his pants, zipping as he walked. He shoved his gun into his waistband and grabbed a shirt. "Let's go."

Ethan held up his hand. "Wait. Clay, we think Conway's taking Evie to Caroline's house. We'll go there. You head for the police station. Evie called and told Dana where Alec was being held. Someplace in Gary, Indiana. Mitchell said she'd take care of it."

"I'll take care of Stan, Randi, and Alec," Clay said, buttoning his shirt. "You go find Evie."

Evie dropped the phone just as Jane left the shop, another bottle of water and three packs of cigarettes in hand. Tried to control her breathing. Tried not to look guilty. Jane got in the car, lit a cigarette, and started the car. Then calmly reached for her cell phone and pressed a few buttons. Examined the display.

*She knows. She'll kill me now.*

Instead, Jane just smiled. "Thank you. She's such a suspicious soul, your Dana. Hard to draw out into the open. But thanks to what I'm certain was your truly believable performance, I imagine she'll be meeting us right where I want her."

Evie's mouth dropped open and Jane laughed as she pulled the car back on the road.

*Chicago,*
*Friday, August 6, 4:50 a.m.*

They were a quarter mile away when she saw the glow in the sky. Ethan hissed as he saw it, too, and Dana's heart stopped. "Caroline's house is on fire." She hit the gas, careening into the front yard with a squeal of brakes. She was out of the car and halfway to the house when Ethan caught her, holding her with both arms banded around her waist.

"Let me go!" she was screaming, crying, fighting him. "Evie's in there. She's going to burn her to death."

Mia's car pulled up behind them and she was out before the wheels came to a stop, her police radio at her mouth. "We need fire and medical personnel at the scene. *Now.*"

A minute later, an SUV screeched to a halt and Abe jumped out and ran to the house, only to back away from the already intense heat. Mia turned on Dana with narrowed eyes. "What the hell are you doing here?" She looked up at Ethan. "What are you thinking about, bringing her here?" Without waiting for an answer she followed Abe up to the house, a handkerchief over her mouth and nose.

Ethan took Dana by the shoulders, shook her gently. "Where is Caroline's son?"

Dana blinked, "He's at Max's mother's. They all are. We should call and see."

"Give me the number," Ethan said. "I'll call."

She stood, transfixed as flames leaped toward the sky, waiting for Ethan to finish talking with Max's mother. *Evie is in there. Oh God, oh, God. Please let them find her. Don't let her burn. Please.*

"Tom's at Hunter's mother's," he finally confirmed. "Mrs. Hunter is on her way over. I told Max to stay with Caroline just in case."

The next minutes crawled like molasses in winter. Details registered with clarity as Dana struggled to stay focused. To stay sane. *Evie was in there. Burning.* Three fire trucks from two separate towns showed up, Wheaton and nearby Lawndale. Two firemen braved the flames to search for Evie. The others set about the task of putting out the fire.

Dana and Ethan could do nothing but stand helplessly and watch as the Hunter homestead cracked and crashed and burned. Against the haze she could see dark figures battling the flames with hoses from the truck. Mia and Abe stood closer to the house, their radios to their ears as they paced the allowable perimeter. Dana started running to the house, struggling against Ethan's grip, when one of the firefighters emerged.

Empty-handed.

*"No."* She could feel the scream in her raw throat, but the sound was lost in the roar of the flames. "She's in there." She lunged forward, free of Ethan's restraining hands, her feet running, stumbling toward the house. Her ears ignoring his shouts to stop. She fell and picked herself up, each sobbing breath burning more than the last.

"Dana, stop!" Ethan was behind her, grabbing a handful of her shirt.

She wrenched away, and ran up to the firefighter who was now talking to the second man who'd come from the house empty-handed. She grabbed on to his coat, gulping for air. "Please." Tears were running down her face, burning her eyes. "Please look again. I know she's in there."

She tensed as a fit of coughing racked her. "Please."

The men looked at each other, then over her shoulder at Ethan who was gently pulling her hands from the firefighter's coat from behind her. "Nobody's in there that we could find," the first man said.

"Are you sure she's in there?" the second asked.

"We're not sure of anything anymore," Ethan said grimly. "Come on, honey. Let the men do their jobs." He tugged until she sagged against him weeping and gasping.

A third firefighter was pulling a hose around the front of the house. "Get out of this area," he yelled, just as a crash shook the ground. Not needing to be told twice, Ethan scooped Dana up in his arms and ran, her hands clutching his shirt, her face pressed against his chest. She was sobbing uncontrollably, hysterically, and the sound broke his heart.

She yanked on his shirt, helplessly. "She's in there, Ethan. I know she's in there. Please make them go back."

Ethan turned, walking backward, his eyes on the upper windows. If she was in there, she'd have inhaled a hell of a lot of smoke by now. A pane of glass from one of the upstairs windows shattered and rained shards of glass around them. Ethan hunched his body over hers and kept moving.

"Sir." He looked over his shoulder to see a female firefighter approaching, settling her hat more firmly on her head. "My name's Stephanie Kelsey, sir. I'm an EMT with the Lawndale Fire Department. My partner over there asked me to see to the lady."

With quick hands Kelsey helped him ease Dana to her feet. Dana gave them no struggle, now standing quietly, her eyes fixed on the house, tears still running down her face. Kelsey tipped Dana's face up and away, searching for obvious injuries. "Did any glass from that window get her?"

"I don't think so."

"She's in shock."

He looked at Dana's eyes, riveted to the flames. Shock was very probable. "She's been through a lot the past few days," he said. "She's exhausted."

"We'll fix her up. Don't worry. This way." Kelsey led them around the far side of the house. Ethan frowned. This wasn't where the ambulance had stopped. The hairs on his neck lifted and it was as if a brick hit him square between the eyes. The poor fit of Kelsey's coat registered. And the tennis shoes on her feet.

A trap. It was a trap. *Conway.* Skidding to a stop, he wrenched Dana from the woman's grasp and drew his weapon from his back waistband. *"No."*

But he was a beat too late. He thought it even as Conway's gun flashed silver in the glow of the conflagration, lifting, pointing straight at his face. Another crash shook the ground as timbers fell inside the old house. No one would hear them here. No one would hear a cry for help. Or even a gunshot. It would sound like crashing timbers. *Hell.*

*"Dana, move."* He saw a flash of white in front of him, heard Dana cry out a split second before a blast knocked him back, knocked him to his knees. Sent waves of burning pain down his chest. His right hand fell open and his gun dropped to the grass.

He'd been hit.

He'd been hit and it hurt. *Dammit, it hurt.* His left hand instinctively rose to the wound, pressing hard against the blood that had already soaked his shirt.

"You!" He could hear Dana scream it, her voice hoarse from the smoke.

He blinked up, saw Dana's hands vised

around Conway's wrist, a look of raw rage on her face as she battled Conway for the gun. "You did this." Tears still coursed down her cheeks. "Goddamn you, you did this."

He remembered the gun pointing in his face, but the pain was eight inches lower. She'd tried to stop Conway from shooting him, kept her from getting a head shot. The thought penetrated the pain as Sue grabbed Dana's arm and twisted it behind her. Shoved the gun to Dana's head. The barrel of the gun pressing the bone behind Dana's ear was silver. Dana's .38. He'd been shot with Dana's gun. Dammit, it hurt.

Sue was dragging her away. The thought pierced his mind sending a burst of adrenaline to his legs. With a roar of his own he lurched to his feet, grabbing his gun from the ground with his left hand. He made his feet move. Stumbled. "No." He gritted it out as Conway pulled Dana farther from the house, one arm around her throat, the other hand holding the gun to her head. "You can't have her."

His vision grayed and he fell to his knees. He could see Dana's eyes in the light of the blaze. Wide. Terrified. Her hands clawing at Conway's arm. Fighting to get away. Then her head jerked sideways when Conway jabbed the gun harder and her struggling ceased. Now she backed up, moving like a robot, her eyes shifting from the burning house to him.

He pushed himself to his feet once again and staggered after them, only to see Conway dragging her to a white car with a light bar mounted to its roof. She forced Dana into the front seat and slid in beside her. Ethan could see the emblem of the Wheaton Fire Department painted on the driver's door. The white car crossed the grass along the woods that bordered the Hunters' home, heading for the lane that led to the main road.

*Help.* He needed help. Suddenly the two hundred feet to the house seemed a thousand. Trembling, he dropped his gun, fumbled for his cell phone. Watched, detached, as the phone slipped to the ground from his hand, slick with his own blood. And he remembered Dana's dream. The blood on her hands. The face on the body had been hers.

*Not today.* He fell to his knees, searching for the cell phone in the dry grass. Wiping the palm of his left hand dry on his pants when he found it. She wouldn't die today.

The sky had just started to grow light when Sergeant Elliot of the local Wheaton PD introduced himself. "You mind telling us what this is all about?"

"No problem." Mia looked around as another car came to a squealing halt just beyond the fire truck. A tall dark man jumped out and started running in their direction. A tall blond boy got out of the passenger side. Tom. He was helping an older lady up the lane, past all the parked cars. "Looks like the family's here. That's David Hunter, brother of the man who lives here. The young one's Tom Hunter."

Elliot frowned up at the house. "Dr. Max Hunter. I know him. Coaches my son's basketball team at the Y. His wife was hurt in a hit-and-run Monday night." He turned to her, his brows bunched. "This was deliberate, Detective. We found empty gas cans inside the house. What the hell's going on here?"

"I think I can explain most of it. Just wait." She looked up to David Hunter when he ran up to them, breathing hard, his face a mask of dread. The ground shook as another timber crashed inside the house and Hunter grabbed her arm.

"What happened, Mia?"

"We think Conway set it. Dana got a call from Evie about an hour and a half ago. Evie had managed to sneak Conway's cell when she stopped to get gas. Dana met us here." Mia's heart skipped a beat, then another as a notion embedded itself. And grew. "Oh, God. Where's Dana?" She whipped around, saw Abe talking to the Wheaton fire chief. "Abe, *where's Dana?*"

Abe's head lifted, his eyes instantly alert, looking around. "I don't see her."

Beside her, David Hunter whispered, "Oh, God."

The fire chief frowned. "The lady with the short red hair? She tried to get my men to go back in the house, to look for the missing girl. Her boyfriend carried her away."

Another firefighter stepped up, wiping grime from his face. "I saw them go with an EMT."

"Describe him," Mia said tersely.

"Not a him," the firefighter said. "Her."

The Wheaton fire chief looked sick. "We don't have any female EMTs."

The Lawndale firefighter faltered. "Neither do we."

"Fuck," Mia hissed. "Which way?" The

firefighter pointed and she was already running when the cell phone in her pocket started to ring. A glance at the caller ID made her blood run cold. "Where is she, Buchanan?"

"She's gone. White car. Fire department."

Mia rounded the corner of the house, her eyes searching. "Where are you?"

"Horseshoe pits. Dammit." His voice slurred.

Mia looked over at David Hunter who was running alongside her. "Where are your horseshoe pits?" Hunter pointed and Mia squinted in the gray semidarkness of the dawn. And saw Buchanan, crawling across the grass. "Shit. He's hit." She turned, walking backward. "Abe, Conway took her in a white fire department car."

"We passed one on the way in," David said thinly. "Turning west on the main road."

Abe was already on his radio, calling for backup. Sergeant Elliot was running for his own squad car and the fire chief was barking for his EMTs to assist.

"Detective, wait." The firefighter who'd seen them leave with the EMT pushed through the mass of gathering uniforms. "She was wearing full gear. With Lawndale's insignia."

Mia grabbed the fire chief's arm. "Make sure all the Lawndale men are accounted for. You may have one down."

People were running, hands pushing him to the ground, cutting his shirt off his body. Ethan blinked up and saw two EMTs frowning down. "Are you hit anywhere else?" one asked and he managed to shake his head. His eyes flicked left, saw Mitchell, her face grim. "She got her, Mia. Dressed as an EMT. Tricked me. Dammit."

"I know, Ethan."

"Stop talking, sir," the second EMT ordered.

"Took her," Ethan said, ignoring him. Full awareness washed over him and a sob rose in his throat. "Find her," he said hoarsely. "She fought like hell. Saved my damn life."

Mia grabbed his bloody hand, squeezed. "I will. I promise."

"Back, please," the first EMT ordered. "On my count. One, two, three."

Ethan groaned when he was lifted onto a gurney. Strapped in. Felt the tears spill from his eyes. Looked up to see Max Hunter looking down, running alongside the gurney as it bumped over the uneven ground. *Hunter can't run,* he thought dully, remembering the man's cane. He blinked, cleared his eyes. *David Hunter.* In love with Dana. Couldn't blame the man. Damn easy thing to do, fall in love with Dana Dupinsky. *Might even try it someday myself.*

"*Buchanan.*" David's shout cut through his mental wandering and he looked up, fought to focus. "Did she hurt her?" David was asking. "Please. Is Dana alive?"

"She was." Ethan gasped for a breath. "I tried to stop her, but I couldn't. I'm sorry, Hunter. I tried."

"Back off," the EMT shouted. "One, two, three." Another groan as he was lifted and pushed into the back of an ambulance.

"Where are you taking him?" Hunter shouted.

"County. He's got one hell of a hole in his arm. Local unit's not equipped to deal. Now move." The EMT sat next to Ethan and the doors slammed shut. "I'm going to start an IV, sir. You'll pull through just fine. You've just lost a lot of blood."

He gritted his teeth as the EMT packed his shoulder with batting. In his mind he saw Dana's terrified eyes as she was dragged away. "I've lost a hell of a lot more than that."

"Well, that was fun." Sue settled into the driver's seat of a gray Ford Taurus with a merry chuckle. "Nothing like a little excitement to get your blood moving in the morning." She turned to Dana with a smile as they moved down the highway, away from Caroline's house. Away from Mia and Abe. And Ethan. "So good to see you again, Miss Dupinsky."

Dana sat in the passenger seat, staring at this woman she'd welcomed into her shelter one week before. She'd shot Ethan. *With my gun.* He'd lost a lot of blood, but still he'd tried to come after her again and again. *He'll be all right,* she told herself. She pushed her fear into the box. *Someone will find him soon.* Locked the box shut. He'd live.

*I, on the other hand, may not.* They'd left the fire department car along the side of the road and Sue had pushed her into this car, which she'd apparently left for this purpose. Mia would know she was gone soon and if Ethan was still conscious, he'd tell them about the fire department car. Mia would find her. Eventually.

Mia would search just as she was

638

searching for Alec and Evie. *Alec.* Hopefully he was still in the motel in Gary and the police had found him by now. If not, Dana would try to give them as much time as she could to look. She wouldn't let on that she knew all about Sue and Alec. She would know this woman only as Jane, and her son was Erik.

"What have you done with Evie?" she asked coldly and Sue cocked a brow.

"Got her little phone call, huh? I was hoping you would. You're damn hard to find."

"Where is she, Jane?"

Sue sneered. "Look behind you."

Dana did, twisting to see into the backseat. And saw nothing. Just a worn blanket in a heap. Her blood went cold. Sue was taunting her. Evie wasn't here. "Is she dead?" Dana heard herself ask, her voice flat.

"No. Probably just asleep. Give her a poke. Have a reunion on me." Then Sue laughed. "Sorry. Your cuffs are in the way. I'll give her a poke." She reached over the backseat and groped at the air and realization hit Dana with stunning force.

Evie was gone. *Escaped.* It had still been dark when they changed cars and Sue had hurried. She hadn't looked. Evie was gone. *Safe.* Triumph flared and Dana tamped it down. Made her face angry. "Don't touch her." *Don't realize she's gone. Not yet.*

Amused, Sue shrugged and put her hand back on the steering wheel. "I'll do more than touch her soon enough. So will you."

What would have been terror became fury and again Dana tamped it back. Put a note of fear in her voice. "What are you talking about?"

"You'll see soon enough."

"Where is Erik, Jane? Is he all right?"

"He's fine," Sue said blithely. "I'd be more worried about yourself, if I were you." She turned, her face abruptly contorting into a frown. "But you don't worry about yourself. You're too damn busy meddling in the lives of everyone else."

Dana looked at Sue's hair, dyed brown now. *She's still planning to use Beverly's ID,* she thought, a fresh wave of fury mounting. "You changed your hair."

Sue turned her head and blinked her eyes. Her brown eyes that had cost an innocent optometrist his life. "Eyes, too. It's just a whole new me."

"What are you planning to do to me?"

Sue laughed. "It's more like what you two will do to each other. Your dead ward will be found shot with your gun, holding a quarter-kilo of very good quality coke. You'll be next to her, your throat slit. Add to that the forgery business you have on the side and I think the authorities will add it all up. Dana Dupinsky, forger and drug dealer, using her shelter as a base of operations. You and Evie have been fighting all week — so many clients will have to swear to it. I think Scarface will cut your face before she tries to slit your throat, give you a scar to match hers. You'll be angry, and *pop* — she'll be dead."

Dana could only stare, horrified at what she'd planned. "Evie would never hurt me."

Sue's teeth flashed in a grin. "Of course she wouldn't. But I would. And I'll enjoy it, too. Now I know how to cut a throat and have my victim survive. If you do survive, you'll wake up handcuffed to a hospital bed." She sighed lustily. "The guards are going to love you, sugar. Possession, forgery, murder. If you live, you'll be inside a good long time."

"You've given this a lot of thought," Dana said steadily and Sue looked grimly satisfied.

"Not as much as I've given to other matters," she said. "But enough."

Mia slammed her car door, hearing Abe do the same behind her as she ran up to the fire department car. Empty. Behind it sat a local squad car. An officer stood next to the abandoned car, looking grim. "Nothing inside," he said, "but we found somebody."

Mia's heart leaped into her throat. *Dana.* "Dead?"

"Unconscious. She must have hit her head on a rock when she rolled down that little embankment. I called for an ambulance." Mia was already scrambling down the side of the hill, sending little rocks flying. The officer's partner knelt on the ground, blocking her view. Then she was around him and dropped to her knees, equal parts relief and shock.

"Abe," she shouted. "It's Evie."

He picked his way down more cautiously, his face tight. "One up, one down," he said. "I just heard from Sergeant Elliot back at the Hunters' house. They found the Lawndale EMT. He's on his way to County with a nine mil in his chest."

"But Buchanan said she had Dana's gun."

Abe went down on one knee, gently brushing dirt and rocks from Evie's cheek. "Like you said, Mia. Conway keeps her business separate from her personal. Dana, and Buchanan by association, they're personal."

*Chicago,*
*Friday, August 6, 8:30 a.m.*

Well, Sue knew now that Evie had escaped, Dana thought as her knees hit a concrete floor with a loud crack. The shove from Sue's foot still throbbed between her shoulder blades; Sue's roar of outrage still rang in her ears. Her jaw still throbbed from the blow Sue had leveled fifteen minutes before when, approaching the city, Sue had pulled into an alley to switch cars once more only to find the back floorboard empty. She'd raised her fists to Dana's face, but another blow didn't come — then. Instead she'd taped her mouth, her eyes, pushed her to the floorboards, and brought her here. Wherever here was. They'd come down two flights of stairs, through two doors that sounded heavy as they'd closed behind them.

Dana bit back a cry when Sue ripped at the tape that covered her eyes, taking part of her brows with it. Grimaced at the sight of the pile of used rubbers and rusted needles six inches from her knee. Squinted up at Sue who stood towering in front of her now, fists clenched, her whole body shaking in anger. *It'll be now. She'll kill me now.*

She'd always thought she'd feel fear. Always battled the fear. Shoved the fear in the box and locked it tight. But now, looking up into the face of this woman who'd killed so many with such callous disregard, there was no fear.

Just grief. It welled from deep within, pressing hard on her chest, swelling to close her throat as she thought not of the moment, the now, but all the things she'd miss. Caroline. The new baby. Evie. David and Max and Tom and Phoebe. Her family.

And Ethan. He'd been right after all. Life was too precious to mindlessly barter. *Even mine.* This . . . this overwhelming sense of loss . . . She'd never stopped long enough to realize this was what she wagered every time she put her life on the line. Never let herself weigh the gain, the prize, against the price. Had she, she might have still put her life on the line, every time, but in doing so, she would have counted the cost. Which would have made the prize even more precious. That's what Ethan had meant about sacrifice.

The kind of sacrifice she was not prepared to make today.

So she straightened her back and stared up at Sue Conway who was visibly pulling herself back together. The woman rocked back on her heels, crossing her arms over her chest, her breath coming more slowly now. She was back in control, her eyes now flatly assessing. "Adopt, adapt, and improve," she murmured.

The tattoo, Dana realized. Adopt and adapt. That Sue had most definitely done.

Then Sue smiled and Dana felt cold, despite the stagnant heat of the room. She pulled a cell phone from her pocket, punched a few buttons. "Donnie, there's been a little change in plans . . ." She looked annoyed. "Of course you get your party. Would I lie to you? I'll be picking up the guest of honor, though . . ." Annoyance became a frown. "I already told you that I don't trust you. I don't trust anybody, but it doesn't have anything to do with trust. Just logistics. I'll pick her up. You just bring the boys and any other party favors your hearts desire . . ." She looked down at Dana with that chilling smile. "I've just added another course to the menu, that's all. Do you remember my place? Two buildings south, in the basement. Ten o'clock."

Sue slipped her phone back in her pocket and shouldered a backpack. "Let's stow you where you won't be seen. That way you'll be a nice little surprise for the boys. I've got a few more things to do before the festivities begin. As much as I love to see you on your knees, you need to get up." She sliced the twine that held her ankles together and, her hand fisted in Dana's shirt, dragged her to her feet. "Walk slowly and don't try anything."

Dana made herself walk, her legs shaking beneath her as Sue pushed her forward, her own .38 shoved at the base of her skull. Her stomach roiled as she understood what Sue had in mind. Sue had been assaulted repeatedly by that guard . . . Fred Oscola. She meant Randi Vaughn to suffer the same fate. *And I'm just another course to the menu.*

*Chicago,*
*Friday, August 6, 8:30 a.m.*

Her head . . . *hurt.* And the lights . . . too bright. They hurt her eyes, so she closed them.

"Evie? Honey, open your eyes."

Evie struggled, opened her eyes, saw David's face. Awareness cut through the fog. His smile was watery and she knew it would be bad. Still she asked. "Dana?"

David's throat worked as he swallowed hard. "She got her. But Mitchell and Reagan are looking. They want to talk to you, find out what you saw. Wait. I'll be back."

He was, a few minutes later, Mia and her partner with him. Mia leaned over the bed, a tired smile on her face. "You're with us again. Where did she hold you, Evie?"

Evie's eyes filled. "I don't know," she whispered. "She kept me blindfolded. I know it was hot and I know kids came in to smoke pot a few times. It was in the city, but I don't know where. I'm sorry, Mia. I called Dana, and it was a trick." Tears wet her cheeks. "She couldn't find Dana, so she used me to lure Dana out."

Mia patted her hand. "How did you get away, honey?"

"She left me in the car, in the back on the floor. I wiggled until I could sit up, then I pulled the door lock with my teeth." Her head hurt. A lot. Evie couldn't hold back a groan and David was there on the other side of the bed, holding her hand.

"How did you open the car door?" Mia asked gently.

"She'd tied my hands in front of me before, when she wanted me to use her phone to call Dana." Her lips quivered and sternly she pursed them. "But when she left me there, she tied them behind my back again. I had to twist until I could pull the door handle. I fell out, onto the ground next to the car, but I didn't want her to see the open door, so I —" she remembered the triumph she'd felt when she'd landed on the ground, the look of the open night sky — "I kicked the door shut."

"Smart thinking," Mia murmured, her smile still in place. Still tired. "What then?"

"I thought if she came back, she'd see me, but I couldn't get away, because my feet were tied, too. So I rolled down the hill to hide, but it was steeper than it looked." She looked away. "That was pretty stupid."

"No, it was pretty smart. You hit your

head," Mia said. "But you'll be fine." She squeezed the hand David held. "Dana will be so proud of you, honey. You were just great. We found Alec because of you."

*Alec.* "Is he all right?"

Mia smiled sadly. "He will be. Now you rest so you can see him when he is."


*Chicago,*
*Friday, August 6, 8:30 a.m.*


Marsden hung up the phone with a trembling hand. "That was her."

James hung up his own extension. "I know. Ten o'clock tonight. What's the significance of this place?"

"Basement of an apartment near where she lived when she got sent up. She hid there."

"And she'll be there?"

"She's bringing the guest of honor," Marsden said bitterly.

Randi Vaughn, née Miranda Cook. "I take it you're disappointed the party's canceled."

"I was looking forward to it, yes."

James stood up, slid his gun in his shoulder holster. "Look, Marsden, I don't care if you have your revenge. From what I

649

heard, you deserve it. But you breathe one word to Sue Conway and you won't live to see tomorrow. Understand?"

Marsden's smile had claws. "Yeah. I understand."

James tossed a stack of bills to the table. "Your finder's fee as we discussed. Thanks."

# Chapter Twenty-three

*Chicago,*
*Friday, August 6, 10:45 a.m.*

Ethan came awake slowly, cognizant of little things at first. The rhythmic beep of the monitor, the smell of the antiseptic. The fact that his arm only throbbed now. The white-hot pain was gone. He looked straight up into worried black eyes. Clay. Just like the last time he'd woken up in a hospital.

"I'm here, Ethan. You're going to be fine."

And it all came flooding back. *Dana.* Ethan struggled to sit up, only to be gently pushed back down.

"Easy, buddy," came Clay's smooth voice.

Ethan grabbed Clay's wrist weakly. "Dana?"

Clay hesitated. "She's still missing."

His head was fuzzy. Too fuzzy to think. Too fuzzy to fight the panic. "What time is it?"

"Ten forty-five on Friday morning."

Ethan jolted. "Five hours, dammit."

"You've been in surgery, Ethan," Clay said. "The bullet went straight through your upper arm, but it nicked an artery. You lost a hell of a lot of blood out there. They had to stitch your artery back up. It took a while, but they say you'll be on your feet by tomorrow."

Ethan blinked and Clay's face came into focus. "Not tomorrow. *Today*."

Clay shook his head. "We'll see, E."

"Did you find Alec?"

Clay's expression was grim. "He's here. The Gary police found him at a motel near an old school and a restaurant with a chicken on the roof. Sue had given him too many Phenobarbitals and he slipped into a coma. They airlifted him here."

Ethan fell back against the pillow, the very word a blow. "Coma?"

"Reversible, Ethan," Clay said. "The doctors are filtering his blood. They say they've had good success with Phenobarbital overdoses in children his age. He should be awake in three or four hours. Randi and Stan are with him now. And, Ethan, they found Evie."

Ethan was afraid to ask. "Alive?"

"Yeah. She was unconscious, but she

woke up right after they got her here. Mia insisted they bring her here. She's trying to keep everybody together."

"Where is Mia?"

"Looking for Dana."

Panic swelled again and with it the need to . . . do something. But he couldn't even lift his head on his own. "Conway will kill her," he whispered. "Dammit, Clay, she should have run. I told her to run. But she stayed." His vision started to blur again and he closed his eyes. "Conway had the gun pointed right at my face. She was going to blow my head off, but Dana grabbed her arm." A wave of fury swelled. "Why didn't she run?"

"Maybe . . ." Clay cleared his throat. "Maybe she thought you were worth saving. The nurse is giving me a dirty look, so I'll wait outside. Rest. I'll be waiting for you to wake up."


*Chicago,*
*Friday, August 6, 2:30 p.m.*


"Anything?"

Mia glanced over at her lieutenant who leaned one shoulder against the wall next to the map of the city where pushpins marked all the places Sue Conway had been in the course of her miserable life. Lieutenant Marc Spinnelli's face was concerned, his eyes kind. Mia gritted her teeth and dragged her eyes back to the map. Right now, she didn't need concern or kindness. *Right now, I need these damn pushpins to rearrange themselves in an arrow, pointing to where Sue Conway's got my friend.* But of course they didn't.

"No. All Evie could tell us was some kids came in to smoke pot."

"That narrows it down a bit," Spinnelli said dryly. "Mia, you're weaving on your feet and this case is too close now. Go home and get some sleep. I'll have Murphy cover for you."

Mia looked over her shoulder to where Abe was diligently reviewing the old case files. "Abe's still here, I'm still here. I'm sticking, Marc. But thanks."

Abe looked up with a frown. "I keep coming back to the time gap — the two days where Sue was unaccounted for right before her arrest. The anonymous call came on a Tuesday reporting a ring using a child to smuggle drugs. We know now the anonymous caller was Randi Vaughn. Narcotics found a neighbor who could match visitors to the apartment with suspected dealers from a photo array."

"That was Jackie Williams, the woman who was murdered yesterday," Mia said.

"Well, that Wednesday they got a warrant for Randi's apartment and found the stacks of empty baby formula cans, but no coke. That night they picked up Donnie Marsden and six other men in Marsden's apartment, all cutting coke into dime bags. They found two cans of formula packed tight with coke that they hadn't even started cutting, but Sue wasn't there. Marsden and the others swore they didn't know who she was or anything about a baby."

"Even though they were surrounded by baby formula cans," Spinnelli said dryly.

Abe slanted him a look. "Drug dealers lying? Tell me it isn't so." He riffled through the papers, found the one he was looking for. "Conway isn't arrested until two days later. She came slinking up just after midnight on Friday and Jackie Williams called the cops."

"She'd been hiding." Mia blinked at the words in the report. "Where was she hiding?"

"That's what I'm trying to figure out. The report doesn't say. Narcotics was afraid she had a hiding place for the baby they hadn't found yet — or that the baby was dead. They wanted to catch her with the child. They found her pulling the stove away from the wall, but she wasn't looking for the baby, just for cash she'd stashed, which was gone."

"It makes sense that she'd go back for money over her son," Mia said. "Sue hid somewhere for two days — that's symbolic. Let's find out if the arresting officer remembers something that could help." But before she could pick up her phone, Abe's rang. "I'll call," Mia said, grabbing the old case file. "You get that."

She'd rounded the other side of their desks to her chair when Abe abruptly stood up, sending his own chair rolling backward. "You're kidding," he said, motioning to Mia to wait. "We'll meet you there." He hung up with a grin. "Guess who just tried to break into the Vaughns' room at the Excelsior? Donnie Marsden, the leader of Sue's drug running ring. He had a hotel passkey. Murphy's bringing him in as we speak."

Spinnelli took the case file from Mia's hands. "I'll have someone track down the arresting officer. You two go find out what Marsden knows now that he didn't know then."

Ethan stopped in the doorway of Alec's room, grateful for Clay's steadying hand on his back. His legs trembled beneath him, but they would hold him up. So many had paid such a price for Sue Conway's revenge. Grimly Ethan wondered how much more they'd have to pay before this was over. How much he'd have to pay. Dana was still gone.

But Alec was safe. Evie was safe. And Ethan knew that's exactly how Dana would choose it to be. She hadn't gone meekly, like a lamb to slaughter. Or blindly, as if it meant nothing. She'd gone kicking and screaming and fighting. Afraid. A shudder convulsed him and he had to lean against the door frame for support, his skin had gone clammy and cold.

"Don't think about it," Clay murmured. "For now focus on the fact that Alec is alive. The doctor says he'll make a full recovery, even though he doesn't look like it now."

What Alec looked like was a small ghost lying there in the bed, his skin nearly as white as the sheets. Tubes seemed to run everywhere. But his chest did move, shallowly. Stan was standing to one side, his expression unreadable. Randi looked up from her place at Alec's side and gave Ethan a watery smile. "You shouldn't be out of bed," she said softly.

"I tried to tell him that," Clay said. "He doesn't listen. He wouldn't even sit in the wheelchair I appropriated."

Ethan ignored them both, slowly shuffling to the bed, careful not to jar his right arm, immobilized in a sling. "I needed to see him myself," Ethan murmured. He sank into a chair, light-headed from the trek to the pediatric ward. "He woke up?"

"For a little while," Randi said. "The doctor said he'd sleep a lot still. Ethan . . ." Her voice wobbled. "How can I thank you?"

Ethan looked up at her, took her hand, and squeezed it. "You just did. We're clear."

Stan cleared his throat, his words forced and hard. "Thank you, Ethan."

They were the first words Stan had spoken to him since that night on the dock at Wight's Landing when he'd begged his help. *Do it for Richard,* he'd said. *You owe him that much.* But sitting here, looking at this child, Ethan knew it had been as much about what he'd owed Alec than what he'd owed Richard. He'd been given a responsibility he'd neglected. For two years he'd been Alec's godfather, but he'd wasted that time. He'd claimed that Stan wouldn't let him be part of Alec's life, but that had been an excuse. The truth was he had closed the door to his emotions. Until Dana had opened it back up.

Ethan looked up at Stan. "You're welcome. We're clear now, too."

Alec's eyes fluttered open, widened at the sight of Ethan sitting by his bed.

Ethan took one of Alec's thin hands in his left hand, gently. The bones in the boy's hand were like brittle sticks. Regret slashed through him when he realized he couldn't communicate with his godson face-to-face. He'd had two years. He should have learned sign language by now. It was a mistake he would soon rectify because when this was over, he *would* be part of Alec's life. "Randi, can you tell him something for me?"

"Of course."

"Tell him that I'm proud of him." He waited while Randi signed the words. Alec's eyes flew to his, large and gray and haunted. "Tell him that Evie is all right." Alec sank into the pillows, relieved. "Tell him that Evie told us how he spoke to her, that that was how we found him. Tell him Cheryl would have been proud of him, too." Alec's lips trembled and his eyes filled with tears, but he blinked them away, his expression becoming hard. He tugged his hand free of Ethan's and signed something back to Randi.

"He wants to know if they caught the woman with white eyes." Randi expelled a breath on a shaky laugh. "He calls her the Bitch. I can't scold him for it."

"Tell him not yet. We will, though. Ask him if she kept him anywhere except the motel."

Alec watched, then shook his head. Signed something, his eyes too old for his face.

"He wants to know why she took him. Why she killed Cheryl and Paul," Randi said. "I don't want him to know about Sue, Ethan."

Ethan looked up at her with a frown. "He'll know sooner or later, Randi. But when you tell him is your choice. For now, my priority is getting Dana back alive." He turned back to Alec, met the boy's wary stare. "Ask if he remembers the lady with short red hair."

Alec nodded. "She was Evie's friend. She was nice," Randi interpreted. "Why?"

"Because she's gone now, too." Alec's eyes flew from his mother's hands to Ethan's face, shocked. "I need to know anything else he remembers."

Alec went still. Then his hands moved slowly. And Randi's voice thickened as she voiced every vile thing her son had seen. "Ethan, he doesn't know any more. I'm sorry."

Ethan squeezed the boy's arm lightly. "I'll be back to see you later." He stood up, met Stan's stony expression. "I will see him, Stan. I've more than earned the right now." He waited until he and Clay were in the hall. "Later, can you do me a favor?"

Clay looked suspicious. "I'd say anything, but an hour ago that got me in trouble with the nurses for buying you a fresh shirt and helping you out of bed."

"This one won't get you in trouble. When the dust clears, can you run to a bookstore and buy me a sign language book? It's about time I started being that boy's godfather."

Clay looked back at Stan. "He's going to need one. And you'll be a good one, Ethan. So now you'll go back to your room and lie down?"

"No, next I'm going to see Evie, then I'm walking out of this place to see

Mitchell and Reagan and you're not going to say a word when I do. In fact, you'll drive me there."

"Ethan —"

Ethan was focusing on walking the length of the hall. "I'm serious. I don't want —"

"Ethan, wait. I have a call coming in." Ethan turned to see Clay pulling his cell from his jacket pocket. "Mitchell just called," he said. "They might have a break."

*Chicago,*
*Friday, August 6, 3:55 p.m.*

The alarm woke her up. Yawning, Sue hit the snooze. This hotel room wasn't as nice as the one she'd reserved in the Excelsior, but that place was crawling with cops. This place was still nicer than the dump where she'd stashed the kid. She'd drive out to Gary and get him in a few hours, hide him in the basement where Miranda would meet her end.

Sue felt a tingle of excitement. Soon she'd be able to watch Miranda Cook writhe in pain, forced to commit acts she never dreamed possible with men who had years of anger stored up. Six angry men could do a hell of a lot of damage to one woman. It was smart to have Dupinsky as a second course. Once those guys got started, one victim would not be enough. She'd give them Dupinsky while she went on to deal Miranda her final hand.

Miranda would be broken and bleeding, but conscious. Sue would make sure she was conscious. Because, when it was Sue's turn, she'd bring out the kid. Sue hoped he'd still be alive after making him take all those pills. She wished she'd shown a bit more restraint, but at the time she'd been so damn mad that he'd tried to escape . . . She lost her head. If he died, though, it wouldn't matter. Sue could say the kid was alive and make Miranda believe it. She'd always been able to make Miranda believe anything she wanted her to.

Sue would lay the kid where Miranda could see him as she endured her last moments on earth. Sue would torture Miranda as she'd tortured Miranda's mother in Florida, with small painful slices and bone-crushing blows. Miranda would beg for mercy, but there would be none. And then, when the pain was so great, so . . . immense, she'd give Miranda the most crushing punishment of all.

One little pill. Guaranteed to kill one person quickly. Miranda would then have the choice. End the kid's life mercifully or her own painlessly. A true "Sophie's choice."

If she knew Miranda, the woman wouldn't make the choice. She'd lie there slowly bleeding to death as Sue sat back and watched. But that would be okay, too, because perhaps worse than the physical pain would be Miranda's knowing that she *would* die and that afterward the boy would continue to lie beside her. Unprotected. For hours, days maybe. Alone. Starving, dehydrating. The seizures would come without his meds. The kid would die and Miranda would die knowing she could do absolutely nothing to stop it.

Then, and only then, Miranda would truly know the meaning of being powerless.

It was a good plan, if Sue did say so herself. She hopped out of bed, a spring in her step. The nap had refreshed her. Tonight would be busy and tomorrow she was driving to Toronto where she'd reserved a flight to Paris under the name of Carla Fenton, an ID there was no way the cops could trace. *And by five o'clock Eastern time today I'll be rich.*

With the time difference, that was only a

few minutes away. Smiling, she pulled her new laptop from her backpack, paid for with cash from the Vaughn trial deposit. The laptop was equipped with everything a wealthy woman would need, including Internet access so she could gain easy access to her own accounts without relying on Internet cafés. And without having to show ID every time she wanted to take a quick peek at her millions.

She'd been careful with the IDs she'd stolen, she thought as she powered the laptop up and plugged it into the phone. She never actually used any of the credit cards, so they couldn't trace the dead bodies back to her. The Internet cafés just held the card for insurance. They only ran the card through their register if you didn't pay with cash and she'd always been sure to pay with cash. Therefore, she'd never be traced to the pediatric nurse or the waitress. If Bryce kept his mouth shut, she'd never be connected to any of it.

It was nearly five on the East coast. The Vaughns would have put the money in the first account by now. She got to the bank's Website, tapped in the account number, then *Walter1955.* Good old dad. *If he could only see me now.* He'd botched a tiny job, a convenience store for God's sake. And she had just pulled off a heist worth five million. And better still, Miranda Cook would finally get her just desserts. She'd —

The hourglass stopped turning and Sue frowned. The money wasn't there. The account was empty. They should have deposited it by now. Her heart started to pound heavily. Maybe they wouldn't pay the ransom after all. Dammit, she needed that money. Wanted that money. She set her teeth, hard. *They owe me that money.*

Compulsively she brought up the second account, the one only she knew about. *Walter1987.* And froze. Stared. *Impossible.* The account was empty.

*Impossible.* There had been over nineteen thousand dollars. *It was all gone.*

*They knew.* Somehow they'd found her second account. Her blood ran cold as her brain raced. How had they found her? How had they known? She'd told no one about the second account. *No one.* But somehow they knew just the same. Her stomach settled and once again she knew calm. She needed to get the kid. A promise was a promise after all. The kid would be returned to the Vaughns in five million pieces.

"So what has he told you?" Ethan asked as he made his way into the detective's bullpen, leaning on Clay's arm.

Reagan looked up from his computer screen and exchanged a look with Mitchell. "You're only encouraging him, Mia. He needs to be in the hospital."

Mitchell shrugged. "They were here. It seemed more trouble to send them back to the hospital than to sign them in with a guest pass. Sit down, Buchanan, before you pass out."

Ethan took Mitchell's chair, his arm throbbing, but his thoughts were on the slime the police had caught breaking into Randi's hotel. "What has Marsden told you?"

"Not much," Reagan said. "He's got a hotel passkey and won't say how he got it."

"Sue gave it to him," Ethan exploded.

"Of course she did," Mitchell snapped back. "But he isn't admitting it." She softened marginally. "I know you're frustrated, Ethan. But we're doing all we can."

"Marsden's lawyered up," Reagan added glumly. "We can't touch him now."

Fury seethed and with it sharp panic.

667

"Dammit. He knows something. He must. Give me five minutes with him and you'll have everything you want to know."

Mitchell pinned him with a glare. "Control yourself or you go back to the hospital."

"Easy, E," Clay murmured behind him. "These guys are on your side. We all are."

Shaking, his heart thundering, Ethan tried to control himself. "I'm sorry." He flattened his left hand on his pants' leg, smeared with blood and grass stains. He refused to close his eyes, because every time he did he saw Dana being dragged away, wide-eyed and terrified. He swallowed hard and grimaced when Clay put a steadying hand on his uninjured shoulder. "I'm sorry," he repeated. "I . . ." He looked up, met Mitchell's round blue eyes. "I keep seeing her . . . She was so scared."

Mitchell flinched. "I understand, but we have to stay calm. If we don't, we won't find her."

"All right. I'm calm." He wasn't, but that wouldn't change until Dana was safe. "This guy, Donnie Marsden. He was one of the guys who got arrested with Conway all those years ago, right? So his breaking into Randi's hotel room is not a coincidence, right?"

Mitchell nodded. "Right."

"So he's part of whatever Sue planned."

"Maybe. If he is, he's not saying. Right now, all we can charge him with in relation to *this* crime is B and E."

"Unless you can tie him to Sue in the last week," Clay said. "Then it's conspiracy."

"She must have called him," Ethan said. "Have you checked his phone records?"

"His LUDs from this week," Reagan said flatly, lifting an inch-thick printout. "Turns out Mr. Marsden is a bookie. Takes hundreds of calls every week. More during basketball season. We're lucky he's only running numbers for baseball and the ponies this week. We're checking his incoming calls to separate out any 'legitimate' gamblers from Sue."

"The old case files show Conway was hiding for two days before they caught her," Mia added. "We're trying to figure out where. Dana was sure this would be symbolic, so the hiding place might pan out."

"And finally," Reagan sighed, "we asked Sheriff Moore to visit Bryce Lewis in jail once more, to see if there's anything else she can get out of him. Beyond that, we'll take any and all ideas that don't get us in trouble with Internal Affairs."

Ethan slumped in Mitchell's chair. "I'm sorry. I know you're doing all you can."

"Ethan, I've been in your place before," Reagan said, his eyes intent. "It was hard as hell knowing someone had taken somebody I loved. We want Dana back as much as you do and we understand what you're going through. But you need to let us do our jobs."

"Go back to your hotel, Ethan," Mitchell said softly. "I promise I'll call you the minute we know something."

Ethan pushed himself to his feet. "All right." He let his eyes take one last sweep of Mitchell's desk, the folder that lay open on her blotter. Then he stopped dead, his heart in his throat. "Clay, look at this."

Clay looked down at the pictures. "Marsden's mug shots?"

"Look at the face, the chin."

"My God," Clay muttered.

Wincing, Ethan reached to his back pocket for his wallet and fumbled it open, one-handed. "Clay, help me get out the pictures." Clay did and Ethan flipped through his photos, stopping when he got to a picture of Alec taken last year. Clay pulled the picture out of the plastic casing and put it next to Marsden's mugs.

Reagan gave a low whistle. "Looks like Sue and Donnie did more than run drugs."

Mia shuffled the papers in the case file. "Marsden's statement at the time of his arrest has him swearing the baby Sue used belonged to her friend. He thought the baby was Randi's because she took care of Alec, even then." She met Reagan's eyes with a satisfied little smile. "I bet he doesn't know he's a daddy."

Reagan picked up Alec's photo. "It might not make a bit of difference if he does, but I say let's go give the man a cigar."

Mitchell paused on her way out the door. Frowned. "You guys can't stay here alone."

"Then we're coming," Ethan said.

"You keep quiet," Mia warned. "One peep and you're gone. Got it?"

"Yeah," Ethan said grimly. "I got it."


*Gary, Indiana,*
*Friday, August 6, 4:55 p.m.*

*He was gone.* Sue clenched her teeth as she drove by the ratty little roadside motel, now strung with yellow crime scene tape. The kid was gone. He'd been found this

671

morning when, according to the guy who'd sold her cigarettes in the convenience store half a mile away, at least ten police cars converged on the motel, dressed in SWAT gear. They'd come out with the kid and airlifted him to County General in Chicago.

Sue stopped at a pay phone, dialed County General, and chose "Patient information."

"I'd like to get information on an Alec Vaughn, please."

There was a short pause. "The computer says he's in stable condition."

"Thank you." Slowly Sue hung it up, every dream in her head crashing around her ears. There would be no luring Randi Vaughn from her hotel. There would be no revenge. There would be no watching Donnie and the boys pound Miranda Cook into hamburger. There would be no Sophie's choice. There would be no cutting and crushing.

Ten years. She'd waited ten fucking years.

For nothing. *Nothing.* She had nothing.

With a small roar of frustration, Sue turned her car back to Chicago. She had only one more thing. She had Dupinsky. Donnie and the boys would have to make do with her.

*Ocean City, Maryland,*
*Friday, August 6, 6:00 p.m. Eastern*
*(5:00 p.m. Central)*

Bryce Lewis's lawyer smacked his briefcase on the table impatiently. "If you don't have any more deals, Sheriff, we have nothing more to say. You're wasting my time and yours."

Lou Moore bit back the urge to tell the public defender to . . . Restraining herself, she leaned forward to snag Bryce Lewis's gaze. "Bryce, I need your help. Your sister left that little boy for dead this morning. Forced him to take half a bottle of his epilepsy medicine."

"My client can't help what his sister has done in the time since they've separated."

"Of course not. But, Bryce, there's something you need to know about this boy." She pulled a copy of the Clark County birth certificate proclaiming Erik Conway to have been a live birth to mother Susan Conway. Father unknown. She slid the birth certificate across the table. "The boy is your sister's son, Bryce."

Bryce's head whipped around, his eyes narrowed as he read the birth certificate. He looked over at his attorney. "Is this legit?"

The defender picked it up. "It's a faxed copy. I can't tell."

"It is," Lou said. "Bryce, please listen to me. I saw the way you reacted when I told you about Paul McMillan's body the first time we talked. You aren't cold like her. A woman tried to help this child. This morning Sue shot the woman's boyfriend and kidnapped her. We know she intends to kill this woman. She didn't succeed in killing your nephew. Thanks to this woman and others, we found him in time. But our time is running out."

"What kind of deal are you offering?" the defender asked.

Lou sighed. "Bryce, you're involved in a murder and a kidnapping."

"Wait," the defender interrupted. "If the kid was his sister's it wasn't a kidnapping."

Lou didn't take her eyes off Bryce Lewis. "But Miss Rickman was kidnapped, transported over state lines, and murdered, Bryce. You participated in this felony. I can only make recommendations for leniency. The DA makes the final call. But helping us find this woman would go an awful long way."

Bryce stood up, stiffly. "I'll think about it."

"Don't think too long. We think this

woman will be dead in a matter of hours."

Bryce's stare was cold. A week of jail had hardened this boy. "I said, I'll think about it."

*Chicago,*
*Friday, August 6, 5:10 p.m.*

Ethan frowned at the two-way glass. Reagan and Mitchell had been in with Marsden for twenty-five minutes and not once had they shown the damn picture of Alec or *mentioned* Alec.

"Why aren't they telling him about Alec?" Ethan muttered.

"Sshh," Clay murmured. "Because they're damn good cops. Hell of an interrogation."

"Glad you approve," their lieutenant said dryly. Spinnelli had arrived a minute before they'd started the interrogation. To Spinnelli's left stood the assistant state's attorney that Abe Reagan had called to expedite any deal making they'd need to do.

Clay shot Spinnelli an even look. "I meant it."

Spinnelli lifted a brow, not taking his eyes from the glass. "So did I, Mr. Maynard."

"Clay," Clay said.

"Clay. But I'm still Lieutenant Spinnelli to you," Spinnelli said, his mustache twitching.

"Understood. Sir," Clay added with an intentional hesitation. "Look, Ethan," he said quietly. "Mitchell plops Marsden's AZT on the table, he's got AIDS, and he doesn't want to die in prison, right? Reagan pounds him with the bookmaking charges, lots of years. He's about to spill Sue on his own. They're saving the picture in case he needs one last push."

"I'd like to give him one last push," Ethan growled. "Randi betrayed him as much as she did Sue. If he got that AIDS while he was in prison, he's got even more of a grudge. He was breaking into that hotel room to pay Randi back." And the very thought sickened him.

"Yeah, but why now?" Clay murmured. "Why does Marsden try to grab Randi this afternoon? If Sue had been orchestrating it, she would have had him wait until after five."

"When the five million would have been deposited." Ethan blew out a breath. "You're right."

"Yes, he is." Spinnelli looked at Clay with critical eyes. "You quit DCPD. Why?"

Clay's face hardened. "That's my business. Sir."

Spinnelli considered him another moment more, then nodded. "Fair enough."

Marsden slumped in his chair sullenly, his lawyer whispering in his ear. Marsden nodded and the lawyer looked up. "What kind of deal are we talking?"

"That's up to the state's attorney's office," Mia replied smoothly. "We don't make deals, we make *recommendations*."

The lawyer frowned. "What kind of *recommendation?*"

Reagan leaned forward, his eyes narrowed. "Marsden, we know why you were going in that hotel room. You and Conway planned some kind of revenge. But you're not charged with that. Yet. You go down with Conway and that's going to be a conspiracy charge, because we *know* what she has in mind. We want Conway more than we want you. Right now. But if we find her first . . ." Reagan shrugged. "Recommendations are out the window. Tell us where she is and we recommend the SA stick with the bookmaking charges."

Marsden shifted guiltily and said nothing.

Mitchell shoved a chair against the table making both Marsden and his attorney jump. "You know, I've had about enough from the two of you. If you don't start talking in thirty seconds, I'll *recommend* the SA add kidnapping charges and murder."

Marsden jerked. "I didn't do any kidnapping or murder. I never touched the lady."

Mitchell leaned in close. "Because you didn't get the chance. But we're not talking about Mrs. Vaughn, we're talking about the kid."

Marsden jolted to his feet. "Whoa. I don't know anything about any kid."

Mitchell and Reagan shared a long look. Mitchell shrugged. "Okay, so you don't." And with great drama she looked at her watch. "Fifteen seconds, Mr. Marsden."

"Dammit, I don't know nothin' about no kid!"

"Five seconds." Mitchell shrugged again. "We're done. Hope you find a prison doctor you like, Mr. Marsden. You'll be spending a great deal of time together in the foreseeable future." Her hand was on the door when Marsden threw himself back in the chair.

"It must be the Vaughns' kid," he snapped. "Sue said she was getting Miranda Cook back to Chicago because she had something Miranda wanted. I didn't know she was Randi Vaughn until I checked the hotel register. But I haven't seen any kid."

Reagan leaned forward, perplexed. "Why do you continue to protect this woman?"

Marsden sighed. "Because she's going to get it from somebody else besides you guys. And I'd rather see her dead than have to go back to prison."

Reagan nodded. "Lorenzano?" Marsden's eyes widened. Reagan chuckled. "We know lots of things, Donnie-boy. So Lorenzano got to you? How much was it worth?"

"Fifteen thousand," Marsden mumbled.

Mitchell sat on the edge of the table. "Fifteen Gs'll buy a lot of AZT. I might have done the same. So you sell Sue to Lorenzano. I take it he knows where she is right now."

"He knows where she'll be at ten tonight."

"And what happens at ten tonight, Donnie-boy?" Reagan asked.

Marsden stared up at the ceiling. "Me and the guys Miranda sent up get thirty minutes apiece to do whatever we want."

Ethan covered his mouth with his hand, and managed to muffle the gagging he couldn't stop. "She won't have Randi," Ethan whispered, horrified. "She has Dana."

Mitchell's face was a stony mask. "Well, that's about as disgusting as I've heard in a while. What was in it for Sue?"

"She got to finish her off."

Reagan raised a brow. "And you took that to mean?"

"Kill her."

Marsden's lawyer held up his hand. "I want an SA in here now."

"That's my cue." The prosecutor nodded to Ethan and Clay. "Gentlemen." A half minute later the interview room door opened and the prosecutor walked in. "You rang?"

Marsden's lawyer gave him a dirty look. "Fancy meeting you here."

The prosecutor slapped his briefcase on the table. "If he tells us where she is and agrees to swear to everything we just heard, we stick to the bookmaking charges."

"You're offering what?" the lawyer sneered.

"Seven to ten. He does three inside. If he's still alive at the end of three years, the remaining will be in a work program. It's a damn good deal."

Marsden scowled. "It's a fucking death

sentence. Three years. *Fuck*."

Mitchell pulled her chair close to his. "You think she's better off dead than with us? Maybe you wouldn't be so charitable if you knew the one other thing we know."

Marsden hesitated. "What other thing do you know?"

Reagan pulled the picture of Alec from his pocket. "The child you used to run drugs all those years ago wasn't Miranda Cook's son. He was Sue's son."

Marsden's face bent in disbelief. "No fucking way. Even Suze wouldn't do that."

"Oh, she did that," Mitchell purred. "And a hell of a lot more."

Marsden went very still. "What did she do?"

"Well, she kidnapped the boy in the last week and murdered eleven people. And she left the child for dead in a Gary, Indiana, motel with half a bottle of Phenobarbital in his gut. But that's not the worst of it, Mr. Marsden, at least not from your point of view." She leaned over and plucked the photo from Reagan's fingers, placed it in front of Marsden.

"Recognize him, Donnie-boy?" Reagan asked acidly.

"You should, Mr. Marsden." Mitchell leaned close to Marsden's shaking body.

He'd seen it right away, Ethan could tell. "He's yours. She used your son to smuggle drugs. She left him to die today. She's planning on getting a five-million-dollar ransom from the Vaughns. Do you still think she's better off dead than with us?"

Marsden drew a breath. "Abandoned apartment building on Central." He looked up at Mitchell who was already running for the door. "Is he alive? My son?"

"No thanks to Sue Conway," Mitchell snapped.

"I want to see him."

"Work it through the lawyers, Donnie-boy," Reagan said. "Mia, let's go."

Ethan burst out of the back room, Clay at his heels. "I'm going."

"You're staying," Reagan gritted. "Full body armor, Mia." Then Mitchell and Reagan were gone, leaving Ethan standing there shaking, holding on to Clay.

"Don't even think it, Ethan," Clay warned.

"I'm going. You can stay or come with me."

Clay rolled his eyes. "Damn. Let's go."

# Chapter Twenty-four

*Chicago,*
*Friday, August 6, 5:40 p.m.*

Dana jerked awake when the outer door to the basement slammed. Someone was coming. She blinked, trying to see something, anything, but the blackness was absolute. The mice, she'd discovered, sounded a whole lot bigger in the dark.

She had no idea what time it was, but thought it must be getting later in the day because the heat wasn't nearly as oppressive as it had been. Her muscles ached from lack of movement, the plastic cuffs holding her wrists and ankles immobile. She was tired and hot and incredibly thirsty. And as the day waned, she became increasingly terrified. She tried to compartmentalize her fear, but it was quickly becoming way too big for the box in her mind.

The footsteps were coming closer. It wasn't joint-smoking kids this time. Her heart started to beat hard and fast in her chest. *Don't let it be Sue and her friends.* Because Randi Vaughn wasn't here. *Only I am.* Pictures of what lay ahead had been running through her mind all day, because it didn't take a rocket scientist to figure out what Sue had planned for Randi. Sue equated sex with power, punishment.

Whatever followed would be worse than Dana's worst nightmares. They'd hurt her. Then they'd kill her. She'd never see her family or friends again. Evie, Caroline, Mia.

*Ethan.* She'd never feel him hold her again. Never have him soothe her fears. Never have him make her feel . . . whole. He made her feel whole, she'd realized. Physically and emotionally. Last night he'd been so right. He'd gotten too close and she'd pushed him away. She deeply regretted that. She would make that right, if she lived to see him again.

The overhead light came on and she blinked. Then a few seconds later she was looking up at Sue Conway looming over her, her light eyes narrowed and furious. *No lenses,* Dana thought. *She's back to blue eyes.* But there was no time to wonder why, no time to be afraid as Sue delivered a quick, vicious kick to Dana's ribs, sending her sliding face first across the dirty floor, her cuffed hands unable to break her fall. Another kick sent pain radiating up her spine, a third, her thighbone. Then Sue was crouching down. She caught handfuls of Dana's shirt and threw her against the concrete wall.

*Something's gone wrong,* was all Dana could think through the haze of pain. This was not the self-possessed Sue who was adopting, adapting, and improving. This woman was one step up from a snarling cornered animal. Joy speared through the pain. They must have found Alec. Without him, Sue's plan fell miserably flat.

The joy was short-lived, replaced by another wave of pain as Sue's fist plowed into Dana's cheek. Tears stung her eyes and she flinched away, unable to shield herself from the next blow. Or the next. She hadn't been beaten like this since Charlie. Or her stepfather. She wasn't able to control the cry of pain when Sue ripped the tape from her mouth, yanking a layer of skin from her lips.

"You will pray to die," Sue said harshly. "You will beg me to kill you before I'm done."

Dana drew a deep breath, the first she'd been able to draw since Sue taped her mouth shut hours before. *How many hours? What time is it?*

"You must have lost Alec," Dana said and experienced the pleasure of watching Sue's mouth drop open in momentary shock. But once again, the pleasure was short-lived. Another hard blow to her jaw had Dana testing to see if her jaw was broken. Still, something drove her to push this woman. "You really should be more careful with your son, Sue. This is the second time you've lost him. It's becoming a habit."

Sue's eyes narrowed. "What do you know?" she asked in a terrible voice.

Dana shoved back her fear and met Sue's gaze unflinchingly. "I know quite a bit about you, Sue Conway. In fact, I know a great deal more about you than you know about me."

"So tell me," said a male voice and Dana's eyes jerked up over Sue's shoulder, just as Sue shoved her against the wall, wheeling to face him.

A man in his late forties, perhaps his early fifties, approached, a nasty-looking pistol in his hand. He had the appearance of a distinguished thug, his silver temples lending him an air of dignity. In a flash of cognition, Dana realized who he was, and why he was here.

"You're Lorenzano," Dana said and watched his mouth quirk up.

"So you know about me as well." He advanced a few steps, his weapon steadily trained on Sue. "I've been waiting all day for you to arrive Sue. You can't hide from me."

"I did hide from you, James," Sue said, "until somebody sold me out. Who was it?"

"Donnie Marsden."

Sue flinched. "Little fucker," she muttered. "Did he hold out for more than fifteen?"

"No," James said cheerfully. "He was cheap, but I won't be. Bryce told me what you're up to, Sue — kidnapping a child, demanding a ransom. How much did you ask?"

"Go to hell," Sue snarled.

"Five million," Dana answered and Lorenzano looked impressed. Sue shot her a glare.

"You still owe me for tracking down Randi Vaughn's mother," Lorenzano mused. "And you owe me for a rather large hospital bill. I want seventy-five percent of the five million."

Sue's eyes dropped to the gun in his

hand. "Fifty percent," she countered.

Lorenzano looked surprised. Suspicious. "I'm surprised you'd agree to anything."

"That's because she knows that there is nothing," Dana supplied. "Fifty, seventy, or hundred percent of zero is still a big fat zero. Which is what she'll get from the Vaughns."

Sue turned and leveled an icy look that sent a shiver down Dana's spine. "Shut up."

"No, tell me more," Lorenzano said. "Who are you, by the way?"

"Sue's worst nightmare," Dana answered evenly. "I'm a meddling social worker."

Lorenzano lifted his heavy brows. "A social worker. Did you give her a place to hide?"

"Unknowingly, yes."

"So how do you know there's no ransom?" Lorenzano asked.

"Because the police found her online off-shore account and took every penny."

"How do you know all this? Are you a social worker" — his eyes narrowed — "or a cop?"

"A social worker. My boyfriend is a P.I." Dana gave Sue a cool look. "And the god-father of Alec Vaughn." And once again she had the pleasure of seeing Sue's face flatten in shock.

Lorenzano's grin flashed white in his tanned face. "Well, well. How interesting that our paths cross so. Now, Miss Social Worker, it's time for you to go. There's the little matter of unfinished business between Sue and me." He fingered his throat. "I need to instruct Sue in the proper art of throat slitting. She didn't get it right the first time."

Dana's eyes widened as he pointed his gun at her chest. Then she sucked in a breath as a revolver fired and with a gurgle Lorenzano dropped to his knees, looking down at his chest in shock. A red stain was already spreading across his white shirt. A few seconds later, he was on his back. Sue stood, Dana's gun in her hand, eyeing him with disdain.

"Sonofabitch," she said. "There's no way in hell I'm letting him kill you. You're all I have left." She grabbed a handful of Dana's shirt and hauled her to her feet. "I've got one evening with you, social worker, and when it's over, you'll be in hell."

"And you'll be in France?" Dana spat. "Carla Fenton?"

Sue blinked, then smiled. "Thanks to you, yes. Too bad you used your talent for charity. You could have made a decent living as a forger."

The thunder of footsteps on the outer steps startled them both. "Fuck," Sue snarled and turned Dana's gun toward the ceiling. A second shot took out the overhead light and plunged them into darkness. The .38 was shoved against Dana's temple and Sue's muscled forearm came across her neck, pressing until her windpipe was closed. "Say a word and you're dead." Then she dragged Dana backward, deeper into the basement.

Dana's heart quickened. The cavalry was here at last.


*Chicago,*
*Friday, August 6, 6:00 p.m.*

Ethan waited until the car stopped. Barely. He was out of the passenger side and moving toward the back end of the line of squad cars that lined the street outside the abandoned apartment building.

Ethan stopped at the last squad car, breathing heavily. He looked at the building, watching as a dozen men and women in full battle gear surrounded the perimeter. He didn't dare go closer. Clay was watching with a critical eye, nodding his approval. That meant a great deal, Ethan thought. Chicago PD knew what they were doing. They had the situation under control. Ethan started to get his pulse under control, too.

"They'll get her out," Ethan murmured.

"Of course they will," Clay said.

"They have to get her out." Ethan heard himself saying the same thing and wondered how many times he had. But Clay kept saying back what he needed to hear.

"You'll get her back," Clay said firmly. "She's a strong woman. She'll last."

*She'll last.* She would. Dana Dupinsky was not a woman to quail at a little danger. Hell, Ethan wished she'd quail a little more. She wasn't a woman who would leave at the first sign of trouble. Until that moment, he hadn't been aware that that was what he'd been waiting for. A woman who would last. One made just for him. She would. She was.

Clay tensed and Ethan jerked his attention back to the black-clad SWAT team. "What's wrong? Why aren't they going in?"

Clay moved his shoulders restlessly. "I don't know."

Then a shot was fired and Ethan's heart simply stopped beating. It came from inside the building. Where Dana was. "Oh, God. Clay." He grabbed Clay's arm as the SWAT team moved, running down the steps into the building's basement.

A second shot was fired. Inside the building. And they waited, he and Clay. Waited for action. For information. For anything. But they heard nothing at all.

*Wight's Landing,*
*Friday, August 6, 7:00 p.m. Eastern*
*(6:00 p.m. Central)*

Huxley followed Lou into her office. "Did Lewis help us?"

"No." Lou rubbed her forehead. "Dammit, Huxley, Dana Dupinsky was such a nice person, too. A little too much of a Joan of Arc at times, but really, really nice. I think she and Ethan Buchanan would have had a good shot at something."

"You think she's dead, then?"

"If they don't find her soon, she sure as hell will be."

Dora appeared with a bottle of Tylenol. "Call on line three. It's that Sheriff Eastman."

Lou leaped for the phone. "This is Sheriff Moore. What happened?"

"Act of God," Eastman replied. "Out of the goodness of his heart, Lewis wants you to have his sister's cell phone number. It's the only other thing he knows about her."

"I've got a pencil, give me the cell number."

*Chicago,*
*Friday, August 6, 6:05 p.m.*

"Police!" Mia followed the tactical team down the stairs and through the inner doors to a black cavern. Not a single beam of light seeped in from the outside. One of the officers found a light switch, but no light appeared. They fanned out, taking shelter behind support beams and anything else large enough to shelter a body. Another officer shone a light around, finding the ceiling light. It had been shot out. So one of the shots hit the light, not a person. The flashlight illuminated the floor in a two-foot-wide swath, stopping when it came to a body lying on the floor.

Mia let her breath go when she saw it was a man. "Dana?" she called. Praying for an answer. A moan. *Something.* Nothing. Disappointment speared deep.

The leader of the tactical team appeared

at her side. "We're going to get infrared goggles," he said quietly. "Then we can see her."

Mia looked around, her eyes struggling with the darkness. "We'll stay here."

Dana's breaths came fast and shallow. *I hurt.* Her ribs and back ached from Sue's kicks, her face from her punches. But all the pain seemed like nothing compared to the cold pressure of her own gun jammed against the base of her skull. They were in a back corner of the basement now, her cheek pressed into the thin chicken wire of a storage stall. At one time families had stored their belongings here. If Mia didn't hurry, Dana would die here. Sue certainly had nothing to lose at this point.

Sue stood behind her, her body taut, her breathing soundless, her free hand closed around Dana's throat. They were cornered. Mia and the police covered the only exit. *How careless of Sue,* Dana thought numbly. Choosing a scene for her final revenge with only one way out. *Let's see her adopt, adapt, and improve her way out of this one.*

Then abruptly Sue's thumb was crushing her larynx and the gun shoved even harder against her skull. Sue's breath was in her ear, her whisper barely audible, but the meaning clear just the same. "One sound and I blow your head off. On your knees."

Trembling, Dana complied. The thumb eased off her larynx but the gun was still jammed against her head, cold and hard. Another slight rustle was followed by a sharp click. The tip of a very sharp blade took the place of Sue's thumb against her throat. A switchblade. Dana's stomach churned. The knife Sue had used to cut that guard's fingers off. And to slit Lorenzano's throat. *That's what she was going to do. She's going to slit my throat.* It would be soundless, unlike the crack of her .38.

She felt Sue's silent chuckle, a slight bobbing of the blade against her throat, and then the sharp pressure was gone, only to reappear at the plastic band binding her ankles. One, two, three sharp slices with the knife and the plastic band binding gave way.

"Stand up," came the breathless whisper. Sue's forearm came around her neck and together with the upward pressure of the gun at her head, Dana rose to her feet. She stumbled at first, her feet numb from hours of disuse. Sue leaned in close. *"I said walk."*

Dana walked, backward through the darkness, praying she didn't stumble again. Her eyes were becoming accustomed to the darkness. They were in a hallway and she could just make out the outline of elevator doors. A service elevator, she thought, just as she was jerked to the right, toward the wall. Toward another door.

*So there is another exit. I should have known Sue wouldn't be so careless.*

It was all she had a chance to think before Sue pushed her through the door. The arm around her neck loosened as Sue grabbed the door to keep it from slamming shut. They were in a stairwell, light dimly visible five or six flights up. "Move," Sue snarled and pushed her up a flight of steps. "I'm going out and you're coming with me. I will kill you if you make one move, one sound I don't like. Do you understand?"

Dana nodded once, but that was apparently good enough.

Mia's chin jerked up at the sound. "What was that?"

Abe was moving quietly forward. "It came from the back." He tucked his chin down to talk into the radio mike on his vest. "Cover the back exit. She may be coming that way."

"We could really use those goggles," Mia grumbled into her own mike as she followed Abe, shining her light along her path. "If she's here, we're sitting ducks with these lights."

Spinnelli's voice was tinny through her earpiece. "The goggles are on their way down. As far as we can see, she's still in there, Mia. Keep back and turn off your lights."

Both she and Abe flicked their lights off immediately. But neither one of them stopped moving. Dana was in here somewhere. *Alive, she prayed. Please just be alive.*

He'd crouched outside desert caves, waiting to storm terrorists armed and salivating to kill him. The moments before those cave raids had been harrowing. Terrifying. But nothing like the moments Ethan stood with his eyes glued to the basement entrance of that damn building. Waiting for a movement. Any indication of what was happening below.

But the minutes ticked by and there was nothing. Until one of the guys in black charged up the stairs. Beside him, Clay narrowed his eyes. "He's getting night-vision goggles. It must be darker than a tomb down there." He instantly flinched as he said it. "I'm sorry, E."

Ethan barely heard him. He was staring at Lieutenant Spinnelli, standing off to one side, his face etched with worry. "Spinnelli knows what's happening," Ethan said desperately.

"And he won't want us bothering him now," Clay said firmly.

"He liked you, Clay. See if he'll tell you *something*. I have to know if she's alive or . . ."

Clay shot him a frustrated look. "All right." He shrugged out of his suit coat and pulled his gun from his back waistband, shoved them at Ethan. "Hold these. I don't want anybody shooting at me for carrying a concealed."

Ethan watched Clay approach Spinnelli, point to the building, then back at Ethan, and Spinnelli wasn't throwing him out. Clay was talking earnestly with the lieutenant. Ethan's eyes were trained on Clay, watching his face for any sign of news, good or bad, when Clay's phone started buzzing. Ethan jabbed his hand into Clay's pocket and flipped the phone open, not stopping to check the ID. "Yeah?"

"Maynard?"

Ethan blinked. "Sheriff Moore?"

"Yeah. Why do you have Maynard's phone? What happened to him?"

"Nothing. I'm just holding his coat. Why?"

"I have a message for Mitchell. I've been calling her cell and getting voice mail."

Ethan straightened abruptly, ignoring the resulting pain shooting down his arm. "She and Reagan think they've cornered Conway. They can only get to Mitchell by radio now."

"Then give her this." Moore rattled out a phone number with a Maryland area code. "Bryce Lewis gave us Sue's cell. Call me when the dust clears."

"Thanks." Ethan's heart was beating faster, this time with hope. If Conway had her phone, the ringing might be enough to distract her, or at least locate her down there in the dark. His pulse was throbbing hard in his arm as he started toward Spinnelli, awkwardly shoving Clay's gun into his back waistband as he walked.

Then all hell broke loose behind him.

*"Hold it! I said hold it!"*

Ethan stopped and spun toward the noise, grabbing his car when the ground continued to spin. CPD had surrounded the building, but all the activity now centered at one first-floor exit where two officers stood ready, their weapons locked and loaded.

It was Conway. And Dana. With a gun to her head, just like the last time he'd seen her.

Ethan's gut pitched as his mind struggled to process the sight. Conway had Dana pulled tight against her body, her forearm against Dana's throat. Dana was a human shield.

Conway took in the scene with a snarl. "Put down your guns or she dies."

Ethan held his breath, waiting what seemed an eternity until both men slowly lowered their weapons and stepped back. Conway jerked Dana forward and Ethan's heart stopped. One side of Dana's face was black and bruised and her shirt was covered in blood. Her feet moved awkwardly and Conway dragged her the next few steps. "Move your feet, Dupinsky," she growled. "Or I swear to God I will blow your fucking head off."

Desperately Dana stared at the officers who held themselves motionless as they passed. "Clear this area," Sue demanded. "Get on your radio and tell everyone to move out." The hand holding the revolver jerked and Dana flinched.

She hadn't seen him yet, Ethan realized. Neither had Conway. He stepped back slowly, not wanting to attract their attention. Crouching behind his car, he pulled Clay's gun from his waistband and positioned it next to his foot. He could still see them. He could hear Dana's stumbling steps. They were coming closer. He fumbled with Clay's phone, dropping his eyes to the keypad long enough to punch the number Moore had given him. Then he dropped the phone, picked up the gun and stood.

And took Conway completely by surprise. Her pale blue eyes widened, her nostrils flared. She yanked her forearm harder against Dana's throat. "Get back," she hissed, "or I'll kill her. I swear to God, I'll kill her while you watch. I have absolutely nothing to lose."

*But I do,* he thought. *I have everything to lose.* Dana was staring at him, but he didn't let himself look in her eyes. Couldn't allow himself to be distracted. Instead he looked right into Conway's pale blue eyes and murmured, "Dana, be ready."

A second later Conway's cell phone trilled sharply and her head moved to locate the noise, her hand bringing the revolver away from Dana's head and around in a reflexive sweep that lasted less than a second. A second in which Dana wrenched her shoulders and dropped to the ground like a lead weight, Conway's revolver following her path.

Dana lay on the pavement panting, her body crunched, protecting her torso. Trembling with rage, Conway pointed the revolver straight down at Dana's head. "Step. Back."

Ethan calmly fired instead. One shot, to her upper arm. *Quid pro quo,* he thought as she staggered back, her low scream of pain tearing the air. As if in slow motion her hand dropped open, Dana's .38 sliding to the pavement and the ground shook as no fewer than ten uniformed cops charged the scene, weapons drawn, all pointing at Conway.

Then everything sped up, Ethan dropping Clay's gun on the trunk and himself to his knees beside Dana. Clumsily he pulled her to him with his good arm as she shuddered, her face buried against his chest, her hands still bound behind her back. He wrapped his hand around the back of her neck, cradling her against him, burying his face in her hair.

In the background he could hear officers shouting for EMTs, somebody reading Conway her rights in a voice loud enough to be heard over her vicious cursing. But none of it mattered at the moment. All he wanted to hear was Dana's ragged breathing. All he wanted to feel was her pulse thrumming under his fingertips.

And it occurred to him that they'd been here before, a week ago. He'd been on his knees beside her, feeling for a pulse. Full circle. Right place, right time.

"Are you all right?" he whispered in her ear and she shuddered again, violently. But she nodded, pressing her forehead hard against his chest, sending icy pain down his arm. But the pain meant nothing. She was alive. That's all that mattered. "Look at me, baby."

She lifted her head and met his gaze, her eyes haunted, then glassy as they filled with tears. "Ethan," she whispered. That was all, just his name. It was more than enough.

Gently he threaded his fingers through her hair and brought her unbruised cheek to his uninjured shoulder. Pressed a kiss to the top of her head and shuddered out a breath of his own as familiar figures converged. Reagan and Mitchell. Spinnelli and Clay. Mitchell saw Dana kneeling in his arms and picked up her pace, stopping to get a scalpel from one of the EMTs who was strapping a still cursing Conway onto a gurney. Crouching beside Dana, she quickly cut the plastic cuff from her wrists.

"You need to get to the hospital," Mia said unsteadily.

Dana straightened her spine, rubbing her wrists reflexively. "No, I don't. I'm not hurt."

"You've . . ." Mia drew a deep breath. "You have blood on your shirt."

"Not mine." Dana looked over her shoulder at Conway being wheeled toward an ambulance. "Lorenzano was standing too close to me when she shot him. He was going to kill me, but she shot him first." She looked up at Mia anxiously. "Where is Evie?"

"She's fine, Dana," Mia told her. "She got a bump on the head escaping this morning, but she should be home with Max and Caroline as we speak."

"Good. And Randi Vaughn?"

Ethan took her wrists, gently massaging them one at a time. "With Alec in the hospital."

She closed her eyes, her shoulders sagging. "She was going to . . ."

"We know," Mia murmured. "We were afraid she'd do it to you."

"She planned to." Dana swallowed hard. "She planned to."

"Well, she didn't," Reagan said kindly, going down on one knee next to her, offering his hand. "Can you stand up?"

Between them, Mia and Reagan pulled Dana to her feet, led her to an ambulance where an EMT waited to check her out. Clay offered his arm and Ethan pulled himself to his feet, not taking his eyes from her face.

"You did good, E," Clay murmured. "How did you know the number?"

"Lou Moore called you with it." He glanced at Clay from the corner of his eye. "She seemed upset when she thought something had happened to you."

Clay bent his lips. "Interesting. Are you planning on relocating to Chicago, E?"

Ethan's gaze was back on Dana's face. The EMT was strapping a blood pressure cuff to her arm when she found Ethan staring and gave him a wry little smile. He hoped for the EMT's sake that she wouldn't need a shot. "And if I did?"

"I'd be happy for you."

"And the business?"

"Details, E. Just details. You can do your computer bit from anywhere. We'll work it out. Now, go to her. You know you want to."

Ethan started walking.

"You should have your ribs x-rayed," the EMT said and Dana frowned at him.

"Why? You won't put a cast on broken ribs. They just have to heal on their own."

He just sighed. "I suppose it wouldn't do any good to tell you that cut above your eye needs stitches?"

"None whatsoever," she answered, staring at Ethan, who'd started walking her way. Nothing or no one on earth could look better than Ethan Buchanan. *He saved my life.*

"Where did you get the cut, Dana?" Mia asked. "There were lots of nasty things on the floor in there. You might need a tetanus shot."

The word *shot* jerked her from her thoughts and Dana recoiled. "No shots."

Ethan stopped at her side, a rueful smile on his face. "She's afraid of needles."

The EMT shook his head. "She appears to be physically fine. She could use stitches, but I won't push it. She really should get a tetanus shot, though. Do what you can." He packed up his kit. "Sign this form officially refusing services and you can go."

Though her hands ached, Dana signed quickly. "I'd like to get out of here."

"And we have a report to write."

Mitchell dusted the top of Dana's head and Ethan could see her hand tremble. "You're dirty, kid. Go home and take a bath." She walked over to supervise the ME's office who'd come for Lorenzano's body. Reagan watched her go, then gave Dana a hug.

"She cried," he murmured. "She never cries, but when she found you'd been taken, she sat down and cried like a baby. Call me if you need anything," Reagan said walking away, leaving Ethan and Dana finally alone. He walked her to his car and gently pushed her to sit sideways on the back seat, her feet on the pavement. Then he looked his fill, cataloging each of her features in turn. His mouth tightened. "She hit you."

"She was in a bad mood when she lost Alec again," she said lightly.

"Are you hurt anywhere else?"

"I'm stiff. I may have a bruise or two." She took in the sling on his arm and the blood on his pants. "I think you win for worst injuries."

"Minor," he insisted and she shook her head with a smile.

"Tough guy." She brushed at the dirt on her shirt. "I think we tie for being dirty though."

Ethan took her left hand, then her right, inspecting them. "Clean," he pronounced and she smiled, bigger this time.

"Yeah. For once in my life my hands are clean." Their eyes locked and her smile faded. "You were right, you know."

He took her chin in his hand and gently touched her chafed lips. "How?"

"It's only a sacrifice when you know what you have to lose."

He shuddered, thinking about what he'd nearly lost. "What would you have lost, Dana?"

"My family," she whispered. "My friends. And you, Ethan. I would have missed you, so much." She closed her eyes and he felt her tremble. "You said you'd gotten too close. You were right, Ethan. I wasn't looking for a relationship. I tried so hard not to meet anyone." She looked up, her brown eyes turbulent. "I didn't want to meet you."

Ethan cleared his throat, but his voice still came out rough. "I remember."

"But I did meet you, and that was fate. Now I get to choose my path."

"You've been choosing your path all along, Dana."

She was quiet a moment, considering the profundity of his words. "Yes, that's true. And while on some levels I've chosen well, others I've chosen poorly."

"I think that's called being human. You didn't answer my question, Dana."

"I'm getting there." She drew a breath. "I'm trying, anyway. You told me that we are the thing that gives us the most satisfaction. Do you remember?"

How could he forget? "It was right before we made love the first time."

She looked up at him, her eyes now intense. "Yes. For me, Ethan, that satisfaction comes from helping people. You were right. It was a penance. But it was also my chosen path. I hope the penance is gone. But it's still my path."

He cupped her cheek in his palm, caressed her bruised skin with his thumb. He needed to touch her. "It doesn't have to be a single-file path, Dana." He held his breath, waiting.

She leaned into his hand, closed her eyes. "I was hoping you'd say that. We've gone too far to be just friends, Ethan. Whether we'll be family . . . I don't know. It's too soon to say." She lifted her eyes to his, vulnerability in their brown depths. "But I want to find out."

He lowered his forehead to hers, gently. For now, it would be enough. "So do I. For now, you've got a family that's worried about you. Let me take you home, Dana."

# Chapter Twenty-five

*Chicago,*
*Friday, August 6, 8:45 p.m.*

Clay stopped Ethan's car outside Max Hunter's mother's house where no fewer than ten cars lined the suburban street. "You want me to wait for you two?"

"If you don't mind," Dana answered. "I'm not going to stay long. Caro and Evie need their rest, and quite frankly, I need a bath."

Clay grinned back at her. "Well, I wasn't going to say anything, but yeah, you really do."

Dana chuckled. "What was that Lou Moore said about discretion being the better part of valor? You try spending all day in a sweatbox surrounded by garbage and see how pretty you smell. Ethan, are you coming?"

He'd been staring at her silently, as if just waiting for her to ask and was relieved that she had. "Yes, I am." Ethan slid out from his side of the car, even more gingerly.

She knew his head hurt like hell. He'd had another "episode" while they were sitting in the police station, waiting to be debriefed. He'd gone untreated this time as his packet of medicine was somewhere near Caroline's horseshoe pits where he'd fallen to his knees that morning. It was hard to believe so much could happen in less than a day.

The two of them looked like casualties from a battlefield, dirty and bruised. They were, Dana supposed. They'd been processed by Mia and Abe, interviewed by the press, and checked out by the EMTs, and now all Dana could think about was a long, hot bath. And sleep. She let her eyes travel up Ethan's body as he straightened with difficulty. And, of course, sex. Even battered his body turned her on and she felt a pang of guilt at the rise of desire. He was in no shape for anything like that tonight. She had to laugh at herself. *Neither am I. But I'd sure like to try.*

Ethan was taking in the cars lining the street. "I think half of Chicago must be here."

"It's the family," Dana said. "They come when there's a crisis."

Ethan walked her to Max's mother's front door and Dana hesitated. "I don't know what to say to Caroline and Max, Ethan. Their house is gone. It was a local landmark. It had been in their family for generations."

He knocked with his good hand, then slid it around her waist. "You didn't burn their house down, Dana. Sue did. Besides, don't you think your safety means more to them?"

The door was opened by Max's mother, Phoebe, who uttered a startled cry at the sight of Dana on her doorstep. Immediately Dana was enveloped in a hug that made her bruised ribs wince. Phoebe cried over her and kissed her and did all the fussy things mothers do. "I'm so happy to see you." She looked at Ethan with a raised brow. "Your war he-ro," she said and Dana laughed.

"Caroline's been talking."

Phoebe let Dana go with a grin. "And shopping. It's a humbling sight to see a woman attack three catalogs and QVC both by phone and online. Makes a woman proud." She held out her hand to Ethan. "It's nice to meet you, Ethan. You're always welcome in our home." She pointed to the back. "Caroline's back there, holding shopping court."

It took them a while to make it to the back as Dana was passed among all the Hunters, hugged and kissed and cried over. She'd expected them to be here for Evie and Caroline, but was taken off guard at the outpouring of love for herself. By the time she got to the back bedroom her own eyes were misty and Ethan was giving her an I-told-you-so look.

"How many does that make, Max?" Caroline was asking when they went into the bedroom where she lay flat on her back, looking up at the TV mounted from the ceiling.

"Four king sheets, two queen. All blue," Max answered dutifully.

"Good. Evie, now we need some white sheets. Four king, two queen."

Dana's lips curved as Evie ordered more bedsheets, the item up for grabs on the QVC screen. Evie sat in the chair next to Caroline's bed, wearing a bandage on her head and a robe, but overall looking none the worse for the wear. Dana waited until Evie realized she was there, new tears stinging her eyes when Evie leaped from the chair, a cry of delight on her lips. Then Evie's arms were around her, holding on so tight Dana gasped for air.

But she hung on just as tight, rocking Evie where they stood. When she thought she'd burst, Evie pulled back, framing Dana's face with her hands. "You're here," Evie said unsteadily. "You're really here."

Dana smiled at her. "I'm here. All in one piece." She held Evie at arm's length, studied her with a critical eye. "You're looking pretty good yourself, considering."

Half of Evie's mouth curved up. "I've certainly looked worse." She raised her eyes over Dana's shoulder. "You're Ethan Buchanan."

Ethan's hand rested lightly on Dana's back. "I am. It's nice to finally meet you, Evie."

"And you, Ethan." She didn't drop her eyes, meeting Ethan's gaze directly. "You saved her. Thank you."

"You're welcome," Ethan said quietly. "Thank you. You saved Alec."

Ethan never blinked at Evie's scarred face and Dana watched Evie's tensed shoulders relax. Her own heart tumbling, Dana wondered if it was possible to fall in love over something as simple as a direct look. But she knew it wasn't simple at all. It was common decency. It was who Ethan Buchanan was.

Recovering her composure, Dana tilted

714

Evie's head sideways, checking out her bandage. "I thought I'd have heart failure when I realized you'd gotten away. Resourceful."

Evie cocked a brow, amused. "*I didn't need a SWAT team to spring me.*"

"Just the entire Wheaton fire department," Caroline drawled from the bed. "Come here, Dana. I need to look at you."

Dana sat on the edge of the bed, patient as Caroline scrutinized her, cataloging every bruise. Then Caroline's lips trembled and her eyes filled. "I needed to see you for myself."

Dana dabbed at Caroline's wet cheeks. "I heard you came through today with flying colors. No contractions and the baby is stable."

Caroline's laugh was shaky. "To stay stable through all this, this baby will be the most easygoing child in the world."

"Or the most strong-willed," Max countered. "I'm betting the latter."

Dana grinned at them both. "What are you shopping for?"

"I have a whole house to refurnish," Caroline said, a gleam in her eyes. "And insurance money to do it with. Evie's helping me with linens and accessories. I assigned Max's sister to buy the furniture herself."

Dana's smile dimmed. "I'm sorry. Your house . . ."

"Is just a house, Dana," Max said firmly. "We'll build a new one. What's important is that we have all of you back." His voice roughened and he cleared his throat. "Safe."

Reaching over Caroline, Dana grabbed Max's hand. "Was anything left?"

He shook his head. "Not much. Tom and David are over there now, sifting through the rubble. What the fire didn't get, the water from the fire trucks did."

"Leaving me with nothing to do for the next few weeks except lie flat on my back and shop," Caroline said firmly. "Ooh, look. Now they're doing lamps. What do you think?"

Dana twisted around and looked up at the television. "They're hideous, Caroline."

Caroline smiled benignly. "I like them. Evie, let's get two for the spare bedroom."

"Ooh, look, cookware online," Evie said, mimicking Caroline and pointing to her laptop with a grin. "Copper pots."

Dana laughed. "My cue to leave." She dropped a kiss on Caroline's forehead. "I'll come by tomorrow and smuggle you in a chili dog."

"Which will then terminate any and all clandestine activities," Caroline murmured, just loud enough for her to hear. "We're too old for all this cloak and dagger stuff, Dana. Besides, this baby's godmother needs to stay out of jail."

Dana's lips twitched. "Yes, ma'am."

*Chicago,*
*Saturday, August 7, 10:25 a.m.*

The phone woke him. Groaning, Ethan fumbled for the receiver with his good hand. His right arm throbbed like a bitch and he felt like every inch of his body had been pounded with a meat tenderizer. "Yeah?"

"It's Mia. You guys alive?"

Ethan blinked at the clock. They'd been sleeping for nearly twelve hours. "Kind of."

"The fog after an adrenaline rush," Mia clucked sympathetically. "Is Dana awake?"

He peered down through eyes that felt like they'd been rubbed with sand. "Kind of."

"Well, tell her I have someone here that

717

she'll want to talk to."

Ethan shook Dana's shoulder. "Wake up."

She made a grumpy sound. "Don't want to."

"It's Mia."

Glaring at him, Dana pushed her hair from her eyes and took the phone. "Hello?" Instantly her expression changed and she sat up. "Naomi, sweetheart." It was a soft croon. Motherly. Ethan racked his brain, then remembered. Naomi was the daughter of Dana's former client. The one who'd been killed by her husband the week before.

"I'm fine, honey. I'm really fine . . ." Dana smiled. "I've wanted to see you all week . . ." Her smile faltered. "I know, baby. I know what happened . . ." She swallowed hard as she listened. "Ben might have those dreams a long time, Naomi. Are you sleeping? . . . Of course I will. Today. Put Detective Mitchell back on, okay?" She sighed and rubbed her forehead, waiting. "Where are they, Mia?" She winced. "Is it a good foster home? Those babies have been through hell. They need to be with people who can help them deal with the trauma. When can I see them? . . . Fine, then. I'll meet you in the hotel lobby in an hour." She hung up the phone and sagged back into the pillows with a sigh.

"The Goodman kids?" Ethan asked.

"Yeah. I kept thinking this whole thing was over for me, but it's just starting for them."

"You'll be able to help them through it," he murmured.

She closed her eyes. "I'm going to try. I'm sorry, Ethan. I know you drive home with Clay tomorrow to clear things up in Maryland. I wanted to spend all day with you, but those kids have been hanging on for over a week now."

He'd been planning to ask her to come to Maryland with him, but now he knew he couldn't. "They need you, too."

She opened her eyes. "Too?"

Her sad smile made his heart hurt. "I told you I needed you, Dana. I didn't mean for just one night or just to get me through this thing with Alec."

She regarded him evenly for a long moment. "Then I think we should start working on those details that stand in our way, Ethan. Your residence and my work."

Panic started to gnaw at his gut. "I need to be close to Alec. If Randi chooses to keep him in Baltimore, I need to live there. Would you live there with me?"

Indecision warred in her eyes. Everything she had, everyone she knew, was here. He knew that. He knew what he was asking and what it would cost her to agree. He honestly didn't expect her to, so he was stunned when she nodded.

"Ethan, I woke up again last night." She grimaced. "Same dream, we were just back to my mother's face. But you were there and you put your arm around me and held me."

"I don't even remember waking up."

"You didn't. You just did it automatically. I've never had anyone make me feel like you do, Ethan. I can't walk away from this. From you." She reached up and ran her fingers down the stubble of his cheek. "I owe you so much. You saved me, but not just from Sue.

"You saved me from myself, Ethan. That's what Evie meant yesterday. That's what I mean now. What I want now is the time to find out if what we have is the stuff that lasts forever. Like Caroline and Max have. Like Richard had with his wife. If I have to move to Baltimore to have that time, I think I owe it to us both, don't you?"

He swallowed hard, humbled and moved. "Yeah, I do." He kissed the corner of her mouth, still raw from her ordeal. "Did I hear you tell Mia you'd be ready in an hour?"

Her little smile became big and instantly his body responded. "Fifty-five minutes now."

"How long does it take you to really get ready?"

"I'm a low-maintenance kind of girl. Wash and go. Twenty minutes, tops. So we have thirty-five minutes, Ethan." She eased him to his back, her hand flat on his chest. "And given your current condition, I think you should let me do all the work." Her hand moved lower and she chuckled. "Well, maybe not all."

Ethan shuddered out a breath. Arched as she took him in hand. "Stop talking, Dana."

"Yessir."

# Epilogue

*Chicago,*
*Saturday, October 9, 3:30 p.m.*

Cheers erupted, the noise startling him for a split second, then Tom Hunter gave him a gentle shove, pointing to first base. Alec dropped the bat and ran as fast as he could, hitting the base in a slide. Proudly he stood up, brushed himself off, and looked to third where Ethan stood, giving him the thumbs up. It was a party with the Hunters, an outdoor picnic with a softball game. He knew most of the Hunters. Most of them had visited him in the hospital. They were celebrating the fact that Max and Caroline's new house finally had a roof. They hoped to be in it in time for Christmas, Tom had told him.

*Told him.* Caroline's son Tom Hunter had talked and Alec had listened. He'd guessed at some of the words, read Tom's lips, but in the end, he'd understood on his own. He'd made strides with his new therapist. Not a private one as Cheryl had been. He still missed her. But this new lady was almost as good. She worked in his school, the public school he'd started last month. Here in Chicago, back in his mom's hometown.

Alec frowned. His mom. Not Sue Conway. Randi Vaughn was and would always be his mother. And Stan Vaughn, no matter what he had done, would always be his father. Alec knew what his father had done. He'd read the newspapers. He knew his father would serve time. But that was small compared to the hurt in his mother's eyes when she'd told him his father had cheated with other women and that she was divorcing him.

She'd worked it out with Uncle Ethan so that they all moved back to Chicago. A grandmother he didn't know had died recently and left them some money. Enough for a little house of their own. But they seemed to spend more time with Dana and her family.

He watched Evie take the plate, clutch the bat as best she could. He got ready to run. He was getting good at running. He and Ethan ran every day. He was stronger now, and faster. And when Evie bunted the ball, he ran his fastest and made it to second while Ethan sprinted for home plate where Dana greeted him with a big sloppy kiss.

He'd gotten used to them kissing. They did it a lot, especially today, since they'd started today's party announcing their engagement. Ethan had told him that morning, when he picked him and his mom up. Told him with his hands, signing the words. Ethan's signs were clumsy, but he was trying, even taking a night class at the local college. Ethan had learned more in two months than his father had learned . . . in his whole life. But he wouldn't think about his father now. Tom was at bat and Alec wanted a run on his personal record.

"Look at him," Dana murmured, leaning into Ethan. "He's having the time of his life."

Ethan pulled Dana closer, her back to his front, his arms around her waist. He rested his chin on the top of her head and watched Alec poised, waiting for Tom to hit the ball out of the field. "He's having a good time," Ethan said, watching Alec's face. "I'm glad we did this today. Stan's trial started yesterday. Alec's been a little depressed."

Dana sighed. "Why Stan didn't just take a plea and save Alec and Randi the pain?"

"I used to make excuses for him, to try

724

to understand. I guess, sometimes you just can't." Stan would be found guilty, they knew. He'd probably serve only a year or two in a minimum security facility, but he'd lost his family in the long term, more because of his infidelity than his financial dishonesty. Clay's cooperation would ensure Stan's conviction as well as guaranteeing no charges were filed against Clay. That had been a huge relief.

An even bigger relief was the future Sue Conway faced. The State's Attorney's offices in three states were going for the death penalty — Illinois, Maryland, and Florida. But even if her miserable life was spared, she'd never walk the streets again. There was consolation in that fact, even if it didn't eliminate Dana's or Alec's nightmares.

Ethan kissed the top of Dana's head. "Looks like Naomi and Ben are having a good time." Dana had applied for guardianship of Lillian Goodman's children. She'd tried to go for a legal adoption, but their murdering father blocked them, suing for his parental rights from jail, but Dana wouldn't give up. She planned to fight for these kids, to give them the life Lillian had wanted them to have. The life her own mother hadn't fought to give her.

"They are. Phoebe's just taken them under her wing like they're her own grandchildren."

"She's good at that." Phoebe Hunter had accepted Ethan into the Hunter clan as well. "She reminds me of my grandmother. Who would have loved you, by the way."

Dana twisted to look up at him, a smile in her eyes. "Thank you." She glanced down at her ring. "I showed it to Caroline last night. She said that I should keep you."

"I'm so relieved," Ethan said, only half in jest. He owed a lot to the woman who'd insisted Dana have dinner with him that night more than two months ago. That day in August changed his life, gave him Dana, gave him Alec. "Will they come today?"

Dana resettled her body against him, burrowing closer, and as always, the feel of her against him sent his body into overdrive. Dana gave an extra little wiggle to let him know she hadn't missed a thing. "Probably not. It's a little too chilly for the baby."

The baby Caroline had given birth to barely a month before. Two weeks early and, thankfully, healthy. Caroline and Max had named the little girl Mary Grace. Dana told him that had been Caroline's name before Dana had given her a new identity. That the baby carried Caroline's old name was a fitting tribute to both women's courage, Ethan thought. He splayed his hands across Dana's midsection wondering when they'd have a child of their own. But child of their own or not, they were destined to have a house full of children.

"I saw the realtor this morning," he said, not sure which was more exciting — the realtor's news or the fact that he'd driven himself to the appointment. He'd been episode free for nearly two months now. It was amazing what the capture of a homicidal maniac could do to reduce a man's stress level.

Dana jerked around, her eyes wide. "The realtor? Why didn't you say something?"

"You were busy showing everybody your new ring, that's why. The realtor said we can get the house for the price we offered."

Her face lit up like sunshine. "Oh, Ethan."

He kissed her smiling mouth. "Soon you'll be able to take on another six or seven foster kids." After soul searching, Dana had decided to shift her life path. No longer would she be meeting battered women in bus stations in the middle of the night. No longer would she be a target for irate husbands. Together, they'd decided to offer shelter to children victimized by domestic violence. Ethan didn't think there was another person alive who could fill that vision better than the woman who now looked up at him as if he'd hung the moon. "And," he finished, "I got that new client yesterday. They've had their server hacked by high school kids three times in the last month, so they want me to get started right away. The advance will cover the down payment on the house."

"I love you, Ethan."

The simple sentence hit him hard, just as hard as the first time she'd said it, shortly after that day he'd almost lost her. She'd visited him in D.C. and they'd gone to the Eastern Shore. He'd shown her the place where he'd grown up and in the quiet of a sunset on the bay he'd held her and she'd said it. And it had been so natural to say it back. Just as it had been every day thereafter, and every day for the rest of his life.

"I love you, too, Dana." He gave her a nudge. Alec was at third, a hopeful look on his face. "It's your turn at bat. Hit it out of the park so Alec can make home."

She did and Alec ran, his face one big grin as he crossed the plate. "I did it," he said.

"Yeah, you did." Ethan slapped him on the back. Watched Dana round the bases. *And so did I.*